Between Love and Ruin

M.A. Frick

Also by M.A. Frick

Scan the code for an up-to-date directory of books by M.A. Frick!
More dragons await...

To those who would risk dragonfire.

Prologue

KALLIAS

There's nothing quite as degrading as tucking in a tunic and buttoning trousers in front of a crowd. Especially after being caught with my son's promised splayed over my desk, hips bucking between her legs like a rutting dog.

My glare locked on Egath. The ambassador hadn't turned for the hall as a proper man would. No—he lingered, watched my disgrace with a flicker of amusement.

"Out!" I snarled.

The Velli at least retained enough self-preservation to flee.

Tallon had no such instinct.

He dropped into a chair, legs crossing at the knees, polished boot bobbing with smug ease. A smirk clung to his face like oil. I turned to Greaves and flicked my chin toward the door.

My best friend gripped his dagger, second-hand shame blooming over his cheeks. He was only a guard. The fault sat square on my shoulders—heavy as the mantle of Radaan. It bore down on me while Tallon watched, eager to witness me crack and break.

"Go." My tone was cold. Even. Measured.

All the things my heart was not.

Greaves left in silence.

My chest ached, hollow where Nienna's presence had been. She was gone. Out of reach. No undoing it now. Rage simmered in my veins, licking hot along my skin. Guilt curled in my gut, disgust tinting my features—an audience beheld my lowest fall, my greatest mistake.

I rounded my desk, avoiding the shards of broken lantern glass and spilled ink pots, trodding on reports scattered in the heat of passion.

Fury clawed at my throat, squeezing, threatening to garble what I needed to say. I bottled my rage, preserved it. My hands formed fists at my sides as I leaned against the desk's edge, hooded eyes narrowed on Tallon.

"You planned this." Not a question. This was no coincidence. Not when Nienna had just caught him with Fyrn, and somehow, Ronan and Egath stood at his side. This reeked of cold calculation—too much like his mother.

"Planned on you taking my betrothed over your desk?" He let out a breathy, mocking laugh. "No, I can't say I ever thought you would be so foolish. But when I realized you were trying to replace me, I saw an opportunity. You taught me well."

"Your mother taught you." The words tore out, thick and sharp with past mistakes. I'd allowed Eldeiade to dig her claws into him for far too long.

"Like it or not, I'm your only heir." His voice dipped, poison threading each word. He wouldn't let me take another woman. He'd drag Radaan back to war if it meant his position remained secure.

"Tell me, Father." He leaned in, a gleam of vile curiosity in his eyes. "How was she? We heard her through the door. Tell me, did she spread her legs without–"

I lunged. Fingers snared in his tunic, I yanked him forward and slammed him onto the desk. My fist met his jaw with a crunch.

"I'm done with you!" My snarl ripped free as I dodged his wild kicks. I struck again. Satisfaction sparked through my limbs with every blow. "You never deserved her. I never deserved her! And yet she came. She was willing to marry you!"

He cried out, snatching the mantle's chains, jerking me closer.

"You ruined everything, boy!" Pain burst through my hand as his nose gave beneath another strike, but the satisfying bloom of crimson made up for the discomfort.

"I bled for peace! You've destroyed it!"

"You did that!" he spat, swinging at my face.

I dodged the blow, then picked him up, only to slam him down again.

"I never lifted her skirts. You defiled her!" He snapped his legs up, kicking me hard in the chest.

I staggered back, trembling with fury.

"I've never touched her, Father! You ruined her, not me!" His hair fell into his eyes as he scrambled off the desk. He shoved it off his face before jabbing an accusing finger my way. "You broke Radaan's peace! You crushed the people's faith! If this brings war, it was you who lit the fuse—and now I'll have to pick up the pieces!"

Each statement was a strike to my heart, cleaving it to shreds. I messed up, crossed too many lines. I brought her here. Kissed her. I didn't stop her, didn't push her away.

He was right.

"You will pick up nothing." I bit down against the words I wanted to spew. He would never rule Radaan. I'd sooner crown a commoner before placing the kingdom in his hands. "I'm not dying anytime soon, Tallon. My death is the only way you will ever gain this mantle."

He screamed—a raw, feral thing—and lunged. "That can be arranged!"

I caught his blow and slammed him against the wall, fingers locked around his throat. The rush of it—pleasure and rage, melded together. He bled where I had once held Nienna with tenderness.

"Try, boy. Just try." I pressed close, breath hot at his ear. "I dare you."

His skin felt too soft. Thin and warm and vulnerable. Snapping his neck would take nothing. No one else would have to suffer under his torment. Crimson spilled over my knuckles, and my gaze fixed on the drip. The urge to finish him tightened around my lungs like a noose.

A knock came seconds before the door burst open. Greaves strode in. Darius and Fallione loomed behind him, flanked by Threshers.

Tallon clawed at my sleeve, straining for breath. His gasp was a wet, gurgled sound as his throat worked beneath my palm.

"Your Majesty." Fallione's gaze swept the room, then landed on me. "Shall we call a private council?"

"No need."

I dropped the prince, letting him crumple. Discussions couldn't fix this. An act of war cannot be taken back after it's committed. Nienna was gone. My people had seen too much. No decree could erase the images scorched into their minds. No gesture would restore their shattered trust.

"I would have a word then." Darius' lips curled with disgust. "In private."

I stepped forward with a snarl. "No."

Tallon scrambled. Greaves moved fast, pinning him to the floor. I glanced over my shoulder, sneering as Greaves ground Tallon's hand into the carpet. A shard of glass fell from his grasp. Once disarmed, he adjusted his position, ramming his knee into his throat. The prince wheezed through bared teeth.

"Threats are one thing, boy," I said. "But an attempt on my life? That's treason." I shook my head and pushed past the others, taking my leave. "Lock him away."

In the hall, nobles loitered at junctions, gazes averted, though they snuck glances my way—at the king who ruined his kingdom.

Bile scorched my throat.

Blood glistened along my knuckles. With a grimace, I inhaled and exhaled, attempting to quiet my fury. Lashing out wasn't how a king should act. That was the man in me. But how long had I ruled as one and acted like the other?

When had I set aside the mantle? I wore it daily, yet it hadn't anchored my thoughts in weeks.

I was a fool. Tallon's head belonged on a pike. Every part of me screamed to secure a ship, to chase Nienna across the sea.

But my wants meant nothing.

Radaan didn't need another man. She needed a king. And kings listened to their advisors. Kings endured.

"Your Majesty." Fallione fell in step beside me, his strides matching mine down the corridor. "Perhaps confinement to his rooms would be more fitting."

"Treason, Fallione," I growled, lifting my chin with a glare as a noble dared meet my eye. He ducked behind a plant, hiding as I passed.

"Considering the circumstances..." Fallione trailed off, unwilling to voice my shame.

I damned myself enough.

"To his rooms." I raked a hand through my hair when Greaves joined us. "He doesn't step foot outside them without my express permission."

"It shall be done." Fallione bowed and veered off down a hall, damage control already underway.

The walk to my chambers passed in a haze, my fury and grief bleeding into one indistinct throb. I shoved the door open and went straight to the bathing room. My hands plunged into the frigid basin, scrubbing Tallon's blood until the water turned pink.

I gripped the edge of the counter, staring at my reflection.

The man in the glass seemed older than I remembered. Dark hair still clung to middle age, but my eyes had dulled, my brow lined deep. Not regal. Not wise. Just spent.

When we were discovered, Nienna looked up at me, panic bright in her gaze. She trusted me, expected me to have an answer. She believed I'd protect her.

But I couldn't even protect myself from my son. I couldn't save her.

Hatred ignited in my veins. I roared and hurled the basin. It struck the floor and shattered—like the fragile peace I carved for Radaan. Gone in one reckless moment of passion.

Each breath scraped my throat as pink water crept across the wooden planks.

Thoughts swarmed, unrelenting and vicious: her brother snatching her away; her dress—torn by my hands as if I were some unchained beast; the shame as she was forced to strip tangled trousers from her feet after she tripped.

Guilt boiled, blistering my chest, searing my soul.

I ruined her.

Furious tears scorched my eyes. Tallon was right. I hadn't just ravaged Radaan—I wrecked her. What prince would marry a princess so disgraced? Who would see past the ruin to the woman spun from sunshine and dragonfire?

I whirled, driving my fist through the mirror. Silvered glass cracked in spiderweb rings, warping my reflection. Blood seeped from my knuckles.

I had destroyed everything.

The scent of roasted meat turned my stomach. Empty chairs hemmed me in, carving the hole in my heart wider. Stares pressed down, thick and heavy, adding to my mantle's weight.

Fallione was absent. Only Darius took up a seat at my table. Threshers loomed in the shadows while those present carried out hushed conversations through muted, forced smiles. No doubt every topic focused on a princess and their king. Forbidden lovers—a scandal dressed in silk and secrets.

Traces of their hushed questions flitted through the dining hall. How long had the affair gone on? Did Tallon know? Could the Chosen of Elohios truly be so deceitful?

I shoved my chair back. The court rose. Not for respect—never for the man beneath the mantle—but out of hollow tradition. The honor I earned through battles, through blood, now ash in their mouths.

Greaves shadowed me as I swept past the high table. Silence trailed me like a ghost of my own making. Every stare clung to me. My chin lifted, though shame burned hot along my throat. Guilt and loathing coursed through me, a toxic poison.

Beyond the hall, I tugged at my tunic's laces. I needed kahve. And air.

My chest locked. Nienna's face blinked into memory—perched against the balustrade, arms folded, wind tugging her hair.

I clawed the thought away and stormed the corridors. Servants scattered. Staff turned to shadows, vanishing from sight.

The kitchen, once alive with clangs and chatter, sat still. No spice in the air. No cider. Only kahve's bitter, earthy musk drifted through the space. It beckoned me.

Igor knew I needed something stronger tonight. Of course he did. Rumors spread like mold in the palace—quiet and all-consuming. A disease.

The short man bowed low as I reached the doorway, then met my stare with a flick of sorrow in his gaze. His mouth dipped.

Disappointment.

Wordless, he ladled dark liquid into a gilded cup, then passed it to me with a crumbling attempt at a smile.

"Thank you." My voice didn't shake, though something inside me did. I turned away.

Steam rose in curls. The black surface rippled, reflecting my fractured thoughts. Greaves reached for the drink, and I handed it off, a wince catching as my bandages bit into my raw skin.

He sipped, grimaced, then returned it. He never developed a taste for the stuff. Hated it nearly as much as Nienna.

When she tried it, her face conveyed everything. She never admitted her repulsion—the furrow between her brows and tight, forced grin had given her away. She drank it only because I did.

A sharp breath filled my chest as I climbed the iron staircase. She once asked about it—the intricate design etched into each step. Her curiosity was a muse for my soul. I told her stories I'd never breathed a word of before. Tales of my mother, my past, parts of myself I held close. She listened.

She cared.

My fingers brushed the giant bug engraved on the post, wings fanned in delicate, impossible lines. Fragile, minute details.

She asked questions no one else bothered to.

I closed my eyes, mouth pressed into a line, then climbed higher.

Outside, sunlight flooded the balcony, gold and cruel, a mockery of my retreat from the dining hall. Sandstone shimmered beneath the fierce rays as if bathed in flames.

How long until she reached Draconia's shores? She wasn't dressed for dragonflight. With no land between her homeland and mine, there would be no place to rest. Just endless sky and sea.

I set my cup aside and braced my palms against the smooth stone, my head bowing low.

"How do I fix this?" The words rasped out, hoarse and thin. Strangled.

I had to find a way to appease Draconia. Ronan threatened war if we tried to stop them. Gods knew I'd already given them plenty of cause. Violence was well within their rights.

And Nereus, Dragon King of Draconia, Lord of the Wild Shores, never left a vow unfulfilled.

Purged in dragonfire.

That was it, the only thing capable of eradicating a Draconis Blood Oath. Vengeance would be his to claim.

I had to prepare my land, my people. Dragons would fly to Radaan.

And still—my thoughts chased Nienna.

She had her brother, his dragon. Surely she was safe.

She would arrive in her homeland broken, exhausted. Her father would rage. And all of it—every bruise, every tear—would be mine to answer for.

I pictured her descent: Gyrak's wings folding; Ronan helping her down; the sunshine hue of her golden hair dulled; skin smeared with dirt; garments torn; eyes wet with unshed tears.

Elohios, spare me.

Nereus would raze Radaan to the ground.

I hurled my kahve, watching it crash far below, lost somewhere in the tangled ruins of the queen's abandoned gardens. The act did nothing to calm my rage. This torment had nowhere to go but inward.

Radaan would burn.

And I would watch it.

Chapter One

S hivers tormented me. My teeth clattered, limbs curling against the last person I wanted near.

Ronan.

Fear of what Gyrak and my brother would do if ordered to remain in Reem—as if I could even force such a thing—had dulled to a bone-deep numbness. Helplessness rooted in my marrow.

Hours passed with my breath timed to Gyrak's wingbeats, trying to stay warm. Ronan's leather-clad arms cinched tighter around me. I stiffened, resisting the urge to shove him off. Rage burned low. He tore me from Radaan.

And I despised him for it.

But more than that, I hated myself.

This was my fault. Kallias was ruined. And me? No man would dare touch me now, not after I'd warmed the hands of a king. Worse still, Ronan radiated fury. His rage clung to the air, thick and brittle. He didn't understand. Never tried. He built his truth and sealed it shut, too wrapped up in his own conclusions.

If he had the power, he would've declared war the moment he saw me on that desk. But breaking a blood oath was only an act of war.

And only our father held the authority to declare it.

The dread in my gut hadn't moved in hours, its burden familiar and heavy.

Father.

Fresh fury surged as I tugged at my torn dress. No breeches. My bare thighs scraped raw against the saddle's leather. He dragged me from Reem without warning. No time to change, to *breathe*.

Humiliation threatened to drown me as I remembered Kallias' mouth on mine, the sound of tearing fabric when he finally tossed caution to the wind, surrendering to his hunger. Gods, the way he'd held me against the wall, letting me feel his need... how my touch slipped beneath his belt...

And then—shame. That filthy shame rippled through me as I struggled out of tangled trousers while my brother dragged me down the hall, my screams trailing behind us.

He would, no doubt, spit every graphic detail of how he found me once we landed on Draconis' shores.

I had to find my mother first. Father couldn't hear this from Ronan. It had to be her. She might—*might*—understand.

Hours wore on, leaving only my worries for company. Tallon planned this. Every piece. He knew I would find him with Fyrn, that I'd run to Kallias. He set me up, and I fell into his trap headfirst.

But how much did he know? How had he learned of my brother's arrival while I was kept in the dark? I never received word that my letters survived the storms. Did *he* send for Ronan?

Bile surged, burning my throat as I thought of Kallias facing Tallon's poison. He was nothing like his son. The king faced his problems, didn't stalk from the shadows. He fought.

Tallon just waited... lurking, picking bones clean. A vulture.

All this time, I toyed with Kallias, teased him, stole moments I never earned. I pushed him against his gods, against his people—and for what?

Guilt caved in. Tears stung, and I ducked my head against Ronan's shoulder.

Kallias was a good king. Loyal. Unyielding. Honest.

He once promised he'd ruin me, but I ruined him, shattered his future. I dragged Radaan toward another war with Vellos... Because of me, there would be no dragons sent to aid them.

I couldn't let my father retaliate.

Shame burned hot, swallowing me whole. Without help, Radaan might fall.

I sagged, all strength sapped from my bones, and I dozed, finding pockets of sleep between stabs of guilt. My ribs ached with emptiness.

I'd left my heart behind.

In Radaan.

Gyrak keened, wings twitching as he dipped, then surged upward on a fresh updraft.

"You'll kill him!" I screamed, slamming my shoulder into Ronan's chest. The massive black dragon had faltered twice since dawn. We still soared leagues above the ocean, no hint of land in sight.

Gyrak was young, but the flight across the sea dragged on for days without sleep or rest. The poor beast was spent by the time they arrived in Reem. He'd needed a chance to recover before returning to Draconia, but my brother hadn't granted him that mercy.

"He can make it!"

Ronan braced himself as Gyrak huffed and lifted his neck, shielding us from the wind. He gripped my shoulder and shoved to his feet, then staggered forward, balancing across Gyrak's midnight spine.

The sun beat down, warmer now, but the absence of Ronan's body heat hit me at once. I wrapped my arms around myself, a shiver crawling down my back.

He scowled, stumbling toward the edge where the dragon's scales sloped to the open sea.

"Not shy anymore, are you?!" he shouted, fiddling with his belt to relieve himself. "See one, then you've seen them–"

"One more word, Ronan! Say it, and I'll toss you to the jellyfish!" I screamed into the gale, twisting back toward Gyrak's spiny neck.

To keep his head upright in flight strained him, but it was the only time riders could relieve themselves midair. Another reminder that the system wasn't built for women. My options were to hold it, or disgrace myself. Not that the beast would care, but my brother—and every Draconis alive—would never forgive me for such an insult.

"It's your fault he's in this state!" Ronan growled.

That broke the dam. I snarled, yanking my boots from the stirrups.

"Sit down!"

"No!" I shouted, clawing my way free of the saddle. My boot slipped over a smooth scale. Wind tore my split dress open, fabric flaring. My bare legs shone in the sunlight, but Ronan's clear gaze remained on mine. "You don't get to order me! You never have!" My voice cracked. "This is your fault! You never listen—you do what you want and damn the cost! You forgot your place!"

"I'm the heir! You're just a–"

My fists slammed into his chest. His body pitched over the dragon's side.

Ronan's shout vanished into the roar of the wind. I stumbled forward. He caught a current, spinning into a free fall. His dragon bellowed, wings folding as he twisted midair. I screamed, nails scraping for purchase.

Gyrak surged upward, his head snapping my way, using his snout to shove me toward the saddle. I kicked against his back, boots slipping on his slick scales. He growled, teeth nipping at my feet.

"I'm trying!"

Motions frantic, I swung my leg over just as Gyrak rolled into a dive. Air punched from my lungs. My fingers flew over buckles, yanking the straps tight around my calves. I knew what came next. I wouldn't hold on–

Everything went black.

I snapped awake with a jolt. My head slammed into a wall of dark scale. Pain burst across my tongue where my teeth bit down. I braced a hand against the dragon, scanning the sea below.

A deep growl rumbled from Gyrak's throat as he beat his wings, climbing again. His tail skimmed the water.

Ronan hauled himself over the dragon's shoulder, face livid.

"You wicked hag." His breaths panted, harsh and strained as he slid in behind me. His chest crushed against my back. "You could've died!"

My heart twisted, heat knotting beneath my ribs. Gyrak would have saved Ronan first. He always would. His bonded, his rider—more important, more valuable. Even with Ronan's freefall, I was the one hanging by a thread.

Something warm smeared across my lips. I wiped it away, scowling at the crimson staining my hand.

"Sea beneath, sister. You already looked bad enough!"

The urge to shove him off again nearly won. "You should have let me prepare!"

"You don't get it." He wrapped his legs over mine to steady us as Gyrak climbed. Each wingbeat shuddered through the dragon's frame. "It wasn't just me, Nienna." He shrugged off his leather jacket. "You were... *on display* like a common whore."

I snarled, throwing an elbow into his gut. I knew what happened. The memory was carved into me—no escaping it.

"Shut up and listen."

He caught my arms, forcing them into his jacket. Heat bled into my bones, and I hated the comfort it gave. He didn't let me speak.

"All of them saw you. Tallon. The Velli. Half the palace! The oath—he tore it apart. You both did." His voice cracked, faltering. "Don't pretend you understand how it felt. To see you that way—my sister–"

He hesitated. His breath hit the back of my neck. "Sea beneath, how could you?"

"How could I what, Ronan?" I turned my head, anger rising—but already retreating like the tide. "Fall in love? You weren't there. You don't know how it felt. He was the only one who cared about–"

"Our people are starving," he spat. "And you think a man twice your age—willing to void a *blood oath*—loves you?!"

Helpless tears burned behind my eyes. That was all he would see—an aging king, dishonorable and treacherous enough to break a blood oath. A man who treated the threat of dragonfire like smoke in the wind. To Ronan, Kallias mocked Draconia's warnings, taking advantage of me to do so.

No, my brother wouldn't believe anything I said. I could only hope that my father might see reason.

By morning, Gyrak faltered. Ronan stayed silent, his face pale and drawn. He refused to speak to me. He offered a strip of dried meat from his pack, avoiding my eyes.

The black beast glided on updrafts, wings trembling in the breeze. A young dragon could make the four-day trip—but a return flight with no rest had never been done.

As the day wore on, we sank lower. Gyrak's talons skimmed the water, cutting silver ripples across the waves.

I ground my jaw tight. We were too far from Radaan to turn back, too distant from Draconia to push ahead. No land between us—only sea. We had no choice but to fly.

When night fell, cold pressed into my skull until my head throbbed. Ronan's water supply had dwindled to its last few drops. His reckless flight from home was catching up. Gyrak panted, steam gusting from his nostrils, each breath ragged as he fought to stay aloft.

"Brace yourself!"

I blinked, headache blurring my thoughts as I grabbed the saddle's edge. The stars flickered on a still, glassy surface. No storm churned above. What would impede our flight?

Gyrak dropped like a stone, crashing into the sea. I screamed, nails biting into leather. Ronan yanked me tight against him as seawater surged up our legs. The dragon flailed, wings sprawled, struggling to stay afloat.

Cold punched through my dress and soaked into my boots. Panic scraped its claws across my throat. Gyrak huffed, curling his wings, dipping his head to the black water.

Never in our known history had a dragon landed in the sea. Fear of the dark abyss was as much a part of them as their scales or flames. Gyrak shuddered beneath us, and Ronan slumped forward, his forehead resting against my shoulder.

"He needs to rest."

Heat prickled across my skin, feverish. I ignored it. The water below my boot looked endless and cold. Resting his wings wouldn't help if he couldn't take off again.

Would we die here? Stranded with a waterlogged dragon?

Ronan sagged into me, his breath warm and shallow. I bit my cheek. I would keep watch. They had to rest. Even if I hated them for it—right now, they needed me.

A distant wail pierced the silence. I jerked upright, rubbing my eyes. My brother's chest weighed against my back. The sound had cut through the dark—sharp, eerie, not wind, not waves.

Another cry followed—high and thin. My heart stuttered.

I slapped Ronan's thigh. "Wake up!"

He jolted, gripping my shoulder. I twisted, scouring each direction. The sea was empty. The sky untouched. Dawn barely kissed the horizon. There was *nothing*.

"We need to go! Now!" I slammed my fist into Gyrak's side. The dragon groaned, shifting, weariness making him sluggish. His nostrils flared as he sniffed the water.

The call rose again—closer. Beneath us.

My heart lurched to my throat, panic flooding my veins with icy terror. I pounded my fist into Gyrak once more. His massive wings snapped open, slapping the sea. Too heavy. Not enough lift.

The shriek shattered the air, deafening. I clutched onto Gyrak, fingers scrabbling across damp scales. Ronan cursed, fire sparking along his palms. His flames lit the water in flickers, but the inky depths below stayed black, endless.

Gyrak thrashed. His wings pounded. His neck stretched, desperate to take to the sky.

This was why dragons avoided the open ocean.

A swell rose around us. The sea heaved in a towering wave. My scream choked in my throat, dead before it could break free. The beast blocked out the stars—colossal, white-fanged. Moonlight glinted off jagged teeth.

Ronan shouted. Fire burst from his hands, flaring into the beast's cavernous maw as it closed in.

"Fly, Gyrak! Now!"

I slammed my palm against his scales. A jolt of raw power surged through my arm. The dragon shrieked, twisted, claws ripping through briny spray. His talons found the monster's face, raked toward a black, glistening eye.

A shark? Or whale? No. Something worse. Bigger than anything I'd seen.

I clung to the saddle as the creature snapped sideways, its ivory teeth snaring Gyrak's rear claw.

Ronan threw more fire, light blazing off barnacle-crusted skin. Gyrak bellowed as the monster bit down. With a wrenching cry, he tore free—sacrificing a toe—and scrambled atop the creature's head.

The beast recoiled into the depths.

Gyrak seized the moment. His wings struck the air with deep, jarring force. We rose.

I gasped, clutching the dark scales as we took flight. Ronan pressed against me, arms locked tight around my waist. His chest was stone—rigid, tense.

He demanded the dragon fly without rest.

Now Gyrak bore the cost.

We rode in silence as the sun ascended. Gyrak's low whimpers filled the space between each labored wingbeat. Ache settled in my bones. Heat blistered beneath my skin. Sleep pulled at me, dragging me under in fits. Ronan shook me, his voice cutting through the fog—but not far enough.

I only wanted to rest.

The deeper I sank into its embrace, the harder it became to rise.

Eventually, I stopped trying.

Chapter Two

Trees swallowed Kallias, his green overcoat vanishing into the forest's shadows. I opened my mouth to call him back, to beg him to wait, but no sound came. The air scorched my throat, and my silken dress clung to my sweat-slicked skin. A thorn bush snagged my skirts, slicing into my leg. I gasped, yanking on the fabric, eyes searching the tangle of branches.

A flash of green, then a glint of gold. Silvered hair caught the light before vanishing behind a massive oak.

"Kallias." The word rasped from my throat, my body straining to force it out.

Why was he leaving? I needed him! Words burned in my chest—I had to tell him how sorry I was. I ruined everything. Somehow, I had to make it right—to grant him the peace he'd spent years chasing.

I tore my skirts from the thorns, took one step—then a branch looped around my waist.

A deafening roar pulled me from my delirium.

Ronan's arm crushed my ribs as I dangled from the saddle, my foot wedged in the stirrup.

My heart lurched, and I flailed, clawing at Gyrak's scales, the jagged ridges biting into my palms.

Spray hit my face, the salt burning my cuts and scrapes as I righted myself. Gyrak flew so low, his bloodied paw skimmed the sea. Each wingbeat dragged, his breaths ragged and rattling. I turned—and bile surged up my throat. Ronan's features had gone gray, his skin slick with sweat. His eyes clamped shut, nostrils flaring with each staggered inhale.

Another roar tore through the sky. The cadence knifed through my skull.

I knew that sound.

Argos swept overhead, a shadow vast enough to smother Gyrak. His midnight neck stretched out as he dipped his head and sniffed. He glided past, careful not to jostle the smaller dragon. My father rode him, a narrow silhouette turned toward us, his face blurred, the details lost in distance.

Weakness lapped at my strength. The adrenaline from waking did nothing to hold me upright, and I slumped against Gyrak, his obsidian scales trembling beneath me.

"Almost home." I pressed a hand to the dragon's side, stroking. My blood smeared against him, catching the light like spilled rubies.

Argos huffed and circled to guide us in—but Gyrak wouldn't reach the Spire. The landing sat far above. Too far. We'd have to touch down on the shore, adding to our humiliation.

My body ached with fever, every muscle protesting each tiny movement, though my shame blazed hotter. My failure would be laid bare for all to see.

I hadn't trained for dragonflight—never crossed the sea like this. My skin burned. My mind swam. Ronan's jacket held my shredded dress together, but it wasn't rider's gear.

Gyrak groaned, and his wing folded with a snap, sending us crashing into the surf. I shrieked. My brother's arms locked around me as the weight of a dying dragon slammed into Draconia's shallows.

Ronan crashed into my back, and my skull cracked against Gyrak's neck. Pain split my vision. Salt water blasted upward, stinging like thrown gravel.

The beast let out a broken cry, fighting to stay upright. Staggering, he found the sand, dragging his wings through the surf, his head hung low.

Argos circled once, then dove for the beach.

Gyrak barely reached dry land before collapsing. The ground trembled as our father's dragon landed nearby, a living shadow that devoured the sun. The massive beast snarled, then nosed Gyrak's wet wing with a puff of contempt.

My brother sagged against me, unmoving. "Ronan." The name peeled my lips. My voice cracked.

What price would he pay, forcing his dragon through such strain?

Draconis poured from the seaside homes, drawn by the crash.

I had to *move*, had to stop my father before he plunged into war with Radaan. With Kallias.

My fingers fumbled at the straps binding my leg, too weak to undo the buckles. My head swam as I leaned sideways, straining to free myself. They held fast. Ronan's weight pinned me. Pain pulsed behind my eyes while my hands trembled, useless.

Father climbed Gyrak's shoulder with fluid ease, navy leathers gleaming with silver thread and pearls. He drew a knife and sliced the straps clean through. The blade hovered at the skin of my thigh, and his piercing gaze flashed from my leg to my face.

"What happened?!" Concern warred with his rage. His brow knit, lips peeled into a snarl as he wrapped an arm around my waist, but I reached for him first.

"Please—don't–" My voice cracked. My eyes burned, but no tears came. We'd gone too long without water.

My father carried me down, setting me on the sun-warmed sand. "Is Radaan at war?"

"No." I choked on the word, desperate to get more out around my slow tongue.

"Then they shall pay." Crimson bloomed beneath his white beard, and his gray eyes sparked as I gasped, clutching his chest.

"Fa–"

The world pitched. His arms caught me before I hit the ground.

"Erin!" His bellow rang out, cold and authoritative. A king's command.

"I've got her, Your Majesty!"

A woman sprinted to my side, canteen in hand. She knelt, bracing her knee behind my back. I leaned into her thigh, grateful for the support. A thin smile split my lips, and fresh blood trickled down my chin as Father turned to climb Gyrak again—for Ronan.

Argos snorted at Gyrak's collapsed body. The smaller dragon couldn't lift his head. His sides heaved, panting in ragged bursts that kicked up sand around the gathering crowd.

I slumped into myself, eyes fixed on the waves churning between the dragons. Ronan's jacket hung heavy on my shoulders—I pulled it tighter, swaying. Sitting upright cost more than I had. Muscles screamed for rest. Nausea twisted my gut, and the ground trembled, as if we hadn't landed at all.

I planted a bloody hand on the beach. A shell bit into my palm, sharp and real, but it didn't clear the fog from my mind.

"Princess, here." Erin swept blonde braids over her shoulder and pressed the drink to my lips.

I tried to lift my hands, but they fell weak and useless in my lap. Cool water met my tongue, though my throat refused to swallow. Liquid spilled down my chest, soaking my torn dress. I coughed, each spasm draining what little strength I had left.

"Abyss!" she hissed, yanking the canteen away.

"Ain, Baer—see Ronan to the Spire," Father called out, voice steady and sharp. "Ned, take your crew. Make sure Gyrak is fed."

Sunlight lit the blue of his leathers, wrapped snug around his broad frame. His body bore the power of a Dragon Rider—solid, honed, unyielding. Two men stepped from the hushed crowd, lifting Ronan between them.

Then Father turned toward me.

My chest splintered. A sob clawed free. He dropped to his knees beside me, jaw taut, eyes fierce. His palm cupped my cheek, rough and warm.

"I will see you to your mother," he said, voice thick with grief. "Then I fly for Radaan."

"No." My hand shot up, fumbling for his. "You can't." My words slurred, tongue heavy and slow. The world spun, blurring the edges. "Please. You don't know-" My head tipped back, and I slipped into blackness.

Sweet humming tugged me from sleep. Dreamless, or maybe not—I let the images slip away, unwilling to chase them. They'd only remind me of what I lost.

"Tea, now."

The sound strangled me. My mother. Her voice cracked something deep. My soul yearned for the calm she carried, the protection she offered. My heart splintered, knowing she alone might understand what Kallias meant to me.

She would be pivotal in avoiding war.

My eyelids stayed shut, too dry to wrestle open, and my tongue scraped across the roof of my mouth, attempting to shape coherent words that refused to form.

Arms lifted me. One eye cracked as a teacup pressed to my lips. The scent hit first—water lilies, soft and clean—then peppermint, sharp enough to clear the fog in my head.

She tilted the cup, and I sipped. Too sweet. My body jolted, adrenaline rushing in a hot surge. The next sip came briny but cool, and my throat remembered how to work. I trembled, forcing down the tepid tea.

Only when the cup emptied did she let me sink back. She passed it to a servant, her blue sleeve nearly brushing the stone floor before she snatched a cloth from a basin.

Her graying, golden curls rose in pinned swirls, a silver crown tucked among them. As she wiped my face, her expression softened, a faint smile tugging at her lips. She pressed the cool cloth to my eyes, easing the sting, soothing the itch and ache.

"Mother–"

"Hush. Your brother will inform Nereus."

I lurched upright. "Ronan?!" The name distorted, mouth thick and uncooperative.

"Do not rise, Nienna." Sparks lit in her gaze. "Speak, if you must. But if you brave the Cireendium, Kalepsi will spirit you away to the Nest."

Across the room, the servant glanced our way, lips drawn tight as she set the kettle on the hearth.

"Ronan cannot tell Father." I tripped over my words, cringing. Shame pooled in my stomach.

"He sees to your brother as I see to you." She sat back in her chair, studying me. "Can you not trust him to speak true?"

My gaze dropped to the silk gown clinging to my skin, clean and unmarked. "He'll lie." I bit down hard as her brows arched beneath the crown. "He doesn't understand."

"You were attacked. That's plain enough to see–"

"By Ronan!" I snapped. "He did not attack me!"

"Who?"

"Kal–"

My mouth clicked shut, teeth catching my broken lip. Blood seeped onto my tongue, sharp and metallic. I glanced at the servant. Mother needed to know. Rumors would spread soon enough, but not like this. The staff didn't need to hear my confession.

That I loved him.

That I broke him—and left.

"Aine, leave us, please." Mother's voice dropped, cool as water over stone.

I kept my eyes down. She already knew. The words I'd used. The defense I'd given. I had to make her believe Kallias hadn't done this.

Aine bowed and slipped through the door.

In the quiet, I steadied my breath, forcing my thoughts to fall into place. I needed a logical argument, something my parents would hear.

They'd brought me back to my old rooms. Sunlight streamed through windows cut into the dark stone. Warm tapestries hung in waves of gold and indigo, ocean sunsets locked in thread. Intricate woven rugs adorned the floor. Shells, driftwood, and hanging abalone disks shimmered along the walls, pale rainbows swaying in the still air.

My chest ached. I never thought I'd return. I was promised to another kingdom. Meant to be a bride, not a shameful whisper. But here I was—not as a cherished princess, a daughter of honor—but as a stain on the name I carried.

Not just mine. Kallias'. My father's.

Guilt settled across my shoulders, and I buried my face in my hands. My fingers scrubbed at the raw, chapped skin as if I could scrape away days of regret.

"I made a mistake," I whispered, voice muffled through my palms. Fingertips pressed to my aching eyes. My body craved a bath, a meal, a tincture for the hammering in my skull.

But war would not wait.

The bed shifted beneath my mother's weight, and her arm enveloped me, pulling me close, anchoring me to her chest.

"Tell me everything."

So I did.

She let me bury my face, arms wrapped tight as I poured out every detail. Dry sobs clutched my throat, choking off words as I spoke of Tallon's cruelty—of Kallias' quiet kindness. I omitted the assassination attempt and Tallon's attack. She only needed bones—the thinnest skeleton of truth. Shame seared my ears when I reached Kallias, and I chose each word with care. But she was my mother. By the slow, steady inhale as I said his name, she knew who had my heart.

Explaining how I found Tallon with Fyrn was easy, but when I got to the study, my mouth seemed to forget how to speak.

"And when I ran, I... well, I thought–" I broke off, heat crawling up my neck. I was a fool. Naïve. A pawn in Tallon's game.

"You ran to his father."

Mother's words hooked into my soul, wrenching it. I hated the way she said that. Kallias was so much more than Tallon's father. But to them, he'd be nothing except the man who tried to bed his son's betrothed.

She sighed, arms slipping from me as she stood. My hands dropped from my face. My eyes stung with tears I hadn't shed.

She smoothed her fine blue gown. Her expression turned unreadable. "Should we expect a babe?"

"No!" My gasp tore out of me. I yanked my neckline higher, cheeks flushed with horror.

"Don't act so shocked. You show up near death, on dragonback, your dress in tatters, legs bare—then tell me your brother caught you in a compromising position with the King of Radaan." Her head tilted. Her glare cut straight through. "Be mindful, Princess. Radaan has committed an act of war. We are a wingbeat from raining dragonfire from their sky."

I shut my eyes. Helplessness rolled over me, pulled me under. If she couldn't understand, who would? I only wanted to protect Kallias. But how?

"Nienna." She stooped down to brush the matted hair from my brow. "Rest later. Save your emotions for another day. Right now, *we* find your father—and explain."

I managed a fragile nod.

She offered a tight smile, the fine lines near her eyes deepening. "Wear blue, not green." She turned on her heel, heading for the dressing rooms. "He doesn't need reminders of Radaan."

She helped me dress, pulled my hair back as best she could. Four days of wind and flying reduced it to a nest. As we walked, she bore most of my weight, guiding me through the corridors and into the Spire's inner halls.

I focused on my strides—one step, then the next. The sharp-sweet burn of peppermint tea lingered on my tongue, but its strength faded fast. We moved too quickly for me to meet the staff's stares or take comfort in the familiar corners of home.

A low hum shivered through the walls as Mother veered into a side corridor, steering us away from the Cireendium. The hum deepened into a growl, flickering the lantern flames.

"Silence, you old bat," Mother muttered.

I smiled, lip splitting. Kalepsi likely heard her and snapped at the air in protest.

The Cireendium lay at the Spire's hollow center—a vast cavern barely big enough for Kalepsi. But the violet dragon would climb down stone and steel to see me—her Dragon's Heart.

"How did you get me to my room?" I asked, tripping over my feet.

Mother caught my arm, hauling me upright. "Zane flew you through the Cireendium while Argos distracted Kalepsi. You probably owe more to Tsunami—the pest nagged at them both."

She referred to the blue-and-green dragon, who had yet to claim a rider or move on to the Wild Shores. A ship-sized dog with wings, an irritating menace—but one we all adored.

We pivoted down another corridor, and the contrast struck me like a slap. Reem's palace breathed warmth—lush with creeping vines, guarded at every turn. The Spire gleamed with polished black stone and mirrored lantern light, yet it pulsed with motion. Servants wandered, their stares blatant, their whispers trailing behind us. One rider in full flight leathers darted past. The only sign of unrest.

A reminder that Radaan had clawed its way from war's shadow—and I was the last thread holding it back from another.

Mother opened the door, and dread punched the air from my lungs.

A massive table took up the battle room's center. Dragon Riders circled it, flight leathers creaking, goggles slung around necks or perched on windswept hair. Silence crashed into the space as every gaze snapped to me.

Shock. Outrage. Faces sharpened with both. A few drew in sharp breaths—but my eyes found only my father.

He leaned over the table, goggles clenched in one fist. His other hand fell from where it had gestured across the map—toward Radaan. His blue uniform stretched over corded arms and broad shoulders. He wasn't soft. He was a warrior, poised for battle.

Jagged shells crowned his epaulets, the mark of the Dragon King—as if the circlet nestled in his white hair left any doubt. His flushed face twisted with fury, jaw twitching beneath his snowy beard as his gaze flitted between Mother and me.

I froze. Part of me longed to run to him, to bury myself in his arms and let him shield me from those gawking stares. The other half itched to flee—to escape the outrage smoldering behind them.

"Nereus. A word." Mother's voice held no room for refusal. Her hands dropped to her sides, chin high. Sunlight caught the gold and silver in her hair, setting her crown ablaze.

"Wait in the hall." Father's order cracked through the silence.

He stepped from the table as the riders murmured their respect and filed out. His hand—calloused, warm—cupped my cheek. My throat burned with the rise of familiar tears as he brushed his thumb over my skin.

"Nienna," he said, voice cracking as he tugged me into his arms.

A sob tore free as he folded me into him. His scent wrapped around me—salt and wind and Argos' smoky musk. Safe.

He pulled back, wiping the lone tear that slipped down my wind-chapped cheek. "I will kill him."

No.

The warmth of his embrace turned to frost. My heart stalled.

"No, Father–"

"I told him," Ronan's voice slurred from the chair, drawing my attention. He looked like death. Pale skin. Dark hollows under his eyes. "Everything, Nienna."

"You didn't *know* everything!" I hissed. "Father—call off the riders."

The tenderness in Father's face vanished, scorched away by rage. "I'll fly to Radaan. We have an oath to uphold."

"This wasn't his fault!" How much had Ronan told him?

"This time? Or the times before?" My brother's sneer cut as if a blade plunged between my ribs.

"It happened before?" Father jerked back, hand dropping as if I'd burned him.

"No! Nothing hap–"

"Bucking between your legs like–"

"Ronan! Mind your tongue!" Mother hissed, her command a whip crack. "See yourself to bed."

"I'm a rider first. The Dragon King rallied his riders." My brother slumped deeper into the plush chair, eyes closing.

"You're in no state to fly," she said, then pressed her hand to my shoulder.

I bit my tongue against berating him further. He nearly killed Gyrak, flying off in a rage. Mother had to put him in his place. I had no authority over him beyond the dinner knife I would gladly stick him with when I got the chance.

He groaned, eyeing our father with a heavy-lidded stare.

"Bed."

Father's growl turned his voice to gravel. His face shut down, but his eyes speared through me, piercing mine as if he saw into my soul, laying bare all my secrets. My spine stiffened, and the room tilted beneath the weight of his glare. The hairs on my nape bristled.

"Fine!" Ronan flung his arms and dragged himself upright. He shuffled out without sparing me a glance.

As the door clicked shut, I deflated, my shoulders caving in. Mother guided me to the chair my brother abandoned, and I sank into the thick cushion, rubbing scabbed hands over my tender face.

"Nereus, hear her," she said.

"Ronan filled me in." His words were so cold. Detached. Wroth.

"He doesn't know the whole story." I wrapped my arms around myself, braving my father's fury. "He waited all of a breath before threatening to burn Radaan."

"That's where we differ, Nienna." His nostrils flared, and the leather of his goggles creaked beneath his tightening grip. "I wouldn't have waited. I would've set her ablaze then and there."

"Stop–"

"Did he rape you?"

I flinched. "No!"

"That doesn't save him." Teeth bared, my father scanned the window above my head as if even looking at me soured his stomach. "He swore an oath—in blood—to protect you, to wed you to his son. And instead, he attacked you!"

"That's not what happened!" I screamed, matching his shout. "I love him!"

He froze.

Mother shut her eyes. Shame thundered in my chest. I'd said too much. But I couldn't let him believe Kallias hurt me.

"It was *my* fault." The words cracked in my throat.

A vein pulsed at Father's temple. He didn't move.

"I pursued him." My voice trembled. "Please—don't fly to Radaan. Kallias–"

"Signed a Draconis Blood Oath." He cut me off. "His life is forfeit. And if a king's life is forfeit—so is that of his nation."

"We cannot sustain a war on foreign lands," Mother snapped.

His glare sliced toward her. "You're taking her side?"

She met his ire, unflinching. "I stand with Draconia. As *you* should."

"Our daughter was," he choked on the word, jaw working as if the words tasted foul, "violated! I won't need to start a war. I'll set Reem ablaze!"

What else could I say? I would've begged—on my knees—if it might make him reconsider. But it wouldn't. The sight would only enrage him further. Draconis did not beg.

"Nereus," Mother's tone softened.

He inhaled through flared nostrils. Argos roared outside, stone quivering underfoot.

"She's here. She's safe," she continued, hand pressed to his chest. "I'm not saying let it go. Retribution will have its place. Just—give her time."

My head fell forward in shame, and my nails dug into my sides, clawing at my sanity. He hated that I was hurt, but didn't see that he was still causing me pain.

I stood, one hand braced on the chair as I lifted my chin. "I gave my oath."

A lie.

To my father.

Hidden under the perfect mask of a princess raised at court.

He dipped his head, gaze sharp beneath his thick brows.

I left no room for dispute, barreling on. "A Draconis Blood Oath can only be purged in dragonfire." I struggled to keep my voice even and clear. "Are you prepared to slander the Draconis name—and burn your daughter alive?"

He shrugged off Mother's hand, prowling closer. I held my ground as he gripped my chin, eyes boring into mine. My skin prickled, palms growing slick.

Could he see the lie?

Did he know?

Had I destroyed the final remnants of my father's trust?

"I have not tarnished our name." Resignation colored his tone, and I smothered my hope. "Go to bed, Nienna."

His hand dropped, and I staggered as if it was the only thing holding me upright.

"Sea beneath," he muttered.

Before I could blink, my feet left the floor, and he hauled me into the warmth of his chest. Medals dug into my cheek, his leathers creaking with every stride. I didn't protest. Couldn't. I just let myself be held.

He said nothing as he kicked the door open and carried me past the riders in the hall.

I should've objected. A princess would have.

But I was too tired, too hollow, my soul too broken.

He made no promises as we strode beyond Kalepsi's wailing, or as he laid me in bed and brushed hair from my face. No comments, no accusations. My chest throbbed, tight with a plea I couldn't voice—that he'd swear to leave Radaan alone.

But I remained silent.

And he left without a word.

Chapter Three

Mother's hand stayed firm on my elbow as we climbed the long winding staircase to the Nest. A full night's sleep, hot food, and fresh water had begun to rebuild my strength. But my thighs and calves, softened by Radaan's flat plains, protested the endless ascent

A sharp pang cut through me. I buried it fast, embracing the burn. I couldn't afford to think of Radaan.

Oils coated my cheeks and split lip, shielding the raw skin. My hands lay swaddled in linen, hiding the gashes from clinging to Gyrak's scales. Nothing could touch the bruises under my eyes—the price of slamming my head against his neck.

I looked wrecked.

A battered shell for a soul in shreds.

Breath rasped in my throat, and I slowed, squinting toward the black passage above. Mother shifted the lantern, golden light flashing across the cold stone walls.

So different from Radaan, where life couldn't be contained.

A throaty croon rolled down the stairwell, followed by heavy sniffing. A faint smile tugged on my scabbed lip, and I forced my legs onward.

At last, we reached a landing. Mother turned the lantern low and hooked it on the wall.

"She'll be insufferable," she muttered.

I chuckled and pushed at the door. It flung wide. I hadn't set foot through before a golden eye blocked the way, the slit pupil tightening as it swept my frame.

"Kalepsi." My throat tightened. I raised a bandaged hand, pressing it to her cool, dark cheek. "Let me in."

With a sharp huff and one last scan, her great head withdrew. I stepped inside, and wind rushed past, tearing at my skirts now that the windbreak no longer shielded me.

A wall of purple scales nudged me deeper into the chamber. I strode over sun-bleached bones and crumbled shells, careful not to slip on the gouged floor where dragons once quarreled. Kalepsi herded me toward a hollow carved in the black stone.

After a gentle push, I stumbled forward, catching myself against a pale-blue egg the size of a barrel. It jostled the others. A myriad of colors and patterns swirled across their thick, dimpled shells, but I knew from experience it would take more than a tumble to break one.

Kalepsi's tail looped around me, pressing me into the Nest. Curled close, she shut the world away, and I laughed up at her as she dipped her head low, pulling in a long, slow breath.

In the shade, her scales blended into near-black. In sunlight, they bloomed violet like wildflowers after rain.

"You laid a clutch." I eased her tail aside and lowered myself against the curve of an egg.

Only hers ever grew this large. The older the dragon, the bigger the egg. Younger beasts laid smaller ones, and their hatchlings took years to grow strong enough for a rider. Kalepsi's hatchlings could carry someone before their first year.

Not always a good thing. Riding a half-grown dragonling invited disaster. Gyrak and Ronan proved that. They'd been insufferable. He'd bonded as a boy when the black hatchling barely held the strength to lift him. A horse-sized beast flitting through the palace had been a nightmare.

Father once grounded him, forced him to walk everywhere for a week. *'A dragon is not a ride,'* he had said. *'Not a shortcut.'*

Kalepsi hummed, settling her head on paws the size of my body. Her nostrils flared. She could smell my unease. I'd be stuck here until she deemed me healed, but after keeping the Spire awake all night with her howls, she'd earned her peace.

Draconia could rest. That was enough.

"I am fine."

She snorted, one lazy eye sliding open like she knew better.

"I'm here. Isn't that what you wanted?"

Grief tightened my lungs, and I dug the heels of my palms into my eyes. Kalepsi might've craved my return, to have me cradled in her Nest, but she wasn't the reason I came back.

My body was mending, but my heart would never fully heal. In the night, I wept like a child, stunned by the simple fact that I once again could. Visions of Kallias, alone, facing his people—Tallon—haunted me. I mourned him, but fury flared hotter at the thought of Tallon poised behind his father's throne, undermining him. Waiting.

Kalepsi's thick tail trembled, muscles shivering against my side.

"Kalepsi, let me in," Mother called from beyond the scaled wall.

The dragon queen didn't move. Her gleaming eye narrowed on me, reading the cracks I couldn't speak aloud. Time stretched, wordless.

Because I wasn't fine.

My heart ached. I shattered my name, turned Father against me, pushed Radaan to the brink of war, and abandoned Kallias in the storm I stirred. Every thought curved back to him.

What would life look like without him?

Cold. Miserable.

I tasted passion, felt what it meant to love. Kallias was strong, steady. A true king—not perfect, but powerful. Fierce. His presence lifted his people, stoked their spirit. He was everything I wanted.

No one else matched his fire with restraint. Nobody saw the world as he did—with that rare blend of resolve and mercy.

Not that anyone would have me now.

A princess caught mid-betrayal, with a man who wasn't her betrothed. Who would trust me to remain loyal? Unless he chained me like a prisoner. Locked me behind iron bars.

My fingers closed around my throat, eyes clamped shut, fighting a silent scream against my constricted airway.

There was nothing left. I had to face what waited: the hollow stares tinged with the slow dying of trust; the hunger we'd share, born from my failure.

Arms crossed tight, I met Kalepsi's eye. Still as stone, she studied me—pupil thin as a thread. I didn't look away. I bared my soul, letting her see my pain, my ruin. There was nothing either of us could do about it.

I dropped my gaze, unable to handle her scrutiny any longer.

Silence thickened. Only the wind's sharp cry and distant gulls competed with the dragon fleet roaring offshore.

At last, Kalepsi eased aside, granting my mother entrance. Queen though she was, she waited for permission like everyone else. She stepped forward, brushing her fingers across the dark violet scales for balance, casting a glare up at the massive beast.

My mask slid into place, concealing my damaged heart to deal with later.

She settled beside me, sighing as her spine met the bronze curve of a nearby shell.

A low chirp broke the quiet, followed by a gust of wind and the heavy thump of wings. Roars rolled over the Spire, a cacophony of dragons banking just outside.

"Tsunami's being a menace," Mother muttered.

"At least the riders stayed behind to rein her in." I kept my voice even. Father didn't ride out yesterday, but he also wouldn't speak to me. He locked himself in his war room, only leaving to fly Argos, who passed the time hurling boulders off the sea cliffs, sharing his rider's fury.

"She tipped a ship last week." Mother pinched the bridge of her nose.

"Black fish?" The great whales often traveled in pods. Dragons loved them.

"Crab."

Tsunami's favorite. When haulers dragged in a net, they were expected to alert Artorius and his rider to deter her from sinking the ship.

I chuckled, wrapping my arms around myself. "Where was Artorius?"

"Patrolling the south. There are stirrings in the Wild Shores. Your father's sending more riders to keep watch."

"What's happened?" I tilted my head, latching onto this new information. I was a Draconis princess once more. My place was here, my mind needed to be, as well.

"Nothing alarming." She gave me a faint smile. "Argos feels it, and your father doesn't want to lose our hold."

We had planned to expand to those lands, as we were the only island with dragons. Unbonded beasts roamed there, so no other isle could claim it.

But we needed resources to settle.

Resources Radaan had once promised.

I nodded and leaned back, eyes falling shut. "You've planned everything for the Awakening?"

"There's always more to do, and your touch would be welcome with the decorations. Williard swore he'd retire from kite-making when you left. Perhaps you can coax him into one more year."

A bittersweet smile teased my lips. The Awakening marked the end of whirlstorm season. It also signaled the start of Hatching Days, when the eggs cracked open. Draconis celebrated with songs, dancing, feasts, and kites soaring overhead. A time steeped in joy and reverie.

Williard was a wizard with kites, and one of the island's finest Vessels. He funneled magic into paper and string, turning sky into canvas. Trails of color drifted behind his creations, glowing like comets. Father himself once gave him the power to fuel them.

Memories stirred: bare feet pounding sand, wind tugging my hair, a dragon kite trailing golden dust. He was my favorite kite maker.

But if I visited now, would he see the same sweet princess who once raced through the tidefoam? Or had I been reduced to a stained name, a fallen daughter?

Self-doubt soured my stomach. I hated this endless cycle of questioning my worth. Would anyone welcome my return?

"The Kulletti recently arrived for the Awakening. Join us for dinner."

"Already?" I scoffed. They never failed to needle Father, hinting we should gift them dragon eggs. No matter how often we explained that dragons chose their riders—*not* us—they ignored it. Their people settled on the island nearest the Wild Shores decades ago, and to this day, remained dragonless.

"They wouldn't dare be late," Mother muttered. "They'll drive your father mad. If it weren't for their pearls, we'd have cut ties long ago."

Kulletti pearls shimmered with multiple colors, but the rare crimson ones held the most worth. They were the only thing that gave them standing among the island nations.

I thought of Radaan, how jewels gleamed on goblets, rings, and every unguarded corner. Gems flowed there like water. Here, pearls were our riches. No room for quarries, no stones to mine. But one day, expanding our homeland might give us that.

Kallias wore no gems on his yoke. Just beaten gold, etched with vines and filigree. No rubies. No opals.

Why?

I pushed the question aside. "If Kalepsi lets me go."

The dragon queen's eye narrowed, and I grinned as wide as my injured lip allowed. She stayed still, watching, asking without words if I truly meant it.

I didn't.

Nestled between eggs warm with life, a steady heartbeat pulsing behind me, a wall of thick scales pressed at my side, and only my mother for company—alone with the wind and remnants of death and birth. I could hide here forever.

But I was a princess.

Duty came first.

Guilt lanced through me.

Mother lingered for hours, catching me up on everything I'd missed. She spoke softly, coaxing me into conversation when my thoughts strayed to Kallias, threatening to pull me under.

Eventually, she rose to check on the Kulletti, leaving me alone again with Kalepsi. I crawled to her great head and curled against the curve of a thick golden horn jutting from her jaw. My cheek pressed to her warm scales, and tears returned. She chuffed and rumbled beneath me, steady and deep. My sobs scattered into the wind. The pain tearing through my chest eased, if only a little, with her near.

But I couldn't stay buried here forever.

The sun sank low when I left the Nest. I felt hollow. No more than a shell, cracked and worthless, but one that remembered how to move. I was home now. I would not hide from my family or from duty.

By the time I reached my rooms, my knees trembled from the stairs and the ache of hunger. I shouldn't have gone to the Nest on an empty stomach, but calming Kalepsi mattered more.

"Princess Nienna."

Freya rose from a chair in my receiving room, a silver tray balanced in her hands. "I began to wonder if you'd ever return."

The sight of her hit me like a wave. It shouldn't have. Everything felt foreign, even her presence in my quarters—though of course Mother would assign her here. She knew who I'd need.

"Scythe is dead." I closed my eyes as the words escaped. They weren't what I meant to say, but I couldn't bear to watch surprise bloom across Freya's face.

Silence settled. The three of us—Scythe, Freya, and I—once stirred chaos through the palace halls. Scythe stuck close, sworn to my service, while Freya floated wherever she was needed. Yet she always found us to join the mischief.

Her loss wasn't mine alone.

"I know."

Freya's lips pressed into a sorrowful curve. Her red hair sat coiled in a bun, with sun-kissed wisps slipping free. Freckles danced across her cheekbones, a cruel contrast to my battered skin.

"Did you burn her?" she asked, shifting toward the dressing room with the tray.

"Yes." The word scraped my throat. I remembered the smoke curling upward, thick with oil and fury. No dragons lit that fire—only torches and man-made flame.

"Then she is with us," she said. "In the air, the wind, the sky. Maybe she'll return as a dragon one day."

"She'd be worse than Tsunami." I slumped into a chair and reached for the tray she placed on the small table.

Freya laughed, hands on her hips as she surveyed the racks of dresses lining the walls. I eyed the food—seaweed cheese, kelp chips, dried fish. Sparse, compared to Radaan's tables, but it would hold me through until dinner with the Kulletti.

"Red," she said, lifting a dress to the light.

Crystals shimmered along the high collar, scattered down the sleeves, clustering at the wrists. The front split open, rider-friendly, though I doubted I'd need that tonight.

I winced. "Maybe I shouldn't stand out."

People would stare. The riders, my family—they understood what crossing the sea demanded. But nobles, ambassadors? They'd see only the fallen royal.

"You're Draconia's princess," Freya snapped, spinning to face me. "Raised by dragons. Eyes will follow you no matter what you wear."

I dragged both hands down my cheeks. "I should eat here. Skip dinner."

She inhaled deep and released it slowly, as if leashing herself. Then she stood over me, stern and resolute. "You can't undo the past. You move forward. Head high. Let them whisper if they dare. You were raised among dragons. Do not cower before nobles."

Her words echoed something Edith once said. The memory stung. Edith still waited in Radaan. And Father? He'd ride for her or demand her returned on a ship—and be tempted to burn it down after she disembarked.

Freya was right. Better to face it now. Hiding would only make it harder later. I nodded and bit into a piece of crisp fish.

"But you'll tell me everything tonight," she said with a wink.

I cleared the tray and let her dress me. The crimson fabric hugged my throat and waist before loosening at the hips. The split revealed deeper red trousers tucked into dark boots. She hooked black pearls onto my ears and pinned my hair high, sliding the silver tiara into place.

Tonight wasn't the night to shrink. I needed armor, even if it sparkled.

Freya worked carefully over my face and hands. She masked the bruises beneath my eyes, dabbed red stain over my split lip, then oiled my raw cheeks one last time.

When I looked in the mirror, I didn't seem like someone who had just tumbled down the Spire.

"You don't have to wait for me," I called over my shoulder as I reached the door.

"Oh, I do. And I will. Happily." She smiled, plucked a book from the shelf, and sank onto the chaise. "Go remind them who the Dragon's Heart is. I'll be here, waiting to hear every detail."

Peace settled over me as she flipped the book open and disappeared behind its pages. Returning to Draconia wouldn't be easy. But with her and my mother, I might manage.

I slipped from my rooms and moved into the corridor. No clatter of armor trailed me. No guards shadowed my steps. The absence struck me, strange and comforting in equal measure. This was still my home. No one would dare touch a Draconis.

The empty halls shimmered under lanterns. Black stone gleamed like quiet water, each flicker caught and mirrored. Thick rugs muffled my feet while paintings of dragons soared through vibrant skies; sails snapped beneath silent storms. I knew these images—the waves crashing against hulls, light glinting on scaled wings. Still, I missed the greenery of Radaan's palace. Life pulsed in every corner there. Flowers spilled from vases while vines crawled up pillars. Vibrant and unrestrained.

I pressed a hand to the hollow in my chest, the ache unreachable. This was my future. The past couldn't be undone. As Freya said—I could only go forward.

I steadied my breath and continued on. Servants passed like ghosts in the corners of my vision. I headed toward the Cireendium—the Spire's heart.

These halls ran shorter and narrower than Radaan's. Before long, the passage opened into the vast hollow of the Cireendium. Sound swirled through the circular chamber. I stepped to the railing and leaned out. The void stretched into black, far enough to steal breath. The Nest crowned the Spire, and high above, a purple snout nudged over the ledge. Kalepsi's golden gaze caught mine. She crooned, her voice rolling through the open space like thunder.

Heads turned. Staff and nobles drifted to the railings, peering up at her.

Heat crept up my neck. Eyes clung to me, too many and too sharp. A few bowed when they noticed my gaze, then scattered, retreating to whatever task they had abandoned.

The Cireendium spanned eight levels. Every inch of the Spire was accessible from here, though reaching the higher levels was faster with a dragon.

I brushed the railing with my fingers, hiding a smile as I descended. The fifth level, reserved for royals, was the only place Gyrak was allowed to land. As they grew, dragons were permitted in the Cireendium, but they caused chaos. Riders discouraged it, with Argos enforcing order.

Most beasts obeyed.

Tsunami didn't.

I reached the fourth level—the last one open to the public—where the dining hall waited. The library stood nearby, tempting in its silence and promise of answers. I wanted to vanish into those shelves. Research blood oaths. Search for anything to preserve Radaan's ties.

Instead, I turned toward dinner.

Zane flipped a dagger into the air, his attention fixated on the spinning blade. He caught it.

Then dropped it with a curse.

"Try catching the hilt next time," I said.

He scooped it up, brushing his red hair from his eyes. "Princess. Good to see you." His voice still held the edge of youth. One of the youngest riders, though his dragon Naneki wasn't strong enough to carry him yet. He trained with the others, regardless.

"Has everyone arrived?" I asked, leaning past him for a better view.

The hall brimmed with nobles. Laughter and conversation filled the space. The scent of grilled fish curled through the air, sharp and salty.

His black leathers creaked as he leaned with me. "Aye. They've started without you."

"They didn't know I'd be coming." My stomach turned. I could still back out. Try again tomorrow.

"Well," he said, grinning, "you'll make quite the entrance. The Kulls are already pestering the king."

"Kulletti," I corrected. I let the *aye* slide, but not that. They hated nicknames.

I ran my tongue across my split lip and stepped past him, head high.

The din faltered after six paces. Then someone spotted me—and silence dropped like a dead fly.

I kept my eyes on the dais. My father's table. Smaller than Kallias', stone-built and three steps raised. My mother dabbed her lips and rose. Father stood beside her, face a stoic mask, mouth hard.

Jehoikim, chief of the Kulletti, was the last to rise. My gaze met his and my stomach twisted. Beady black eyes raked over me. Feathers and shells hung from his braids, brushing the sash across his chest—bare skin beneath.

"Nienna, please join us," my mother called, motioning to the chair beside her.

Ronan stood behind our parents, his face painted with concern.

I wanted to throw a fork at him.

Instead, I crossed the room. The hem of my gown split as I climbed the steps and took my place.

"It's good of you to come," my mother murmured as she sat.

I flicked a glance at Father. He stared down at the crowd, jaw tight, refusing to meet my eyes. He sank into his seat with heavy resolve, and the rest of the room followed.

A servant placed a bowl of crab soup in front of me. No piles of food. No spices dancing in the air. Just briny fish and salted kelp.

A reminder of what I ruined.

By my third bite, Jehoikim spoke.

"It appears Princess Nienna is without a husband."

It took every ounce of training to cover my flinch. My mother's hand trembled as she reached for salt. I sat back slowly and looked at my father, who tapped the table.

"She has returned," he growled. The flush beneath his white beard darkened. His mouth curled with barely restrained fury.

"I assume you'll be seeking another match," Jehoikim pressed, dabbing his lips. His eyes latched onto mine.

"I will not," Father said, leaning back. "You're not known for your tact, Jehoikim. Choose your words carefully."

"No offense meant." The man laughed. "Alliances are valuable. We have the best ships in the sea. The brightest pearls. Endless crystal caves. A union between our nations would yield treasures beyond count."

Surely he was not trying to barter for my hand.

I clenched the napkin in my lap. If he'd take me ruined and ragged, his might be the only offer I'd get.

But Father would never allow it.

He leaned forward, sparks crackling at the edge of his spoon. "Caves explored by Draconis' Vessels. Pearls gathered by Draconis' divers. Ships crafted from Wild Shore lumber, secured by my Dragon Riders. Tell me, what benefits could you offer in exchange for my priceless treasure?"

I shrank in my seat, a child again, longing to hide behind him.

"No one else would have her, now that–"

The spoon shot forward. Mother's hand snapped to Father's wrist, her intervention halting the utensil before it stabbed into Jehoikim's eye.

The man bolted upright, but an invisible force pinned him. He shouted. Argos roared overhead, stone trembling beneath our feet. Silence fell. The spoon hovered, unmoving.

"If you speak of my daughter again," Father hissed, "I will scoop your greedy eye from its socket and feed it to you."

"Chief Jehoikim." My voice held firm, though my thoughts frayed and my heart thrashed against my ribs. "I'm granted the right to select my husband. I may accept or refuse the match."

My confidence cracked, but I feigned steel, lifting my chin and locking eyes with the chieftain in what I hoped resembled a dragon's glare.

"I would not choose you."

The spoon clattered to the table. Father had dropped the magic. Across from me, the portly man squirmed, his squinted gaze flicking between us, sweat shining at his temples.

"The Dragon's Heart has spoken." Father's voice rang through the hall—measured, cold, final. "So have I."

He surged to his feet. We scrambled up in his wake. Without a glance, he spun on his heel and stormed down the steps, his cloak snapping behind him. He barked a command at Zane as he passed.

The warmth of his support turned brittle, withering into shame. He couldn't even bear the sight of me.

I locked my jaw and swallowed the rising ache. Jehoikim still watched. I was a princess. I wouldn't accept defeat.

Chapter Four

I t was late when I finally retreated from the dining hall. *Staggered* might've been the appropriate term, but I clung to retain any shreds of my remaining dignity.

"Nienna!"

My brother's voice flared something hot in my chest. I refused to slow, pushing toward our floor.

"Wait!"

"I don't think I will, Ronan," I snapped. "You didn't."

"Stop." He hissed the word and snatched my arm.

I whirled, my palm cracking against his face. The sound echoed down the Cireendium's stone corridor.

"You stupid wench!" he snarled, grabbing for my wrist.

"Don't call me that!"

I jerked against his grip, but he held it fast, blue eyes blazing. A handprint bloomed across his cheek, filling me with a wicked sense of satisfaction.

"Then stop acting like one! I came to help you!"

Voice low and venomous, I leaned in close. "I don't *want* your help!"

He could go fly around on his dragon, play his games, make his hot-headed impulsive decisions and pretend nobody ever bled for it. I wanted no part of that world.

"Too bad."

He bent at the waist, slamming into my stomach, wrenching my battered body over his shoulder like a bag of sand.

A strangled squeal slipped out as I choked off a scream, driving my fists into him. He grunted, legs stretching into long strides up the path.

I clawed at his jacket, yanked the hem loose, and dug my nails into his back. Pale flesh split from the sting of my grip, drawing blood. My fingers still ached from gripping Gyrak's scales, but they didn't falter now.

"Sea beneath!"

Ronan pinched my thigh—hard—and I drove my nails deeper.

"Put me down!"

"Will you listen to me?!"

"No!"

He swatted back at my hands, but couldn't dislodge me. His pace broke into a run, charging toward our floor. I tore red welts up his skin, fighting with the only teeth and claws I had.

He kicked through my door, barreled for the chaise, and threw me down. I landed in a heap beside Freya, who scrambled upright, eyes flicking between us.

"Out!" Ronan barked.

"No! He's just leaving." My lip curled with a snarl. "He knows his sister needs time to recover after being dragged across the sea on a spontaneous *four-day* flight. And she's not a *rider!*"

"I walked in on a man *Father's age* groping–"

"Leave!" I lunged at him, shrieking.

He caught my wrists and shoved me back toward the chaise with ease. Ridiculously strong. Freya took that as her cue and bolted out the door, leaving me and my brother locked in a silent war, both breathing like cornered beasts.

His chest heaved. Red blurred my vision.

He opened his mouth. I hurled an embroidered pillow at his face.

"Don't you dare say a word, Ronan! You have no idea what you stole from me!"

His grimace showed more pain than defiance. "I didn't know you *loved* the old man. Not that it would've made it better!"

"He's not old!"

"He could be your *father!*"

I shut the door to my thoughts, retreating behind walls he had no right to breach. I didn't need to fight him, and I owed him no explanation. He had his chance to understand and spat on it. Let him believe whatever he wanted. It changed nothing.

I rose and crossed the room, flinging open the balcony doors. Warm wind shoved past me, lifting the curtains in soft waves. I wrapped my arms around myself and leaned on the rail.

Above, the stars burned. The same stars that hung over Radaan.

Was Kallias staring at them now?

My soul reached for the starlight, searching for him. That quiet, intangible connection. Whatever we had, Ronan shattered it. My heart ached with the loss, as if something vital had been ripped out.

My brother stood just out of arm's reach, gazing skyward. A dragon's shadow blotted out the stars for a breath.

Gyrak. Probably circling to come to his rider's aid.

"I'm sorry I hurt you." His words held weight—mourning and regret carved into every syllable.

But an apology couldn't fix this. It wouldn't undo what he'd done or return me to Kallias' arms.

"Don't you see how wrong it was?" he asked, voice quiet, pleading.

Wrong.

The word struck like a dart. I rejected it, pushing it aside.

I loved Kallias. He was loyal, strong, *good*. Someone like him, the love I had for him—it couldn't be wrong.

Cursed, maybe. Doomed. Star-crossed.

But not wrong.

He sighed before trying again. "I'm not asking for your forgiveness–"

"You'd never get it."

"Abyss, let me finish! I never meant to hurt you. I reacted and–"

"You gave in to your temper, your dragon doing nothing to steady you," I hissed. Angry tears burned trails down my cheeks. "You weren't a prince—or a rider. You were a child. And because of that, you failed to analyze the situation. You didn't *stop*. Tallon used you like a hammer to a nail, and you let him."

"Quite the accusation coming from a princess bedding her betrothed's father." His gaze darkened. "Did you ever *analyze* what you risked by welcoming that beast into your arms?"

I had. A thousand times. I told myself why I couldn't, *shouldn't*. And yet, the pull remained. We were meant for each other, two halves of a whole. We saw the world the same. Understood duty. I was just born in the wrong generation.

"I love him."

"*Loved*."

"Love," I bit out. "You can't kill something like that, no matter how far you drag me away."

"Listen to me, Nienna."

He stepped closer, and I turned on him, fire rising in my throat. If he dared lay a finger on me, I would murder him. A screech split the sky, and a dragon streaked overhead. Green scales shimmered so close I could've reached out and touched them.

Ronan tracked the beast, then returned his attention to me. "I love you. I know you *think* you care for him, but I... I don't—*can't*—understand that." He ran a hand through his shaggy blonde hair, the light from my room catching on the shadows under his eyes. Proof his body was still recovering from the flight too.

"I couldn't live with myself if I left you there. Maybe I judged too harshly, but I don't think I was wrong. As a rider, I have to do what I believe is right. We'll never see eye-to-eye on this, but I want you to know it came from love."

He licked his lip, flexing his jaw as he stared at me, waiting for my understanding, for grace. He craved to uphold his own honor, but he never gave thought to mine. No, he dragged me through the halls with a torn dress. Hauled me like some scullery maid caught in scandal. Let every passing eye judge what he didn't care to protect.

He *humiliated* me.

That wasn't love.

His brow furrowed, lips pulled into contemplation, arms crossed tight as he glanced out to sea.

"Done?" My question rasped through a constricted throat.

"I guess so."

"Then leave."

He sucked a breath through his teeth, shaking his head. Then, with a resigned shrug, he left.

Tears chilled on my skin with the breeze as I faced the moonlit water far below, watching the moon's reflection dance across the waves.

And suddenly, I *knew*.

My knees hit the stone. A sob tore from my throat.

The sea, the stars, the moon—I faced north. Beyond that horizon lay Radaan. I reached out, trembling.

If he were here, he'd make sense of this mess, know what to say, have the right laws memorized. He'd figure out how to move forward.

But didn't he already? We both knew it couldn't happen. The best we could hope for was keeping the dragons in Draconia.

He let me go.

He let me go.

In my mind's eye, panic flashed across his features as he weighed every outcome, ran through each possible solution—coming up short.

There was nothing. We had nothing.

My hand slammed against the stone.

I would never see him again. There was no *us*.

I hated love.

When Freya returned, she peeled me off the balcony floor and cleaned me up enough to crawl into bed.

The sun rose, cruel and blinding, dragging another day behind it. And with it, the drive to chase whatever scraps of hope remained.

"I'm going to the library." My voice cracked the silence.

Freya didn't flinch. She paused mid-braid, eyes locked on my reflection in the mirror.

"Looking for inspiration?" she asked, fingers resuming their work. She wasn't as fast as Edith—my heart splintered a bit more.

Kallias wouldn't let anything happen to my maid, but being stranded in a foreign kingdom on the edge of war would never be a comfortable situation.

"Perhaps."

She hummed, frowning as she tugged a stubborn strand into place. The tangles from the flight had taken forever to comb through. My cheeks no longer felt stretched raw—oils were finally working. My lip had begun to scab, slow to heal, and the bruising beneath my eyes deepened to dark, yellow-ringed shadows.

Freya caught my gaze in the mirror. "They'll get worse before they improve."

"That's what the healers said."

She finished the braid, and I slipped on worn boots while she straightened the room. When I reached the door, she followed. I turned, ready to object, but she beat me to it.

"Two sets of eyes are better than one. I'll help you search."

"Did Mother tell you to babysit me?" I scoffed.

"She didn't need to." She crossed her arms over her chest and arched a daring brow at me. "Your state last night said enough. And look at that! Lucky for you, I'm free today."

I narrowed my eyes, lips pressed tight. She had a point. She'd grown up in this palace, understood its rules and buried meanings. Between her and Mother, they were the only ones who at least pretended to understand how I felt.

I sighed, showing my resignation. "Fetch me a cup of travel tea, then meet me there."

She grinned and waved me off, splitting directions.

I crossed the Cireendium, slipping through an arch carved straight into the stone. The room beyond had low ceilings and narrow aisles. Shelves pressed in on all sides, a maze perfect for children to hide in, but a headache for adults.

"Princess Nienna." Kienna rose from her desk and bowed. Her brown hair slipped over one shoulder, resting on her white robes as she straightened. "May I assist you?"

My gaze wandered the rows—tomes stacked with rigid care, shelves coiling like vines deeper into shadow. Dust and parchment clung to the air, musty and warm, steeped in memory.

To find what I sought would be akin to searching for a crumb on a beach.

Pointless. Because it didn't exist.

Teeth clenched, I forced a thin smile. "Everything you have on blood oaths."

Whether it was instinct or preparation, she nodded and tapped her nose. "One moment."

She referenced a massive directory on her desk—a book that would strain every muscle to lift. Nearly as tall as my torso, it held all titles housed in our halls. She jotted down a few titles, then gestured toward the narrow aisle.

"I'll fetch you a few to get you started, then search for more while you read. If you'd rather wait in the study, I can bring them there."

With a polite nod, I turned down a tight path to my right, brushing my fingertips along the rows of worn spines. I had weathered so many stormy afternoons tucked between these shelves. This felt like being among old friends.

I paused and pulled a tattered green tome free, its pages heavy with detailed sketches of dragon anatomy.

A sharp ache pierced my chest. Another book. A couch beneath me. A hand on my ankle. My back pressed to the shelves. Lips—fierce, greedy—on mine. I slammed the cover shut, pushing the memory down.

My boots made no sound as I crossed the quiet library, chin lifted, moisture blurring my vision. In the study, I strode past sagging armchairs and low, cluttered tables ringed with lamps and magnifiers. A towering window spilled the only natural light. Mage lights fed by Vessels lit the interior, but daylight only touched this spot.

The sky was heavy with clouds, rain ticked against the glass. Whirlstorm remnants.

I stood there, looking out across Draconia. Four cities—K'lan, K'seer, K'dan, and K'bar—stacked like layers of an unsteady cake. I was too high to make out faces, but wagons shifted near the harbor, unloading food into the Eye, the city center.

More fish—more kelp. More lotus. With the treaty void, we'd need to trade with the Innaku for wheat. The largest island in our sea, infamous for selling their own to stem overpopulation. Slaves worked to the bone, harvests sold to the highest bidder. Their king ruled with an iron fist.

I wanted nothing to do with them, but hunger left little choice. Too many suffered hollowed cheeks and shaking hands. Malnutrition. My people were starving. The Ivetti orchards would only go so far.

A soft scuff broke the quiet. Kienna's boots. She placed three books on a table, muttering to herself, a quill tucked behind her ear, dripping ink on her white shoulder. I smirked as she drifted back into the stacks, adrift in her own thoughts.

I sat and pulled the stack closer, reaching for a mage light. It hovered, a glowing orb the size of my fist, anchored in a silver base etched with runes. Bright. Well-fed.

It pulsed, casting soft shadows across the open pages. I touched the base. Warm. Alive in a way I'd never understand.

Shame pricked the flesh along my forearms. Magic, the heritage of my people, and I couldn't touch it. Ronan had no such trouble. He breathed life into them without effort, long before he was named a rider. He never mocked me. Pity, though—that he offered freely. I would have preferred his teasing. Instead, I watched him dim his power out of mercy.

"Tea, my lady?" Freya asked, placing a silver tray down. She poured a strong green brew for each of us, then settled beside me. When she plucked a book from the stack and sipped, her eyes scanned the cover.

"If there's anything on blood oaths, I want to see it," I said, wrapping my fingers around the cup. Salty peppermint clung to my tongue, heat curling down into my stomach.

"Breaking them, perhaps?" She cracked open the book and took another sip, indifferent, as if she hadn't just asked a question that bordered on treason.

"If you find anything." I held her gaze, then dropped into the texts.

Hours passed. Kienna returned again and again, arms full, muttering half-formed thoughts under her breath. The tomes contained plenty of information: blood oaths forged by kings, burned fleets, duels to stave off dragonfire—often ending with the oathbreaker dead. Nothing useful. No path out. Most references bound queens and kings in alliance. Breaking a Draconis Blood Oath exacted too great a price to be done often.

When my eyes drooped and the teacup had emptied, my mother appeared, glancing over the chaos of open books. Freya rose and greeted her quietly, but the queen said nothing, just studied the spines and scrawled notes.

"What time is it?" I asked, rubbing the burn from my eyes.

"Nearly dinner." She nodded toward the darkened glass. "Perhaps your research can wait until tomorrow."

A whole day gone, filled with dusty pages, and still no answers. Frustration clenched in my chest. I stood and stretched, arms high, a loud, ungraceful yawn escaping me.

"Nienna," Mother chided, lips pursed.

"I'll take dinner in my room," I said, nudging the chair back in place.

"And let Chief Jehoikim squirm unopposed?" She pressed her finger to the mage light. It flared, pulsed, then burned brighter, as if newly fed.

Jealousy prickled through me.

"You should be there. A symbol of strength." She straightened. "You delivered a blow last night. Now follow through. Sit tall. Don't cower. You refused him—make sure he doesn't mistake it for doubt."

I bit the inside of my cheek. Freya's raised brow and crooked smile met my gaze.

A princess wouldn't retreat.

"Freya, I've a dinner to prepare for."

Chapter Five

I arrived at dinner on time, before the first dish was served. I ignored Ronan's stare, but sought a single glance from my father. None came, still avoiding me.

Jehoikim locked eyes with me as he approached the dais. I met his attention with a relaxed face, though my gaze dared him to ask for my hand again.

Father clenched his spoon, glaring at the island chieftain across the table. The second night of soup marked either the depth of our desperation or a continued threat, with such utensils at my father's grasp.

I dropped a seaweed crisp into the broth, watching it sink and swirl. The space buzzed around me. Lanterns and mage lights bathed the walls in warm gold. Their glow skimmed the polished black stone, throwing reflections that made the space feel larger than it was. Long tables filled the chamber, brimming with guests—less so with food. Smaller than Radaan's grand dining hall, as was everything here.

We were only a small isle nation. I once believed this land to be vast. Now it felt like a droplet beside Radaan's ocean.

My thoughts broke—fractured with the ache of wondering what he was eating.

I forced it away.

A roar shook the Spire. An indignant shriek followed. Father's head snapped up, his brow fixed in that permanent scowl. Conversations quieted but didn't fall silent. Dragons argued often.

"Tsunami," he muttered, shaking his head and returning to his soup.

"What now?" Mother asked.

"Taunting Argos. Flirting for a dance, then darting off. If she keeps it up, he'll ban her from the island."

"She wouldn't stay away," Ronan said, pushing his empty bowl aside. He always ate like someone might steal the food. "Something's keeping her here."

"Regardless, Argos is the strongest bull. He alone decides which beasts remain and which leave."

Mother set her spoon down. "Let him. She has sunk too many ships."

Shock surged through me. Since when did we decide which dragons belonged?

"She refused the tithe," she added.

A cackling chirp rang through the Cireendium—Tsunami's laugh.

"She's only playing," I said. Tsunami was large, fast, and clueless. Like a pup too big for her paws. A rider would temper that immaturity, but for now, the dragons corrected her as best they could.

Father's eyes speared to mine, and I wilted beneath the intensity. "Play is for hatchlings and children," he said. "She's old enough to know her place."

Were we still talking about Tsunami?

Mother rested her hand on his arm. "Nereus, have we received word from the Ivetti concerning the Awakening?"

"They will send what we asked."

Father sat back in his seat. His stare clung to mine for a breath, then dropped. My breath hitched in my chest, air rushing into my lungs as if I'd been drowning.

Abyss, he loathed me.

The urge to flee rose, sharp and sudden. I gripped my napkin, knuckles pale. I wasn't a child who ran when scolded. If he meant that as a rebuke, I'd take it as a woman.

Mother found me in the library's study the next morning. I sipped my tea, letting the salty mint settle on my tongue as she approached with a worn leather book in hand.

"Back at it, I see," she murmured, stopping at the table to flip covers and skim titles.

I shrugged. "I've nothing better to do."

"You might spend time with your people instead of your books." Her gold dress whispered behind her as she crossed to the window. She paused in a shaft of sunlight and studied the cities below. "Draconia is hungry—for food, for inspiration. If you can't feed them, walk among them. Bring the Dragon's Heart to the people."

Grateful Freya wasn't here to add her voice, I stared at the silver in Mother's hair. "Shall I paint for them?"

I was a princess—trained in courtly customs, raised to sip tea and dab pastels on canvas.

She turned, half-shadowed in the glare, but her disapproval pressed into my skin like thorns. "You are the symbol of hope. Of a better future–"

"Ruined that one, didn't I?"

"Nienna." She stormed toward the table and slammed a book down, gaze full of fire. "Self-pity does not become a princess."

Dragon Queen, indeed.

I bit my tongue. The words I wanted to hurl scorched the back of my throat. She'd stood by me, helped convince Father to stay. I didn't want to drive her away. I needed her.

But pretending this was just another inconvenience—a minor nuisance I could brush off and smile through—hurt.

"What would you have me do?" I bit out, glare sharp as glass.

Her eyes glittered, lips tightening with approval. "See Williard. He'll find something for you."

She didn't wait for an answer; only walked away, trailing gold and silence behind her.

Williard. Kite maker. Steady as stone. A pillar of K'bar. He would know where the peoples' pain festered most. But what good could I do? A tarnished princess dressed in shame. I blew a strand of hair off my cheek and shoved aside the book Mother left.

Gold glinted in the corner of my vision. I frowned, tugging it closer. *The Heart of Dragons*, the title stamped in flaked, gilded filigree across the cover. I'd never seen it before. The leather felt unfamiliar beneath my fingers, its pages worn and tattered. A strange scent clung to it—dried herbs, old smoke, something sharp underneath.

The spine gave with little resistance, pages crackling as it fell open.

The Tale of Nienna, the First Dragon's Heart.

I frowned, squinting at the faded ink.

Born Year 17 After the Calamity, daughter of Mad Queen Violet and King Beorn.

The Calamity—the whirlstorm that stranded the dragons in Draconia—was common knowledge. So was Queen Violet; her portraits lined the second-floor gallery, painted in varying shades of red.

But this? Nienna?

How had I never known?

I closed the book. The leather cracked beneath my palm, rough and dry. With all the books held by the Spire, it would seem impossible to read them all—but I had. I knew every title, every shelf.

This one wasn't from here.

It was Mother's.

The binding sagged again, yielding to the same page; it read:

Queen Violet's obsession with dragons is chronicled in the Book of Queens, a tale of its own. When she became with child—her only—the obsession reached a pinnacle. She demanded access to the Nest, where the beasts had driven out mankind. Every request was denied, resulting in the tragic deaths of three maidservants.

In the throes of childbirth, she defied her husband, King Beorn, and ascended the Spire. Riders Silva and Quinn lost their lives upon entering, attempting to clear a path for their queen.

With a trail of blood in her wake, Violet forced her way inside. Dragon Queen Yuleni, enraged by the scent of flesh drawing other beasts to her Nest, fought off the bulls in an attempt to defend her clutch. Violet crawled toward the eggs, and there, amid the unborn hatchlings, she gave birth.

When bloodlust dissipated, Yuleni moved to strike the queen—but hesitated at the sound of a newborn's wail. Whether from curiosity or pity, she spared the child.

Little Nienna survived—but became bound to the Nest.

When the new mother attempted to bring the young one back to the Cireendium, Yuleni blocked her path. Violet then placed the babe in a bed of bone and shell, then entered the Spire, leaving Nienna to the dragons.

The Wild Princess, more dragon than human—this is her tale. The story of the Dragon's Heart.

I spent the rest of the day reading about Nienna, eating only when Freya brought me a small tray of pickled herring and dried grapes.

She was the first ever given to their kind. So soon after the Calamity, little was known about the bond between dragon and rider. They'd abandoned the babe to chilled winds. Her only warmth was the sweep of scaled bodies and her mother's breast, offered when she deigned to nurse her.

At two, Yuleni allowed her into the Spire. The child cried, restless, never calm until she returned to the creatures that had claimed her. Even then, she displayed the ability to hold and use magic as any Vessel, but with the exception that all dragons heeded her—not only the bonded ones.

That struck me. Was every Dragon's Heart different? Or was I simply obscure?

My mother loved me, stayed by my side. But I was an empty Vessel. Dragons only treated me the way they did because of Argos; the black bull would rip apart any beast before he'd let them hurt me.

Night fell. I carried the book to bed, declining dinner in the great hall.

The first Nienna used magic freely, tied to no single dragon—gifted, they said, by her link to Yuleni. Another skill I lacked. The words depicted her as wild, unpredictable, touched by madness like her mother.

At fifteen, she vanished into a whirlstorm on the back of a young dragon. Never returned.

I closed the book gently. Freya had dozed off on the chaise, a thick tome titled *Acts of the Kings of Draconia* slipping from her chest.

Why would Mother give me this? Did she want me to fly off into a storm? Was this a lesson in lineage? A warning of madness in my blood?

I groaned and collapsed into bed, blowing out the candle. Let her speak in cryptic riddles. Tomorrow, I'd demand clarity.

I set the book between our plates, raising a brow at Mother. "You named me after the first Dragon's Heart?"

She looked up from her meal, sunlight pouring through the windows behind her, turning her pale hair to spun gold. I joined her in the private dining hall, noting the empty seats where Father and Ronan should've been.

"It seemed fitting," she said, dipping a thin slice of bread into thick broth.

I folded my skirts and sank into the chair beside her with a quiet huff. "You didn't know I would survive."

"Dear child," she laughed, "from the moment I conceived you, you were a stubborn, determined thing. I told your father I would risk the bloodlust of dragons if it meant giving you the best life possible. If you'd died, Kalepsi would've turned on me next. Naming you wouldn't have mattered."

The best life? They had no way of knowing it would be the only title I'd ever claim.

"Why leave it?"

She paused, chewing a dainty bite, eyes drifting toward the far wall where family portraits hung. One depicted the day Gyrak claimed Ronan. Mother and Father sat upon their thrones while I stood on the landing, arms flung wide like wings.

"You're searching to break the blood oath."

Not a question. Not a challenge. A truth. Her certainty made me scan the room for eavesdroppers, but we were alone.

"Do you know a way?" My voice dropped low, hushed, ashamed to even ask.

"If I did, do you think I'd keep it from you?" Her eyes studied mine. Narrowed. Crow's feet deepened at the corners. "You're my daughter. I want you to be happy. If it was possible to release King Kallias from the threat of war, I would tell you."

She stared into her bowl. "I know of nothing but death and dragonfire. Still, widen your search. Don't just study the Oath—look inward. The magic in his blood binds your father—drives him toward vengeance. That same blood runs through your veins. And I hate watching you rot in a library, clawing at loopholes set in stone. You should embrace your status, your power, not run from it."

"You want me to forget him." I leaned away, tucking the sting of betrayal away. My blood may have come from the Well of Draconia, but I was a faulty Vessel.

"I want you to remember who you are." Her hiss cut sharp, and her fingers curled over mine. "Love hurts. But you were the Dragon's Heart before you ever met him. If he changed you for the worse, then I'm afraid he's hardly worth the days and nights spent in a library searching tomes that will give you no answers."

I jerked my hand back and rose. Her words sliced deep, stripping away hope I'd barely dared to hold. I thought she'd understand. Maybe she did. But I wasn't just a daughter—I was a princess. Locked into a tidy, little mold. Expected to fill it.

"And if Father died," I said, voice rising, "would you mourn him for three days, then carry on, unscathed?"

She sighed. "Kallias Sunspear is not dead."

"Yet."

The door creaked. We both turned.

Father entered, boots striking hard across the floor. Ronan trailed after, goggles pushed into his hair. He dropped into a chair, snatched a slice of bread, and slathered it in marmalade without looking at me.

"Father." My voice caught. He seldom spoke to me now, and when he did, it cut.

"Nienna." The word fell cold.

Dread crawled through me, icy and sharp. How much had he overheard?

Did he know what I was trying to do?

He took the seat beside his queen, set his flight goggles on the table, and reached for his bread.

"How was your flight?" Mother nudged the conversation elsewhere, pushing her bowl aside.

"Well enough. We may fly to Little Island tomorrow. I want to see how the crops fare."

"What did you plant?" I asked, hoping to ease the tension. The isle was too small and wild to house anyone, but we'd tried to tame the hills with crops.

"Mostly potatoes. A few orange trees." He grunted and shoved a bite into his mouth, eyes never meeting mine.

"The last whirlstorm tore through it." Ronan spooned up broth. "Might've shredded the lot."

"If it did, we'll replant," Mother said.

"Any word from the Innaku?" I asked, sliding into a chair.

"Jain and Naksula left this morning to check in." My brother drained his bowl and set it aside. "If we're lucky, they'll bring fruit. I'm sick of fish and kelp."

Guilt struck hard. I stole a glance at Father, who wouldn't look at me either—but the crimson flush under his beard said he blamed me as much as I blamed myself.

If I hadn't ruined the union, we'd have more food than we could carry.

"We eat what the common folk eat," Mother reminded. "If we share the harvest, we all survive."

"We need to colonize the Wild Shores." Ronan leaned back, raking fingers through his hair. He tore off his goggles and tossed them on the table.

"You can be the first to move in," I said.

"No dragon will stay the night," Mother warned.

"Gyrak can leave him there."

"You wound me, sister!"

"Enough." She pushed to her feet, brushing Father's shoulder. "I'll check on the kites and see K'dan about supplies."

"Take three crates of dried grapes. They're low," Father said, turning to kiss her hand before she left.

My heart twisted at the tenderness between them. I wanted that. Those small, intimate moments. I'd had a taste once—with Kallias—before it all collapsed.

The ache curled inward, sharp and familiar, a craving I didn't know how to name.

"I'll be in the library." I pushed out of my seat, ready to follow.

"Oh, Nienna?"

I froze. Glanced back.

Father stood and crossed to me.

"Seeking to break a Draconis Blood Oath is treason."

"Going to hang me?" I bit my lip, the sting sharp. My mouth always moved faster than my wits; provoking him never led to anything good.

"You? No." His boots thudded past. At the doorway, he glanced back. "But don't drive me to fly Argos north."

I spent the day in the library. Was it rebellion? Determination? Hope? A refusal to accept defeat? I didn't know. Freya brought tea. Kienna brought books.

Dusty tomes and brittle parchment buried the study table. Mother's words gnawed at me—something about magic driving Father to retaliate. The texts offered little insight. Most claimed honor alone compelled men to fulfill their oaths. Only one mentioned King Durani, nearly two centuries past. His dragon urged him to secure an oath of protection for his queen with the Innaku. She died of sudden illness in their care. Durani lost his mind soon after.

Blood oaths were supposed to be symbolic.

There was no magic in them. No bond to twist a man's mind. Surely, I didn't have to fear my father unraveling just because I kept him from flying to Radaan.

Chapter Six

I squinted at the leather boots and trousers Freya set out for me. She pulled a sapphire-blue dress from the rack, silver threads catching the light as she hummed and laid it across a chair. I hadn't moved from the threshold of my dressing room, still staring as she bounced about, brimming with excitement.

It reminded me of Scythe.

"Those are traveling clothes," I said, when she snagged a pale-blue shawl that shimmered like fish scales.

"Indicating we will be walking today."

"I walk every day." I tried to keep the bite from my voice, but it slipped out anyway.

"You've not been to the cities since you returned," she said, planting her hands on her hips, leveling me with a challenging glare.

"I have other things to do."

"What? Spend more weeks buried in books? You're so pale, you're an embarrassment to Draconia. A ghost! And for the love of the sea, you need a deep-fried fish or two."

"Then I'll ask the cook for one. I'm not going anywhere today."

"Don't make me get your mother."

I scoffed. "Threatening to tattle?"

She shrugged, stepping closer. "If you'd rather I tell her I'm worried about your health and fetch George to confirm it and prescribe a walk on the beach, I will."

I didn't budge. She paused before me with a mischievous grin. George, our healer, had long been wrapped around her finger. If she called, he'd come running, and agree without hesitation: I needed air and sunlight, and the dragons' landing wouldn't suffice.

The idea of facing my people was worse than weathering the stares of the nobles. I had finally managed to bore them. Jehoikim stopped pursuing my hand, and the lesser lords no longer circled like sharks scenting blood.

I was the returned princess. Nothing more.

But to face the hollow-eyed mothers, the gaunt children—the consequences of my selfish actions—I couldn't do it.

"Shall I fetch the queen, or are you going to get dressed?" Freya challenged.

Kallias would see his people. He wouldn't hide from pain. He'd bear their grief and press forward.

I frowned when my heart gave no reply. No ache of longing. No rush of memories threatening to drown me in misery. Just cold. Solid. A stone had settled in its place.

There was my answer. I could handle my people's sharp accusations and condemnation. It would shatter like glass against my hardened heart.

With a dramatic sigh, I pushed past her. She hummed her approval and helped me dress for the high winds of Draconia.

By the time we reached the highest commoners' level, my thighs burned from the descent. Freya may have been right about my inactivity.

The ground floor teemed with voices and movement, the noise near deafening. This was where the common folk petitioned the nobles. Once a week, my father descended to hear their pleas, though matters often filtered to him all week long.

We slipped into the crowd at the base of the stairs. For a breath, I let myself hope this might feel like before, no different from previous years.

A shoulder clipped mine—bony, hurried. I turned with the motion. The man wore a tattered tunic and offered a hasty glance.

"Your Highness!"

He froze. Gaze wide. Recognition dawning.

"The princess!"

"She's well!"

"Dragon's Heart!"

The swell of voices rose around me, and I swallowed against my tight throat as I forced a smile. Bows dipped; eyes stared.

I had to get out.

Panic seized my chest.

These people were here seeking aid and answers. Aid I should have been able to give them—but I returned empty-handed, more burden than blessing.

A hand clamped over my clammy palm and yanked me through the swell of bodies. Freya pushed through the crush, moving like she meant to clear a path.

The stench hit first. Sour sweat and spoiled fish. My stomach rolled. Elbows clipped my ribs. Fingers grazed my skirt. Voices rose, calling my name—pleas for me to hear their needs. Freya didn't slow.

We burst through the stone arch of the Spire, stumbling into open air. Shadows pooled behind us where the crowd still pressed close, their faces upturned. Freya guided me toward the carriage, where two white horses stood calm and poised, a vision of grace compared to the prancing war beasts of Radaan.

A guard in pale-blue livery opened the door. Sunlight blazed down. I gripped his gloved hand, grateful for the barrier between skin. Once inside, I wiped my damp palms on my dress as Freya climbed in after me, securing the latch.

Outside, the black stairs coiled toward the Spire behind us. On the opposite side, a vast open clearing yawned—one of the few spaces left untouched. Father would address Draconia there with Argos, his voice carrying across the space. Everywhere else, apartments and shops crowded the land.

"Williard first, then fried fish," Freya said. "Unless you've got another stop?"

I shook my head, gaze drawn to the window as a flicker of shadow crossed the sun. A chirp broke through the light. I squinted into the glare—Tsunami's tail, green and blue with flecks of gold, swept overhead.

"She's going to pester me all day," I muttered. She couldn't resist anything with wheels. Or wings. Or noise.

Sure enough, she followed as the carriage rolled through the heart of Draconia. We veered southeast, toward K'bar—city of trades and craft. K'lan held the harbor. Goods moved from merchant to laborer along the main route, and somewhere above it all, Williard's shop perched.

K'lan teemed with life. Youngsters darted between wagons, chasing rag balls. A red-haired girl tackled a boy, setting off a pile-on. Nearby, mothers worked—fingers weaving, curing strips of sharkskin, attention flicking toward the wild swarm while other women labored with their husbands on ships.

Laughter cracked the air. Brine thickened with the scent of dye. As we crossed into K'bar, lye stung my eyes, sharp enough to draw tears. Soap-makers lined the road, their faces swathed in cloth against the fumes.

Draconis worked hard for what they held. They built their legacy with blood and grit. Nothing was given, and nothing was taken. We *earned* the respect of our dragons.

The carriage slowed, too wide for the narrow lanes curling between the stacked stone buildings.

There were too many people. Crammed in tight. Pressed shoulder to shoulder. The memory of Radaan's open plains—bare, boundless, terrifying—rose sharp in my chest. This place had always felt like home. But now? We were ants, piled high, scrambling skyward with nowhere else to go. The sea pinned us in. There was no way out. Only up.

Dragons or no, we would have to expand to the Wild Shores soon. We had no choice.

The carriage rocked as the guard dismounted and swung the door open. I took his hand, skirts brushing the sand-packed road.

Freya followed, arm flung wide as a boy darted past me. "Back to K'lan!" she snapped.

"Probably an errand," I said, unconcerned. Some parents encouraged their young ones into trades early. Technically forbidden until age twelve, but rules bent when there were mouths to feed.

"They belong in the safe havens with the rest of the children," Freya muttered, moving ahead.

The alley pinched so tight we walked single file, brushing shoulders with passersby. Recognition flickered across sun-browned faces. Men and women bowed in awkward dips, as if unsure how to treat me. Some smiled. Others frowned and hurried on.

Their uncertainty mirrored my own.

Part of me was overjoyed to be back, wrapped in the cozy chaos of this close-stitched city. But I longed for vast green fields, the open sky, the wind.

I needed a good flight. A real one. I'd only ever ridden with my brother or father, and for whatever reason, asking either of them felt as if admitting defeat, surrender.

I didn't stop to analyze that.

We passed oil refiners, tanners, dyers, weavers—the woodworkers came last. Williard's shop stood ahead, its door painted in festive red and green. Inside, mage lights flared so bright I had to blink against the glare.

Mikal wore his flight leathers, goggles dangling loose at his neck. His wiry frame angled away from us, hands clasped with another man's. I halted without thinking, my greeting caught behind my teeth.

An older man stood nearby. His graying brown hair hung in a braid, paint staining his worn clothes. His gaze latched onto me, a slow smile deepening the creases across his weathered face. A neat gray beard framed his chin and upper lip. He raised a finger, eyes flicking toward the two men.

Kites lined the far wall—bright, dyed sealskin in a dozen styles—but my focus returned to the pair.

Mikal's back was stiff. The act of filling a Vessel was never easy. To open oneself meant letting the rider in—baring their soul, thoughts, and fears. Most chose their rider with care, knowing they might witness their innermost reflections.

It took intense concentration not to be distracted by the other person's mind. Even a disciplined Vessel couldn't hide everything. Elmo would be near. Dragons never strayed far when channeling, needing proximity to keep the current steady.

Mikal stepped back with a grunt, cracking his neck left, then right.

The younger man—tanned skin, black hair—shook out his fingers before folding his arms.

"It never gets easier," he muttered, looking away.

"With time." Mikal turned to Williard. "Keep an eye on him. The magic is for kites," he said, cutting a sharp look toward the apprentice, "not for making fish dance."

Freya snickered, drawing Mikal's green gaze to mine. He grinned, then shuttered it back into a modest nod. "Princess. Good to see you out and about."

Middle-aged now, Mikal wore his years in the corners of his eyes, sun-etched and faint, though he hadn't lost that sly charm.

"I heard Williard's not making kites for the Awakening." I stepped deeper into the room, tracking the brilliant displays lining the walls. "Shame. I expected more of him."

"My greatest fan moved across the sea," Williard said, his voice dry and brittle as driftwood bleached by sun. "I told you—I made my kites for a certain princess."

A smile tugged at my lips. "Well, I've returned." I spun, catching the warmth in his broad grin.

The apprentice scoffed. Every head turned. Williard's brows furrowed. Mikal's hand dropped to his dagger without a word.

"Something to say?" he asked.

The young man's dark eyes darted from face to face. Freya edged closer. Her presence settled my nerves.

"We didn't expect her back," he bit out.

"So soon," Williard added, tone soft. "Princess, you haven't met my apprentice. This is Kai. He's gifted at crafting and imbuing kites."

"And making fish dance," Freya muttered.

Mikal hadn't taken his eyes off the boy. "Abusing magic will cost you your Vessel status," he said, voice low. "I shouldn't need to remind you."

"Thank you for coming." Williard forced a smile in an attempt to dismiss the rider. "Kai, why don't you check the market for ash? You'll require more for the dragon kite."

The apprentice shrugged and made to brush past, but a leather-clad arm stopped him.

"You've not greeted your princess."

My heart seized, screaming to just let the man go. His gaze carried the weight of every failure we'd tried to solve with the treaty—the famine, the crowding, the bitterness. He blamed me.

I wasn't ready to confront that.

Kai froze. So did Mikal.

"Pay your respects," the rider growled.

Dragon Riders knew no more than the common folk regarding the details of what unfolded between me and Kallias. But they served my father—loved him, were loyal to him. Elmo answered to Argos and Kalepsi. I was the Dragon's Heart and earned their love. Not a single rider had ostracized me, at least not yet.

Kai's dark eyes snapped to me, thick with hatred and heat. Dread twisted in my gut. Mikal was turning this into a spectacle, and I loathed him for it.

"Let him go." My voice rang steady, my chin lifting a fraction under the burden of a forced smile. "I'm sure he's in a hurry. The Awakening nears, and a missing dragon kite might be blasphemous." I flavored it with humor, but the words burned bitter on my tongue.

That accusation in his gaze would only fester. I'd been lucky not to be caught by another commoner who hated me as deeply. He would only be the first. I had to learn to let it go.

A low snarl thundered above us. Elmo's cry mirrored his rider's fury, but Mikal dropped his arm. Kai dipped his chin, cut me a glare, and stormed out.

Williard heaved a sigh and settled onto the workbench. His fingers traced the kite's frame as he shook his head. "The boy is passionate. Young."

"Foolhardy," Mikal spat. "Princess, perhaps you shouldn't be outside the palace without a rider."

I recoiled, stunned he'd suggest it. "I am among my people." My scowl cut sharp. "I am Draconis."

"A *limited* Draconis." He grimaced, rubbing his neck.

My inability to hold magic—a subtle hint I couldn't defend myself against a Vessel if they were to attack.

A terrifying thought.

"Tensions run high," he continued. "So many were planning to settle on the Wild Shores with the help of Radaan—and the promises of an abundance of food—it will take time before they forget that."

They wouldn't. My people would never forget what I promised when I agreed to marry Tallon. And they wouldn't brush off how I'd ruined it all.

What had he seen in Kai's mind? In others'? How much hatred simmered beneath the surface? I trusted Mikal not to hold back from immediate threats. He'd act. But even so, the warning settled between us like smoke too thick to breathe.

"She isn't alone," Freya cut in. "Zane filled me yesterday. Nothing will happen to Her Highness."

My smile wavered, but I forced my unease to roll off my shoulders.

"I didn't come here to argue over my safety. I came to talk about kites. If you have thoughts on the subject, stay. If not…"

Mikal lifted his brows, hands raised in surrender. "No harm meant, Princess. I'll see myself out." He slipped through the door without another word.

When it shut, my shoulders sank. The weight of masking, of posturing, pressed in on me. I was still a princess. But pretending I was the same girl who left Draconia felt harder than climbing the Nest's stairs.

"Come here, child." Williard patted the bench beside him.

I crossed the room and flopped down.

"Don't let it eat at you," he said. "It will pass."

"The emotions may fade, but they'll never forget."

He reached out, patted my hand. A rare display of affection.

"I promised them everything." No tears came. I felt hollow. Empty. My attention drifted to Freya as she settled across from us. "A better life. A future. I returned with nothing."

"It's not your fault, dear."

My eyes flew to Freya's. Her gaze warned me to stay quiet. Radaan needed to carry the blame. No one knew the extent of my treachery.

The old man went on. "Everyone knows King Kallias attacked you."

I stiffened. Pulled away.

He had been my mentor. My friend. A guide through my youth. I couldn't let him assume the worst of Kallias.

Everyone pointed fingers—at him or me.

If I wanted acceptance, I had to allow Kallias to take the fall. The truth would turn them against me. They'd choose Kai's hatred over understanding.

Flying into a storm like the first Dragon's Heart seemed more appealing by the day.

But I couldn't let Williard believe a lie.

"He didn't attack me," I whispered.

Freya's eyes squeezed shut. Her grimace said enough.

Williard sat silent for a moment, then shifted. "Of course, dear," he murmured.

He didn't believe me. If I told the truth—that Kallias and I loved each other—they'd laugh. Call him a monster. Easier to cling to the story they preferred than accept what didn't fit.

Guilt carved into my chest like a dragon's claw.

Either way, I lost. Stay silent and let them believe a falsehood, or speak and be scorned all the same.

I was living a lie.

Chapter Seven

S mall bones bit into my palm as I steadied the child's hand beneath the bowl. His white teeth flashed in his tanned face as he grinned up at me, the burden of his hunger pressing heavy on my heart.

It was agonizing not to slip him an extra slice of bread, but grain rations left no room for mercy. I smiled anyway and scooped an extra heaping of fish.

"Hurry, eat it while it's hot," I said, shooing him off. He gave a sloppy bow and skipped away, broth splashing onto the sand.

"Wasteful," Freya muttered, shaking her head.

It had only been a few days since I last spoke with Williard. He'd nudged me toward the soup kitchens, told me to find my footing in a place I could help and be among the people.

I resisted the urge to swipe my sleeve across my face, then forced a smile as I studied the line. Dozens waited—mostly women and children, a few elders, a scattering of maimed men.

The soup pot had dwindled. Miral, who ran this kitchen, was slicing the last loaf of bread so thin the crust curled.

Too many mouths. Too little to fill them.

Guilt coiled through what was left of my heart, constricting around it like a serpent. The Tithe neared—our weekly offering when the boats went out at first light, all their catch given to the dragons.

It was tradition. Necessary. But we were never this unprepared. If the kitchens ran dry now, they wouldn't reopen when people needed them most.

"A princess. Serving soup?" A young man strode toward the counter, cutting the line.

The crowd parted with shallow bows. His smirk found me. A silver-leaf crown caught the sun in his shoulder-length blond hair—worn like a weapon, demanding their respect.

"Adoni," I said, sealing my thoughts behind training. Calm. Distant. Measured. "I didn't know the Innaki had arrived."

"Hit the shore and practically ran straight to you, my princess." He grinned, sliding in front of a mother cradling a child.

"I can't imagine you running anywhere." I gave a polite laugh, though I wanted to shove him back and return to work. The Innaku ships had been expected this week, but I should have heard the dragons herald their arrival.

"True. A prince does not run." He tilted his head, a lock of hair spilling across sun-kissed skin. "Hence why I said *practically*. You Draconis are so literal—oaths and all."

My stomach tightened. A quiet insult, dressed in charm. I pressed my lips into a tight smile and glanced at the crying child behind him.

"You might've been better welcomed at the Spire." I offered the suggestion like a gift.

"So you've stepped down from greeting dignitaries? Has your father disowned you?"

No. Adoni would never take a hint.

"It seems I'm needed elsewhere." I turned to Miral and wiped my hands clean on a cloth. I had to tour a man-child around the island.

"Will you be needing me, Your Highness?" Freya asked, eyeing him like he smelled of rot.

"No. Stay and help."

"I'll see you at dinner." She gave Adoni a side eye.

I hurried out the back of the kitchen, tugging at my hair and smoothing my dress. A smear of soup stained the hem—something he'd notice and mention. I didn't care what he thought; only how I appeared. Beauty had become armor. It masked the bruised pieces inside, a flimsy shield against my people's disapproval.

Adoni stood exactly where I left him, forcing my people to step around him for food. My blood boiled. He blocked the path on purpose—a show of power. But they were commoners. He had nothing to prove.

"This way, my prince," I called, gesturing toward the beach. He moved slow, stretching his long frame, adjusting the white linen draped over his chest.

It was impossible not to compare him to Kallias. Adoni knew he was handsome. Perhaps he was—but beside the King of Radaan, he seemed unfinished. His skin peeked through the folds of his toga, muscle carved from youth, not effort. He hadn't grown into a man.

A dazzling grin lit his face as he approached, toga pristine, sun glaring off the fabric like polished bone.

I didn't know why it irritated me.

"Immaculate manners, as always. I thought Radaan might have changed you." He laughed, falling into step as I led him toward the sea.

My jaw tightened. No reaction. I'd known Adoni since birth—four years older and enamored with *his* Dragon's Heart. It used to be cute. Now it grated. He was harmless, but smothering.

"How were your travels?" I asked, watching the waves crash against the shore. Two dragons soared above, shadows etched across the sky.

"Smooth. Though Father wouldn't stop droning about marriage."

"Twenty-four and still without an heir," I scolded. "Your father's lineage is in peril."

He laughed and held out his arm, guiding me toward a boulder. "If he looked hard enough, he'd find no shortage of his line."

I gave him a glare. He only chuckled and dropped onto the stone beside me.

Birds shrieked overhead, circling for crumbs. My people lingered behind us, silent lines measuring our every move. To the left, a jagged outcrop marked the rock gulls' nests. To the right, a distant dock shimmered in the heat.

"Tell me, are the rumors true?"

Wind whipped my hair across my face. I brushed it out of my eyes. "Which ones?"

"Fair point," he teased. "You came back and lit gossip like dry tinder."

"And here I thought your lands escaped our drama."

"Hardly. We thrive on your antics."

He meant they waited for cracks of weakness to exploit. Innaku played nice, but they were the sharpest teeth behind the smile. The largest island chain. Grew the most crops.

When I didn't answer, he pried again. "Did the king attack you?"

I rolled my eyes. The question burned on every tongue.

"No? Doubted it, to be honest." He propped his elbow on his knee. "If he had, your brother would've razed Radaan."

Ronan certainly tried.

"You were caught with him, though?" he pressed.

I clenched my jaw, tipped my face to the sun, and closed my eyes.

"Father warned me about you," he continued. "Said you'd been compromised."

Same song from every noble and envoy. If the king didn't hurt me, I must have begged for it. Must have laid back and spread my legs like a proper little whore.

I bit my cheek, trying to wrangle my rage as I planned my escape.

"Was he at least a good lay? He's got to have, what? At least *forty* years of experience."

"Adoni." I snapped, turning on him. "Prince or not, you don't speak of another king that way. When I decide you deserve an explanation, you'll get one."

He grinned, eyes wrinkling with delight. Bile rose in my throat.

"That good?"

Thank the gods I didn't have magic. Or a dragon.

I'd have killed him.

A shadow swept over us, blanketing the beach. I looked up. Artorious flew low, wings stretched wide, scales gleaming like oil-slick armor. He circled once, a deep growl rolling from his chest. His gaze locked on Adoni.

I wasn't the only one who disliked the prince.

No saddle marked his back. I wondered if his rider sent him to keep watch. Mikal had made a habit of tracking me. Another leash I didn't need.

"You're weary from your travels. Careless with your tongue." My voice stayed low, even.

"Fine, fine." He raised his hands. "I surrender. No more prying."

Liar.

"How fare the crops?" I asked, trying to turn the subject.

"A whirlstorm clipped our eastern border. Flattened the outer villages." He sighed. "But it broke over the bay and twisted north. Tianna's breath saved us again."

The Innaki goddess. Her southern winds pushed storms off their shores.

"The loss?"

"Measured. As always." He turned to me with a crooked grin. "Draconia will eat."

Disgust curled in my gut. I hated that we relied on Innaku for bread. Even long after Father's death, Adoni would never let Ronan forget it.

And it was my fault.

I smiled despite the crack in my spirit. Everything reminded me of what I'd done.

Pain had become a part of me.

The island prince wanted to sit beside me in the dining hall, but Ronan called him away. My brother never liked his fascination with me, though I no longer trusted his judgment—not after he gave his blessing to Tallon. I'd known Adoni for years. Harmless, save for his sharp tongue. But Tallon... I shivered. Malice burned in his eyes. His words sliced deeper than steel. He thought drawing a blade would send me running.

I didn't run—I was taken.

The library tempted me, but I'd scoured each shelf. Dug through every tome I could touch. Scribes were still chasing leads—any mention of oaths or the Dragon's Heart.

None spoke of breaking a Draconis Blood Oath.

The last sliver of hope faded with the setting sun. I sat on the beach as the waves danced and stars blinked to life overhead, hollow. The fire had gone out. No spark. No drive. I still wanted to help my people, to grow our borders, feed the starving—but even rising each morning felt like a mountain. A task. A punishment.

I was a princess. Dishonored, scorned, reputation in ruins—but dutiful. My mother never wavered. She worked tirelessly, always preparing for the Awakening. I wouldn't quit. Not for pain. Not for shame.

"Isn't it past your bedtime?"

I spun around, kicking up sand, to see Adoni. He padded across the shore barefoot, moonlight tracing the lines of his tawny skin as he pushed his hair back from his face.

"I outgrew bedtimes years ago," I said, my heart thudding. We were on the northernmost beach, as close to Radaan as I could reach. Stone outcroppings hemmed us in.

He dropped onto the sand beside me without invitation, his hip brushing my hand.

I recoiled, clasping my palms in my lap, gaping at him. "Do you make a habit of invading people's sanctuaries?"

"You seemed lonely."

"Your rooms face south."

"Maybe I needed a night stroll too."

I narrowed my eyes, letting him see my skepticism.

"Peace, Nienna." My name on his lips dug into me. He'd said it before, but tonight it scraped against old wounds. "Where's my Dragon's Heart, the girl I used to play with?"

"I'm not *yours*, and I think you've outgrown playing."

"Gracious. Radaan made you bitter. What did their king do to you?"

Nothing. Everything. None of it was his business. Adoni hadn't earned that truth.

"What do you want?"

"Company."

I folded my arms tight, tempted to tell him where to shove that request. I came here to grieve. To unwrap the bandages holding the pieces of my heart together and survey the damage. Take note of what was left. Sitting next to a prince was not the time to do that.

The night was quiet. No gulls. No dragons. Just waves striking the stone. The breeze carried a chill, but the sand clung to the sun's heat, soaking through my thin dress and breeches.

"What was it like?" His tone held a strange wonder.

My teeth ground together against the irritation. "What?"

"Radaan. Being abroad."

I searched his voice for mockery. Found none. He'd always wanted to see more of the world. I could answer a few questions.

"Big."

A laugh burst from him. He tipped his head back, shoulders shaking. I smirked.

"Well, it is."

"I don't doubt it," he chuckled, leaning on one hand. The movement brought him closer. "But I expected more eloquence from a princess."

"It's spacious. Roaming. Capacious. Voluminous."

"Yes, thank you. I'm beginning to grasp the size."

I rested my cheek on my knee, watching him. His dark brown eyes locked on mine. He winked.

"It's beyond anything you've seen, Adoni. Land stretching forever. Endless plains. Mountains as tall as the Spire and wider than some islands. They run like a god's spine through the continent. It was... humbling."

"You? Humbled?"

"Here, Draconia is... well, we have–"

"Dragons," he finished. "You're at the top of the food chain. You rule the skies."

"Yes, as we would there, too. But the scale—it dwarfs even dragons. They could fly for days and still not reach the edge. I'm not sure it ends."

"I wish I could see it." His voice dropped to a whisper, his eyes on the sea.

I wanted to tell him he could. Buy a ship. Chase the horizon. But Innaku princes didn't have that luxury. He was bound as I was—married to diplomacy, anchored by bloodlines.

"And Radaan's people?"

Kallias or Tallon? The question hovered on my tongue. I bit it back.

"Proud. Loyal." I scoffed and turned toward the waves. "Much like our own. But worn thin. Tired. Their palaces gleam, their feasts are endless—gods, the food! But gold can't fix everything. They've bled in war nearly as long as I've been alive."

"And Vellos? Did you see their lands?"

"I was only there a few months." My laugh came brittle. "But the Velli ambassador visited. Egath, that was his name."

I shuddered. Sharp teeth. Rotten magic that made my blood rebel. He and Tallon had secrets, of that I was certain. Maybe now Kallias would find the truth buried between them.

"You're more worldly than I am, Princess."

I wrinkled my nose at the surf. "And yet, here I am. Back where I started."

Alone.

"It's not so terrible," Adoni murmured. He reached up, brushed a loose strand from my face, tucking it behind my ear. "Your people love you. The dragons still fly for you. You'll ride them to the Unknown Shores one day. You're the beginning of an empire."

I lifted my head, staring at him. "I brought Radaan to its knees. Destroyed the peace we needed. Broke my vow to feed our starving. I'm not a beginning, Adoni—I'm the ruin at the end."

"You're wrong." He cupped my cheek. I flinched, but didn't pull away. "You came back. You can start again."

His eyes burned, hunger glittering behind his tenderness. Not a boy anymore. A prince. A tactician. Reaching for power.

I shoved his hand aside. "Abyss, I'm a fool."

"Wait!" He caught my wrist, yanking me off balance as I tried to stand.

I twisted, straining against his grip. "Let me go!"

"You're not listening!"

I kicked him in the shin. He grunted, then lunged, knocking me flat in the sand.

Cold panic sliced through me. I gasped, searching for a blade. Tallon's face flickered in my mind. I reached for Adoni's hips. Nothing. No weapon.

"I hear you just fine!" I screamed through clenched teeth. "You want my crown—and I thought you were my friend!"

His weight dropped on me like a beached whale, pushing the air from my lungs.

He was going to kill me.

A dragon roared in the distance. Adoni's mouth crashed against mine, shattering every coherent thought.

I screamed into him, twisted, lunged to bite his cheek as my nails tore down his arms. He cursed, seized my wrists, slammed them into the earth. His knee jammed between my legs, shoving them apart.

Real horror settled cold in my chest. No one knew I was here. No bonded dragon heard my cry. The Spire lay too far. He was too strong.

"You gave yourself to an old man who had nothing to offer!" he snarled, fighting as I bucked beneath him. "I have a nation! What could he offer you? A storming pat on the head?"

"He'd give me the world if I asked!" I shouted into his face. "A dragon will eat you. Get off!"

"My precious Dragon's Heart," he breathed, lips and teeth and tongue burrowing into my neck, "They don't answer you. And no one would believe you didn't want this—not even your family."

Was he right?

Would my father believe him? Had I tarnished myself so badly they'd all think I wanted this?

Tears burned down my cheeks. I dug my fingers into the sand and thrashed, every nerve alive with panic. I clawed inward, searching for anything—any scrap of power, any spark.

Nothing came.

"It won't be bad," he said, mouth dragging a wet trail up my neck, to my ear.

I threw my head sideways. Bone cracked. Light exploded behind my eyes, but he yelped. I drove my knee into his gut, kicked. He let one wrist go, grabbing for my leg, and I raked claws across his face.

The ground shuddered.

Then something dark barreled into him.

Adoni vanished. I toppled after the blur that hit him. Scrambling upright, I bolted the other way and ducked behind a scaled foreleg.

A dragon loomed above, its massive paw nudging me beneath its chest. In the low light I couldn't make out which one, nor the rider who had come—but I heard grunts. Fists meeting flesh.

The earth heaved again, followed by a shriek. Tsunami had arrived. And she was furious. Her hiss split the air. I clung to the dragon's leg, rough scales biting my palms, and peered through moonlight at the shore.

"Storming son of a squid!" my brother roared. He hauled Adoni up by the hair. The prince swung, landing a fist in his gut.

Ronan doubled over.

Tsunami lunged, neck weaving low across the sand.

I bolted from under Gyrak, sprinting toward them. We couldn't kill him. He fed our people.

"Ronan! Adoni!" I screamed, charging to intercept them, racing Tsunami's strike.

Behind me, Gyrak let loose a roar, reared, and slammed into the ground. The shockwave sent me stumbling. My brother staggered away, dragging a hand through his hair, while the island prince struggled to his knees, rage simmering in his eyes.

My strides halted beside Ronan, chin raised like steel. "I am the Dragon's Heart, Adoni Innaku. I am never alone."

Then her jaws descended.

Chapter Eight

"She's a riderless dragon—it's a known risk when they come to our shores!"

"He was the crown prince of Innaku! Their ambassador! And we don't have so much as a shoe latch to show for him!" Mother snapped at Ronan.

We sat cramped at the table in my parents' chambers. Father's glare pinned me with suffocating force. I couldn't read him anymore. Did he blame me? Did he hate me even more?

I huddled beside Mother, a thin blanket over my shoulders. It did little to fight the slight chill in the salty air, but offered some defense against the tension curling through the room.

"Send Tsunami to their coast," Ronan muttered, rocking his chair back on two legs. "Let them take it up with her." Blood streaked his cheek. Sand clung to his tangled blond hair. His torn tunic hung crooked from the fight.

Mother pinched the bridge of her nose, as though the pressure could hold back her temper. "We cannot afford vengeance—we need their supplies!"

"Draconia flies for Innaku." Father's voice hit the table like a dropped blade. All eyes turned to him. His gaze never left me—as if I held the answer he wouldn't say aloud.

"Fly?" Mother echoed. "Nereus, do not act in haste."

She'd caught the word. He hadn't said sail. Flying the dragons meant war.

"Their prince attacked my daughter," he growled, teeth clenched. At last, his stare broke from mine and turned to her. "That was within their ability to control. Tsunami eating that flaming son of an eel was beyond our responsibility."

"Gyrak was present. He could have prevented it."

"Whose side are you on, Mother?" Ronan snarled. "Adoni would've raped Nienna if I hadn't stepped in!"

He slammed his chair forward, all four legs thudding hard against the floor.

"Don't you dare accuse me of betraying my daughter." She spun on him, eyes sharp as sparks. She jabbed a thin finger toward his face. "Watch your temper—and your tongue. One day this burden may fall to you, and, dragons above, may you have a steady voice of reason at your side!"

"Voice of reason?" Father leaned forward. "Tell me, then. Why can't I fly for Innaku?"

Mother straightened in her chair with a pointed look at Ronan. "Innaku is too large. You cannot hold it with dragonfire, not when we need it for its resources. You burn the fields and they're worthless to us—and they won't forget."

She pressed on, tone flat. "We don't have the manpower to colonize a land that size without leaving ourselves exposed. And if you start a war among the isles, the Kulletti will strike before you can blink. Dragons or not, their warships could reduce the Spire to rubble. And the Ivetti? They'd be caught in the crossfire. Resources are scarce as it is. Add a war and our people will suffer even more."

"She's right." My voice broke. I loathed how weak that made me feel.

Father's stormy eyes traced back to me and I frowned, trying to weather his glare.

"Tsunami avenged my honor. As a dragon, Draconia is her haven. King Galdoni knew the risks when he sent his son. They've seen their bloodlust—how instinct takes over. If we strike Innaku now, we lose the potions keeping half our children alive."

"Pah!" Ronan spat. "If I hadn't seen the attack myself, your defense might convince me–"

Blue sparks burst across his mouth, silencing him. His chair scraped back as magic shoved it from the table.

"Another word, and you're grounded a week." Father's voice cracked like thunder. He pointed, the dismissal plain.

Ronan threw up his hands, then stormed out, slamming the door behind him.

"He'll be worse than you," Mother muttered, face buried in her palms.

Father didn't speak. His silence burned hotter than words. He stared at me still—white brows drawn in what I hoped was contemplation, not accusation.

"The Innaku wait for our response," she continued, trying to draw his focus away.

He pushed to his feet, shaking his head. "Nienna, why is it always you?"

Shame sealed my throat. This wasn't my fault. Not this time. The island prince saw weakness—thought I'd grovel for a crown without seeing that I already gave everything that mattered. My heart. My soul. Both belonged to someone else.

I would never marry. Never bear children.

Besides, after Radaan and now Adoni, men would keep their distance. I'd become a cautionary tale—untrustworthy, cursed, or worse, a death sentence wrapped in a pretty dress.

I couldn't possibly sink any lower.

Sunset found me on the landing, legs dangling into the wind. The sky blazed—a riot of pinks, purples, and bruised blue streaks, screaming for attention. Dragons echoed its cry, their roars tearing through the painted heavens as they darted between clouds like living fire.

But my gaze stayed fixed on the endless northern sea. My mind clung to a continent hidden by distance, tethered by something I couldn't name. An ache pulled in my chest—as if unseen fingers clawed outward, reaching for the missing half of my soul.

Kallias.

I could dance through courtly games, charm diplomats, and endure the whispers that skittered down the Spire's halls. But the emptiness in my chest? It gnawed at me. Unraveled me with a silent, ceaseless hunger.

Every sun-thirsty plant straining toward a window. Every mention of trade routes or harvests. Even when someone so much as uttered the word *goat*, the void inside me tore wider.

How was he surviving? Did he feel this too? He had years on me. Did time dull the pain? Did duty weigh less on stronger shoulders?

A tear broke loose and traced a hot path down my cheek. I shut my eyes, throat clenching as I pictured his silhouette—broad, unyielding. No, it wouldn't be easier for him. But he'd shoulder the burden, as always. He would never let Radaan down. Too loyal. Too strong.

He was probably arranging another marriage for his wretched son.

A sob clawed free as Tallon's face collided with Fyrn's in my mind. My fist cracked against the stone beneath me. The sea looked serene—mocking me with its calm.

My heart kicked against the injustice. Fyrn didn't suit him. She had nothing to offer and knew it. How had I missed the way she looked at him? I assumed she tolerated him, grew up with him. I never guessed she wanted him.

She got her heart's desire—regardless of the cost. But Kallias and I? We were cursed from the beginning.

It. Wasn't. Fair.

I hugged myself. Wind curled around my dress, tugging it like a child seeking attention. Kallias would arch a brow if he saw me perched on the edge—just as he did in Phares.

Back then, he flinched when I leaned over balconies. He hated heights. Hid it well, but not from me. I remembered the strain in his jaw as we climbed Sol's mountain path.

Footsteps scuffed behind me, and I straightened fast, wiping the wet from my cheeks. I met my father's frown as he stared over Draconia. Wind toyed with his white hair, but didn't ease the tension in his brow.

I sniffed, laced my hands in my lap, and blinked the rest of the tears away. I buried the broken part deep where he wouldn't see.

With a sigh that carried too much weight, Father sank beside me. His boots dangled off the edge, silver buckles catching the sun's last breath. He crossed his arms, leather creaking faintly with the motion.

Neither of us spoke as the light bled from the sky.

I had never felt so alone. A failure to my people. A shame to my parents. Too soft. Too easy to use. And the man I loved bore the blame for what I let happen.

"Your mother fears you hate me." The words scraped out, as if he loathed having to say it.

I stole a glance. His beard twitched. He still wouldn't look at me.

"I don't," I whispered, curling my arms around my knees.

"You don't act the same." His voice dropped. "You came back... different."

"You haven't treated me like your daughter since I arrived." I pressed my face into my knees.

And I *was* different. I was cracked. Splintered down the center.

He inhaled, then tipped toward the sky as Argos soared overhead. "Do you remember when you were small and insisted on sleeping out here? You wanted to watch the sun sink into the world and rise again on the other side."

"If I recall, you banned me from doing exactly that."

I had been obsessed with the idea—catching the day as it emerged. I always fell asleep before it rose, only to wake with a dragon curled around me like a living shield.

He grunted. "Do you remember why?"

"Because I was a princess, and princesses don't bed down beneath the stars." I scoffed. "They sleep tucked in satin and feathers."

He chuckled, head shaking. "As if."

"You *yelled* at me," I shot back. "Carried me inside like a sack of grain, tossed me in bed, and screamed that princesses belonged indoors."

"I don't *scream*," he said, arching a brow. I narrowed my eyes in return. "What you forget is the tumble off the Spire."

I frowned, trying to recall. The landing had always felt like home, as if I were tucked away in the skies. Surely, I would've remembered if I fell off the edge.

"You were fevered. Sick. I shouldn't have let you sleep out here, but your mother insisted the air would help. I was working late when Argos roared through the bond—you were falling."

Cold spread through my limbs.

"He caught you." His jaw tightened. "But it reminded me—if you fell, no matter how fast I was, I couldn't save you, couldn't protect you. I had to rely on the dragons. Argos placed your small, fragile, wingless body in my arms and–" He stopped, breath sharp. "I nearly lost you."

He dragged a hand over his face, fingers raking through his beard. "When I put you to bed, I wasn't angry at you. I was furious with myself. I let you stay out there, knowing the risk. If anything had happened... I wouldn't have forgiven myself."

It all made sense now. His fury. Mother's reassurances. As a girl, I forgot his sharpness quickly, slipping back into adoration—but I never slept on the landing again.

"Why didn't you tell me?"

"No Draconis should ever fear the sky." His stare pierced through me. Pride and worry tangled in his gaze. "Every time you venture here, Argos flies. Always ready. When you lean over the Nest, when your feet dangle off this cursed edge, his roar floods my mind. And I see it again—your fall—through his eyes."

He released a long, slow breath. "No, Nienna. I was never angry with you."

Not then. Not now. Tears welled, and I pressed my lips together, holding them at bay.

His gaze softened. A grimace tugged at his mouth as he caught the tear streaking down my cheek.

"Disappointed?" The word cracked in my throat.

My teeth clenched, bringing an ache to my jaw. I just wanted him back—my father, Dragon King of Draconia, fierce and overprotective, full of laughter and endless warnings. I needed his arms around me, to hear everything would be alright. That no matter what I'd done, he still loved me.

"We can't change what happened or how it happened." His voice dropped low. He brushed the tear away with a thumb rough from years of sword hilts and reigns. "But I will never forgive that man for how he broke you."

"Father–"

"Don't." He tapped my lips with a finger, silencing the protest. "I still rage. My oath calls for vengeance." His expression flared contempt. "But I will never stop loving you, Nienna. You are my daughter. My blood."

I shut my eyes. My heart cleaved. He hated Kallias—but he was safely on the other side of the sea. Father had come to offer peace. A truce. He came to *me* to reconcile.

He was my father. My family. And I had walked in like a storm, torn open the court with truth and grief, thrown my word against my brother's, confessed love for a man I should never have touched. I shattered a blood oath and expected him to welcome me with open arms.

Nothing about this was fair.

His strong arm wrapped around me, tugging me against his strength. A sob tore loose as I crumpled into him, resting my head on his shoulder.

Solid. Steady. Safe.

He was still my father—my home.

Chapter Nine

The next morning brought worse news. The Innaku were sailing home, pulling every one of their people from our island.

We ate a meager breakfast. Tension crackled between my father and me, frayed further by the steady stream of messenger doves and Chief Jehoikim's demands for answers.

If he didn't back off, Argos might eat him.

I ended up in the soup kitchen again, sleeves rolled, ladle in hand beside Freya and Miral. Together we fed the crowd—our people—though a hush hung over them, a shadow of grief clinging to their shoulders. The cries of rock gulls echoed above their murmurs. They'd watched the Innaku ships vanish over the horizon—along with our last steady supply of bread.

It wasn't my fault this time, but I still stood at the center of it. Disaster spiraled around me like a whirlstorm, dragging everyone into its eye. I was a curse in human skin. The story of Nienna, the first Dragon's Heart, resonated with me. She vanished into the sky—and I wished I could too. If I knew how to fly alone, I might not come back.

An elbow jabbed my ribs. I sucked in a sharp breath as hot broth splashed down my front.

"My apologies, Your Highness!" Freya deadpanned, her reproving expression unrepentant. "Perhaps it's time to return to the Spire?"

The sun had begun its descent, orange bleeding into the clouds. I'd spent the day in the heat, handing out portion after portion, yet the line stretched on.

Some would leave hungry.

I bit back a curse and glared at her. "I'll stop when the beach is empty."

"Begging your pardon, Princess," Miral said, passing another steaming bowl, "but we're nearly out. Best you go on."

I glanced at the hunched woman, shawl clutched tight as she peered into the pot. She was right. We'd refilled it four times from the mage light bubbling in the corner, but it wouldn't last much longer.

The line had thinned. Mothers clutched tired children, some already turning away, heads bowed—not all would eat tonight.

"Come, Princess. King Nereus will be waiting." Freya gestured toward the narrow door at the back of the kitchen. I managed a tight smile and placed the ladle beside the steaming pot.

"I'll return in the morning!" My voice carried to Miral over the clatter of pans and hiss of boiling broth.

She nodded without looking, busy with another bowl.

We had barely stepped down the stone stairs before Freya cornered me.

"They won't starve. This is just extra to their rations and whatever they can buy. You act like they're wasting away."

"They are," I snapped, slipping into a shaded alleyway between buildings. The sun couldn't reach us there.

"Are we out of fish? Kelp? Salt?" She scoffed. "Have the coconuts fled the island? No, they'll grumble, but they'll endure."

I bit the inside of my cheek. She wasn't wrong, but the knot in my chest didn't loosen.

There was nothing I could do now.

Onward.

She caught my silence and sighed. "You need to leave the mainland."

"I just got here." My laugh came bitter.

"Ask your father to take you to the Wild Shores. Maybe the dragons will settle with you there."

"Argos and Artorious won't even stay the night. And you think *I* can soothe them?"

"You're the Dragon's Heart," she said. "That title means something. You calm them in ways riders can't."

I wasn't so sure. My father had more sway over the dragons than I ever would. Still, she had a point. My body was nothing more than a brittle shell painted with forced smiles. I craved an escape—the opposite of the girl I'd once been, the one who begged to stay among my people.

Draconia held a piece of me. Mother always told me I belonged elsewhere, that my future was across the sea. Now, my heart lay there too—and this place no longer felt like the home it once was.

"Perhaps I'll visit one of the islands after the Awakening," I said, mostly for her sake.

She shook her head, looped her arm through mine, and together we walked toward the Spire. Narrow passages twisted like snakes between old walls. Around us, commoners drifted home, shoulders heavy with fatigue. The scent of brine clung to the air as we pressed on.

When we reached the palace, the sun had vanished. Green and gold scales blocked the doors in a living wall.

"What are you doing, Tsunami?" I laughed, stepping toward her. She lifted her head, tilting it as she studied me, golden membrane sliding over her eye in a slow blink.

Her body uncoiled in a stretch, claws digging into the stone steps like a waking cat.

"Father won't be pleased," I said, climbing the dark stairs to meet her.

She snorted, unimpressed, and sank onto her haunches, peering down.

Dragons were sentient, though more beast than man. She wasn't a dog to command. Intelligence glimmered in her gaze—a question I couldn't begin to guess at.

I slipped free of Freya's grip and stepped forward. Tsunami towered above me. I had to crane my neck to meet her eyes.

"Princess?" Freya's voice wavered, unsure. I had no answer for her.

Something inside me stirred. A spark, a tug—intuition, raw and insistent. I frowned and reached for her. She wasn't mine, wasn't anyone's. All my life, she'd ignored me. She wouldn't choose me now.

Still, a strange sensation pulled tight beneath my ribs.

Tsunami snapped her jaws with a sharp clack, biting the air. I yanked my hand back. A warning—one dragons gave each other.

With my palm to my chest, I stepped away. The sensation pressed, persistent and aching. A low trill rose from her throat as she dipped her head and sniffed my hair. Her breath stirred the loose strands, and I smiled.

Then she turned.

I backpedaled, letting Freya tug me toward the doors as Tsunami's wings unfurled. Leathery and vast, they snapped wide. She launched skyward, beating the air. Dust lifted in her wake. I shielded my eyes and rubbed at the ache in my chest.

"What's wrong?" Freya asked, glancing at my hand as she steadied me.

That pull tightened, then eased. I didn't lower my palm as Tsunami vanished into the night. Relief and worry twisted together.

"Ever since I've come back... the dragons feel different," I murmured, searching the stars for her shape.

"Their scales?" Freya sounded doubtful.

How could I explain it? I wasn't a rider. Their thoughts couldn't reach me. I was just the grown version of the babe they hadn't eaten. But since returning to Draconia, it felt like they *knew*. Knew when I needed them. Adoni's attack shouldn't have stirred them. And yet it had.

Ronan's answer echoed in my head: *Gyrak heard you.*

"It's nothing," I said, brushing her off as we entered the Spire's first level. Mage lights flickered between lanterns, catching the black stone like flecks of obsidian.

"It's never nothing with you." She snorted, linking arms with mine as we climbed the stairs.

We rushed to clean up. She slipped into the servant halls, and I made for the dining room. Zane stood guard, flipping his dagger with lazy precision, catching it midair with a wicked grin.

"No comment, Princess?" he asked as I approached.

"You meet expectations," I said. "A rider should know which end of a blade to hold."

He recoiled with mock horror. "You wound me."

"Better my words than your knife." I laughed and strode past him. The scent of fish broth and kelp wrapped around me, fragrant and briny, richer than what we served on the beach.

Scarcity didn't discriminate.

A dull ache pulsed through my heart again. The Innaki abandoning our shores wasn't just a signal—it was a warning. But until word came, we could only wait.

Adoni was Galdoni's only heir, but the king could still produce another. I mourned the boy I once called friend, but the grief had torn itself to pieces. I didn't know how to feel anymore.

He thought I was *easy*.

Retaliation hadn't crossed his mind. He thought I would fold. Surrender.

My stomach soured.

I approached my father's table with a careful grin. He greeted me with a clenched jaw and a terse nod.

But he saw me. That counted.

These were hard times for Draconia. He hadn't smiled in public for weeks. I missed the days when we'd fly with Argos, his arms around me, the wind a song and the sky a promise.

Now everyone had a scheme.

"You're late," Mother whispered, dipping her bread into her soup.

A servant placed a portion in front of me. Bits of fish bobbed in the broth.

"I was feeding our people."

Across the table, Ronan cleared his throat and raised his brows at his empty bowl, refusing to meet my eyes.

Mother caught it. Her gaze snapped to him, daring him to look up.

"Tomorrow you'll be better used in K'seer," she said. "The stage needs your touch."

"Something you can't do?" I kept my voice low. Nobles didn't need to hear bickering between a queen and her daughter.

"I could spend my days in beach kitchens." Her tone lowered. "However, there are duties that demand more of me."

I pressed my lips together. Her words stung, despite their gentle delivery. I'd spent weeks hunting for impossible answers in the library and sweating in the kitchens, trying to atone for something no one asked me to fix. Perhaps it was selfish either way. Both were for my own benefit.

This mess was *mine*. Our people needed something to lift them. The Awakening would remind them of what we still had—an abundance of fish, music, community.

Dragonlings.

We would not perish or starve.

The festival, a symbol of hope, meant rebirth after the storms that assailed our islands.

Our people needed that reminder.

So did I.

Haldor, an aged rider, burst into the dining hall and drew my gaze. He didn't move with his usual ease. His stride had urgency—long legs devouring the space between us. He raked a hand through gray-brown hair, eyes flicking to me as he stopped at the base of the dais.

"Rise," Father said, dabbing at his mouth with a napkin, his frown deepening. The table quieted, every noble straining to eavesdrop while pretending to eat.

"There's been a message." Haldor's voice, low but clear, reached the family with ease.

"From?"

He hesitated. His gaze cut toward me, uneasy.

What did I do now?

Haldor bent close to his ear, a hand steadying on Father's shoulder as he whispered, lips hidden.

Argos roared.

Porcelain rattled.

Father shoved back his chair, snarl curling his lip. "Nyxaria, come with me."

Mother and I set down our spoons. Ronan rushed to his feet, already tensed to find Gyrak, to take flight.

My breath hitched. Sky above, had the Innaki declared war?

I scanned the table. Jehoikim's beady eyes narrowed, studying my family. He wasn't panicking—so it didn't concern him. But then who?

Father stepped away. Mother and Ronan flanked him.

I moved to follow—whatever it was, he'd need all of us.

"Nienna, stay."

I froze, mouth half-open. I swallowed the protest and sank back into my chair.

"You've only just arrived," Mother called over her shoulder. "Join us after you've eaten."

She took Father's arm. Ronan followed, expression taut.

Dismissed. Left alone in a room full of nobles who no doubt blamed me for the disruption—probably a correct assumption—waiting for me to slip up.

I drew a breath, slow and deep, and leveled a smile like drawn steel. Then dipped my spoon back into the soup.

If Father wanted me here, I'd stay. Maybe he needed someone to watch the ambassadors. Still, the message gnawed at me. I didn't know who sent it. Or what it said.

Endless possibilities swirled in my head, and somehow I was sure none of them were right.

The day's heat blistered against my back. Sweat slicked my skin as I reached for the last length of cloth. The gold shimmered under the brutal light as I draped it over a green so deep it pulled my thoughts across the sea.

My foot slipped. A yelp broke loose as Freya cursed and grabbed for me. I dropped the fabric and snatched the rungs, fingers closing on rough wood. It jolted but held.

"Sun above!" Freya's knuckles had turned white on the rails. "Let me move the blasted ladder!"

I groaned and climbed down. She was right. I shouldn't have reached that far. The heat had frayed my patience—this task couldn't end fast enough.

"You were *so close!*" Ronan's voice came from the beach, a stone's throw away. Gyrak's wing stretched wide over him, casting a generous shadow.

Of course he wanted me to fall on my face while he stayed in the shade, complaining his black leathers weren't suitable for stationary work in the sun.

I didn't bother to give him a response. Freya and I repositioned the ladder against the platform. I'd been assigned to decorate the dance stage—my mother's attempt to make my work more 'acceptable' for royalty. Honestly, the whole thing needed saving. The poor woman who'd started it chose brown and green in honor of the earth.

A noble sentiment. But not a joyful one.

I accented in gold. The palette tugged at my frayed heart, but I claimed coincidence.

Freya steadied the ladder as I climbed again, reaching for the fallen cloth. The stage stood raised above the beach, ringed with tall poles. I secured the fabric to ropes strung from pole to pole, the drapes catching the breeze as if the wind danced with us. Mage lights would hang among the cords. Dragons would paint fire in the sky during the Awakening.

Some days crawled; others vanished like smoke on a windy day.

Nearly a week had passed since Haldor's message. When I reached Father's level that night, he was flying with Ronan, and Mother warned me to give them space. All she'd said was war—and nothing more. She left me with orders: prepare for the Awakening, stay clear of the nobles.

"A little to the right," my brother called.

"I'm going to kill him," I muttered, shoulder pressing into the damp strands of hair clinging to my face.

"I have a dagger," Freya said from below.

A snort escaped as I adjusted the fabric, then tied it off.

"Too tight–"

A roar cut him off.

Gyrak jerked his head up, dropping his wing over Ronan like a tent flap. I twisted, gripping the ladder as the black dragon snorted, tongue flicking the air while his rider thrashed beneath the leathery membrane.

"What is it?" I shouted, as if the beast might answer.

A chorus of roars and shrieks ripped across the island, sending rock gulls screeching for their nests. I snapped my head around. Dragons launched skyward from every direction, wings slicing through the air as they surged north.

Gyrak snarled and sprang upright, lifting his wing.

I scrambled down the ladder while my brother brushed off his leathers, muttering curses. Gyrak let out another growl and tossed his head toward the northern shores, eyes slitted.

"Ronan!" I called over the sudden clamor. Workers shaded their stares, gazes tracking the beasts spiraling overhead.

What could stir them like that?

He hesitated, spun to Gyrak, then sprinted to his leg, clambering up without pause.

"You slimy suckerfish!" I snapped, tearing after him. Whatever drove the dragons to frenzy—he wasn't leaving me behind.

My dress tangled around my legs, nearly pitching me into the glittering sand. I grabbed a fistful of fabric and sprinted across the beach. Ronan leaned into the saddle as I vaulted onto Gyrak's paw, slipping where his missing toe left a hollow. A midnight head swung toward me, breath hot and rancid. I locked eyes with the yellow glare and didn't flinch. He would take me. I'd ridden him before—with my brother. I wouldn't dare try another dragon, not even Argos.

Teeth the length of my arm snapped inches from my face. I exhaled hard, then scrambled up the side, fingers clawing at the saddle's straps.

"Stay here!"

"I'm not your dog," I spat, climbing behind him and locking my arms around his waist. "Tell me what's happening!"

Gyrak launched skyward. The force slammed my jaw shut. Ronan grunted as I clung tighter, hands clenched in front of him. Black scales shifted, muscles coiling, wings unfurling to catch the wind. Gyrak hurled his neck forward, leveraging his bulk, jostling us with each beat.

My throat tightened as the northern port came into view, the air swarming with dragons. K'lan shimmered beneath the chaos. Innaki ships would have arrived from the east, landing farther south along the border. We'd have heard if they passed through the outer isles.

It couldn't be.

Dread stole my breath. Panic swelled. My vision blurred.

He wouldn't.

Gyrak cut through the sky. Ronan pulled his goggles down while I pressed my face into his shoulder. Wind clawed at my eyes when I tried to look. I gave up and held on, whispering prayers to Veridis—or any god listening—that he hadn't sent a ship here.

We dipped low. Gyrak groaned as he fought to land on the choked beach. Dragons packed the shore, scales glinting in a riot of colors. Some stood knee-deep in the surf, riders still mounted.

My gaze swept the water. Hope curdled. Air fled my lungs.

A Radaanian banner snapped from the mast of a sleek ship.

Ronan dropped from the saddle without waiting. Across the way, Father dismounted from Argos' massive shoulder. The black bull snarled, lips curled, eyes murderous.

I swung my leg over and slid off Gyrak—graceless, stumbling through the sand as I raced after them.

Dockhands bolted from the green-flagged ship, retreating behind the wall of dragons. No one wanted to be caught in the blast.

And that's what the ship risked.

Ronan and I sprinted after Father's navy coat. His shoulders squared, his stride relentless as he charged the ramp. Radaanian crew leaped from the vessel, ropes in hand to moor it.

"You get a single breath to haul anchor and leave our waters!" Father thundered.

My boots thudded on the dock. I grabbed Ronan's arm, holding him back. We didn't need more kindling thrown on this blaze.

"Begging your pardon–" one began.

"But they're under my orders."

My knees buckled. A sob caught in my throat.

Kallias stood atop the ship. Greaves loomed behind him, his shadow as always. Sunlight flared against the golden mantle. The wind stirred his silvered hair. I couldn't see his face at this distance, but I knew that voice. It clung to my nightmares.

Argos roared. The blast whipped the sails and strained the ropes that held the ship in place.

Ronan yanked me to a stop behind Father. A ramp crashed down from the ship's deck, thudding hard against the dock.

He shouldn't be here.

Even in my wildest dreams, he never dared. He couldn't. Father would kill him.

"Don't do it." Father's voice dropped—quiet, deadly. A promise.

The air swirled around us, tugging at my dress. Sparks crackled over his clenched fists, blue and bright.

Kallias stepped onto the ramp.

Argos lunged. Water exploded beneath his pounding stride. His gaping jaws rushed past me—teeth wide, aimed at Kallias.

I was wrong.

Argos would kill him.

Chapter Ten

KALLIAS

"No!" Nienna's voice split the salted air, sharp as shattered glass.

Gods above, if the last thing I saw was her face—wind teasing sunshine strands of her braid—the mad sail across the sea would have been worth it.

Even I flinched when the black dragon—vast enough to eclipse our ship—recoiled from Nienna's cry. Its horned head snapped toward the clouds.

I moved one pace closer to an enraged father with murder carved into his stare.

His dragon shrieked, a bone-rattling sound, then hurled fire above me. A warning. He wouldn't hesitate again.

I advanced.

Greaves' armored tread echoed behind me, no balm for the thunder in my chest. Doubt fused with grim resolve. If this ended in my death, so be it. I would die chasing the one I loved.

Nienna was worth it.

Another step.

Nereus, King of Draconia, loomed ahead. Snow-white hair and a trimmed beard marked his age. Though leaner than me, his navy leathers clung to a warrior's frame. Ice-pale eyes burned beneath furrowed brows, his face reddened with fury.

I could have sworn blue sparks danced in his glare.

Another step.

He moved, bridging the last of the distance. My boots hit the dock. His hand shot out, seizing the front of my overcoat.

"It was a mistake coming here," he spat, yanking me close.

I grabbed the collar of his jacket, gripping him with as much force as I dared. My fingers twitched above my sword.

"I've come for a private word. King to king." I knew the risk. Fallione waited aboard the ship. No one else would disembark until I secured our safety.

Nereus hissed, his lip curling in a snarl. "You are no king."

"Then man to man." I was in no place to test him, but my life was already forfeit. He hadn't killed me yet. That counted for something.

"Man? No *man* would have done what you did." His tone dripped acid.

"A man recognizes his failures and seeks to right them." Our noses were breaths away, each of us clinging to the other with barely restrained violence. I'd stood on countless battlefields, but nothing prepared me for the Dragon King's fury. Whatever held him back was wavering—and fast. Even the Velli's threat paled in comparison to this king's wrath.

"Father."

My breath lodged in my throat. I refused to look past him, not yet. I needed to face Nereus first, explain what happened. Right my wrong. Only then could I ask her forgiveness.

And pray she still wanted me.

Gods, if she didn't–

"You want me to hear you like a man?" Nereus stepped back and shoved off my hold. "So be it. You'll be escorted to the landing as the criminal you are, tried for your crimes against Draconia—"

"Father!" Nienna's voice broke in a quiet plea.

"—And against my daughter."

His fist lashed out. Reflex saved me from a shattered jaw. His knuckles grazed my chin as I dodged, and the blow sent me staggering.

Elohios—did he pack that punch with magic?

I steadied myself, ignoring the throbbing sting as he spun on his heel. Above me, his beast loomed, saliva dripping from fangs longer than my legs.

Ronan held Nienna back, but I couldn't look at her. Not yet. The king came first.

"You, to your mother!" Nereus pointed at her, then to the smaller black dragon—Prince Ronan's mount.

Tried as a criminal, but not eaten.

Elohios guide me.

"Haldor! Mikal! Escort him for trial."

Riders dismounted from their red and green dragons as Ronan hauled his sister off the dock. My teeth gritted at the sight of her struggling against his grasp. She argued, words too low for me to hear, gaze flashing over her shoulder, searching for mine.

Her cheeks were thinner, her skin sun-darkened. At this distance, the blue of her eyes was almost indiscernible.

A growl snapped my attention downward. I'd stepped toward her. A wall of obsidian scales slammed down, and an orange eye pinned me in place.

Pulse hammering, I resisted the instinct to draw my sword. A single wrong twitch would mean my end. I inhaled through my nose, calming the urge. I faced death countless times—dragonfire would simply be a quicker path.

Ronan's dragon launched into the sky, and I tilted my head, chasing one last glimpse of Nienna. A speck against the clouds. Then gone.

The larger black whipped its head toward me, knocking me off balance, and I steadied myself on the dock as it retreated into the water. The movements sent waves rocking the ship.

My attention shifted to two men advancing.

Riders, clad in black leather. Knives strapped across their bodies like scales. One unhooked a chain from his belt.

I was a king.

My throat tightened. I stared into the older man's eyes—anger glinting in the dark brown.

"Your men remain aboard," he said.

I dipped my head. "Agreed."

The younger man jerked his chin toward my shadow. "Including him."

There was no avoiding it. Greaves would never stay behind. He was bound to me. Leaving me would destroy him.

"Where he goes, I go," he growled.

"He's going to his death." The older rider pushed past me, and it took everything I had to remain still when he grabbed my sword.

My eyes drifted shut as the blade scraped free of its sheath.

The wave of vulnerability hit harder than expected. My weapon was gone. Cold steel bit my wrists as they wrenched my arms behind me.

"I go with him." Greaves stated.

Even if I commanded him as king, he wouldn't turn back. I had no right as a friend to send him away while I marched toward what could be my end.

"Your choice," the younger rider muttered.

Greaves had planned for this—left most of his gear on the ship, surrendered the rest without a fight.

A crowd gathered along the shore. Nereus meant to make a spectacle. I had disgraced him and his daughter in front of our courts; he'd return the favor now. Behind the cluster of uneasy faces, a jagged black tower loomed from the island's center.

The stone drank in sunlight, casting a deeper shadow. That grim fortress was Nienna's birthplace—and my doom.

I lifted my chin as Nereus mounted his dragon, its wings tucked, its scales dull and broad as shields.

"Let's go."

A rough hand shoved me forward, and I stepped toward the watching crowd.

If I wanted Nienna, I would suffer this. I would endure, bear this burden. Radaan whispered blame into every painted smile. She would have suffered worse at court, her reputation in tatters.

I did that. I humiliated her, and now her father answered in kind.

A hand pressed between my shoulder blades, steering me toward the pale sand. The silence was unbearable. A gull's cry rang from above. Waves battered the shore. Every face fixed on us—children peeking out from behind robes, women with sharp eyes and squared shoulders, men instinctively moving to shield their families.

Wood gave way to soft sand as the dock ended, and the crowd swallowed us. No words. No murmurs. Just tension thick enough to choke on.

We moved toward a narrow break between red brick buildings. They stretched skyward, as if they'd run out of land and grown desperate to escape the earth. Their shadows fell over me like a cage. Was this how Nienna felt under the mountain? Trapped. Compressed. As if the city itself pressed in, intent on crushing me.

The alley narrowed until only the rider and I could walk abreast. Doors creaked open. Faces appeared, vanished. Shock and fury etched every expression.

It was a public shaming. The King of Radaan, shackled. Paraded about like a criminal.

To them, I was worse. I had tarnished their princess, shattered a sacred oath, abandoned a people who needed food and supplies.

In their eyes, I was the enemy.

Breaking the treaty had been an act of war. Yet I hadn't left it there—I sailed straight for their shores. A smaller vessel meant fewer supplies, but more speed. Less of a threat. Better odds of arriving without being turned to ash.

Even now, I couldn't make sense of it. Fifteen dragons on the island and none intercepted me. The alarm sounded only when I neared the harbor. Was that Nereus' idea of mercy?

I sent him a dove days ago. His answer came on bloodstained cloth. A warning. Come, and die. But he hadn't killed me at the docks. Did Nienna stay his hand—or was he playing at diplomacy?

The rider yanked my elbow, jerking me around a corner. My boot caught a step. I stumbled, lips curling into a snarl.

Behind me, the scrape of motion—Greaves was ready to fight the city itself for my sake, or die trying.

"Move!"

The command struck like a whip. I was shoved toward a mass of civilians. They cried out, scrambling away, vanishing into shops or homes. Were these homes? Storefronts? I hated how little I knew. I had never stepped foot on Draconis soil. Now every crack in that ignorance cut me.

I assumed we headed toward the Spire—my trial waiting. But what would that consist of? King Nereus as judge and jury, or a full council? I hated not knowing.

If Nienna stood at my side, she'd know how to navigate this, but she was with her mother.

But I was the Gods' Chosen. Golden Warrior of Elohios. I survived nearly two decades on the war front. I would endure this too.

My mantle chafed at my neck, dislodged from my hands being pinned behind me. Each step dragged metal against raw skin. I had refused to approach Nereus without it. And I wouldn't remove it. Not yet. It reminded them who I was. Reminded *me*.

The space between structures trapped heat. No breeze cut through. Though shaded, the alley sweltered, and sweat beaded on my brow.

After an eternity, we burst into a clearing boxed in by red-clay brick buildings. They walled off a grassy plain—where a jade and gold dragon waited. It crouched low, tail lashing like an angry cat, its head tilted at us in quiet appraisal.

The rider behind me gave a grunt of disapproval. Overhead, a crimson beast plunged from the clouds, ivory claws outstretched. The green one snapped its gaze skyward and loosed a roar that rattled the mantle across my shoulders.

The red beast veered off, circling above the clearing. I barely had time to wonder who it belonged to—clearly not bonded with the riders escorting us—before I was yanked along the edge of the plain, steered wide of the sweeping tail. Eyes the color of sunbursts tracked me, predatory and unblinking, like a giant feline stalking its prey.

Its gaze unsettled me. Tension coiled in the air, thick as smoke. It wasn't only the crowd pouring in from the narrow paths between the buildings—it was the beast itself. Untamed. Feral. Not bound to any man.

The Spire loomed overhead, a towering omen, a herald of death. A black seam split the open sky, but I didn't dare lift my head to follow its peak—my mantle had already slipped too far.

A rough hold dragged me up the steps. I stumbled, caught myself. I refused to fall. Not here. Not now. I wouldn't humiliate myself further.

Massive doors, carved with ancient sigils, gaped open. Inside, a crowd pressed in around the entrance. Awe and dread pooled in my chest as we stepped within.

The center was hollow—a cylindrical core bored through the stone. A ramp spiraled along the edges, not unlike the tunnel leading to Clay's manor. Balconies jutted out above me, where faces leaned over the railing. Murmurs and gasps slid down the walls, coiling around me like a constricting serpent. They pulled me forward, beginning the long ascent.

I lifted my chin, fixing my eyes on the path ahead. I didn't need to provoke or threaten these people. Nereus wanted them to see a prisoner. But I was Radaan's king, and I'd walk with dignity. I would not slump like some whipped dog.

The ramp wound upward, endless. My thighs screamed with the effort. Sweat beaded along my brow, and I cursed the droplet tracing my temple. I didn't want to look defeated—but this was all part of Nereus' plan, and resistance meant nothing now.

At last, the incline gave way to flat stone. A crowd of Draconis in earth-toned garb filled the chamber. Their clothes weren't tattered, but bore evidence of labor. The women wore split skirts and trousers like the ones I'd seen Nienna wear so many times.

They shoved me forward through the crush of bodies. The ceiling stretched far above, voices bouncing off the stone. To my left, a dark throne rose on a platform sculpted high above the floor, visible even to those crammed near the back. Small balconies honeycombed the walls—like a termite nest carved into the rock. The Spire had to be hollow, riddled with unseen halls and passageways.

A thunderclap of wings tore my gaze toward the massive opening at my right. My spine snapped straight. Nereus' dragon landed on a stone outcropping, neck snaking into the tower's heart.

I clenched my jaw and held my ground as the crowd shrank from me. The beast halted a handspan from my face, lips peeled back. Its snarl sounded like boulders grinding down a mountainside.

Still, I wasn't dead. Yet.

Its jaws snapped shut with terrifying speed. I winced, bracing for the strike. It didn't come. The dragon lifted its head instead, golden eyes searing into mine, pupils thin and sharp as knives. Nereus slid down its shoulder and landed with fluid grace, armor whispering as he hit the stone.

He marched straight toward me, fury etched into every step.

I needed a private conversation, a chance to explain. But from the fire in his eyes, he meant to make a spectacle of this. Nothing I said would stop him. It would be my word against his son's. I could only pray Fallione's counsel had earned me some ground.

He sneered as he passed. I turned, careful to keep my attention on his silver-threaded blue leathers, though every instinct screamed not to turn my back on his dragon.

Right now, Nereus was the greater threat.

He spun and dropped onto the black-stone throne. The stairs beneath bore sea beasts and waves, but dragons held dominion at the top.

"Kneel!"

A hand shoved hard between my shoulders. I hit the floor with a grunt. Pain flared through my knees, but I stayed upright, jaw clenched as I stared at Draconia's king.

"Kallias Sunspear," Nereus thundered. His voice rang through the Spire, silencing the murmurs. "Have you come here to die?"

Chapter Eleven

NIENNA

Ronan's hand snagged the back of my dress, but I jerked free, slipping down Gyrak's shoulder before his claws touched stone.

"Nienna, stop!"

As if I ever obeyed my brother.

Gyrak's talons struck the landing with a thunderous crack. I hit the ground beside him, stumbled, snatched up my skirts and bolted for the throne room.

Kallias was here.

He came for me.

But instead of joy, terror sprouted in its place. Here, in this cursed stronghold, Father would kill him. I'd already begged, pleaded—he chose Ronan's lies instead. Kallias would only stoke that fury, incite his rage, and there was nothing I could do to stop it.

The vast sea protected him. My lie about the blood oath, flimsy as it was, had kept him hidden. Distance had dulled Father's wrath—but now?

He was *here.*

I tore across the wide space, feet slapping the marble, heart in my throat. Empty corridors blurred past. Servants scattered from my path, eyes wide, but I didn't stop. No time to offer apologies.

Father would treat him as a traitor.

A man who defiled his daughter and mocked a sacred oath. Perhaps I could plead madness on his behalf. What sane person dared defy a promise backed by dragonfire? Maybe I could twist the truth before the judgment fell.

I threw open a door. Four noblewomen shrieked, bolts of silk fluttering as they rose. Mother's gaze snapped to mine, sharp and assessing. Her pale brows dipped, and I opened my mouth too late.

"We will discuss the festival later, ladies." Her tone sliced clean as a blade. She stood and rushed toward me, her dress twisting around her like wind-driven sails, features set into a hard mask.

I swallowed whatever I meant to say. The women of K'seer didn't need Kallias' name whispered in their halls.

It was delaying the inevitable.

Mother swept past, already striding down the corridor. I had to jog to catch up.

"Where is he?" she hissed as I matched her pace.

Somehow, she knew. Dread curled deep in my belly.

"Father's bringing him for trial." I panted, pressing a fist over my hammering heart.

She stopped cold and pressed her eyes shut, tension rippling off her like waves crashing against stone.

"He came here to die." Her whisper splintered something inside me.

Tears burned, demanding release. My breath shuddered. If she didn't see a way out—there wasn't one. She knew Father's mind better than anyone. His flaws. His oaths. The cracks in his logic. She might have shielded me before, but not now. Not with a king's life at stake.

No.

I wouldn't accept that. He came for me. He crossed the sea, knowing the cost—and still, he came.

I lifted my chin, spine rigid. "I can't let that happen."

Mother yanked me into a spare chamber and slammed the door. Dust-veiled sheets cloaked the furniture. A single shaft of sunlight pierced the gloom.

She faced the window, voice cold. "Remember your place."

Her words struck like a slap. Ice spread in my veins.

"Your father warned him not to come," she said.

"Maybe he brought Edith!" My arms wrapped around my ribs, nails digging deep.

"You don't understand." She turned, pain carved into the lines of her face. "Your father signed a blood oath. So did Kallias Sunspear. They agreed—you were to be given to Tallon of Radaan. No man would touch you. The king vowed to protect you, to present you to his son. Kallias broke that bond. There's no twisting it. He took what was promised."

"We never—nothing happened!"

"Ronan says otherwise. And his presence here proves it."

"Does it?" I snapped, fury flaring hot enough to scorch away fear. "He came because he's *honorable.* He cannot let a lie stand. Elohios wouldn't bless a liar."

"And this god blesses him for defiling the future bride of his son?" Her voice struck like a whip. "His honesty means nothing now." She shook her head, the sunlight catching the silver threading her hair. "He broke an oath signed in blood. Our oaths are not empty vows—they bind life and magic. The power in your father's soul has gnawed at him for weeks, demanding retribution. The lie you told—the one you *thought* protected him—only delayed the eruption."

I flinched, shame burning across my cheeks. "You don't *know* I lied."

Her glare hardened. "Your father is a Well. You think he didn't *feel* your deception? Magic ancient as the bones of this kingdom flows through him. The only thing that stopped him from burning Radaan to the ground was his love for *you.* That restraint will vanish the moment Kallias stands before him."

She paused. "A dove arrived days ago. Kallias begged for safe harbor. We denied him, and Nereus gave fair warning that if they set foot on our shores, they'd be slaughtered as traitors."

The message. The one I thought came from the Innaku—it had been *his.*

My throat closed tight.

Father wasn't just a Vessel. He was an abyss. A Well with no bottom. His power built over years, calm on the surface—but beneath, a molten fury.

And I was the exact opposite. I couldn't hold magic in. It seared through me and left nothing behind.

There were tales of my father holding off an entire whirlstorm, shielding Draconia in his youth—and his skill had only deepened with age. If the magic tied to the oath was unraveling, fraying his control and demanding release, it was a volcano sealed by will alone.

"There has to be something—a way around this." Either that, or I'd figure out how to smuggle him off the island. I wouldn't let my father be his executioner.

Mother pressed her lips together and shook her head. Her hand settled on my arm. "The only thing you can give him now is comfort in his final days."

I jerked away, vision blurred. I spun and tore down the corridor, cutting through hidden passageways wedged between walls and winding above the throne room. The narrow tunnel spat me onto a stone balcony veiled in shadow.

Below, Father sat on his throne above a crowd so dense it bulged against the doors. Every soul had come to witness history's claws sink in.

The Dragon King would kill the King of Radaan.

Kallias knelt. Haldor stood beside him, hand twisted in Kallias' hair, forcing his head up. Rage surged inside me, coiled and sharp. I lunged toward the railing, teeth biting into my tongue to stifle the cry in my throat.

Then he looked up. Sky-blue eyes locked on mine.

My heart cracked.

That gaze—steady, unflinching—I knew it. His face had thinned, cheekbones carved sharper. Scruff shadowed his jaw, grown thicker, as if to hide the hollows in his cheeks. Silver had threaded his temples.

He would never let me steal him away.

Haldor noticed me. He yanked, forcing Kallias' attention forward, toward the throne.

My nails scraped the stone railing, the cool grit unwavering beneath my fingertips. A distant dragon's roar echoed the scream in my chest. Kallias was a king; he deserved more than this spectacle.

The crowd stirred. Ronan pushed through the bodies, halting beside Mikal—who restrained a seething Greaves.

The man looked ready to vomit or kill. His face burned red, muscles stretched near breaking. His gaze locked on Kallias, twitching at every movement Haldor made, as though his body trembled on the verge of violence.

He was watching his friend's death sentence.

"I've come to clear your daughter's name." Kallias' voice rang out, thin but unshaken. The words echoed through the hall. Father let silence steep before answering.

Mine. Not his.

Father's fingers tapped the throne's armrest, silver rings clacking sharp in the hush. "Nienna was deceived. Manipulated by a man twice her age."

A palm clamped over my mouth and yanked me into the shadows. I shrieked into the grip and drove an elbow into ribs.

"Don't!" Freya hissed in my ear, pulling back her hand. "You'll only make it worse!"

"It's a lie!" I snarled, twisting to reach the rail again.

"And shouting it now fixes everything?" Her arms locked around me. "You wait. You watch. Think like the royal you are."

I bared my teeth and shoved free, lunging toward the edge.

"My daughter needs no forgiveness," Father said. "The monster who defiled her is the criminal—and will pay."

"I offer my life—"

No.

Tsunami screamed past the landing, wings slicing the air, her cry shattering the sky.

"—I ask for Nienna's hand in marriage."

King Nereus exploded from the throne with a roar, a blur down the steps. He seized Kallias' coat, dragging him upright. Greaves lunged, Ronan and Mikal barely holding him back.

"You *dare*," Father growled, almost lost beneath Argos' thunderous shift. The dragon stretched its neck, sparks smoldering between its fangs. "*Dare* ask for my daughter—after swearing her to your son?"

Kallias, taller by a hair, met his fury with that same unshaken stare.

"I ask for her hand."

Father's fist snapped forward, crashing into Kallias' face. "You swore a blood oath and broke it! Your life is forfeit—you've lost the right to request anything, least of all *her*!"

Freya grabbed my arm as I flinched.

Kallias' head whipped back from the strike, magic trailing the blow. He steadied himself, rolled his neck, lifted his chin. Blood traced a slow path from his nose. "I offer a new oath. Grain for your people. Trade with the continent. A stronger alliance—and a vow to make your daughter happy." His voice rose, addressing the crowd. They needed to hear.

"You don't speak of her happiness," Father spat, releasing his coat with a shove. "Not after twisting her into ruin."

Kallias staggered back, boots scuffing stone. He looked up—straight into Argos' gaping maw.

"Kallias Sunspear, king who doomed his nation, you do not deserve a quick execution by dragonfire."

My stomach knotted. I leaned over the rail as if I could listen to my father's thoughts.

"I challenge you to a duel to the death. May you have one final chance at honor."

Blood drained from my face as bile crept up my throat. When Father waved his hand, Haldor jerked Kallias back. The heavy mantle slid from his shoulder, hanging askew.

But those cornflower eyes still found mine.

Tears slipped free. I couldn't speak, couldn't reach him. One word and Father would strike him down. I'd hate him forever if he did. Perhaps he knew.

Haldor led Kallias into the crowd. Draconis parted, cold and disdainful. Some spat. Others looked away.

To them, he was a villain.

They didn't know the truth—that I loved him—or what a monster Tallon had been.

And I could never tell them.

This was my story.

And it was broken. A tragedy.

Freya yanked me back. I wanted nothing more than to collapse. Cry until my bones rattled. I could live with a shattered heart. But I would never forgive my father for what he did—for killing him in cold blood. Magic or not, I couldn't excuse that.

But I was nowhere near finished. I wasn't ready to quit.

I caught Freya's hand, then swiped my tears before dragging her into the tunnel.

"Give me your clothes."

She tried to pull free, but I held tight. "Why?" Her voice sharpened. "What are you planning?"

"Father will have barred me from the dungeons."

She groaned, "Your mother told me to keep you from doing anything reckless!"

"You stopped me from speaking, did you not?" I snapped, tugging her into the main corridor. "Now, as your princess, I command you—hand them over."

We burst into my rooms. I reached behind me and began yanking at the fastenings of my dress.

"And I'll be tossed in beside your darling king if we get caught!"

"Then we'd better not be caught," I shot back. "Now move!"

It didn't take long to exchange clothes. Freya's garments were plain enough to help me pass as a servant. Her hair, a vibrant red, would draw attention, but mine vanished beneath a worn hooded cape. I ducked into the hall, keeping my gaze low and my face hidden.

The dungeon lay below the Spire's main level. A long descent. I moved fast, my thoughts racing faster.

Would I need to drug him? Could Greaves smuggle him out? Every possibility collapsed under the significance of what I didn't know.

People clogged the path. Civilians wandered about in stunned clumps, their shock a shield as I slipped through unnoticed.

The stench hit hard. Damp and dank. Stale and musty. Heavy air pressed close, the reek of mildew clinging to my throat. It seeped into my skin, clung to my breath. Nothing like the rest of Draconia—where sunlight and wind kept the rot at bay. Mage lights flickered, barely more than a glow, swallowed by the dark.

The cells, carved from solid rock and braced by slabs of iron, lined the walls. I veered off the main path, keeping to a narrow trail that curved behind the guard station. Few guards lingered—Vessels didn't need numbers. Their magic was enough to keep the worst prisoners caged with a look.

We'd never had a high-profile prisoner such as a king—and I was lucky to slip into the dark corridors before they brought in more reinforcements.

Cold gnawed at my skin, sank into my ribs and curled along my spine. A tremor rippled through me, but I didn't stop. Kallias needed sunshine—everything in Radaan revolved around it. It was seen as a blessing from his god, and Father threw him in a cave.

Voices sharpened near a bend. I lowered the mage light and tucked it at the base of the wall, casting the corridor in a soft, silvery pulse. This side stood empty. Of course it did—Father wouldn't risk Kallias talking to anyone.

"You were foolish."

My mother's voice. Quiet but cutting, almost lost beneath the thunder in my ears.

"Perhaps." Kallias sounded flat. Tired.

"We denied you safe harbor, and still you came. You have doomed yourself—and if what Nienna claims is true, you've cursed your lands to be ruled by a child."

"Radaan appreciates your concern." His tone shifted into the one he reserved for foreign courts—measured, composed, not quite warm. "However, I left my kingdom in capable hands."

Silence followed, broken only by her sigh. I pressed my back to the cold stone and shut my eyes.

"Why did you come?"

"I told King Nereus–"

"What he wanted to hear." She cut him off. "I'm not asking as queen, but as Nienna's mother. Why are you here? You knew you'd find no kindness on these shores—you're lucky Argos didn't eat you alive. Haven't you broken her enough?"

I clenched my jaw and folded my arms tight. They always blamed others for my wounds. Never saw the way they tore me apart from inside.

"Queen Nyxaria," Kallias said, the tortured soul mirroring my own slipping through. "I came to make it right."

I heard him then. The man I knew.

Silence answered. Thick. Strained.

Far off, something skittered. My eyes flew open—please, no rats.

"Nereus will never grant you mercy."

"Which is why I've asked for a private audience."

"If you met him alone, he'd gut you before you spoke." Her voice dropped. "You tampered with forces you don't understand. And because of that, you've dragged our people into your mess. You will answer for that."

"Do you not fear you're reacting to a half-truth?" Kallias bit out.

"You shattered our trust when you took our daughter—someone else's betrothed."

"I never *took* her!" Steel clanged. Bootsteps followed. "Excuse my bluntness, but I never bedded her—ask her; she'll say the same."

"If I may be bold enough to match your tone, it doesn't matter," Mother hissed. "My son found her sprawled across your desk, half-dressed and face marred with passion. Perhaps you didn't bed her then, but there's nothing to show you've had a shred of restraint before."

Someone blew out a resigned breath.

"You brought this upon yourself, Kallias Sunspear. You stole my daughter and left behind a ghost. She's a shell now, hollowed out by what you did. She'll never come back from this, and you've ensured the last thing she sees is your death. May your soul never find peace."

I winced. If any of what they believed had actually happened, they would be within their rights. My heart broke at how protective my mother was, but she was resigning him to his execution over what they thought was true.

No one spoke. Footsteps faded into the dark. I waited, unwilling to breathe until they passed.

Once the silence returned, I rose and crept around the corner.

Empty. The mage lights flickered dimly, their glow barely enough to show where the cells began. I drew in a quiet breath and moved forward, heart hammering as I scanned for extra guards.

Movement caught my eye at the first cell, and I paused.

Greaves sat on a cot, elbows balanced on his knees, fingers laced tight. His warm brown stare assessed me before he dipped his head in silent greeting, then motioned toward the next cell. He rested his chin on his hands, eyes falling to the floor. Lost.

My chest ached as I passed. I never expected to see Kallias again—let alone here. I wanted him higher. On my floor. Not buried down here.

I stopped.

He sat hunched on the edge of the cot, fingers tangled in his hair. His mantle lay on the far corner of the mattress, the cleanest patch he could find. He raised his head as I approached, and something inside me split.

Blood crusted along his cheekbone. His eyes—drained. Hollow. His expression mirrored my very soul.

Tears blurred my vision. I offered a smile, one I'd practiced a hundred times. It trembled, then gave way. "Greetings, King Sunspear."

His brows pulled low. Hurt etched into the space between them. He braced his hands on his knees and pushed himself upright, gaze darting behind me to the dark hall.

"It's just me," I choked out, hating the steel bars between us.

"Just you." He exhaled, a trace of tension bleeding from his shoulders. This was my Kallias.

"I'm so sorry." The words rasped through the tight knot in my lungs. I reached for his face. "I should have warned you—I should have-"

"Nienna." His palm pressed mine to his cheek. "You are Draconis. I knew."

I slid my hand behind his head, threading my fingers through the short strands and drawing him to me. My lips, salted with tears, found his—bloodied and warm.

He kissed softly, carefully, as if testing the shape of our grief. I smiled against him, rage blooming within, directed at the barrier caging him from me. Heat clung to his skin as if he were sunlight trapped beneath stone. Cinnamon lingered on his breath, sweet and bitter like memory.

My chest ached, the pull to him tearing at my bones. He was safe. He was home. Nothing could rival this. I had tasted the King of Radaan and would settle for no other.

He broke away first, resting his brow against the iron. His gaze searched mine. "Do you kiss all the prisoners?"

"Only the ones who belong to me."

He scoffed, soft lines deepening around his eyes. I had been right. Silver had thickened along his temples and threaded through stubble framing his jaw.

"You shouldn't be here." The words gutted me, tore out my soul.

"Lie." He rubbed his chin and leaned back. "I should have come long ago. I'm late."

"Why now? You knew they'd never accept you. Not after Ronan." Fresh tears slipped down my cheeks, and I let them fall, allowed the anger to scald through the hollows of my ribs like armor.

"I came to ask for your hand. To atone. To right my wrongs."

"*Our* wrongs."

"The blame rests on my shoulders. Nereus made that clear."

"He doesn't know!" I slammed my palm against the bars. "No one will listen!"

"Our reputations are destroyed." He exhaled a sharp breath, bracing himself against the wall. "They trusted us, and I shattered that. I deserve their fury."

Droplets flung from my lashes as I shook my head. "I left to *save* you—and you threw that away."

"To save me, or Radaan? I gave my life to that kingdom. Never once took something for myself." He stepped forward, hand reaching through the bars. "I'm a monster. Selfish. I've tasted joy—held it in my hands—and I *crave* it. Nienna, I need you. I love you."

His fingers curled around the nape of my neck, tugging me close.

"You can't," I whispered. Not now. Not after everything.

His grip tightened as he tipped my chin, gaze unwavering. "You don't get to tell me who I love, Nienna. You don't get to tell me who to pursue."

The confession echoed mine from what felt like an eternity ago.

No, the heart loved who it loved. Sometimes it chose the wrong person, and sometimes it found the other half—but at the wrong time.

"I came for you."

"This will destroy me." My voice cracked. Tears spilled over his hand. "When you draw blades, which death do I celebrate? If you strike him down, Argos will rain fire—you'll be lost to me either way."

"Such faith in your dragons," he said, mouth lifting in a crooked smile. "Yet none for my gods."

"I've never seen them."

I tried to lower my gaze, but he caught my chin with his thumb, lifting me back to him.

"They brought me to you after the mammoth. You bartered with Veridis. I'm breathing because you refused to let go. Exercise your faith, Nienna."

I closed my eyes. Pain tore through me like splitting bark. He wouldn't run. Even if I opened the cell and led him to the sea, he'd stay. Too stubborn. Too righteous.

His lips brushed mine again, light as breath against the iron. I slid my hands through the bars, fists closing around the front of his coat. I pulled him closer. He grunted, and I traced my fingers up the back of his neck, deepening the kiss.

I poured everything into it—ache, hunger, the fear I'd never feel him again. With every ounce of my racing heart, I offered him my pain, my fury, my love. I begged without words.

He gave me the lead. Allowed me to *take,* to be the aggressor. He always did, bearing every burden life dealt him.

And I hated it.

I broke away, breath ragged, searching his eyes. "I need you to fight for me."

"That's why I'm here," he murmured.

"You can't let him win."

His jaw clenched. He winced, then nodded, slow and certain. He had seen it too. My father's blade. My love in its path. I didn't want to lose either of them—but I couldn't sit back and watch Kallias die.

"I will fight for you," he said, "my Dragon's Heart."

Chapter Twelve

NIENNA

I returned to my rooms and barely dressed before dragging Freya to the library. There had to be an answer buried in these pages. Somewhere, a way to sever a Draconis Blood Oath without death.

The sun sank below the sea, casting the room in shifting shadows. Freya read beside me, page after page scoured in silence. Now that I understood the magic binding the oath, scattered clues began to align: fits of blind rage, erratic outbursts of power. It all fit. And still, we had nothing.

Kalepsi's cries filled the night, needling my frayed mind. Whatever she wanted, it could wait.

I hadn't even seen Mother to ask if the duel would come at dawn, or if we'd been granted a brief reprieve. I plunged into the texts, chasing threads that stretched back to the first bonds between dragons and Draconis. Perhaps that held the key.

"There's nothing." Freya exhaled, shoving her book toward the table's center. "If there's a way out of this mess, it's not in here."

I clenched my jaw, snatching the volume she abandoned in front of me. "It's here." The words scraped from my throat, meant more for me than her.

Kalepsi's roar tore through the Cireendium, rattling the Spire; Argos answered, his screech splitting the air. I pressed my fingers to my temples, trying to ease the pressure pounding within.

"Sea beneath, what's set them off?" Freya muttered.

"Argos is angry. Because of Father."

"And Kalepsi?"

"I don't know!" My words cracked. "I don't know anything!" I shoved the book aside, heat burning behind my eyes.

Worthless. A princess. A Dragon's Heart with no dragon to my name—a pawn in everyone's game.

In Radaan, I was treasured. Even in Draconia, I had some standing, a measure of respect. But now, when the man I loved stood on the verge of death—I was nothing. This was my harsh reality. No magic. No power. A voice with no say.

I hid my face in my hands as Freya leaned back, studying me. Pain throbbed waves across my skull. My mouth felt like ash, my fingers trembled, and my limbs dragged heavy and slow. Every bit of my body demanded I rest, but Kallias came for me. He was here, and that *meant* something. A cursed flicker of hope. If he was here, there had to be a chance, some minute shred of a future together.

"I'll get you tea," she said, chair scraping as she stood.

She was just giving me space to grieve. I dragged her into this impossible chase—she was as spent as I was. The sun had punished us all day while we strung those ridiculous drapes, and now my desperation for answers demanded more.

I dropped my head to the table, retracing the same maddening path for the thousandth time.

The blood oath tethered Father and Kallias. Their lives locked to a signature, magic woven into ink and intent.

If there were a loophole, wouldn't Father have told me? Could magic be misled by clever words? It wasn't the runes themselves—it was belief, direction, purpose. When Father sent me to Radaan, he bound that purpose to a promise: I would be Tallon's. When that promise unraveled, the magic must've interpreted it as betrayal.

Too much room for failure. Why were these oaths even still used?

"A princess never slouches."

I jerked upright. Stars burst along my vision. When they cleared, Edith stood by the table—hair pinned in a perfect bun, not a strand astray.

Her mouth curled in a soft, sorrowful smile as she shook her head. "Before you ask, I don't have the answer you seek."

"He treated you well?" My voice was barely a whisper.

"As a king should." Her gaze dropped. "He's a kind soul. So are you both. But you're caught in a terrible web."

I buried my face in my hands. "I can't let him duel Father."

She sighed, then stepped behind me and swept my hair from my shoulders with careful fingers. "It will be tomorrow."

The words hit like a physical blow. My lungs buckled. I folded in on myself, breath catching in a soundless scream. Somewhere above, a dragon's roar rang out—raw, distant, full of grief that mirrored my own.

"The dragons feel it too," Edith murmured, working her fingers through my wind-tangled knots. "If there were another way, your parents would have found it."

"They hate him!" I choked, the stupid, worthless tears leaking out of my eyes once again.

"No," she said, her tone gentle. "They love *you*. For that alone, they would choose differently if they could."

Edith. My nursemaid. My handmaiden. Always steady, always near. She stepped back into her role as if we never parted, her voice full of sense and sorrow. She wove my hair into a braid with practiced hands while I tried to crush the last living piece of my heart.

Why didn't I leave, run home, when I saw Tallon? Why did I go to that library, give in, tease, taunt, push?

Everyone pointed fingers now that he was here—but the blame belonged to me. I tasted passion, lust, and demanded more when it wasn't mine to take. This disaster was my fault, and he bore the burden of it without protest.

"You cannot change the past, Nienna," Edith whispered, pinning the braid around my head with tender precision. "All that's left is forward."

She tugged back my chair, and I faced her, eyes itching and blurry. "Go check on your dragon," she said. "She's been inconsolable."

I forced my feet beneath me, bottling up the pain as I stood. If Kallias was resigned to trust his gods, then I'd trust mine.

The walk to the Nest was quiet. Even the torches along the Spire walls flickered with unease. As I cleared the corridor, a cold gale barreled into me. Kalepsi's tail lashed, nostrils flaring. The violet queen snapped her jaws in my face—sharp and sudden. A reprimand.

"Did you call me just to scold me too?" I bit out, tears streaming. I was so sick of crying. It couldn't change who I was or what would happen tomorrow.

She hissed low, curling her lip to flash teeth—a sign she wouldn't put up with my irritation.

"Am I not enough for you either?" I shouted. "No wings or fangs. No magic. You claimed me as your own, and I have nothing to show for it! A princess of a starving island and a worthless broken heart of dragons!"

Kalepsi threw back her head, rearing up. Her forelegs slammed into the stone at my sides, bones scattering like brittle leaves. Throwing her muzzle at my body, she bellowed, the clamor splitting the night. My ears rang.

I didn't flinch, baring my broken soul to her.

What good was I? What purpose would I ever serve?

Worthless. Shattered. Unprofitable.

Another roar tore from her throat. The force ripped strands loose from my braid. She snapped her jaws and swept a claw toward me. I braced—but she caught me in her grip and yanked me upward.

I clutched her scales, heart slamming against my ribs. She bolted for the Nest's edge.

Then threw me.

Wind tore at my skirts, my hair, ripping the breath from my lungs. I tried to scream, thrashing midair to find a grasp. A snarl split the sky—Kalepsi dove, wings tucked, eyes locked on me. She shot past, twisted, and caught my fall with her back.

I slammed into the hard ridge of her spine and scrambled for a grip. Still diving, she didn't slow. My knees clamped tight to her neck, muscles shaking. My pulse beating through my throat.

Above us, Argos let out a furious bellow; Kalepsi ignored him. She leveled out over the rooftops, wings slicing through the wind. My weight forced downward—once again in subjection to gravity.

Terror chased the grief out of me. I'd never ridden her—or any dragon—alone. One wrong move and I'd tumble off her back. I pressed flat, making myself as small as possible, heart hammering against her scales. The beat of her wings thundered through my body as she soared toward the sea.

The first Dragon's Heart vanished into a whirlstorm, never seen again.

Was that what I wanted? To disappear?

Would anyone notice I was gone?

Mother loved me. I knew that. She saw something in me—though I couldn't guess what it was anymore. Father would pluck the moon from the sky for me, if I asked. Ronan, for all his mischief, would stand between me and death. He'd protect me with his life.

Kalepsi crooned, the sound vibrating through her chest and into mine. She cocked her head, vivid eyes tracking Argos above.

A chirp to my left—Tsunami. She cut into the sky, her body alive with motion, weaving like a snake through star-dappled air. She caught my gaze, flared her wings, and spat a burst of fire, diving through the flames. A trill followed, pleased with herself. She rolled midair, gliding on her back before plummeting toward the city.

I had my family. I had the dragons.

But I wanted Kallias.

A pang of sorrow scored through me, grounding my racing heart. I desired what wasn't mine—lusted after someone who I should have never considered. Now, I ruined both of our lives.

Kalepsi huffed, banking before she reached the sea. I yelped, thighs locking tight as the turn yanked me sideways. A scream clawed its way out when her wing dropped in a heavy downbeat—K'lan spread beneath us, every roof and tower laid bare. She leveled out, giving me a breath's reprieve, then banked again over K'bar.

I frowned. Realization crept in.

When she veered above K'seer, I rested my cheek against her scales, my grip loosening.

She was showing me my people.

I couldn't just vanish into the sky and leave them—not to Ronan, who had the temperament of a crab. He might inherit the throne of Draconia, but he would need a steady voice of reason at his side. Sorrow lanced through my chest.

Tallon would rule Radaan next.

My brother couldn't face him alone.

Kalepsi circled above K'dan, then angled back toward the landing. I frowned with confusion, wondering why she wouldn't return me to the Nest—then saw my father.

White hair stark against the night, he watched us at the tip of the landing.

Argos hovered above us, pulling up as Kalepsi beat her wings, slowing her descent. She dropped hard. Stone cracked under her weight—unbonded dragons did not land with care. My teeth clacked, the copper tang of blood seeping over my tongue. I held tight, breath hitching as her long neck twisted to peer at me. Her pupil widened.

We weren't bonded, but the soft croon she gave—nostrils flared—felt like reassurance.

Father kept his back to us, hands laced behind him, tension rigid across his shoulders. His robe, a shade of summer sky, snapped in the wind. Boots planted, spine straight.

The father I adored. The man fated to kill the one I loved.

He would do it. I had no illusions. As a Well, magic filled his every breath. Faster, stronger, more powerful than any rider. Kallias was a mere mortal. He stood no chance.

Grief sank into my bones, heavy and jagged, iron driven through marrow.

Kalepsi chuffed, lifting her head, teeth clicking together in a sound too gentle for her size. Encouraging. Urging. Like a mother nudging hatchlings from the Nest.

I drew in a breath, but it caught in my throat. When she lowered herself close to the ground to ease my descent, I tucked loose strands of hair behind my ear, then slid down her side. Even so, I stumbled when my boots struck stone.

Her muzzle nudged my back, and I staggered forward—toward him.

With arms wrapped tight around my ribs, I crossed the distance as Kalepsi launched skyward, vanishing into the night.

Father's robe snapped again, revealing his pale tunic and breeches. I stepped to the edge beside him. Wind tore past us. The city lay far below, a sprawl of dim rooftops and glinting lights.

Beyond the cliffs stretched the north sea. And beyond that—Radaan.

"You have to kill him?" My words barely carried, plucked away by the gusts.

"Have you come to make your plea?" His voice cracked, gravel thick in every syllable.

My nose burned, a sign more pitiful tears hovered close. I flared my nostrils, fighting to hold them at bay. "I already have."

He inhaled, slowly. Raised his hand.

Moonlight gleamed on his skin; steam curled from his palm, as though the heat of his magic boiled his blood. He closed his fist, knuckled it behind his back.

"He has done this to himself."

I studied his face. Wrinkles carved deeper than before, eyes raw and bloodshot.

"You will never forgive me. I know that. But he made this choice."

"He came to right our wrongs. He didn't lie." My nails dug crescents into my skin; pain helped. It steadied me. "We haven't lied. He chose honor, Father. You have to see that."

He bowed his head, pinching the bridge of his nose. "This is bigger than *choice*. It's consequence: mine, for sending you to a foreign court alone; yours, for loving a man you were fated to lose." His voice broke. "Do you think I want my daughter—my treasure—to watch me kill the one she..." He faltered, then swallowed. "Loves? I want to see him bleed for the pain he caused you, for his recklessness. But I've never wanted you to suffer.

"Were I a weaker Vessel, the blood oath might only destroy me and Argos. But as a Well? It will destroy Draconia."

Above, stars glittered like frost. Winged shadows slid across them, the slow beat of dragons circling. Their wings a drumbeat of impending doom.

"You don't have to come," he said, low. "Spare yourself. Do not watch."

A breath shook out of me. "I have to."

Silence stretched, brittle as cracked glass.

"I don't hate you," I whispered, a confession tearing its way free—but he needed to hear it. "I hate myself."

Chapter Thirteen

KALLIAS

Mother Veridis, breathe life into my nation. Father Elohios, lend me strength. Forgive me my deceit. Let my actions raise your name, and may my people remember me as honorable—as your servant.

Pain raced up my knees, drawing a grimace, but I refused to move. I had been in prayer all night—if it was night. No windows. No moonlight. Only the dim orbs flickering along the stone walls. I couldn't tell how long it had been since Nienna left.

Or if she meant to return.

Let me see her one last time.

A selfish prayer, but I asked anyway. Just once more, I wanted to feel her touch on my skin.

This was what honor demanded. I wouldn't hide and allow her to take the blame. I was here, facing judgment, paying my penance, accepting the cost. Still, a nagging part of me feared it would end with my death.

Bless me again. Let the Draconis see your light.

I had slain the mammoth. My skin lit with Elohios' power after Nienna and I had tangled ourselves. He blessed me even after I sinned. Radaan knew nothing of that—but Greaves did. And Fallione. My god hadn't forsaken me, though I didn't understand why.

No breeze stirred in my cell, no whisper of approval. The black walls of the Spire swallowed my prayers.

Still, I prayed.

Faint footfalls whispered down the corridor. I stood, knees stiff, legs prickling with blood. Gods, I wasn't young anymore.

"Kallias Sunspear," came a stranger's voice, steeped in disdain.

Greaves' muttered correction poured from the next cell. "*King*."

He hated this place—feared the duel's outcome.

A man stopped outside my bars, his blue-gold tunic catching the mage light's cool glow. The orb bobbed above a small device carved with runes. Its light etched shadows across his severe face as he scowled toward Greaves' cell.

Two riders flanked him, clad in black leathers, hands close to their blades. They watched me as if I were already condemned.

At least they blamed me—not Nienna.

"I'm here to record your final requests," the scribe said, holding out a plank of wood.

"I ask only for a private audience with King Nereus." My spine straightened, rising to my full height. I might be caged, but I was still King of Radaan.

A rider crossed his arms, lifting his chin. "Denied."

"Then I ask for nothing."

"Surely you wish to clear the record," the scribe tilted his head, "provide your honest report?" His tone was accusation enough. He believed the lie.

"If your king will not address me face to face, I have no interest in speaking to you." The words ground between my teeth.

Blame me. Condemn me. Let me bear it all.

"You rape our princess, then come here–"

The steel door of Greaves' cell shuddered with the impact of his shoulder. A rider turned, blade half-drawn, snarl sharp.

"I've *never* forced myself on a woman." The words snapped out too fast, and I cursed myself. I knew better than to rise to their bait.

The scribe's lip curled. "And yet your late queen claimed otherwise."

Bile crept up my throat, and I forced my expression into neutrality. Of course they discovered that accusation. Eldeiade never kept her venom quiet.

I turned away and lowered myself to the floor beside the cot, my knees barking in protest.

"You'll be summoned within the hour," the scribe said. "The record of your death will be sent to your people." His voice dripped with mockery, and I kept my head bowed.

"And you," he added to Greaves, "almost as beastly as your king. Will you return to your ship? Or face your end in dragonfire?"

"I go where my king goes," Greaves rasped.

"Then you shall die with him."

"So be it."

After a scoff, the scuffle of boots pounded against stone, fading down the corridor.

Guilt gnawed at my conscience, thrashing alongside the gratitude knotting my chest. I mourned what he would lose, but there was no point demanding he leave. He might call me King, but he'd pledge Nyryn's vengeance oath without blinking an eye if it kept him at my side.

"Kal." His tone was flat. Resigned. Frustrated.

"You'll have to watch." I didn't say it cruelly. He knew as well as I did—they'd never take me without a fight from him.

"They'll need to hold me back."

"They will." You don't lie to a man who's shared your battles.

A low, choked sound echoed through the corridor. Then the thud of flesh hitting stone.

"I shouldn't have let it go that far," he said.

A smile ghosted across my lips. *Greaves*, letting anything slide? "I recall you dumping cold water on me and pointing out my gray hairs."

"You have no business dueling at your age. You're too old for this nonsense."

I snorted. "You've gone soft. Is your spine giving way?"

He laughed, short and bitter. Then fell silent. I closed my eyes and reached for the thread that bound me to Elohios.

"To the end," he said, voice soft.

A goodbye.

"To the end, good friend."

Cold light caught on the mantle laid across the stained cot.

"We will have it returned to your people." The rider's tone took on an air of respect.

"See that you do."

Leaving it behind fractured something deep in me. I had not crossed the sea as a king. No true leader would chase a woman beyond his borders, abandoning his throne.

No, I left Radaan as a man, and I would face Nereus as such. He was a father wronged. My mantle—symbol of duty—had no place in this. This would be a reckoning between men.

My jaw clenched as I squared my shoulders and turned toward the others in the hall. Three riders, though none held any rope or chain. Greaves stood beside them, his wrists bound behind his back.

Ronan's nose wrinkled at the question in my expression. A snap of his fingers and a flicker of flame danced above them. "We won't need to bind you."

"No, because I go willingly," I growled. The boy grated on me—smug, sharp-tongued. Why any dragon chose him was beyond me.

When I stepped out of my cell, a red-haired rider took point while Ronan gave a mocking bow, palm out.

"After you, Your Majesty."

At least the whelp knew who outranked him. I gave a tight nod and followed the redhead. Greaves and the last rider fell in behind as we wove through the stone veins of the prison.

No other prisoners. Not a whisper, not a face. Either the dragons ruled through fear so complete their cells stayed empty, or Draconia's perfection ran deeper than I dared believe.

They led us up a different path than we'd come. Staring up the narrow stairwell, I narrowed my eyes. The red-haired one clapped, and orbs of light spiraled up from below, whirling past my face. I grit my teeth and resisted the urge to flinch as they blazed upward.

The stairs came in ten-step bursts, doubling back again and again. My thighs burned. My breathing slowed to a steady rhythm. Was nothing on this gods-forsaken island flat?

Perhaps that explained Nienna's legs—why they were so toned.

I bit down on the thought. Here I marched to die, and still, she haunted me.

Part of me hoped she wouldn't come, that she'd spare herself the sight of my demise. But I knew better. She was forged of dragonfire. She would stand and watch, no matter how it broke her.

And I—I held no illusions. She wouldn't root for me. Nor would she pray for her father. She loved him. Spoke of him with reverence.

No one would win today.

If I struck him, if I managed to maim or kill, she'd carry that pain like iron in her chest for the rest of her life. My only path forward meant blood. Her father's. His dragon's. Even then, his riders wouldn't let me live—but this wasn't about them. This was between me and Nereus.

At last, we stopped before a massive entrance. The redhead cast me a look—one final invitation to run. I almost laughed. With Nienna's brother at my back, there was nowhere to go.

He dipped his head. "May you find peace after death."

Ronan scoffed.

When they opened the door, sunlight slammed into my face. I winced, squinting into the blaze, but refused to shield my eyes.

Light poured through the massive archway. The landing loomed beyond. We entered the throne room again—this time, the chamber held fewer people. The empty circle carved into the center had grown.

The duel would happen here.

I rolled my shoulders as a wall of black scales blocked the sun. Eyes like molten bronze narrowed. Lips peeled back. Serrated teeth waited to shred.

A silence deeper than sleep crept in. Only the sharp crack of stone echoed as the dragon stepped forward, claws biting into the marble. People moved aside in practiced silence. It prowled to the throne's rear, coiling around it, eyes fixed on mine. Its tail swung overhead. No one flinched.

It settled behind the throne, tail curling along the stairs. Its horns towered like jagged peaks. A blast of hot air steamed from its nostrils.

The breeze caught Nienna's hair.

My gut tightened. She stood to her father's left, veiled in black. A silver tiara glinted through her braid—the only shimmer on her. Her eyes looked hollow. Her jaw flexed, tight with restraint.

A future queen.

To the king's right was Queen Nyxaria. Her loose curls, once gold, had grayed at the roots. Her frown etched deep into her cheeks. Chin lifted high, she glared as though I were mud tracked across her floors. Her white gown fluttered, untouched by her expression.

Between them, the Dragon King.

White hair slicked back. Beard clipped and sharp. Legs spread wide, he filled the throne as if it had been carved around him. His stare could chase lesser men into the sea. As I approached, his nostrils flared in unison with his beast.

He wore black like his daughter. Dressed for a funeral. The buckled leather armor hugged close, but I saw the clever seams—the fabric beneath for motion, not vanity. Draconis understood the need for movement beneath the strain of dragon scales.

No crown graced his brow. He rose, then descended the stairs to meet me.

Man to man.

Father to monster.

I reached inward, searching for the tether that bound me to Elohios. When my fingers closed around it, I lifted my chin.

"Kallias Sunspear. I've challenged you to a duel to the death." His voice cut like steel drawn from a sheath.

A dragon shrieked above the landing.

My eye twitched, but I held his gaze. "You leave me no choice."

He dipped his head, almost a nod, and extended his palm. A sword was laid into it.

My sword.

He gripped the scabbard and offered it forward. I reached past the hilt, fingers closing over his.

His glare deepened.

"I do this for your daughter," I murmured, low enough to keep the words between us. He wanted a spectacle, but I'd still give him truth.

"As do I." He yanked his hand back, sneering. "You broke a Draconis Blood Oath. Your death, or dragonfire, will cleanse it." His voice rose, echoing through the chamber. "You've chosen the honorable path—taking your sins upon yourself."

I clenched my jaw, holding his gaze.

"Any last words?" His hand drifted to the hilt of his short sword.

"I never broke the oath."

"On Argos' call."

Argos. His dragon.

He stepped away and drew his blade.

My heart slammed against my ribs, but I refused to look at Nienna.

Two paces back, I unsheathed my weapon and flung the scabbard aside. It clattered across the stone.

I cracked my neck, took a breath, then planted my feet, shaking out my sword arm. I would've killed for a spear—or a shield.

The dragon's head snapped skyward, and its mouth tore open in a roar that drowned the world.

I bared my teeth and brought my blade up in time to block the first strike. He moved faster than any Velli. Magic. He used magic to sharpen his speed, to deepen each blow. I parried three times.

Then I felt it—warmth, familiar and wild, spilled through me.

I smiled, teeth bared. Nereus faltered.

Then the light of Elohios blazed through my skin.

Chapter Fourteen

NIENNA

Above me, Argos snapped his jaws, hissing his frustration—but even *he* flinched from the sudden flare.

Kallias' skin burst with the light of the sun before melding to cracks along his hands and neck. His movements sped to match my father's, the force of his blows sending Father staggering back a step.

Was this Elohios' gift? The light Gayle had spoken of? It streaked beneath Kallias' clothes like fire behind a veil. It didn't touch his face, only burned low, hidden, but potent. Whatever its source, it let him match my father blow for blow.

Father's fury deepened, and Argos growled, matching his chaos. They wanted this fight to have a quick end.

My pulse rattled. My palms burned slick. I didn't know how to feel—how could I? No matter the outcome, I'd lose a piece of my heart.

Father ducked under a swipe, lunged. Feet moving faster than my eyes could track, Kallias dodged the blow, muscles bunching under his tunic as he parried. His blade cut upward toward Father's skull.

A dry sob wracked my body, emotion jerking through my chest. I would lose either way. Even if Kallias had the power of a god trickling through his veins, Father harnessed the magic of the eons through Argos.

And so the torture dragged on.

Steel shrieked with each clash. Kings tore at each other for my sake. I was their destruction. Never had I believed I would be a single nation's doom, let alone two.

I was cursed.

Kalepsi's roar rattled the Spire, sending bits of stone skittering across the floor. The dragons grew restless—their king had met his match. At my back, Argos snarled, tension thrumming through him as the fight dragged on.

Pebbles and dust rained down, the throne room trembling beneath their fury.

Father slashed, feinted, swept low. His foot hooked Kallias' knee. Kallias hit stone, rolled, pushed upright in one fluid burst. He met the next blow with a grunt and steel.

Momentum pushed Father forward, and Kallias rammed his shoulder into his stomach. They broke apart, circled again. Vultures over a carcass.

That's all I was. A corpse. No heart left.

Their breaths matched, sharp and ragged. Kallias' disheveled hair clung damp to his brow. A sheen coated Father's skin.

My knees threatened to give out, and my fingers closed around the throne's cool stone for support. I had to stop this. I couldn't stand here and watch. There had to be something—anything.

If I attempted to interrupt, Ronan and Mother would drag me out, remove me from the throne room.

My gaze slipped to my brother as the men clashed in a tangle of blades and limbs. He held Greaves back, Mikal tight beside him. My breath snagged at the sight of Kallias' friend. Veins bulged in his neck, swollen from strain. His fists trembled, teeth bared, ready to charge.

Help me.

My nails scraped into marble like dragon claws, agony crashing over me in waves, and I shuddered.

Please, help me.

Kalepsi slammed into the landing.

Gasps cut the air, and the crowd parted like frost from flame. True fear washed me in terror as she clawed into stone, sparks dancing past violet scales.

Father shifted, attention split between her and the man he meant to kill.

Argos reared, stretching his neck over us and bellowed, a territorial warning that cracked the sky.

Kalepsi crept forward. Her massive form blocked all sunlight, casting the space in shadow.

Help me! I prayed to whomever might hear me. Would Radaan's goddess hear me again? Kalepsi avoided people—she was more prone to eat them than tolerate anyone's presence—and she never left the Nest this close to the Awakening.

She cocked her head, golden eye locking onto mine. Unblinking.

She came for me.

A soft grunt snapped my attention back to the fight.

Kallias staggered, hand pressed against his chest.

No. *No!*

Crimson seeped between his fingers. Still, he grimaced and launched himself at my father, defiant.

My breaths came in quick gasps, refusing to fill my lungs. All the while Kalepsi stalked closer, mouth open, lips curled. She sensed the blood.

Argos roared again, scales quivering with the threat.

Kalepsi snapped her jaws. A rebuke. Then her attention shifted to the fight.

Kallias ducked beneath Father's guard, hooked an arm around his neck, and used the spin's momentum to drive the sword's hilt into his temple. His legs buckled.

A strangled whimper clawed from my throat, tears springing free.

Kalepsi roared, sparks flying from her mouth. Kallias lost his grip and dropped hard to the stone. The men rolled apart, panting, bleeding.

When Kalepsi snaked her head above the crowd and lunged for my father, Argos tore forward, his black belly just over our heads. One final warning. She snapped at the air in front of his nose, then swung toward Kallias.

"No!" The scream ripped from my throat, raw and grayed. It echoed back, pitiful and thin.

Kalepsi froze. Her glittering pupil narrowed, golden fire caught in the slit. Her lips trembled. Everything, everyone, went still.

Kallias lay beneath her, tunic soaked dark. His chest heaved, shallow and fast. The fractured glow of his skin glinted along her fangs.

"Please, no," I whispered.

She wouldn't—couldn't give in to bloodlust. Not with him. Not Kallias.

Her tongue flicked out, tasting his blood.

But her gaze never left mine. Waiting. For what?!

No one moved. Not Father. Not Greaves. Frozen in some sick time loop. I hung somewhere outside myself, as if suspended midair. My scalp tingled, limbs numb. My heart slammed against my ribs.

Kalepsi rolled her tongue, a shower of sparks raining over Kallias.

My vision danced with stars as I struggled for air. Argos vibrated with tension while the realm watched on in silence. Draconia's dragon queen hovered over Radaan's king.

She waited for me. For my permission.

Purge it in dragonfire. Release him.

Kallias trusted his gods. But belief meant nothing when faced with a wall of flame.

He told me to have faith—not in his gods. But my *dragons*.

Tears streamed down my cheeks, and I blinked hard to see through the blur.

Kalepsi inhaled, slow and steady, her gaze locked on mine. She pulled her head back.

"Rise, Kallias Sunspear." My voice cracked, torn from a throat too tight to breathe.

Father stood and backed beneath Argos, giving Kalepsi space.

Mother's hand found mine. Her grip crushed my knuckles, but it wasn't enough to match the pain splitting me apart when Kallias turned my way.

Love wasn't easy. It was a horrible, spiteful thing. It shattered kingdoms. Cleaved souls in two. It ripped everything from me. I had nothing else. No power, no future. Just this moment—and the Queen of Dragons.

Those sky-blue eyes saw me—my soul. And he knew.

I couldn't watch. I was weak. They would kill each other for me, and I would break beneath their fury.

"Rise." I choked, the word a sob, selfish and small.

But love made monsters of us all.

He smiled. A quiet, terrible grace.

I shuddered with a cry, my tears hitting the cold stone. No, he couldn't give me permission, couldn't forgive me for this. I wouldn't let him. It was a twitch, nothing more.

He moved, pushing to his feet. Blood slicked the floor. He dropped his sword with surrender, a sharp, ringing clang as he turned his back on me, facing Kalepsi.

Greaves howled his torment, thrashing against Ronan and Mikal's hold. A sound of rage. Despair. Pure, unfiltered heartbreak.

"Purge him in dragonfire."

And there the King of Radaan stood alone, facing his death.

Kalepsi's maw opened, spreading wide as sparks sprayed from her throat. Then, in a torrent of blinding heat, a deluge of flame swallowed him whole.

Chapter Fifteen

KALLIAS

Everything ached, but the sharpest wound came from the torment in Nienna's eyes. Grief twisted her face. Tears streamed down her cheeks, soaking the front of her dress. Still, she asked this of me.

For her, I would move the sun. I would trade my life for hers. So, I turned to the dark maw stretched wide before me.

And dropped my sword.

For Nienna, I would surrender. She needed my death—asking me to spare her.

I did not fear dragonfire.

A bitter smile tugged at my lips as I watched the dragon's rough tongue scrape the roof of its mouth, flinging sparks that crackled in the air.

Fluid dripped from the glands at the corners of its jaw, and for one breath, I wondered if it only meant to scare me.

Then the flames came.

I clenched my teeth, shut my eyes. Heat slammed into me, a wave of flame wrapping my limbs. My skin blistered under the lick of scorched fabric.

But death didn't take me.

The air scalded my lungs when I tried to breathe, the throne room glowing orange behind my eyelids.

When I cracked them open, heat surged up, circling me in a column of light. The purple dragon exhaled fire—tight spirals rising to the cavern ceiling. Within the blaze, silhouettes twisted, draconic and wild.

I smiled, chest swelling with the burn.

Elohios be praised... and Nienna's dragons.

Someone crashed into my back. I staggered, heat shifting with me as the flames moved in tandem. Arms locked around my waist. I shifted, half-turning, and the violet dragon snapped its jaw shut, cutting off the blaze.

A sob tore from behind me. I stopped moving. Her weight sagged against me.

Smoke curled from the tatters of my tunic. My chest lay scorched bare, hair singed away. The shallow wound across my ribs steamed where fire left it half cauterized.

Small fingers dug into my abdomen—ten hooks like dragon claws dragging through tender muscle.

I pressed a hand over hers and raised my gaze to her father.

"Purged in dragonfire," I said, pitching my voice above the tide of whispers that rippled through the crowd. Let him challenge it.

His jaw clenched, and his grip whitened around his sword. Argos bared his fangs and snarled, shouldering through the gathering toward the landing.

Nereus lifted his chin. "The Draconis Blood Oath is satisfied."

A tremor jolted through me. Her fingers clamped harder, hooking into my muscles. I bit down a groan and waited for her father's verdict.

"Take him to my floor," he spat, then turned, vanishing into the crowd.

I met Greaves' eyes. Deep lines furrowed his brow, but the corner of his mouth twitched—a ghost of disbelief, maybe even pride.

"You trusted your gods," I murmured low, the words meant only for Nienna.

She sobbed into my back, each tear leaving a chilled trail down my spine.

Nyxaria descended the steps, white skirts sweeping across the stone. A hint of the confident queen Nienna would make one day.

The frown between her brows was sharp, but she gave the smallest bow before extending a hand. Masses peeled apart to form a path through the crowd. "This way, King Kallias."

Mouths hung open. Hands covered them. Eyes stared, wide and unbelieving. Whispers passed between them like wind through dry leaves.

"I'm afraid I can't move." I squeezed the fingers leaving gouges in my flesh.

Above us, the dragon made a sound—deep, rumbling. A soft, strange croon.

I craned my head to meet her gaze.

She lowered, bringing an enormous eye level with mine. That iris, larger than my skull, slit to a thread before darting toward the princess behind me. It flared wide, then narrowed as it returned. The dragon exhaled, a breath strong enough to rattle loose stones.

Still, she didn't move away.

Her eye dashed once more to Nienna. Back to me. Another hiss, low and scraping.

"She's waiting for your assurance," Nyxaria whispered.

I dipped my chin, searching for words a dragon might understand. "I will protect her with my life."

The beast snorted, the sound something between disdain and amusement.

Lips touched the burned skin of my shoulder blades. Nienna's hand unlatched from my waist and caught mine. I turned to her, then attempted to wipe the soot and tears from her cheeks, but only smeared them further.

Her eyes were swollen from crying. Her face blotchy and pale beneath the grime.

And I had never seen her more radiant.

But this trial wasn't over.

I stepped the way Nyxaria indicated, and Nienna's fingers squeezed mine. She drew herself up, lifted her chin, and inhaled—her expression hardening into the dignified mask of royalty. One that demanded respect.

We moved through the throng, the queen carving a path toward the exit, following the route Nereus had taken. My spine itched—no doubt the purple dragon tracked my every step, sizing me up like prey. I gripped Nienna's hand tighter and kept going.

The Spire's heart had been carved from black stone, but the walls shone like polished onyx, throwing back the light and lending the illusion of brightness. Thick mats lined the floor, muffling our boots as Nyxaria guided us upward.

We avoided the vast central chamber, instead climbing narrow stairs tucked in shadowed corridors. The tight walls pressed in close, each step more claustrophobic than the last. Everything in this place felt constricted, pinched, rigid.

On the next floor, silence fell like a shroud. This was no public space. We rounded a corner and slipped into a room—and I understood.

Nereus positioned himself behind a chair at the head of a small table, knuckles white on dark wood.

Ronan entered last, swinging the door shut.

No one spoke. We just stood there, tension crowding the air. I looked and felt like a burnt idiot—clothes half-incinerated, smoldered to ash, still clinging to Nienna's hand as if I were a chastised schoolboy.

"Nereus?" Nyxaria asked, voice thin.

His storm-gray eyes met hers. A breath passed. Then he shifted his gaze to me and straightened with a silent snarl. "Let go of her."

My chest tightened. I held his stare and flexed my fingers. Nienna clung tight, but I eased free, not wanting to provoke him more than I already had.

Blowing a relieved breath out, he shook his head. "It worked."

Nyxaria's shoulders deflated. She pulled out a chair and collapsed.

"I can't believe it," Ronan muttered, circling around us.

"If it quelled the oath, then it's settled," Nienna said, lowering herself beside her mother. "He asked for my hand."

"It's far from settled," Nereus bit out, glare drilling into mine. "Just because the magic that demanded I torch your body and toss you to the eels is satisfied does *not* mean I am. You have much to answer for."

Jaw clenched, I nodded. "I requested a meeting prior to the duel." This could have all been avoided had he swallowed his pride and met with me.

"You didn't want to be locked in a room with me then," he growled, rubbing at his brow. "Sea beneath—can you put on some clothes?"

"He's fit for an old man," Ronan said, drawing a glower from both me and his father. He chuckled, dropping his amused gaze.

"I have none." I kept my tone dry. "Greaves could retrieve some from my ship—which you'll be releasing."

Nereus blinked, then his white brows lifted. "I'll be doing what?"

"Releasing my crew and my ship." My words carried no heat—just steel. I didn't want to rile him without cause, but gods, I'd endured enough of his posturing. I lived through his duel, survived a torrent of dragonfire.

"Your oath is satisfied. My people have committed no crime. Let them walk the docks and share the grain we brought." I tempered the demand, the blow to his ego, with a reminder of my own power.

The queen leaned back, eyes on her husband while the rest of us waited.

"Well enough," he muttered.

Ronan groaned while Nyxaria loosed a sigh. At her side, Nienna offered me a quiet smile.

"Let me get him cleaned up," she said, rising. "I'll find him clothes."

"Nienna!" Her mother caught her wrist, throwing a wary glance my way—eyes trailing down my ruined state.

Ronan's face twisted into a disgusted grimace. "She's seen more of him than that, I'd wager."

"Ronan!" Nereus thundered. "Take him. Find something that fits."

The boy scoffed, striding past. "Come on, old man."

I bit down on the retort, turned, and followed. He led in silence through emptied halls—cleared for this moment, no doubt.

Good.

He brought me to a chamber and stepped aside. I entered and stopped just past the threshold.

Light spilled across the floor. The room had a clean, masculine edge. Preserved sea creatures loomed from the walls—monsters frozen mid-lunge. Heavy blue drapes matched Nereus' colors.

I kicked the door shut behind me.

Ronan looked over his shoulder, brow arched in amusement before sauntering deeper into the rooms.

I flipped the lock into place. Just for good measure.

"You're broader than Father, but you could squeeze into some of his old things. That, or provide comic relief until we dig clothes out of your ship. Who knows? Perhaps the dragons will turn it into a game and roast you every time you step outside–"

I seized his collar and yanked him back, slamming him into the wall. Flames sparked to life in his palms, but my fist already flew.

Knuckles crashed into his nose, and pain jolted up my arm. Fire flared hotter from his palms, but I crushed a hand around his throat, leaning close. Let him try to burn me. I survived dragonfire. I could endure this ember-sparked brat.

"It's time you learn what's off-limits, boy," I snarled, tightening my grip.

A dragon bellowed outside—likely his. He shoved both hands against my chest. Heat surged against my skin, then fizzled.

"Abyss," he wheezed. "You're fireproof?"

My grin cut sharp. I squeezed harder. "Taunt me all you want—but you'll keep Nienna out of it."

He bared his teeth, face flushing under the pressure. His knee jerked up, aimed for my crotch, but I snapped my legs together and trapped it.

"I'll make sure you regret *every* slip. Got it?" I eased off enough for him to breathe.

"She's my *sister*, you eel!"

"That makes me your future family," I said, voice a growl. "So, let's play nice, shall we?"

He squirmed against my hold, but it was his penance to pay. The boy had to learn when to bridle his tongue, and if no one else would teach him, I would. I'd bent too long beneath the burden of duty—to Radaan, to my son. At some point, a man had to serve himself.

"Fine!" he choked.

I let go and stepped back. "What happens between me and her is none of your business, understand?"

"You're condemning yourself," he muttered, rubbing his neck. He snapped his fingers; flames sputtered in his palm. He stared at them like they'd betrayed him.

"I'm teaching you respect." I shook my head. "Now get the clothes."

He bared his teeth, but stalked into the dressing room.

That marked the difference between him and my son. Draconia's prince would learn from the correction. Tallon would let it rot inside him like a disease, plotting his retaliation. Ronan would still mouth off—probably about me and

Nienna—but if he breathed a word about our relationship, I'd teach the lesson again.

He left me with a basin of water and his father's old riding leathers.

I eyed them with unease. Donning them felt wrong—almost sacrilegious. But it was what he gave me.

I peeled away the scorched rags, ash falling in soft plumes onto the stone. The mess made me grimace, but there was no help for it. Perhaps they had magic to sweep it away.

The slash across my chest was gnarly. Shallow, but blood oozed in branching trails down to my pelvis. I sighed and scrubbed it clean, wincing as I tugged away fabric clinging to the torn flesh. No sign of cloth melted into the skin where the dragonfire had sealed part of it—but I needed a healer to be certain.

Nothing festered like buried grit in an open wound.

Once finished, I pressed a cloth against the cut and pulled the tunic over it. The jacket followed, buckled tight to keep the bandage in place. I smirked at the memory of Nienna offering to help—gods, she was bold. Especially with her parents near.

In public, she played the part—measured, calm. Around her family, she burned like a forge.

I pulled on the trousers. They hugged my hips too tight, but I fastened them. In the mirror, I studied the fit.

There was power in riding leathers. They wrapped close, fitted for movement and protection. The collar brushed the knot of my throat, and buckles climbed one side of my chest. Small loops lined the waist—likely for knives or rope.

Would a rider need knives? What threat hunted them in the sky?

The black leather threw my silver hair into sharp relief. I shifted closer, frowning at the pale strands. Would she mind that? That I wasn't young like Tallon or some smooth-jawed noble?

I leaned back, palm brushing the tender wound. This was as ready as I'd get. Now came the real trial—convincing her parents to let me marry their daughter.

Draconia unnerved me. The Spire's window sat impossibly high—hundreds of paces in the air, maybe thousands. The city sprawled beneath, its rooftops laid out like Radaan's patchwork fields. Tiny flecks shifted across them, Draconis moving about on their roofs, wringing use from every scrap of space.

My stomach knotted when I got too close to the glass. No human had business being this far above solid ground. I stepped back, gaze drifting to the wild seas. They spread in all directions, boundless. How did anyone live here long enough to settle?

Nienna once said Draconia wasn't small, but beside Radaan, it felt like a splinter. My homeland stretched on forever. From the top of the Spire, I'd probably see water framing every edge of the island.

A knock broke my study.

"Ready?" Ronan poked his head in. His face was clean, but a bruise bloomed under one eye.

It would be interesting to explain that to his parents.

I drew a deep breath, shoulders tight. Sparring Greaves came easy—no stakes, no blood. But wielding Elohios' blessing in a true battle? That demanded more than technique.

I grunted and stepped through the doorway beside him. As we walked, I mapped the Spire—each turn, every stair. I doubted they'd strike inside their own palace. Still, I was determined to know my way around.

In case Nienna ever needed me.

The walk wasn't long before Ronan opened a familiar door. My eyes swept the room, caught on the seating. My jaw ticked when I saw where I'd been placed.

Across from Nereus.

At the far end of the table.

He sat at the head, Nienna nestled to his left between him and his wife. Another setting waited on his right. Ronan didn't pause, sliding into the chair without glancing my direction. I hesitated a moment as all eyes landed on me.

Nyxaria's brows arched. Nereus choked.

But Nienna though, the way her gaze roamed over my body, lingering on my thighs—and the blush that heated her cheeks—had me striding for my seat.

Gods, the woman lit me up like a wildfire choking dry brush.

"Ronan, were there no other clothes?" Nyxaria's tone made it clear Ronan was known for pulling this sort of stunt.

"He's no rider," Nereus snapped.

I sat, tucking my legs beneath the thick wooden table. A bowl steamed before me—soup that smelled of the sea, dotted with fish and tangled greens.

"Has Greaves returned with my clothes?" I asked. No one had greeted me, so I offered none in return.

"We ordered him to rest," Nyxaria said. "Two levels below, on the public floor. He'll return to your service tomorrow once we... settle affairs."

I reached for the spoon, but glimpsed Nereus glaring.

I set it back down, leaned into my chair, and met his glower. "Shall we talk now?"

"And let good food go cold?" He spat. "No."

Picking my utensil back up, I caught Nienna's smirk. She bit her lip, ducking her head to hide it.

The meal was enough to fill the ache in my stomach. The soup tasted like sea brine and old nets. A slice of bread sat beside it—dry, nothing extra. I wondered if the fare was a matter of circumstance or custom. Were they scraping stores clean, or offering only what sufficed?

Nienna had told me her people needed food, but I hadn't realized how deeply. If this was their table, what fed the slums? Malnutrition bred disease. In Radaan, a strong army ate well and moved fast.

We ate in silence. Ronan finished first, chair creaking as he leaned it back on two legs. The room felt tight, homely. It wasn't built for state dinners—more a place for family. Paintings lined the walls: dragons curling above Draconis' shoulders, riders sweeping across skies. A single window framed the night.

Above us, a chandelier flickered—small lights bobbing over carved runes.

I itched to ask Nienna what powered them, but stayed silent.

Nereus rose, crossed the room, and opened a cabinet. He poured amber liquid into a misshapen glass. Bottles clinked. No words.

He hesitated. Then prepared a second.

He'd offer it to me. My pulse jumped. Which would be worse—talking to him while alcohol burned my wits, or refusing it and angering him?

He returned, slid it across the table. I caught it, cool rim slick from sloshed liquid. He sighed and sat.

"I want the truth," he said, voice low and hard. "From you. Nienna stays silent."

Her lips pressed tight and her glare burned holes in the table's surface, but she remained quiet.

"From her arrival?" My chest already ached.

"If that's the beginning."

I refused to rise to the bait. Instead, I settled back. "When Nienna arrived at Reem, Tallon wasn't there."

"Where was he?"

He wasted no time. "Out on a hunting trip I didn't know about. I assume Ronan told you Nienna delivered her seal to me?"

"And it saved your life," Nyxaria said, shaking her head. "Only the Dragon's Heart can bestow the Dragon's Kiss. We never guessed it would shield against dragonfire. There's no record of such a thing."

Elohios be blessed. He'd watched over me since the beginning. I made a note to thank him later.

"Please explain what happened between you two after Ronan left," Nereus said, raising his glass for a sip.

This part twisted deeper than the rest. Speaking my failures as a father was one thing—admitting I fell for my son's bride... Well, it painted me as a monster.

"Nienna was promised to Tallon. I honored that. A ball was held to celebrate their engagement. But over time, the prince proved... unfit to care for her as she traversed our country. I stepped in, trying to ease the burden of her transition."

His fingers locked around his cup. A pulse flared in his temple. Fury lit his gaze. I knew what he wanted, but wasn't ready to hand it over. The *when*. When desire turned to touch. When restraint burned away and lust fluttered to flame.

"If Nienna is bound to silence, perhaps the women should step out." I held his stare. If he needed the whole truth, I'd give it. Let him swing the full weight of his fury at me. He wouldn't break until she left the room.

"And if I want her to verify your story?"

"Have your wife interrogate her—if she hasn't already—and compare notes later."

He drained his glass and stood. Nyxaria narrowed her glare at his back, then leaned to whisper something in Nienna's ear.

Those sea-deep eyes darted from mine to her father. I raised a brow. I'd faced down dragonfire for her, and she doubted I could handle this?

She pressed her lips tight, gave a sharp shake of her head, then followed her mother through the door. Nereus returned from refilling his drink, and I leaned in, arms braced on the table's edge.

"I first touched your daughter weeks after her arrival," I started.

His lip curled in a furious sneer.

"It wasn't sudden. When she landed on my shores, I had no interest in her outside the alliance with my son. I fought the connection between us—she did not."

I let that hang, then pressed forward.

"She cared for my people. For Radaan. There's a strength in her—a sense of duty—that few carry. She's more than a princess. She's a queen in her own right, and revealed as much in my court. Nienna faced crowds, challenged nobles, won hearts. Don't reduce her to a simple beauty I wanted for myself.

"I have remained celibate since Tallon's conception. There's no shortage of women that I could have bedded. As a king yourself, you know this. And yet, I touched no one."

"But you had to have *my* daughter," he snarled.

I eased back, dragging a hand through my hair. "I've made mistakes. But I never crossed a line she didn't invite. I never forced her. Never coerced her."

"She wouldn't know. You're twice her age. You've had years to learn how to prey on younger women. How am I to believe anything you say?"

"Greaves is my guard. He's slept in my chambers, shadowed me since boyhood. Ask him."

"And where was he when you touched my daughter?"

Telling me I was too old for her.

I exhaled, cornered. "I sent him off. Or slipped away."

Nereus tipped his head with a smug leer. A predator with fresh blood on the wind.

"You've got all this magic," I said, jaw tight, "yet can't tell truth from lies? You're determined to cast me as an animal—Elohios knows I've felt like one—but I'm standing here trying to make it right. And you're determined to drag me down."

Ronan kicked his chair to the floor and slammed his palm against the table. "A Vessel!"

"Radaanians are not Vessels," the king barked.

I turned, squinting at the prince. "Vessel?"

"Aye. A Vessel for magic. Riders can pour power into them—and when we do, we glimpse their minds."

The nape of my neck prickled. I recoiled.

"There's absolute trust between rider and Vessel," Nereus said, voice low as he swirled his drink. "We guard their secrets. They respect our gift. We never bond with one who might abuse it. That's why Dragon Riders reserve the right to sift through memory."

My stomach knotted. The thought of someone combing through my thoughts—rifling through what I'd buried beneath decades of discipline—turned my insides to ice.

"It could work," Ronan said, turning toward his father. "He has magic of some kind—we all saw him glowing like a storming firefly."

"That glow is Elohios' blessing," I explained. "Though his gift is fractured here." My eyes swept the stone walls, as if they might explain it. Normally, the light pooled across my skin—whole, unbroken. Today, it flickered and dulled. Dampened.

"We don't believe in gods," Ronan tossed out carelessly. "Father, let me try."

"I wouldn't have you in my head if it spared me from hurling myself off the landing, boy," I hissed.

Nereus scoffed—the closest thing to a smile I'd seen on him since arriving. He dipped his chin, studying me. "And if I asked? Would you allow a father to see whether you speak the truth about his daughter?"

Gods. The library. That hall after the assassination attempt. The manor in the mountains. Would he feel how my pulse jumped near her? Know what lust stirred in my veins? Would it damn me further or clear my name?

Other memories roused from their coffins—dark ones I kept sealed tight.

"What are the risks?" My voice dipped low as caution crept in. No part of me had prepared for this—for Nereus, Dragon King of Draconia, sifting through my mind.

"A bit of mild discomfort on your end," he said, leaning closer, tone needling. "Unless I find a lie."

"I ask that the prince leave."

Ronan balked. "Why?"

"Done," Nereus cut in.

"Father!" Ronan rose, face twisted in protest. "What if he glows like a cursed starfish again and attacks you?"

"I'll give you three breaths before I acknowledge your blatant insult to my ability to defend myself," the king growled.

Ronan scoffed and shoved his chair back, stalking out. "I'll be in the hall."

The door slammed, and I exhaled, letting my weight sag against my seat. "It's no simple thing, allowing someone to crawl through your thoughts."

"And yet I'm meant to trust my daughter with a man old enough to be her father, one found between her legs, insisting he's honorable."

Fair.

"Can I control what you see?" I asked, fighting my cringe.

"You cannot."

"There are things I wish to remain private."

He deadpanned. "I imagine so."

My glare sharpened. "If it concerns Eldeiade, I expect her privacy to be respected."

His brow creased. "Your former wife? Why hide her from me?"

"That's my line." My jaw flexed. No man should have to bear that, let alone watch another witness that shame. Only Greaves knew the extent of what happened behind closed doors—and it would stay that way.

"I can't promise I won't stumble upon it," he said with a shrug, "but I won't go digging. If I sense you abused her though, I'll see you dragged back to Radaan on that pathetic scrap you call a ship."

A slow breath steadied me. For Nienna, I'd endure it. Sun above, I hoped she'd been honest with her mother about how far things had gone.

Nereus rose. I followed. He stepped closer, reached toward my face. I recoiled, neck cracking as I flinched.

"You'll see what I see," he warned, settling his rough palm on my shoulder instead. "Brace yourself."

My grip barely found the table's edge before his thumb brushed my skin—and the ground vanished beneath me.

I sat in the study with Bac'phares while he fumed over the raise in his taxes.

The vision shifted.

Nienna leaned into me, fingers grazing my jaw. I flinched from her pull. "Gods, Nienna, I'm trying to do the right thing." Her touch reminded me she lived. She came to me—needed me. I would burn Reem to the ground if it meant keeping her safe.

The scene fractured.

We spun in a ballroom haze, her breath brushing my ear. My thigh pressed between hers. Her face flushed. I wanted to tear the fabric from her skin and take her right there, with the crowd watching. She matched my rhythm with willing submission, hips grazing mine—gods, what would she be like in bed–

My stomach dropped as the world spun again.

Nienna, Princess of Draconia, arrived, and Tallon was nowhere to be seen. Of course. That scorching son was never where I needed him. She climbed the dais with unsteady steps. Pale. Damp with sweat. Ill?

She bent and pressed her lips to my brow. Fire erupted from her, curling around us in blazing ribbons. This was for Tallon. She belonged to him. And he cast her off as if she were a broodmare he hadn't chosen.

The image bled away.

She pulled my tunic free, hands trembling. Desire and dread surged through my veins. Shouldn't. Couldn't. But I didn't stop her curious exploration. Would she recoil from me like Eldeiade, or would she hunger for me?

Her thighs pressed into my hips. I groaned, teeth clenched. She trailed kisses along my jaw, exactly where I needed her most.

She fumbled with my belt. I seized her wrist, even as my body strained beneath her.

"No."

"Take me." *Her voice cracked. The pain in her eyes cut deep.*

"I cannot."

My thoughts whirled, bile rising in my throat.

She sat between my legs, curled against my thigh, head resting just above my knee. Blood still slicked every inch of me. Lust simmered. But I wouldn't let her go further. She offered so freely what my late wife never gave.

The world spun on its axis.

"Kallias Sunspear," Eldeiade sneered. "They call you that, but you're dull as stone."

I said nothing. Her mockery lost power years ago.

"Come, serve me like the dog you are. That's all you're good for." She flung herself back on the bed, robe falling open.

I turned away, her beauty soured in my eyes. Elohios help me, when would I get her with child?

"Should I send for your guard? Perhaps he would do a better job."

My nails scraped the table. I tried to wrench free.

She'd drawn me. Crude, awkward strokes—but I knew that body, that scar. Gods, the princess—betrothed to my son—drew my naked chest. Why did that stir my blood? What kind of beast was I? I crushed the feeling and returned her sketch. She could draw what she would, it wouldn't affect me.

The floor buckled beneath me.

"Kallias refused the trade I arranged." Eldeiade popped a grape in her mouth. Phares turned to me, annoyed.

"He lost three hundred men in the last battle."

"He hasn't given me a child. I told him to visit the healer."

"He's too hard on the Velli. We should listen to them. Isn't that right, dear?"

"You have one job, Kallias. Can't even sire an heir. A dog could do better than you!"

I tore away from Nereus and lurched over the side of the chair. Dinner surged up my throat. I vomited onto the stone floor—fish, broth, acid. It sprayed from both nose and mouth, burned all the way out. My gut clenched against the violence of it.

Shaking, I gripped the seat and forced my breath into rhythm. Slow. Shallow. The world held still. No visions, no spinning. Only the scrape of wood against stone and the stench of half-digested food.

I straightened and met Nereus' gaze, then dragged my sleeve across my mouth, smearing bile and spit. "I pushed her away."

His jaw flexed. He watched me—not angry. Just weighing something. "You should have pushed *her* away," he said, voice thick with unwanted sympathy. It chafed.

My chin lifted. "That's not your concern. I told you not to pry."

He gave a stiff nod. "Your name is cleared. The blood oath satisfied. As her father, I accept that. The Spire offers you a clean start. Wash up. Tomorrow, we'll speak of contracts."

Relief twisted in my gut, knotted tight with too many memories just below the surface. I shoved them down. Buried them deep where they belonged.

He gestured to the mess. "Forget it. It Happens."

I reached for the mead, tipped it into my mouth, and sloshed it around before I spat it back into the cup with a grimace.

Then I lifted it toward him as if to toast a tentative peace. "To mild discomfort."

Chapter Sixteen

Nienna

"How did you know it would work?"

Mother's question jabbed hard, the one topic I both avoided and craved.

I stared at my clasped hands as we walked. "I didn't."

To admit it out loud felt like a betrayal. How could I ask Kalepsi to set him ablaze if I hadn't been certain he'd survive?

Mother pressed her lips tight. The creases at the corners of her eyes deepened.

She guided me to my floor. I fought the pull to turn back, to head straight for the dining hall. I needed to see him. Touch him. Make sure he was whole. But he had to face Draconia's king first. Nothing I said could soften his image. That was Kallias' burden—to stand tall, speak for himself, likely clash with Father again.

Inside my rooms, she gave a quick glance for Freya or Edith before settling on the chaise. Reclining, she shut her eyes and shook her head. "It's strange. Your father told me about last night. That's the second time Kalepsi has left the Nest near an Awakening."

Queens never abandoned their eggs so close to hatching—not even for their riders. And yet twice now, she came to me.

"They feel different since I arrived." I sank into a padded chair with a sigh. "It's like they understand me."

"They always have." She studied me, a crease forming between her brows. "But this is different. You haven't bonded—we'd know. Still, there's something about you being the Dragon's Heart. I've never heard of anyone immune to dragonfire."

"He's safe. That's what matters."

"Hardly." She straightened, tucking a stray strand into her braid. "This is only the beginning. You're back to page one. Worse, because now he must prove himself to your father. Show this was a misstep, not a pattern. If he can persuade Nereus to let him stay, we renegotiate. If we give you to Kallias, it won't be as a princess—it'll be as a queen."

My stomach clenched, and my eyes snapped to hers.

"To ask for your hand, he'll have to surrender more. I hope he's ready."

I scoffed, still stunned. "He faced a *dragon* and you wonder if he'd give up more for me?"

"That duel—and standing in Kalepsi's fire—was his decision as a man. Brave, yes. But personal. Sacrificing his body is one thing. Giving up his kingdom is another."

He would. I knew it in my bones. Father wouldn't demand the impossible—he'd be firm, but fair. Kallias could negotiate. That was part of being a king. It might take days, maybe longer, but it would happen. Faster than the contract with Tallon. This time, we didn't have to worry about doves and missives crossing the sea. He was here and would see it through himself.

I would be a queen.

My mouth drew down. I'd have to step into Eldeiade's place. Would Radaan welcome me? After everything? What would our reception look like? Where would the wedding even happen? Here in Draconia? There?

So many questions. But I just wanted to see him.

"Tomorrow will be long," Mother said, rising with a breath. "We can't hide in the Spire. The Awakening is near, and we must stand united."

She studied me a moment longer, her gaze quiet, sharp. "He'll stay here. That may help, after what happened with Tsunami and Adoni. But a word of warning, Nienna."

My smile turned smooth—demure, obedient. Perfect.

"Until you're joined, abyss—be careful." Her eyes narrowed, tone dry. "Your father knows you won't keep your distance, but he'll try to make it so. Whatever happens, remember your people. They're watching. Waiting. Their world has shifted—your return, the Innaki, the duel. Be patient. I spent years drilling sense into your skull. Don't let that man's charm pluck it out."

"He's charming!" I laughed.

She rolled her eyes, but offered a teasing smile. She held out her hand. "Remember who you are—a princess, and perhaps, soon-to-be queen. Act like it."

She pulled me to my feet and folded me into her arms.

I gripped her dress, breathed in salt and sun. In spite of everything that had happened, she stayed by my side. Unable to change any of it, but she didn't abandon me.

"Now—off to bed!" She kissed my forehead. "We all need rest after a day like this."

"Hush! They're bound to have Argos and Gyrak lurking in the Cireendium," Freya scolded with a muffled giggle, fingers working through my hair in the dark.

I stifled a laugh and threw my head back, fastening the light cape over my nightdress. Pale-blue silk clung to my chest, lace draped over the bodice and a delicate strip crossed my middle—one of my finest gowns. I squinted into the mirror, nudging the lace into place until it aligned with my navel.

"If you're caught, your father will toss you into the sea," she hissed, still grinning, then smoothed my hair down over my shoulders. "Scandalous."

"Scythe would've kicked me out already," I said, a sharp pull behind my ribs.

Freya paused. Her eyes found mine through the veil of moonlight. "Well. I best make her proud. Shoo!" She pushed me toward the door.

Bare toes skimmed cool stone as I crept forward and pulled the heavy wood open. I peeked into the dim hall.

Draconia slept. In Radaan, the halls glowed, lit bright even at midnight. Here, mage lights hovered in silence, flickering on spent magic, waiting for the Vessels to revive them.

No guards. No footsteps trailing mine.

I slipped into the corridor, clutching the cape tight to my chest. Freya told me they roomed Kallias close—on my floor, not among the nobles below. Perhaps Father offered him that much mercy. A subtle nod of favor.

I kept to the wall, weaving past Ronan's chambers. To be caught by him would mean weeks of smugness. He wouldn't snitch, but he'd never let me live it down.

Rugs detailed with tribal designs muffled my steps, and I came to a stop before a plain wooden doorframe. No engraved flourishes. No gilded trim. Solid. Unassuming.

My throat rasped with dryness, but I swallowed it down and turned the handle.

The hinges held silent. I slid through and eased the door shut, letting the latch settle without a sound. Shadows swallowed the receiving room, but a low, white glow flickered from the next chamber.

Greaves hadn't been returned. He was still grounded on the level below.

Kallias was alone.

My heart kicked. Not from fear—but the rush of secrecy, the draw of seeing him without court stares or whispers behind fans.

I crept toward the doorway.

He lay stretched across the bed, a shaft of moonlight cast over his body like a blessing.

Breath caught in my throat. One arm draped over his face, shielding his eyes. My father's old leathers hugged him well, silver stitching catching the light in quiet glimmers.

My heart slammed into my ribs.

His trousers sat unfastened. Pale skin peeked above the open seam. His hand disappeared under the waistband.

Blood flushed to my face. I stared at the place where his fingers vanished. One leg stretched long and straight. The other bent outward, knee angled wide. Bare feet sprawled across the linens.

So exposed. Unarmed. Beautiful.

I glanced at the window. The curtains stood open. If a rider passed, their dragon might glimpse me through the glass. But I wouldn't close it. Not if it meant dimming the sight before me.

The stone chilled my soles as I padded to the bed and paused. His tousled hair, dark and messy. Lips soft and still. The scruff on his jaw had grown longer than he kept it in Radaan—silver dusted the edges. His leather jacket clung to his chest, buckled to his throat, though one clasp hung loose.

I chewed my lip, nerves humming. My eyes drifted again to where his hand vanished. The heat in my body surged. My thighs clenched, and I bit down on a gasp.

How did anyone resist him?

Tall. Sculpted. Sin incarnate.

A vision flashed—me straddling his hips, jacket undone, lips brushing his chest as I peeled him free of leather. My hands moved lower, my mouth trailing after...

The fingers in his trousers twitched.

I jolted, my knee smacking the bedframe.

Frozen. Breath held. I waited.

He didn't stir.

I winced and placed my palms on the mattress.

He moved.

An arm hooked under mine. In a single pull, he dragged me onto the bed. My head struck near the footboard. His hips pinned me down, one hand catching my wrist, pressing it above me.

A whimper escaped me. His body settled into place—heat and weight claiming the space between us.

Sky-blue eyes blinked, then his brow creased as he scanned the room, muscles taut, every inch of him alert.

My chest heaved in short bursts. My nerves screamed—move, speak, *breathe*. He felt so good against me, his hard frame pressed into my soft curves.

His gaze fell back to mine. "Are you alone?" His voice, hoarse from sleep, rasped across my skin.

I caught my lip between my teeth and his stare dropped to my mouth. I writhed, hips rocking into his. A surge of pleasure cracked through me. My spine arched.

"I came to talk," I gasped, forcing myself to keep my eyes open, to hold his gaze and not surrender to the heat.

His hand shifted to grip my side and he sat back, pulling his body away from me. He drew the cape aside and his stare swept over my gown, darkening. "Gods, Nienna. You didn't come here to talk."

My chest rose in hard, uneven bursts. He winced and let himself drop beside me, limbs stiff, a groan tearing loose as he hit the mattress.

"Sun above," he muttered through clenched teeth. "I feel like a dragon chewed me up and spat me out." His gaze drifted to me, trailing up from my chest before locking on my face.

A twist of guilt pulled at me. I shifted, propping myself on one elbow. "You spoke with my father?"

He grunted and stared at the ceiling, then drew his lids shut. "The man won't give you up easy."

"But he's open to negotiations?" I asked, scrutinizing his every move.

He turned, rubbing his chest with a grimace before pinning me with a sharp look. "Nienna. I'm not leaving this island without you."

My lips curved. The moment his eyes caught the moonlight and his mouth tugged into a crooked smile, something warm bloomed low in my belly.

"We need to talk, though," he said. "And I doubt that'll happen if you stay dressed like that."

I glanced down. The silk clung dangerously close to baring my breasts.

With a sigh, he swung his legs off the bed and pushed to his feet. He moved to the window, scanning the skies—always cautious—then crossed the room to a small dresser.

"You said you love me."

His voice cut through the hush. I sat up straight. The playfulness, the teasing edge had vanished. What remained wasn't regal or commanding, but it carried weight. Not authority. Something more raw. He leaned against the drawers, a twitch beneath his eye.

"That hasn't changed," I said, words tentative, testing the waters.

"I left Radaan with clear intentions. Your father knows exactly why I came." His jaw flexed, hands tightening at his sides. "But I need to know what *you* want."

His stare never wavered. It felt like he expected me to shatter. To back away. As if bracing for rejection.

"Before you answer," he added, raising a finger when I parted my lips, "remember a few things. I'm twice your age. I'll die before you."

"Kallias!"

"You'll get your turn." He lifted a brow, hand raised to silence me. "But let me speak first. Understand?"

I leaned back and crossed my arms, raising a brow of my own in challenge.

He grunted, half-pleased. "I've been married. As much as I wish I could erase that part of my life, Elohios knows you deserve more than someone's leftovers."

I drummed my fingers against my arm, letting him go on about all the ways he thought he fell short.

"Tallon will never accept us. I could exile him to the Valley Beneath, but even then, the people might still resist you. And with him stirring unrest, this won't be easy.

"I say all this to make sure you understand the gravity of what I'm going to ask. You're not just a young woman in love with a boy, but a princess who had an affair with a king. I'm asking you if you want to be my queen."

Sorrow wrapped around my chest, constricting painfully. He thought he had so little to offer, and that hurt.

"My turn?" I asked, voice sharper than intended.

He nodded once, rolled his shoulders, arms folding again as if bracing for a blow. A line creased his brow. I wished Eldeiade still lived, just so I could claw her eyes out for what she did to him.

"Then I shall answer you as a princess destined to one day rule." My tone was flat, the confidence and authority my mother had schooled into me straightening my spine. "As a ruler, I will not run and hide from conflict. Let Tallon throw his fits—I won't tolerate him any longer."

I rose, prowling toward him.

"As a queen, I expect my future husband to face dragonfire for me. If enemies scorched the gates, I want him beside me. I would walk into his kingdom and *earn* his people's love. Honor his name."

He flinched—barely—when I stopped in front of him.

"And to be blunt, I wish I'd met your late wife. Just once. Long enough to slap her for the damage she did."

At that, his brow tightened. But I wasn't finished.

"Your age doesn't scare me. It suits you. Makes you sharper, steadier. And you've proven you can command a court. I won't have to wait for you to grow into the role. You're loyal, and your people know it."

I reached for the button at his waistband and gave it a gentle tug.

"And now you ask if I want to be your queen?" I scoffed, voice softening. "I'd be honored if you'd choose me."

A flicker of pleasure danced in his eyes, and the lines on his brow began to fade.

My touch brushed along something sticky.

I lowered my gaze and rubbed the dark smear between my fingers. "Abyss, you never saw a healer?" The question bit through my teeth.

"Between being torched by a dragon and your father rifling through my head, no—not much time." He exhaled hard and dragged his palms down the bare *V* of skin above his waistband. Blood smeared across his abdomen with a grunt.

"Kallias." Guilt coiled tight in my throat as I reached for the buckles of his jacket. "I'm sorry."

His fingers lifted my chin, drawing my eyes up. The forgiveness in his face hollowed my chest. I had ordered Kalepsi to flame him. I had delivered the command that nearly killed him. Every wound and scar—my doing. My passion. My recklessness.

"Any regrets?" he asked, brushing a thumb across my lips—rough, calloused, tender.

My vision blurred. The sting behind my nose returned as his words from long ago wrapped around me like smoke.

"Many, but you are not one of them."

The corner of his mouth lifted in a smile. Gentle. Steady. He nodded. I turned to his leathers, fumbling at the silver clasps. His hand found my waist—solid, silent, anchoring me. He understood I needed to do something, to help somehow.

He had suffered. Fought. Bled. All for me. A slow heat built behind my ribs, fierce and hollow, demanding I prove myself worthy of it.

The last buckle near his throat gave way. I slipped the silk-lined leather from his shoulders.

"Kallias," I hissed. Crimson spread across his tunic, dark and blooming. Bandages beneath clung wet and useless.

"The jacket kept pressure on it."

"You're in *my* house, drenched in blood," I snapped, shoving the fabric down his arms. "Are you trying to rouse the beasts' bloodlust?"

He rolled his shoulders free with a grunt, muscles shifting under taut skin.

"No one else on this island bleeds?" He asked, tugging the tunic over his head with a wince.

"They know better than to lie in it." I scowled at him. "If you're close to me, then you risk the dragons' attention. Keep it clean and dry."

He glanced down as I peeled the wrappings loose. "Stitches?"

The wound traced a jagged path from his upper chest to the far rib. Not deep—but the day's strain had broken the scab and set it bleeding again. I leaned in, arm stretching behind him to dampen a cloth. The scent of salt, blood, and sweat clung to his skin.

"You might not need them, but the healers know best." I exhaled. "Father should have sent for one."

"He seems content to let me suffer." His laugh rasped low in his throat.

The gash had burned edges where the dragon's fire had sealed it, ugly and raw. It would scar deep—proud, unforgiving. A reminder etched in flesh. I dabbed it clean, relieved to see the bleeding had slowed.

"He's notorious for holding a grudge." I nudged him aside, rummaging for new bandages. "Negotiations start tomorrow?"

"I wasn't told."

"Hold this." I pressed gauze to the wound and handed him the fresh wrap. He pinned the cloth in place. "When talks begin, you've got leverage. We lost our trade route with the Innaki. No word from them yet, but war isn't off the table."

I circled behind him, winding the bandage snug around his ribs.

"An island willing to challenge the wrath of dragons? Have they hatched any?"

"No. Dragons won't settle on Innaku." I cinched the wrap and tied it off. "No, there was an incident and Tsunami ate the crown prince."

His brows shot up. Eyes wide. "They pick humans off as they please? Should I warn my crew?"

"If they stay respectful, they're safe." I stepped back, brushing hair from my face. "Tsunami's riderless. She answers to no one. That's the risk when people step foot on Draconis' shores—you're at their mercy."

"This prince must have done something worthy of their wrath. I'd assume being neighbors, they would know better."

I bit my lip. Adoni had known better. Foolish. Possessive. I saw it now—in the way he lingered too close, how he claimed my title with his tongue as if it were his. It had all been there. I just hadn't wanted to acknowledge it.

"What is it?" His voice tugged at my gaze. His brows dipped in a hard frown as he searched my face. "What did he do?"

Why did I hesitate? Perhaps I feared he'd see weakness. Or was it shame? Adoni assumed I'd welcome a prince just because I once chased a king.

"Nienna, tell me." His hands slipped to my waist, anchoring me as though he sensed the urge to run.

"He moved against the royal family."

Kallias blinked. His eyes sharpened. "He attacked you?"

"He grew up with me." I dropped my gaze, fingers fussing with the edge of his bandage. "I should've noticed the signs. Ronan warned me, but after Tallon, I can't exactly trust his judgment."

He pulled back slightly, scanning me with fresh concern.

"You're well?"

"Only my pride's bruised." A bitter laugh scraped free as I shrugged. "He assumed I'd be easy. Thought I would fall for his future crown. As if that's what I was after in Radaan."

Kallias drew a long breath, his chest rising under my touch. His jaw clenched. "Then it's my fault. You were after a title—but my advances made them think you were greedy. Gods, I'm sorry."

"Your advances?" I smirked, lifting my face. "If I recall, I was doing the chasing."

His head dipped. "I knew what it was. What *we* were becoming. And I let it happen."

I grabbed the damp cloth off the dresser and swiped it low over his open trousers. "Do you know what's happening now?" My voice lilted with challenge.

His eyes fluttered shut as I cleaned the bare skin exposed by his undone buttons.

"We're going to do this right," he muttered. "Not until we're married. I'm not sure how long negotiations with your father will take. If I were him, I'd watch me like a hawk."

He hissed when my hand dipped too far. His grip clamped around my wrist, firm and fast.

"He will count your cycle, and at the first missed bleeding—he'd toss me into the sea."

"Maybe I'll hurry him along."

"Elohios be praised, it can't happen fast enough." His jaw tightened. "Now, your mother's no fool. She's probably watching your hall. Go, Nienna."

"Let me stay," I whispered. "Just a while."

Moonlight caught the silver at his temples as he smiled. "We have a lifetime ahead of us. I'll see you in the morning."

Would I ever grow tired of him being right?

Mother would know I'd gone to him. Ronan might already be lurking in the halls. If Father found out, he'd send Argos into a rage. Still, I didn't care. I hated the idea of returning to my rooms. I wanted him. Now.

I sighed and leaned in, brushing my chest against his as I tipped my chin to offer my lips. "At least kiss me good night."

"You'll be the death of me." He groaned, hand rising to cradle the back of my head. His fingers tensed in my hair. I gasped, and he let go, his eye twitching.

"Just one kiss," he said.

I nodded, teeth scraping my bottom lip. His gaze lingered there, hunger searing his expression, then he leaned in.

His scruff prickled across my skin, his lips warm but unmoving. I smiled into the stillness, letting my mouth part just enough.

With a sharp, breathy sigh, he tasted me, slow and tentative.

I clutched onto him, yanking him flush against me. My tongue flicked against his, coaxing him. He groaned, answering with a fierce plunge that pulled a gasp from my throat. Heat unfurled low in my belly, the kiss dragging out the ache between us.

His fingers tangled in my hair as he backed me into the dresser, his hips pinning mine. We kissed like a battle—urgent, wild, with each retreat followed by a fiercer return. He tasted of cinnamon, hot and spiced.

One hand darted down to my rear, sliding over my curves before continuing down to grab my thigh in a rough grip. His fingers flexed along my leg before they flew open and he tore his mouth from mine.

"Nienna, go," he rasped against my throat, blocking my path.

I stood there, knees shaking, breath ragged. Sea beneath, I needed him to move, to throw me against the dresser and *take* me. My body ached for him, the way lungs burn for air.

But he wasn't ready. Neither of us were.

Honor ran thick in his blood. A kiss could be survived. More might break what we'd built.

With a tortured whimper, I drifted sideways, spine brushing cool wood. I slipped from beneath him. His palms planted firm on either side of the dresser. His head hung low, shoulders tense, shaking with restraint.

"One day," he growled, eyes squeezed shut, "you won't get away so easily."

My heart surged. A thrill bloomed in my chest.

To bring a man like Kallias to the brink—to know he had to hold himself back. That power stole the breath from my lungs.

I wanted to test his control. Push him further. See where he'd break.

But tonight, I'd show mercy.

With a grin, I darted into the darkness.

Chapter Seventeen

KALLIAS

If the trousers were a shade roomier, I'd have no complaints. Instead, I drew a breath, squared my shoulders, and forced the button into place. The leather bit into my hips, but appearances mattered. I had no clue who'd greet me today—and a little discomfort was worth the risk.

Silk lined the inside of the leathers, cool against my skin as I buckled them across my chest. I refused to touch the tunic from yesterday—soiled, bloody, and folded over a chair. The gash along my torso pulled tight with every motion, but Nienna's wrap held firm, clean cloth snug against the wound. Her warning rang in my mind. Walking around soaked in blood only drew attention. If I thought dragons might cross my path, I'd change the bandage first.

A knock echoed through the room as I fastened the last buckle at my throat. For all Draconia's crowded cliffs and winding towers, the rooms were wide and open. Not as ornate as the Golden Palace in Reem, but richer in wildness. Above the bed loomed a massive fish—sword-nosed, preserved mid-leap in a curved arch.

Paintings of dragons covered the stone walls, scattered with flat seashells that caught the light in shifting rainbows. Chains of giant scales hung across from the window, swaying gently with the breeze.

It was all sea and sky—Draconia, bottled in a single space.

Bootsteps padded along woven rugs dyed in bold spirals. I met my reflection, collar smoothed, jaw set.

Greaves strode in first. He moved fast, looping the room, checking the windows, then settling into the corner with arms crossed. Black armor, throwing knives back in place. The tight pull of his mouth said he wanted words alone.

Fallione followed. "Good morning, Your Majesty." His tone warmed the air, though the formality stayed.

"Morning," I returned, turning to face my advisor and friend. Shadows clung beneath Fallione's eyes. His graying hair, tied at his neck, framed an expression sharp with worry and resolve. He held a pile of green and gold clothing.

Greaves didn't speak. Just leaned, watching.

"Your people were relieved to hear you survived the trial." Fallione offered a brief bow, eyes flicking down my frame and back. "I brought your clothes. King Nereus requests an audience now that you're awake."

"These will do." I glanced at the bundle. My sword wasn't among them. "Where's my blade?"

"I'll send for it. Your mantle waits in the receiving room." A pointed reminder—I was king before warrior. "They're planning a celebration in the coming days. If you enter negotiations today, I advise leading with the supplies we brought."

"No. Tell the crew to surrender it to the dock workers." I shook my head, rolled my shoulders, adjusted my sleeves. "Innaku's pressing them. We share our grain first. Let it show our goodwill."

Fallione frowned, gears spinning behind his gaze. "The Innaku supply most of their wheat," he murmured. "What tensions do you suspect?"

"A dragon ate their crown prince."

He paled. Hands tightened around the fabric. "Shall I warn our people to remain aboard?"

"Remind them their king came for peace. If they act out of turn, I cannot save them from their own foolishness."

Fallione said nothing, consumed with thought.

I crossed into the next room. Sunlight fanned over a wooden table where Radaan's mantle waited, its golden weave catching in the glow. My throat tightened.

Greaves stepped forward, lifted it with steady hands, and draped it over my shoulders. The weight no longer pressed—it grounded. Familiar. Welcome.

Relief swept through me.

Elohios' light might've fractured during the trial, but it hadn't dimmed. Not fully. The mantle reminded me I didn't stand here as a man dodging fate—I stood as king, shielded by the might of a nation behind me.

"I'll see that the supplies are distributed and urge our men to act with care," Fallione said, while Greaves secured the mantle's chains. The gold clashed against the black leathers.

"Shall I accompany you to the king?"

"I speak with him alone." I caught the tension in Greaves' jaw. He hadn't met the man—just a dungeon door slammed in his face. "Work with the staff. Make sure Nienna has everything she needs."

"Nereus and Nyxaria?"

"Nienna," I repeated, cutting the thought short with a hard stare. "They'll send their aides to you, but I want *her* informed. No surprises. She's my future wife—and I expect you to speak to her directly."

"Yes, Your Majesty." His tone stayed neutral, but I knew the rebuke hit. I brought him for his value, but he'd be stretched thin—balancing the needs of the crew and acting as Radaan's voice in a foreign court.

"She'll need you," I added, "as the future Queen of Radaan."

"You've secured her hand?"

"No contracts yet." My mouth pressed flat. "But the intention stands. It's known."

"And King Nereus—will he negotiate in good faith?"

He meant: *Will this be a war of words?*

I exhaled, steadying myself. "I crossed the sea for her. Left Radaan to the Threshers. I've sacrificed more than I can name to claim her hand. I offered myself in place of my son. Our tithes will reflect that." I caught Greaves' scowl as he fastened the last chain. "But Nereus is more father than king. He won't surrender her without resistance. He'll press hard. I want this settled quickly."

Fallione hummed, understanding what I hadn't said: time away from Radaan was dangerous.

When I left, the prince was confined to his chambers with strict orders not to be released until I returned. Darius would see it through, but knowing Tallon orchestrated my public disgrace—and wasn't rotting in the dungeon—gnawed at me. If Vellos made a move, Darius would rule in my place. But doves took days to reach us. And our return by sea—weeks.

If Radaan fell into war again, we couldn't afford weeks.

"I'll convey our urgency in the talks," Fallione said, reading my thoughts. "But, a warning, Prince Ronan waits to escort you."

I smirked at the note of disdain in his voice. The boy's insolence grated on him too.

"I'll be off. Report before dinner—or sooner, if needed." I pulled the door open.

Nienna's brother looked up, polishing a pair of goggles. He breathed on the lens, then wiped it clean with silk.

"You look horrible," he said, tucking the cloth away and pushing the goggles into his sandy hair.

"As do you. Take me to your father." I kept my tone flat, noting his black eye. Whether he meant my face or the outfit, I didn't ask. After Nienna left, sleep eluded me. Lust burned too hot. Dawn still woke me, as always. Old habits refused to die.

"He's flying Argos. Hope you're not afraid of heights."

"The only things I fear are your temper and your loose tongue," I muttered.

"Scared of *me*?" He grinned, fingers brushing the bruise beneath his eye.

"Only that you won't survive to see my departure."

He snorted and led the way through the black halls. Sunlight vanished at our backs, replaced by the cool glow of rune-lit lamps. I studied the markings—curious whether they fueled the light or merely sustained it. It was humbling being on a foreign island—thrown into a culture I had read about but never experienced.

My age lent me confidence. Court politics honed me. Nienna didn't have that when she came to Radaan. This kingdom was new to me. I couldn't linger—Vellos' threat made sure of that—but questions still crowded my mind.

We climbed through the Spire's core, and I kept away from the railing overlooking the hollow shaft. Heights didn't scare me, exactly—they unsettled. The Golden Palace's roof had always been a refuge, and during war, with my stay in the mountains, I fought in valleys. Radaanians belonged to stone and soil, not the skies.

A guttural chirp cut the air. I flinched, glancing to the side.

Ronan sighed.

A blur of blue-green sliced past, gold flecks flashing as the creature tore by, its wings snapping like canvas in the wind.

"Tsunami," he called, just as a roar rattled through the Spire. "She's a menace."

I edged closer to the railing and looked up. She climbed toward the black ceiling, slicing through the air before catching a high ledge with her claws and vanishing into shadow.

Another piercing scream shattered the stillness. I clenched my jaw against the sound. How the Draconis hadn't all gone deaf was beyond me.

"She'll outgrow the Cireendium soon," Ronan muttered, leading the way up the next flight. "But for now, it's her escape. She stirs up the others, then flees before they can catch her."

"She hasn't bonded with a rider?"

"Who would want her?" he snorted. "She's half feral."

"A dragon picked *you*."

His brows rose as he shot me a look over his shoulder. "And Gyrak won't take another. We crossed the sea and back without rest. Let's see you manage that."

"Unnecessary exertions." I returned his stare, flat and unimpressed.

His expression darkened, lip pulling into a sneer. "It was the right thing to do—she needed distance. From *you*."

I didn't flinch or respond. The boy itched for a fight, and I owed him nothing.

"Tell me this, King Kallias," he went on. "If you had a sister—or a daughter—and found her tangled up with a man old enough to father her *and* her betrothed, skirts hitched to her hips–"

"Seen a healer about that eye?" I spat, snatching his jacket. Fisting the leather in one hand I pushed him back and forth examining it. "Be a shame if the other matched."

He jerked out of my grip, humor drained from his face. "What would you have done?"

"Listened to the sister I grew up with." I brushed past him as if I knew where I was going. He'd catch up. "The one who understood court politics better than I ever did. Who our parents married off because they trusted her judgment."

"And see how flawed it was?"

"She didn't settle for a prince," I replied, as he fell into step beside me again. "Because a king was in her grasp. I'd say she chose well—for herself and for her nation."

"Blasted kings and their egos," he muttered, forging ahead.

I scoffed. He was well on his way to growing one of his own.

We stepped into the hollow of the throne room, the dais looming above like judgment cast in stone. No banners hung from the arching walls—just glossy slabs reflecting pale light from the landing. The space breathed severity. As if Nereus only ever sat on the throne to deliver punishment.

Deep scars clawed across the floor, remnants of Argos' fury.

Ronan led us toward the open platform. As my boots struck the landing's first stones, my stomach pitched. From below, it looked formidable. Up close, the sheer drop stole my breath. Maybe wings would've helped—or the promise of a dragon to pluck me from death if I slipped.

More likely, they'd chirp at my fall and watch me plummet.

A thunderclap of wingbeats ripped through the air, and I halted as the massive black beast descended, claws raking stone. My pulse startled. The landing groaned beneath his weight.

Argos twisted his head toward us with a growl, foul breath washing over me as he shook his thick neck like a soaked hound. Nereus dismounted in one clean slide, pulling off his goggles and never once glancing back.

He stalked closer, each step heavy with intention. Chin high. Shoulders squared. Storm-gray gaze pinned to mine. A man I'd clashed blades with. My equal—maybe my better—but not someone I ever wanted to meet on a true battlefield.

"Walk with me," he said, his tone clipped. Behind us, Argos hurled himself back over the ledge and vanished into the sky.

I pivoted and kept pace. Another dragon landed, and I caught sight of Ronan tugging down his goggles, heading toward the smaller black.

"The Kulletti demand a meeting." Nereus' voice ground like stone as we turned into a side corridor. "The Awakening is two days away. You know it?"

I hated this ignorance. "A festival."

"*The* festival," he snapped, not breaking stride. "It begins with a night of revelry, ends with the dragonlings cracking shell. Marks a new year. It matters. I've no time to juggle marriage negotiations on top of that."

He wanted to delay. I braced myself. "My nation is without a ruler. It is of the utmost importance that I return soon."

"You wouldn't be returning at all if Nienna hadn't kissed you."

His words hit sharp, but I masked the wince.

He pushed through the doors of the smaller dining hall, the same room we'd spoken in before. His gaze flicked to Greaves, then he dropped into a chair. He gestured for me to sit beside him. A sour, briny scent stung my nose—pickled fish.

I joined him as he bit into toast layered with diced fish and some sort of paste. Greaves hovered close, watching, waiting. Wondering if I'd have him test it first.

But I passed their games. Draconia needed me alive. Poison wasn't on the menu, not when I was more valuable as their ally.

I bit through the paper thin bread. Salt-heavy with a slow, rising burn. I swallowed it down and leaned back.

Nereus nodded, satisfied. "Negotiations for Nienna's hand begin after the hatching. But I have two conditions." He lifted a finger. "First: a Draconis wedding."

"Here?" I asked. If the palace served as host, I could oblige. Ideally, Radaan would witness the marriage—but I wouldn't deny Nereus the assurance of a sealed union.

"And by our traditions."

"I'll need a detailed list. My advisor will see to it."

"Done." He took a deep breath, then raised a second finger. "And I want your word. Swear you'll not touch her until you're married."

Years of court trained me to stillness. But the words struck hard. Had someone seen? Heard?

"I know Nienna," he said, grinding his teeth. "I saw what happened."

He stared at the table as if he didn't want to be reminded of what he glimpsed in my memories.

If he only knew what a breach of privacy that had been for me. I wouldn't have done it if there was any other way. My moments with Nienna were ours. And what of me and Eldeiade? I could only hope he didn't see more than I had.

"I'm asking you as a father," he said, eyes rising like steel drawn from the sheath. "Keep it in your trousers. Show a scrap of respect for me and my station. I want your word no one will find you the way Ronan did. I won't have whispers about my daughter's skirts flitting about my ears at the dining hall."

Could I promise that? Could I resist her—resist myself? Nienna ignited every hunger I had, an addiction I couldn't curb.

But if her father demanded this, I could honor his request.

"I'll not bed her until the wedding. You have my word."

A flicker of guilt burned behind the words. His eyes narrowed. He'd caught the phrasing.

"It's settled then," he said, leaning back. "Negotiations start after the hatching. I look forward to it."

So did I.

It couldn't come soon enough.

Chapter Eighteen

NIENNA

The dancers stomped in time. Shells tied at their ankles clattered with each movement as they chanted. But my thoughts wandered—high above the celebration, tucked in the Spire, wondering what Kallias was doing.

Mother warned me that negotiations shouldn't begin until after the Awakening. Too much had unsettled our people. For now, all focus belonged on the festival meant to reunite us.

I sighed and dragged a quill across parchment, scribbling notes. Assigning the dancer order should have gone to someone else, but the task had landed in my lap. Freya sat at my side on a shaded bench, the image of perfect decorum.

Edith remained on rest since her return, though I had no doubt she'd found a way to stay busy. I needed her with me when I traveled back to Radaan.

When I left with Kallias.

"Thinking about him?" Freya asked.

I frowned and gave her a questioning look.

"You're smiling. You haven't smiled like that since you arrived."

My lips pressed into a line. I rose as the dancers finally slowed, their chests rising and falling in unison. I passed the note to the nearest woman. "This is the order. Make sure Lina gets her gown in time."

She wore simple cotton, cheeks blooming pink as she nodded. Her ceremonial attire—meant to match the others' blue—had torn, and her mother was still mending it. Accidents happened. Even so, I hoped this Awakening would outshine all that came before it.

It would be Kallias' first.

We returned to the Spire, and my thoughts drifted again. Would I get a chance to show him the island before we left? The black beach—the Nest. So much I wanted him to see now that he was here.

He'd be eager to rejoin his people. I could handle them. I had before. But Tallon... what had Kallias done with him? Had he dismissed that betrayal without consequence? A darker part of me burned to return—if only to show Tallon and Fyrn what real love looked like.

Let those monsters rot in their sick affections.

I had Kallias.

Elmo's red tail flashed overhead, slicing through the wind. Tsunami wheeled behind him and I chuckled. She'd grown bolder with each year. Why she lingered around the island without a rider still puzzled me, but I never pretended to understand the minds of dragons.

By the time we reached the clearing, the sun had dropped low in the sky. I tilted my head back and spotted Kalepsi poised near the edge of the Nest. Her violet scales shimmered in the dying light, and a smile tugged at my lips.

What was I to her—some wingless dragonling? Yet she always watched over me. I reached inward. For a moment, I could almost feel a thread tightening between us. My imagination, surely.

Freya hurried to prepare me for dinner. She took extra care with my sea-blue dress, lace pooling over the bodice like seafoam. My hair, braided into a crown, framed the golden circlet she tucked in place. Once she gave her silent nod of approval, I slipped away to the dining hall.

Zane waited at the entrance, tilting his head with a familiar grin. "Hold, Princess," he said, stretching out a hand.

I paused, casting a glance past him toward my father's table. Then I looked back, wary.

"There's a great debate among the riders. No one has the guts to ask."

I relaxed slightly, lips pursed. "Or the stupidity?"

He chuckled. "We all want to know... does he always glow?"

My face scrunched. "Glow?"

"Like during the trial of the blood oath. Is that... normal for Radaanians?"

A laugh escaped me, short and sharp. If it had been any other rider, I might've brushed it off. But Zane was harmless.

"It's his god's blessing," I said, pretending I understood more than I did. "He shines when Elohios grants him favor."

"I knew he had magic!" He grinned.

It was nearly impossible to understand how Radaan could place faith in gods they neither saw nor heard. Did they possess a magic of their own and simply credit it to divine hands? Or had we abandoned gods we once followed?

That was a question for Kallias and me to untangle one night in bed, when sleep refused us.

Hope flickered in my chest, knitting together the broken pieces of my heart as I stepped into the dining hall. We would have years for philosophy. Our convictions aligned—duty, loyalty, resolve—but there was still so much I craved to know. How he thought. How he saw the world.

Back straight. Shoulders set. Chin high. I drifted through the room like a princess worthy of her station. Father remained at the head of the dais, Ronan to his right, Mother to his left. Further down, Kallias held a seat across from mine—but not beside it.

No marriage contract yet. No official place by my side. He sat next to Jehoikim, treated like any visiting sovereign.

Cornflower-blue eyes flicked up, and when I approached, he rose. A flush crept up my neck, and I dipped my head to acknowledge the gesture. A king standing for a princess—it wasn't required.

My stomach curled into knots. Blood beat at my temples. He stayed on his feet, gaze steady, until I slid into the seat beside Mother.

She remained still, watching him as he returned to his chair. "Chivalrous," she murmured, lips curling as she spooned up a mouthful of broth.

Pride flared in my chest. I reached for my glass, hiding a smile. If he'd impressed Mother, that alone could help usher along the new terms between us.

We ate fish chowder—thick, creamy, flecked with herbs—while she peppered me with questions about the dancers. Between spoonfuls and answers, she gave me little chance to study my future husband. Likely on purpose.

Still, I caught glimpses. Jehoikim slouched back in his chair, arrogance draping off him. He talked down to Kallias, despite the king's clear advantage in presence and stature. He played along—leaned aside, sat a fraction lower, subtly offering the illusion of deference.

It was all calculated.

He studied the island chief the way a predator watches prey. And when he understood what made Jehoikim tick, he shifted. Straightened a handspan taller. Shoulders squared. Gold links of his mantle shimmered against the dark leather. He leaned in, gaze unwavering, crowding Jehoikim's space without touching him.

Jehoikim flushed.

The noble beside him froze, soup halfway to his mouth. Slowly, the man lowered his spoon and reached for his napkin, dabbing with a quiet nervousness as he sneaked a glance at Kallias.

"Nienna." Mother's voice cut through, and I masked my smirk, folding my lips tight.

"Shall I repeat the question?"

I blinked, struggling to recall. "No, I didn't see Williard today. I'll check on him tomorrow."

She sighed, eyes darting from Kallias to me with a flicker of irritation. "I'm going to insist on an extended stay after your wedding."

My brow pulled down. "He needs to return to Radaan."

"And you need time to work this out," she said, tone cool. "I'm not sending my daughter to another kingdom as a moon-eyed bride, swooning across the table. You're besotted, and it's painfully obvious."

"You think it will fade?" I shot back, glancing at Father.

He didn't speak—just watched her, eyes glazed in thought.

"I don't make a fool of myself," she muttered, clearing her throat. Her gaze met his, sharp as flint. Color touched her cheeks, and she offered him a pointed glare.

Father took it in stride, then shifted his attention down the table to Kallias. His pale brows narrowed as he lifted his wine. Likely planning a subtle torture for this other king.

Mother's rebuke landed like a blade. I might be younger, but I wasn't naïve. A princess must carry herself above reproach. If I couldn't conceal attraction during a meal, how could I represent Radaan in matters of state?

I pressed my expression into a courtly smile and finished my soup. For the first time in weeks, I lingered. I moved through the room, chatting with nobles, asking about trade and weather, even pearl harvests. I kept clear of Jehoikim but idled near his ambassador, who was far easier to stomach.

Kallias kept his focus trained on the chief and the mayor beside him, but his posture tilted just enough to suggest his ear stayed with me. He leaned. He listened. A small smile tugged at the corner of my mouth.

He was playing the same game I was. And I loved him for it.

Ending the conversation, I strode down the dais—chin high, shoulders squared. No longer was I the cornered, diminished princess who returned from Radaan.

I had purpose now.

I would be a queen.

Wind tore at my hair as Tsunami streaked overhead. Her sea-green scales, flecked with gold, caught the sun's last rays. On the landing's edge, I clenched my core and braced against the gust she left behind.

Far below, scattered figures flowed through the streets—Draconis returning home after a long day's work. One more day, and celebration would take over the island. The Awakening. A festival of song and fire, dancing and games, food and stories passed beneath rising stars.

And Kallias would witness it all.

I leaned back on my hands, head tilted to catch the last warmth of the sun. Strands of hair tickling the backs of my fingers. Would it be braided for my wedding? Plaited and pinned in the traditional Draconis style? Usually, yes—for dragonflight—but none would let Kallias ride. Our ceremony would be bound to the land.

"Ready for the Awakening?"

I opened my eyes. Father leaned over me, white beard pulled to one side by the curve of a knowing smirk.

"I've yet to convince Williard to make a kite for the ceremony." With a huff, I shifted as he dropped beside me, letting him block the worst of the gale.

He gave a short hum, then caught a fistful of my wild hair. With gentle, practiced hands, he coiled it into a knot and tied it at the nape of my neck.

"He's old," he said. "Time he let the others do it."

"One kite's nothing for him," I muttered, laying my head on his shoulder.

"And what if his kite outshines all his apprentice's?" he asked, wrapping an arm around me. "How do you think Kai would take that?"

"They should strive for mastery."

A low grunt rattled his chest. "Kai's got talent, but his pride is barbed. He needs encouragement, not competition. Too much pressure and he'll turn bitter."

"It's an honor to craft the kites for the Awakening," I chafed.

"And it's an honor to rule." His gray eyes held mine, steady and solemn. "People are not alike. You must know them—read their moods, guess their fears. Rule them not just for the kingdom's good, but for their soul's."

I turned his words over in my mind.

How would Tallon react when I returned as his crowned queen? Had his father warned him? Or would I be the surprise that shattered him?

He would rage. Lash out. Possibly worse than before. We would never reconcile. Would Kallias cast him out? Would I be expected to visit him? Or would he demand the right to visit us?

A vision flickered across my mind—Tallon older, silver laced through his hair, hatred burning in his eyes. A villain. My villain. A monster worse than the Velli.

"You're seeing him tomorrow?"

I blinked, shaken free from the image. I wouldn't borrow tomorrow's troubles.

"Yes—I'll make my case one more time."

Father exhaled, slow and deep. "Take Mikal."

"And does Kallias have free roam of the island?"

He stiffened against me, agitation sharpening his gaze. "Last I checked, he was no longer shackled."

"He would respect your wishes if you demanded he stay in the Spire."

"Respect?" He scoffed. "He listens because Argos will swallow him whole if he doesn't."

"And yet, he landed here. Faced your trial."

"He wanted *you*."

I nudged him with my shoulder, a grin teasing at my lips. "He respects you. Honors you. Faced you as a man—now he treats you like a king."

"We'll see once negotiations begin."

"He would give you the moon and all her stars."

"You're worth far more."

My heart swelled, and I leaned in, watching a golden dragon dive toward the sea, talons skimming the surface. Somehow, this second departure felt heavier. The first time, I left with wonder. With dreams. Now, Kallias would be beside me—but I feared how Radaan would respond. Wondered if I could shoulder their scrutiny and win back their faith.

"He may accompany you tomorrow," Father muttered. "But take your maid. Show him Draconia in all her fierce glory. Remind him what awaits should he forget to honor this contract."

I bit the inside of my cheek, smothering my response. As if the trial had not seared that reminder deep into his bones.

Still, I would take Father's blessing. Kallias would walk my streets, see my home—not from the Spire or royal gardens, but on the beaches and narrow roads.

As a common man.

Chapter Nineteen

KALLIAS

She curled against her father, eyes fixed on the sunset. Her hair sat twisted in a rough knot, a leather-wrapped arm draped around her frame.

A black dragon glided past the landing, slitted pupil trained on me. I eased back a step, not meaning to intrude. But Nereus turned, glare sharp, then rose.

Regret stirred in my chest. Their moments together were fleeting. I couldn't say when—or if—we'd ever return to Draconia. At least their bond had endured, despite everything.

The Dragon King adjusted his jacket as Nienna leaned over the edge. My heart lurched into my throat.

She belonged to the skies.

Dragons swarmed the island. Nothing would happen to her.

But they've failed before, allowed her to be attacked by another man. Accidents still happened.

Nereus approached, glower set like flint. I met him straight, spine locked. I wouldn't shirk his challenges.

He sighed, then clapped a heavy hand over my mantle. The added weight dragged at my shoulders, but I stood firm, refusing to shift.

"I didn't mean to impose," I offered.

When he glanced back, Nienna tugged her hair loose, wild in the wind, and his scowl eased, gaze softening. "She's your Tsunami now." He patted my shoulder, shook his head, and kept walking.

I squinted after him. Tsunami? A wave after an earthquake?

Steeling myself, I braved the landing, half-expecting a dragon to knock me aside like a cat toying with prey.

My stomach coiled as my boots scuffed along the black stone. I was bred for the dirt and sand, not sky. But Nienna felt safe here. That had to count for something.

She turned, eyes bright, lips curled in a coy smile. "Care to join me, King of Radaan?"

"It would be my honor, Lady of the Skies." I grunted, glaring down. The stone dropped into air, a void beneath my feet, promising a violent end with my remains splattered against a rooftop.

Still, I sat, muscles locked, every breath wary.

"You won't fall."

Her smirk curved as she hummed. Her joy buzzed through the wind, contagious. I shook my head, easing into her mirth. I wanted to draw her close, pull her to my side, let the world see what she meant to me. But not yet.

Later. After our vows.

"Your father said you're my tsunami." Sunlight broke on the waves, a blinding flare. "Does that make you my doom?"

She laughed, head thrown skyward. Golden locks brushed the back of my hand. I fought the urge to catch a strand.

"The dragon." She pointed toward a blue-green figure tumbling high above. "Tsunami's a menace. It's how we say, *'Now it's your problem.'*"

"I'd take you either way."

She peeked at me, lip caught between teeth. "You have her to thank. She's the reason you were able to land. Father said she claimed the northern sky the day you arrived."

"And he listens to her?" I chuckled. Nereus didn't seem the type to take cues from beasts.

"Tsunami is…" She scrunched her face, tracking a bluish-green dragon banking above. "Well, the beast's more trouble than she's worth. Grown, clever, always stirring up fights and tipping ships."

"Ships?"

"Fishing vessels. A rider's usually stationed nearby to keep her away. She'll dump a ship to grab an easy meal."

"She doesn't hunt on her own?"

"Dragons are opportunistic feeders at heart. When they bond with a rider, many of their wild tendencies are tempered. Tsunami never bonded—she's sharp but untamed."

"Sounds like a scaled babe."

"That would be an accurate description." Nienna hummed, fingers inching closer to my thigh. "A very large one with teeth the size of your arm."

"I saw her when I arrived."

She blinked, confused.

"She landed in the courtyard." My lips formed a line. "Your dragons are larger than I anticipated. Radaan will need time to get used to them."

"What did you expect?" She laughed, relaxing again. "You saw Gyrak."

"I figured he was one of the biggest. With the island's limited resources, I assumed most would be smaller."

"They don't need land—only sky." She smiled, knuckles pressing against my leg. "And they have all the fish they could eat—if they hunt. Argos is the largest. Kalepsi, the queen, second. Their clutch hatches soon."

"And the dragonlings?"

"As large as horses."

"Truly?" I imagined smaller eggs, but Argos' size made that laughable.

"They won't bond with a rider for quite some time. On the Wild Shores, they'd have more experienced parents. They'd grow stronger, bigger. Less chance of them falling to a predator."

"What could possibly prey upon a dragon?" I asked, genuinely curious. Anything out there that viewed the massive, fire-breathing creatures as food… I never wanted to meet it.

"Nothing I've seen. But bonded dragons refuse to sleep overnight on the Wild Shores."

"Hence the reason Nereus only claims lordship."

"We're the only ones who *could* claim it. Our beasts would defend us against their untamed kin—no other island has that. But we can't settle there."

"And have you sent a man-only crew?"

Her brows crept up to her hairline. "You suggest sending men to sleep on a shore that *dragons* avoid?"

I snorted, tilting my head in agreement. "Fair point, but it seems odd."

She leaned forward, dusk spilling across the horizon. "Bonded or not, we are theirs. Just as you trust your gods—we trust the beasts."

Draconia and Radaan—different as stars and soil. But our beliefs were mirrored.

I shifted the topic back to the upcoming celebrations. "And the dragonlings hatch in a few days?"

She nodded. "The Awakening starts before the hatching, then ends with their first feeding."

"I'm eager to see a Draconis festival."

Her eyes glittered, and she ducked her head. Something like nerves stirred in my gut. What was she planning? I'd have to ask Fallione for more details to better prepare myself for whatever unfolds.

"Would you care to join me tomorrow? To see a master kite maker? It's for the celebration."

"Nienna, if you asked me to follow you to a speck of sand, I would."

I was ruined. Her light laughter lifted and vanished on the breeze. Chill kissed her cheeks, painting them a soft red. Eyes the color of the deepest sea sparkled with mischief. At that moment, Radaan and all its troubles seemed so far away.

The carriage—half the size of those in Reem—was made with Draconia's tight streets in mind. As Nienna descended the stairs beside me, I wondered how far this kite maker might be.

Greaves shadowed my steps, blades strapped to his body. Nienna's handmaid, Freya—introduced to me that morning—trailed behind, casting curious glances my way that I pretended not to notice.

I opted not to wear my sword. In Radaan I bore it proudly—a reminder that I was the warrior king Elohios chose. But here—these people needed an assurance of peace.

Two white horses stood at the carriage's head, placid and steady. Their quiet presence brought to mind Nienna's wild ride through Reem. Here, in the city, there was no room for them to panic and bolt. Maybe at the beach, but not in these cramped streets.

All eyes followed us down the stone stairs. Nienna wore violet—the color of wildflowers—with pearls along her high collar, drawing my gaze to her slender neck. The dress bore the typical Draconis split, black trousers tucked into dark leather boots. Her hair, pulled into intricate braids, cascaded like a waterfall to the small of her back.

A servant adorned in blue and silver opened the carriage door and lowered the steps. I offered my hand, and Nienna's delicate fingers slipped into mine, squeezing as she climbed inside. Freya followed, cheeks flushed as she accepted my aid.

Before I entered, I caught Greaves frowning at the skyline. With only a moment's hesitation, I took the spot next to Nienna. When my friend got in, he surveyed the seating with a furrowed brow.

"The greatest risk comes from above." Freya patted the velvet seat beside her. "You have the best vantage point here."

Nienna pressed her lips together, smothering her grin—some shared secret between them.

I adjusted for comfort, and my thigh brushed against hers. The small bench left no room to avoid contact.

When Greaves settled into his place, he angled himself away from Freya. The motion was subtle—but, by Elohios, the woman scooted a fraction closer.

His glare warned me I'd pay for this later.

The heat burning through my trousers was enough to distract me from his quiet fury.

We rolled through K'bar, a southern craft city. Draconia split into four districts, each with purpose. I had walked K'lan—the harbor and trade hub.

Even the city's sounds differed from Radaan's. Here, voices crowded, pressing into ears and mind, and all stacked on top of each other, demanding attention. Dragon roars and chirps echoed in the distance, overlapping the incessant cries of gulls.

Reddish-brown buildings towered overhead, squeezing roads into a tangled web. It would be a terrible place for battle.

Soon, the carriage halted. The door swung open and Greaves was first out—not duty, but by choice. He might give me grief for sitting too close to Nienna in public, but I wouldn't let him forget how he leapt out as if the maid were a flame waiting to consume him.

Greaves disliked attention. Quiet and watchful, he preferred observing to being observed.

After helping the women down, I stepped beside her onto the sand-dusted path.

"And you feared the Andeluith," I muttered, craning my neck to catch the thin line of sky above the rooftops. Down here, no sunlight reached the path. The corridor pressed in, dark and cramped.

"I can still *see* the sky," she whispered, defensive. "And I could climb to the roof in mere moments. I'm not trapped under a mountain."

I chuckled, wrapping the banter around me as if it were armor. In the road, Draconis paused and stared. Their lips parted in disbelief, brows low with suspicion, shoulders tight with disdain. Nienna moved forward, spine straight, demanding their bows and respect with each step.

They parted like a field of wheat beneath storm winds—retreating into doorways, pressing against walls. Greetings came, along with shallow bows, some more shallow than others.

Radaan had pride, but Draconia wielded it as a sword. To them, I had stained their princess—sent her away, only to return when it suited me.

And that was the nicest theory.

Nienna stopped before a colorful door, and Freya swept it open, ushering us into a room soaked in light.

Kites hung overhead and lined the walls—bursts of color and craft suspended in midair. Magical lights glowed along the ceiling, bathing the display in radiance. Every kite demanded attention. They were a myriad of colors and styles, vibrant as wild banners, strung with a precision fashioned by expertise.

An older man rose from behind a counter, smiling wide as he spotted Nienna—only for it to flicker when he noticed me.

Gods, I hated that.

The judgment landed fast, deep, and silent. Still, I'd endure it for the way he lit up at the sight of her.

"Princess!" he called, his graying braid slipping forward as he dipped into a bow.

A younger man stood nearby, arms folded tight, eyes sharp and angry as they darted between us. Greaves shifted closer. I met the youth's glare with my own, cold and steady.

She beamed. "Williard, how are you?"

The younger one didn't move. No show of respect. No greeting. Just that unblinking gaze, thick with accusation.

"As well as these old bones allow," Williard replied, still smiling. "And who might this be?"

I considered looking away from the insolent boy, but chose not to. His tanned skin crinkled as his nose twitched into a snarl.

"Is it customary for apprentices to ignore their royalty?" I asked, chin lifted.

Something in his stance tightened my gut. I wanted to put myself between him and Nienna, shield her from whatever venom stirred behind his eyes.

Freya sucked in a breath as Nienna faced the dark-haired man.

Her silence bristled. I could almost hear the decision forming. Should she demand obedience? Or let it slide? I had already issued the challenge. Would she support it or allow him grace?

And was it worth it?

"Kai?" Her shoulders squared. Voice low, steady.

That's my queen. Don't let them walk on you.

His eyes snapped from me to her. My jaw clenched as his anger shifted with them—no softer, no kinder.

"You may see yourself out," she said. Flat. Final. "I'll make sure Mikal hears of your reluctance to show respect."

He staggered, face twisting, trying to mask the snarl beneath something polite. It didn't work. He gave the weakest excuse for a bow, then stormed out past the counter, slamming the door behind him.

Nienna exhaled, breath long and tired, the tension folding out of her spine, deflating. "Williard, this is King Kallias Sunspear of Radaan."

The older man's eyes, clouded with age, still held a glint of cautious disapproval. "Greetings, Your Majesty."

"Well met." I inclined my head, letting my focus wander to the walls. The room exploded with color, a splattering of rainbow, but as I neared one kite, I noticed the stretched material wasn't fabric at all, but hide.

Of course. Linen and cotton would be harder to source. They wouldn't waste precious fabric on what might be considered trivial toys.

"Please tell me you're not letting Kai make the grand finale kite," Nienna groaned, collapsing onto a bench.

"He needs the experience," Williard replied, easing himself beside her. Paint stained his worn tunic, leaving him as vibrant as the room. "I cannot craft kites for the rest of my days."

"Just this year. Only one more."

It amused me how easily she shifted from royalty to a beloved child. It was obvious she adored the man. There was history between them—and she leaned on that to coax his favor.

"And next?"

She laughed. "I won't be here to nag you about it."

My jaw tensed. Yes, I was taking her to Radaan—but hearing her tell someone she loved that she was leaving twisted something sharp inside.

"Is it true then? Radaan's king has come to take our princess?" Williard's question brought my attention back. His tone stayed even, but his eyes searched mine with the kind of wariness only age could perfect.

There it was. Jealousy tingled along my spine. He had every right to her. She belonged to this land, its people. And I was simply the king who wanted an alliance.

"I've come to unite Radaan and Draconia—through Nienna's hand in marriage." I didn't owe him an explanation, but she trusted him. That was enough.

"To you?"

Whatever answer he preferred, I'd give the truth. "I'm asking to make her queen." I paused. "My queen."

He sat back, expression unreadable. Nienna kept silent, fingers folded in her lap.

"Honorable of you," he murmured.

"Dragon King Nereus would let her go to nothing less," I said, reminding him that I'd earned the right—through fire, steel, and a ruler's scrutiny. I was a far cry from the monster he believed me to be.

He leaned on his cane, thumb tapping the wood. "I don't recall the King of Radaan joining us in celebration before. This is your first?"

"Yes. I'm eager to see it." I motioned to the surrounding kites. "These are works of art. Have they all flown?"

"Most." He rose, shuffling past. "They're sacred to us. They bind sea and sky, giving the common folk a taste of flight. We can't all be riders, after all."

I approached a kite shaped like a seal, flicked the hard spine holding it rigid. "Bone?"

"Fish mostly. Bird bones when we're lucky. Trees are too scarce here."

"I noticed," I said. "And hides instead of cloth. Your bodies are bound to the earth, but your hearts belong to the skies."

His gaze flicked back. "If Princess Nienna asks me to make a kite for you, I will. But she must ask."

So that was it. He thought I pressured her, that I won her by force or trickery, took advantage of her and only wanted to clear my name.

My face fell blank, refusing to show that I'd caught onto his game.

"You would let him fly it? The finale?" Nienna's breathless tone hinted at significance. Perhaps something symbolic.

Here I was, signing up for yet another thing I knew nothing about.

Reckless fool.

"Only if you want it," he said, matching my stare. "You've flown a kite before, dear king?"

It was ridiculous, but I had never.

"I can manage," I answered, tone flat.

Nienna practically bounced on her heels. "It would mean so much to the people, and before negotiations, it would symbolize peace between our nations."

He grunted, finally looking her way. "Then for you, I will make one last kite."

Chapter Twenty

NIENNA

There was pride in the way Kallias observed my interactions with my people. It wasn't just about showing him my world—but also revealing the bond I shared with my kingdom. One I hoped to replicate in Radaan.

After we parted ways with Williard, I brought him to the beaches.

It still surprised me that the master kite maker offered him the last flight. It wasn't something handed out lightly—an honor he didn't completely comprehend.

"The final kite is reserved for one held in high esteem," I said as we threaded through the narrow streets leading south.

"Should Nereus fly it, then?" Kallias carried himself with steady confidence, but his sharp gaze scanned every corner, stall, and shadow before returning to me. He absorbed the world with quiet calculation.

Greaves trailed close, his posture tight, his movements clipped. He didn't enjoy enclosed spaces.

We stepped toward the wide band of sunlight breaking through the alley, the beach waiting on the other side. "The kites are meant for the riderless. A chance for them to soar beside the riders."

He made a thoughtful sound, more breath than voice, then took in the open coast.

The air changed. Brine and salt swept in with the breeze. The essence of fried fish clung thick around us. A gust tugged my dress behind me like a banner.

The beach stretched in bleached white, almost painfully bright under the sun's glare. The people scattered across it broke up the glare—little dots of dark fabric and movement. They clustered near food carts lined along the shore, where fish crackled in oil and steam rose from heavy pots.

Waves moved with lazy rhythm, licking the coast rather than crashing against it like they did on the western shores. It made me think of K'seer—children racing barefoot over wet sand, their laughter rolling through the breeze as they stacked up castles. I'd have to bring him there, too.

Freya strode ahead, her flame-colored braid swinging behind her.

That earned a flicker of interest from Kallias.

"She knows the best foods," I said, grinning.

She beelined for a vivid red cart where a stout man turned skewers over a sizzling grill. His cheeks were flushed from heat, his tunic stained with oil. Sweat gleamed on his brow, and he swiped it with a greasy sleeve.

"Good day!" he called, gaze flicking from Freya to the rest of us.

The metal tongs slipped from his fingers and clanged into the steaming pot below. Jaw slack, he dropped into a bow so low I feared he might tip over.

"Princess—Your Majesty!" he boomed. The words echoed through the midday chatter, and half the heads on the beach snapped toward us.

I lifted my chin, back straightening on instinct. Whispers would follow. The King of Radaan, walking about, eating street food like a commoner?

It wouldn't shock anyone to see Freya and me here. But the fact that I brought Kallias?

That said something. It spoke volumes about the trust I had for him—and them.

"We'll take four Stick'ems with the spicy tartar." Freya spoke with confidence.

Kallias blinked, the only sign he registered the crude name for the treat. I almost laughed at how well he masked his amusement, but I turned my attention to the vendor instead.

"Yes, of course!" The man stabbed polished bone rods through thick cuts of breaded fish, plunging them into the oil with a hiss. Our presence hastened his movements.

Freya waited, patient, coins ready in her palm.

"This is where the workers eat their midday meal," I said, motioning toward the civilians trickling from thin paths between buildings. Weary laborers sat on soft sand, stealing a brief rest, food in hand.

"This is the craft district?" he asked, sun glinting off his mantle. He wore his traditional fashion of green and gold, but donned a tunic and vest over heavier layers. A wise choice in this heat.

"Yes, K'bar is where the makers and creators work," I said. "Districts belong to Radaan. Here, we only have cities. They return home to K'dan or K'seer when the day ends."

Draconia felt so small now. In his country, traveling from one city to another could take days on horseback. Here, we could walk the island end to end with ease.

"I've seen the skill inside the Spire. Your people are talented."

His words brought a pleased smile to my face. Around us, stiff shoulders began to ease. Passerby bowed as they moved through the crowd—busy, but listening. Eyes lingered on Kallias.

"Four Stick'ems with spicy tartar!" the vendor called out, holding up skewers loaded with fried fish, orange sauce sliding down the crisp batter. My breath caught. Messy food and public company weren't the best mix.

It wasn't the act of eating in front of Kallias that bothered me—it was the *staging* of it. A mouthful of dripping tartar in full view of the people? That felt... unseemly. As if a bit of sauce on the chin might chip the polish from our reputation.

As Freya handed out our portions, Greaves eyed his with suspicion, then gave a short shake of his head.

"I will eat later." His voice—quiet, gravel-edged—still startled me.

My friend frowned, casting a bewildered glance my way.

"Perhaps he's not as skilled with Stick'ems as he is with a blade." I chuckled, steering toward a cluster of boulders further up the shore.

Greaves grunted. Agreement or protest—I couldn't tell. Kallias took a bite as we walked. He blinked and cleared his throat.

"Hot?" I asked, claiming a boulder before committing to my own battle with the sauce.

"Both temperature and flavor." He settled beside me, gazing at the shimmering surf. Foam scattered across the tide like dancing lace.

"We get our spices from the Kulletti. Their food makes you feel as if you're a dragon breathing fire."

Right on cue, Tsunami swept low over the water, wings stretched wide. Her eyes caught the light as she veered toward us.

Above, Borj and Artorius circled—the black scales sucking up the sun, white horns shimmering. She wouldn't harass the vendors, not outright. But rules had never stopped her before.

I ate quickly, nose prickling from the tartar's heat. Tsunami's tail dipped, carving through the shallows with a splash.

A chorus of groans and yelps followed as workers scrambled back. She prowled forward, nostrils flaring, her sea-slick head lifted high. Green and blue scales shimmered like wet glass.

Greaves edged between her and his king, every movement coiled tight. Freya huffed and picked up her pace, scarfing the rest of her second stick as if she feared the wild dragon might lunge for it.

"I can't tell if I should worry for my lunch or my life," Kallias muttered, craning back to study Tsunami as she blocked out the sun.

Borj landed with a thud behind her. His midnight beast eased between Tsunami and the crowd, but she didn't waver. Her attention stayed locked—on Kallias.

She snorted. Tongue flicked out, tasting the air.

"Don't make me harm a dragon, Princess," Greaves muttered, one hand already on the hilt of his sword.

I laughed. The movement showed off her fangs and threw small sparks from her mouth—it was a harmless move, but one that could seem threatening if someone wasn't familiar with dragons and their antics.

"She smells something unfamiliar," I said as she lowered her head. Chin resting on the tide, waves frothed around her jaw. One golden eye tracked Kallias, then Greaves, then back again. "You're Radaanian. Apart from your envoys, she's never scented you."

"Exotic," Borj called as he made his way over. The large man strolled across the beach, dark hair wild, grin on full display. "Artorius says you smell like sun and soil, Your Majesty."

Kallias huffed a laugh. "There are worse scents."

Cinnamon and sunshine. His scent. I understood the dragons completely.

Tsunami lashed her tail, flinging seawater across the beach in a wide arc. Artorius snapped his jaws, a sharp reprimand meant to steer her off the civilians. She ignored him. Another snort gusted from her nostrils, followed by a deep inhale like she needed to clear her nose to place Kallias' scent.

I sighed, handed my stick to Freya, and slid off the boulder. Wet sand swallowed my boots. Her eyes locked on mine. She bared her teeth and released a low warbling trill. I recognized it—a sound of frustration.

Lifting my hand, I let her study my approach. If she didn't want me close, she had every chance to show it. Water curled around her limbs as she crouched in the shallows, tail flicking under the surface.

When my palm met her snout, she shivered, muscles rippling. A low click sounded in her throat, uncertain.

"He's mine," I murmured, running my hand along the smaller plates near her jaw. Warm. Almost soft. Those scales held heat like stone in summer.

She blinked slowly. The horned crests above her eyes dropped in a suspicious squint. Then she turned, studying me sideways, head cocked like a dog too clever for her own good. A menace, but with the heart of a spoiled pup.

Artorius clacked his teeth. She shrieked, hurling her massive skull toward him, sparks flying from her mouth. I staggered back, salt spray and heat surging over me as her talons churned the water.

Borj swore and rushed forward to put himself between me and the bickering creatures as I retreated to the beach.

She hissed, lunged like she might strike—but instead flared her wings and leapt skyward. The downforce punched into the sea, sending a wall of water over the shoreline.

Greaves' jaw tightened. He glared after her, unreadable but clearly unimpressed.

"Good day, Princess," Borj barked, already moving, his voice clipped as he joined Artorius. The black dragon's rider crouched low, preparing to follow her into the sky.

I didn't envy him. Babysitting a force like Tsunami required both skill and patience—and even that wasn't always enough. She was half storm, half flame, with a will no dragon could temper.

Kallias had watched it all in silence, leaning against the boulder, shoulders relaxed. But his gaze didn't miss a beat.

"So," he said as I stepped beside him, "is this what my people should expect?"

I shook my head, pushing damp hair behind my ear. "No. Tsunami won't leave Draconia. The dragons assigned to Radaan are older, bonded, and disciplined. She's a rare... exception."

He hummed, thoughtful. "Still. Radaan will have to adjust."

I grinned. "Wait until you see the Awakening."

It began with the dragons' song.

Before dawn's first touch, when light only whispered at the edge of the sky, their voices rose in eerie, powerful howls. Cavernous groaning bellows rolled through the air—much like whales from the deep—vibrating in tandem. A chorus carried from ridge to sea.

The sound pulled me from sleep, lured every Draconis into the damp hush of morning. At the landing, Argos perched at the tip. His neck curved, chin tucked to his chest. He loosed a low, resonant thrum that rattled my ribs, blending with Kalepsi's haunting notes from the Nest above.

Father rested a hand against Argos' shoulder, gaze trained on the horizon. Mother stood behind him, near but not part of the moment. She had no dragon—no place in their bond where their souls melded.

She smiled when I reached her, our pale white robes catching the moon's last light. Her hand clasped mine—steady, warm.

Argos' humming tunneled through my bones, thrumming beneath my skin, sparking urgency. It felt ancient, like the song stirred something buried in the island itself. Magic shimmered in the air—unseen, but impossible to ignore.

The sky shifted to gray, and a bloom of orange spread at the sea's rim. Mother squeezed my hand, and I followed her pointed nod.

Kallias approached the landing, stride sure but guarded. Greaves trailed close behind. Their black attire broke like shadows across the stone. Morning light kissed the edge of his mantle, offering hints of reflection.

He stopped before us, bowed low. "I was sent for."

Father didn't move. His eyes stayed forward, locked on the surf. Argos remained still, lost in song.

"Welcome to the Awakening, King Kallias," Mother said, offering a graceful nod. "I trust your rest was sufficient?"

"Very," he replied, glancing east. "Though I must admit, I don't know how to participate." His eye twitched, but he masked it with a blink.

Control suited him. He didn't like surprises. But here, in Draconia, the rules were different. He'd rushed here, leaving Fallione scrambling to keep pace. No amount of preparation could replicate the rhythm of this place.

"The dragons' song wakes the island," I said, stepping away from Mother to stand beside him. "Some say they were the first to sing the world into being. This is a homage to that lore."

Wind surged through the landing. My skirts whipped against my legs, pulling taut like sails. I looped my arm through his, and he rested a palm on his belt, tucking my hand in close. Mother raised her eyebrows at my move, but let it go, staring back at the sunrise.

"I didn't know they sang," Kallias murmured.

Argos drew in a deep breath, scales shifting over muscle as his chest expanded, his attention locked on the orange halo as it climbed.

"Only for the Awakening," I whispered, barely above the low hum surrounding us. "This song marks the beginning. Riders spend it with their dragons. It will happen every dawn until all the dragonlings hatch."

"Then the festival ends?"

"Not until the first flight and feeding."

He gave a rough grunt, tension slipping from his posture as he turned back to the sunrise. In Radaan, Fallione could guide him. Here, he required more than an advisor. He needed someone who belonged to this place. A partner.

A queen.

I tightened my grip on his arm. Heat curled through my chest. My parents stood beside me, and Kallias let me hold him. For a breathless moment, everything felt aligned.

The dragons' voices rose, reaching higher. A shrill, piercing cry cut through the harmonies as the sun finally breached the sea. Their breaths staggered, one after another, a ladder of sound. The stone beneath us trembled with their song.

Argos braced himself, talons carving shallow grooves into the cliff's edge. His muscles tensed, shoulders locked.

New daylight shimmered on the water, wavering like it strained to break free.

Kallias shifted beside me, glancing toward Argos.

I smiled.

He didn't know what came next. But I did.

"Brace yourself. This is my favorite part," I called over the rising crescendo.

The sun broke free of the horizon, a sliver of light cracking beneath the burning orb, lifting it from the sea. Argos' head snapped skyward. His neck shuddered, and a bone-deep bellow tore from his chest, sharp enough to split the sky.

The cry echoed across the island. Every dragon answered. For three full breaths, the only sound on Draconia was the raw, wild scream of dragons.

Kallias tensed beneath my hand, but he tracked Father, now climbing onto his dragon's back.

With a thunderous snap of his jaws, Argos silenced himself and tipped off the landing in a steep, headlong dive.

Roars fell quiet in unison. Then came the thunder—wingbeats crashing like drums as leathery sails punched into the air.

I craned my neck toward the Nest, pointing. Kallias followed my gesture. Kalepsi leaned far over the edge, morning light gilding her golden horns. Her massive head stretched skyward, hunger to fly tugging her from the clutch she refused to leave. She released a guttural roar that rang like an echo from another age.

Dragons burst from rooftops, cliff edges, beaches—rising in wide spirals around the Spire. Their paths narrowed with altitude, the sky becoming a whirl of iridescence, a storm of rainbow-scaled bodies flashing by.

Wind ripped through my dress, and my cheeks ached from grinning. With the landing's edge beneath my feet, the dragons soaring past so close I could taste the heat off their wings—nothing matched it. It set every part of me alight.

Riders hugged their dragons' spines, molded tight. No wavering, no faltering. They ascended together, one purpose, one breath.

Argos led the spiral skyward, streaking toward the faint stars clinging to dawn.

Then, with a final roar, he curved into a sweeping arc and plummeted. Even Tsunami followed, slicing through the sky in a narrow line. They dropped together, zipping past the Spire like a falling star. Wings snapped open with a deafening crack, just before they hit the rooftops.

Muted cheers spread across the island, celebrating their rise and return.

"We take first meal with the commoners during the Awakening," Mother said, already turning toward the throne room. "Will you join us, King Kallias?"

"It would be my pleasure." He dipped his chin. I brushed my thumb along the inside of his arm as he pivoted to follow.

She led us down the palace terraces to the courtyard, packed shoulder to shoulder with civilians. Blankets covered the dewy grass, and children darted between adults, who carried baskets brimming with food. Dragons landed briefly on rooftops, their claws chipping stone before they leapt away once their riders dismounted.

The scent of warm bread curled in the air—thicker than usual. Where would we get that much grain without an Innaki ship?

I glanced at Kallias.

His bright gaze danced the crowd, radiant with calculation. The fine lines at the corners of his eyes deepened under the sun, but his expression stayed relaxed.

"You brought goods from Radaan." I didn't ask. It surprised me, though. I hadn't expected him to offer them without using them to sweeten negotiations.

He looked down at me. "Your marriage was to secure grain. Seemed foolish to arrive empty-handed."

"And you gave it away for the festival?"

"It matters to your people," he said, guiding me down the steps. "Call it my contribution to the festivities."

I pressed closer, heart warming as I lifted my chin toward the crowd. He hadn't used Radaan's goods to buy favor. He gave them freely—to win the hearts of my people.

By their smiles, it worked.

We waded into the throng. Greaves kept close. A toddler slammed into my leg, let out a delighted squeal, and tore off waving a hunk of steaming bread. I laughed as a sibling scrambled after them with a quick apology.

Draconis overflowed into the streets, spreading to rooftops where blankets had been laid out, legs dangling over the edge. In the center of the courtyard, Edith and Freya waited, a white and silver blanket spread wide enough for all of us.

During the Awakening, royalty walked among the people. No thrones. No ceremony. Just humans sharing food, sky, and breath. A reminder of what we truly were.

Mother lowered herself gracefully, settling onto the crisp fabric. I nudged Kallias down beside her. His brow furrowed, as if unsure about sitting while the masses stood. For most royals, seating themselves lower than their people was a foreign concept.

I dropped to my knees and stared up at him. That wrinkle deepened, then eased as he followed suit. He stretched his legs in front of him, still stiff, still watching.

"We all are mortals," I said, noting the twist in his mantle. I fought the urge to fix it. One day I would. But not yet—not until my people accepted him. "Here, the ground is level."

Father made his way through the crowd, stopping to greet others with a smile and hearty slaps on the shoulder. He was a rider, yes—but still their king.

"Even Dragon Riders come back to earth," I said. "A reminder that the same blood flows in all our veins." These traditions were second nature to me. To him, they were stories, observations scribbled in history books.

Father joined us with a look at Kallias that started hard but softened at the sight of Mother. He sat with a grunt. Edith opened the basket beside her, the scent of jam and bread rose like morning mist from the grass. My stomach tightened.

Two children shrieked with laughter nearby, tumbling across someone's blanket. A couple a few spots over burst into giggles. Joy and mirth spread as if it were a ripple through water, catching on others.

Kallias snorted at their antics, chewing a thick slice of bread. He was different here. Something in him had shifted. His mantle still weighed on him, but his eyes lit with something lighter—curiosity. It lent him an air of youthfulness, watching the Draconis with ease. He leaned back on his arm, noting my father's informality.

This would be my last Awakening on the island.

And I was glad I shared it with him.

Chapter Twenty-One

KALLIAS

The Awakening wasn't what I expected. Fallione roused me early, whispering about customs and traditions. I held on to what I could while the sky still clung to night. I hadn't prepared for a pre-dawn summons—least of all for what happened on the landing.

But if Draconia's queen invited me to share a private moment before I was officially a member of their family, I wouldn't let it pass me by.

Nienna's face lit like a sunrise, and every hour of missed sleep faded behind her glow. Watching the dragons perform their ceremony felt as if I were witnessing a living legend. I wished Radaan's people could stand beside me and see it unfold.

Her joy spilled through her eyes, her smile pulling wide, bright as polished gold. She guided me through each movement, pointing out nuances while we sat among the commoners. No barriers, no thrones—just bodies pressed shoulder to shoulder in the clearing.

We followed the king and queen down winding paths carved between stone homes and woven awnings. We reached the shore where booths lined the beach, colors vivid beneath the climbing sun. Vendors shouted greetings over the surf. Anyone could approach Nienna or her parents. No guards blocked the way. But none spoke to me.

Draconis glanced; they scrutinized my mantle, but they didn't speak.

The grain we supplied had softened their stares. Enough, maybe, to sway opinion. If I wanted Nereus' favor, I needed his people behind me.

The dragons—now that was a different challenge.

The hours blurred, draining me. Greaves stuck to my side, close but never suffocating. He made space when Nienna nudged me toward conversation. But he never strayed far. Not with the beasts gliding overhead, wings outstretched like sails. Ronan sparked flame from his palm with casual flicks, more stage magic than threat, but the message stayed clear—no one dared strike a Draconis royal.

Which made the attack on Nienna back home even more jarring.

No assassin would be reckless enough to target them. Not unless they found her alone. Not unless they knew her gifts were weak.

The thought snagged in my mind, sharp and splintering. She'd been with her handmaiden. Nienna had told me—confessed—she was a poor Vessel.

Who else in Radaan would've known that?

"Kal?" Greaves bumped my shoulder, his eyes raking the crowd.

I blinked. "It's nothing." I shook my head, clearing the hazy thoughts. We never found solid answers about the assassination. This wasn't the place to chase them.

Nienna glanced over her shoulder, lifting her hand to beckon me forward. The sun leaned close to the horizon. My legs ached from the endless walk, joints stiff, back screaming. But gods help me, I wouldn't look weak in front of her or her people.

I stepped in beside her, and she slid her fingers into the crook of my elbow. My thumb hooked around my belt buckle. Together, we led the crowd toward a stage that gleamed under flickering lanterns. They followed like water drawn to the shore.

"It's time for the dance," she whispered, excitement coloring her voice.

"I thought Draconis dances were solo affairs." I drew her closer with a subtle shift of my elbow. She burned with energy. I wanted every spark.

"Most are," she said, eyes flashing. "Though we don't move quite like the Sols."

"Are you performing?" I asked. "Or trying to coerce me into it?"

"When I ask you to dance, Kallias—I won't have to resort to trickery."

My brows climbed. I blinked, wondering just what she would do—and when I would have to learn a new dance. Greaves didn't know a single step of their style.

Mage lights floated above, casting silver across silk banners draped between tall poles. Lanterns swayed gently with the breeze. The illusion of walls wrapped the stage in a soft glow, though it stood open to the tide on one side. The crowd surged closer, and when the king and queen mounted the stairs, we followed.

Our footsteps vanished beneath the swell of voices. A covered section with benches offered the best view, elevated just enough to overlook the display. She tugged me toward the shadows behind her parents, deeper into the corner.

Greaves took his place at my side, and I dropped onto the cushioned bench. Nienna leaned in at once, her weight pressing warm against my arm, and I sat forward to ease the pull in my spine. She'd pulled us off-center—still close, but not obvious.

Knowing her, she chose this spot for privacy.

We were hidden from view against the back wall; the only chance of being seen was by the stage or if her parents turned.

I worried over the latter more.

"The first dance is by Ciana," she whispered as the crowd shifted and settled.

Nereus muttered, rubbing his knee. His wife leaned in, said something low, then pointed across the platform.

Nienna's calf pressed against mine.

I rolled my shoulder, wincing as the chains of Radaan jangled over my chest. Pain bloomed sharp in my joint. I sank into the seat, resigned to the ache until I could finally collapse into bed.

Then the drums struck—deep, sudden, thunderous.

I searched the stage. No sign of them. The drummers had to be tucked near our box, hidden behind the draped panels. The rhythm lasted a breath, maybe two—just long enough to call her forth.

She stepped from the shadows.

Black curls spilled down her back in thick ropes. A stark white dress clung to her bronze skin. Her eyes—dark and unyielding—spoke of island blood. Not fully Draconis, not with that shade and midnight gaze. Their kind wore sunlight in their hair and sky in their irises.

She gripped her skirts and dipped into a bow, snowy fabric billowing around her legs.

"Rise, woman, and tell us your name." Nereus' booming tone cut across the murmurs. Silence followed.

"My name is Ciana, Your Majesty." Her words curled with richness, weighted by an accent I recognized—the same as the Kulletti chief I'd once dined beside. "And I bring you the Dance of the First Light."

The drums erupted.

She spun in a tight circle, faster than expected, then slammed her foot down with an abrupt snap. She faced away from us. A white hood swept over her head, and when she turned...

A dragon stared back.

Gold eyes shimmered in the stitching, so intricately embroidered they seemed alive, watchful.

She danced with the drums, skirts sweeping in wide arcs. This wasn't the measured rhythm of Radaan's court dances—no matched pairs, no slow, precise pacing. This felt like the Sols: quick, sharp, independent.

Nearing the end of the dance, she bent and angled her face to the sky. Fire shot out of her mouth with such force, my hand twitched.

A Vessel.

"She's not Draconis?" I kept my voice low, just for Nienna.

"Ciana's father is," she murmured. Her breath brushed my jaw. "Her mother's Kulletti."

I watched the dancer flick arcs of flame skyward. "So the blood doesn't have to be pure."

"Some mixed children channel it with no issue," she said softly. "Thinking of Radaan?"

"We've no use for magic. But..." I let the words trail. If magic was a usable resource, Clay would find a way to bend it to our benefit.

"They have to carry Draconis in them. No rider would share power with someone outside the blood. It's our inheritance. Even if the blood's thin, any Draconis has the right to be a Vessel—if they can bear it."

"But the riders choose."

"They search the mind." She applauded as Ciana bowed, her dance complete. "The process is complicated. I've only been part of it twice."

A flicker of shame slipped into her tone.

I nudged her knee with mine. "You need no magic, Dragon's Heart."

Her eyes rose to the sky, mage lights casting flickers across her face. "Something's changed since I returned. The connection feels distant. I can't hold their power—but I still feel them. Somehow."

Another dancer stepped forward. The drums surged, loud enough to drown her out. I leaned closer.

"You've searched the records?" I asked. "Of the Hearts before you?"

"There are so few." Her mouth moved again, but the rising beats smothered her words.

I ducked lower, giving her my ear. My gaze stayed forward—on the line of female dancers now circling the stage.

Her lips brushed my skin. Her palm settled on my thigh, fingers pressing into the muscle. Heat flared through me, sharp and immediate. I clenched my jaw, fighting the primal urge to move her hand higher. My body wanted it. I refused it.

"There's a pattern," she breathed. "Most of them went mad."

Her breath lingered on my skin. All it would take was a single turn. My mouth could find hers with no effort at all.

Her mother glanced back, brow furrowed at our position. I didn't bother to smile, blood roaring through my veins. I straightened, shifting so Nienna sat in full view. The queen's gaze dropped to her hand on my thigh. I refused to move, but Nienna caught the warning. Her fingers slid slow across my trousers, a bold stroke, before she folded them neatly in her lap.

She would pay for that later.

The dances spun on into the night. Lore wove itself through chants and movement—the old songs of Draconia, stitched from flame and myth. The dragons. The first settlers. Men abandoned on the island's shore, left to rot but choosing to rise. Prisoners carving a nation from stone and fire.

That was what made Draconis different from their island kin. Fairer skin. Sun-kissed bronze, not as dark. Eyes like glacier water, hair like sunlight. The rest of the archipelago bore night-blessed curls, and irises like rich ink.

Draconis weren't born of this place. Neither were their dragons.

One dance told the story of the first riot—when the sky split with storms and beasts crashed to earth. Windsingers joined the drums. The music surged, raw and guttural. Dancers moved with violence, ripping garments to reveal crimson cloth beneath—blood writ in silk.

When the first bond was forged, the man at center stage clapped, palms sparking. A streak of white light shot from his hands, arching into the crowd. Shouts and cheers erupted.

Nienna's elbow nudged my ribs. A silent command. I rose with her family and joined the applause.

My eyes swept the small amphitheater. "Your brother doesn't attend?"

"He's just a commoner during the Awakening," she said. "You won't see him in the Spire tonight."

Which means one less person walking the halls.

I squashed that thought. I would wait for Nienna, as a proper man would. There would be no hoping she snuck to my rooms.

Nereus and Nyxaria led us through the crowd and across the cleared stage. The celebration had drained itself. Laughter thinned to yawns. Smiles sagged under the lure of sleep. Nienna leaned on my shoulder as we walked, and when her cheek pressed to my mantle, heat stirred in my chest.

Radaan would learn to love her. She would give herself to my kingdom. Win over a people who didn't yet know her worth.

When we reached the black steps that led up to the Spire, the island had gone silent. No dragons cried. No gulls screamed. The night held its breath. Doors shut. Windows dark. The world tucked in.

Inside the palace, lanterns glowed, casting soft amber across stone and steel, but the mage lights above remained cold and unlit.

"The Vessels are relieved during the festival," Nienna whispered, her voice thin in the vast corridor. "The riders won't refill them until it ends."

"Half your light is magic." I glanced up. Another contrast—Radaan would've burned fish oil to keep the night at bay.

"The dragons need that oil," Nereus echoed back from his place ahead of us, as if he heard my line of thought. "Magic is a resource, same as anything else."

At my floor, I slowed, easing out from Nienna's grip. She clung tighter.

"I'll see Kallias to his rooms," she said, tone smooth as ever.

Her parents paused.

Nereus' tired stare sharpened. It landed on me, flint-hard. I clenched my jaw. His suspicion was earned. This was the price of my earlier recklessness.

Nyxaria inhaled, then exhaled slow through her nose. "Come see me once he's settled."

So she'd know the moment Nienna left my quarters. Nereus dipped his chin. The gesture was slight, but heavy with emphasis. A reminder. A warning. His glare flicked past me to Greaves, jaw tightening.

"Good night," I said, offering a shallow bow. Then I turned down the hall.

I could find my way to bed alone. But I didn't send her away. Not with shadows whispering promises just out of reach.

Greaves followed, each step a mirror of mine. A quiet rebuke. One I wanted to ignore. I could dismiss him, order him elsewhere, but anyone watching would know exactly what his absence meant.

"The lights are magicked by people, but why the runes?" I asked, forcing my mind from thoughts better left alone.

"It's easier." Nienna's gaze drifted to the dead mage lights along the wall. "They need Vessels to power them, but the runes are ancient words. They're phrases to help you remember. *Light to glow, to guide. Measured for use inside.* The spell shifts depending on purpose, but Draconis can't enchant without them."

"And any Vessel can refill them?" I asked as we reached my door. I opened it, unwilling to see her go just yet.

She did not hesitate to enter. Behind her, Greaves frowned. His lips pressed to a line, already dreading where this would lead. I waved him in with a jerk of my head.

"Any can, but no two are the same," she said, spinning to face me. Her hands found the chains of my mantle. "Some hold more. Some longer."

I caught her wrist. Letting her unfasten it seemed too intimate. I'd made that mistake once—too soon. Almost gave in.

One day, she'd lift the weight of my kingdom from my shoulders. But not tonight.

Her eyes met mine. Doubt flickered in the ocean-deep blue.

"Greaves can do it."

Her skin felt impossibly soft beneath my grip. Her full lips parted, and need struck like lightning. Watching her all day had ignited something slow and smoldering, and now it boiled.

She would let me.

If I stepped forward—if I leaned in—she would fold into me without question. We were fated. I crossed the sea for her. Braved dragonfire. And stood here, risking everything for me.

But honor demanded we wait.

"When I make love to you, it will be to a queen. Not a princess."

Her mouth curved, sly and dangerous. Challenge replaced hesitation. I released her and pointed toward the adjoining room.

"Go. Wait for me."

She bit her lip, then obeyed.

Greaves moved in with practiced ease, unfastening the chains. His scowl said everything. "You're playing with fire," he muttered, lifting the mantle from my shoulders.

A knock on the door. He shut his eyes for a long breath, and I scoffed, already knowing who it would be.

"It's Fallione. Go eat."

"And leave you alone with her?" His gaze cut toward the bedchamber. "What happens if you break your word again?"

"Go." I shoved his shoulder, too tired to argue.

He huffed but opened the door, letting Fallione inside.

"Your Majesty, there are traditions to marrying a Draconis–" He didn't wait for greeting or permission. Greaves shook his head and slipped into the hall.

"As with any nation," I muttered, walking to the dressing room. A glance told me Nienna remained hidden, uninterested in political counsel.

"You are expected to ride a dragon."

That gave me pause.

"Come again?"

Fallione pinched the bridge of his nose. "The groom is to take his bride on a flight around the island. Most males of the royal house of Draconis are riders. You are not."

I started on the buttons of my vest. Would I need to bond one? Those massive creatures wouldn't carry just anyone. Only their rider.

Except Nienna.

She was the exception. That meant she was safe. I was not.

"Nereus must have known that when he set the terms."

"He refuses to discuss anything with me until the Awakening ends."

I didn't blame him. After the long day, I wouldn't want to be bothered either. It wasn't hard to see why Nereus would turn him away.

"Then we'll discuss it in negotiations."

"I apologize for not preparing you for the dragon song–"

"Fallione." I cut him off, peeling off my vest. He had followed me into foreign lands with no map and no promise of survival. "Keep the ship steady. Stay in contact with Nereus' staff. Advise me as needed. But don't think I expect you to know everything. I'm not a young prince anymore. I can handle myself."

"Yes, my king. I aim to serve." He sighed, voice heavy with weariness. "I am sure you're weary from your travels today."

"I want nothing more than my bed." And the woman already in it.

"If anything pressing arises, I will do my best to inform you prior."

"As expected." I tugged at my sleeves. "Now go rest. Gods know I won't get much." I cast a look toward the other room.

"Good night, my king." The door clicked softly behind him as he left.

I pulled my tunic free, yanking it over my head. My back screamed from the trial and the endless walking. I hissed and tossed it across a chair.

At the basin, I studied the bandage. Crimson bled through the linen. I peeled it off, revealing a scabbed-over gash just above the old scar from the foothills. Another to add to the tally.

I soaked a cloth and pressed it against the wound. Cool water stung. I bent over the basin, scrubbing sweat and grime from my face and hair. After drying off, I left my trousers on. I might enjoy her games, but I knew my body's reaction to her well enough that I didn't trust losing the garment.

Towel slung over my shoulders, I crossed to the bedchamber.

The moon gilded her in silver. Draped in white, her slender form curved atop the blanket. Pale hair spilled across the pillow like silk. She lay facing me, lashes casting faint shadows over her cheeks.

My chest tightened.

She looked fragile—thinner than she'd been in Radaan. I'd done that. Guilt gnawed at me. My mistake hurt her, tortured her, thinking I would just let her go.

Gingerly, I sat on the edge, bending to unlatch my boots. She moaned and wiggled on the bed, teasing a smile from my lips. Kicking my boots off, I set them aside before reclining on the mattress.

There would be more days like this. Duties from dawn until long after dark. A life of serving our kingdoms. If I could give her rest now, I would.

At least one of us deserved sleep.

Chapter Twenty-Two

NIENNA

The next evening brought the kite parade. We walked among the crowd beneath the bruised sky, the air laced with salt and laughter. Rough displays bobbed on short strings, their crooked frames pieced together by little hands. Others soared higher—sleek, intricate, the work of seasoned fliers. The beach stretched under a canopy crammed with color, Draconis kites weaving in and out of clouds like stitched flame.

Ours carried the legacy of our ancestors, their frames constructed unlike any from distant shores—lighter, stronger. The craft passed down through generations, born from wherever they'd first set sail, then refined with magic.

Glowing trails marked the dusk, streaking the air like fallen stars. Swirls of green shimmered alongside veins of blue. Threads of pink and purple danced with streaks of crimson, sunburst yellow glinting in between. Power once locked in dragons now spilled through the hands of common folk, letting them share the sky with their rider kin.

Scaled bodies banked through the upper wind, dipping into the waves, scattering spray with their wings. They chased each other in wide arcs, unbound by any rule but instinct. Overhead, the sunset poured fire through the drifting clouds.

I gripped Kallias' elbow, steering him toward the northernmost edge of Draconia.

This location mattered. Radaan waited across the sea. He should launch the final kite from here.

Mother and Father let me take the lead, though custom frowned on it. He was still a foreign king. But they understood how important this was to me.

We climbed the cliffside path, rocks biting through the soles of my boots, sea wind tugging at my braid. The trail hugged the cliff, sharp and narrow, until the land opened at the top.

Williard waited for us there, the gale snapping at his clothes. A green-and-gold display rested in his hands—dragon-shaped, its wings spread to catch the ocean breeze. Bird bones lined the open mouth, jagged and pale like teeth.

With a slight bow, the master kite maker offered it to Kallias, who accepted with reverence. It fit easily in his arms—modest, unassuming.

I smiled. Appearances could be deceiving.

We stepped away from Williard, Kallias unwinding the cord. His brow tightened as he gauged the wind, fingers careful and deliberate.

"When was the last time you flew a kite?" I asked, eyes on the crowd swelling below us.

"Never."

My chest clenched. I turned, blinking to hide the jolt. "Never?"

"I've seen it done," he muttered, testing the air with his hand.

Guilt rippled through me. I pushed him into this—an act steeped in tradition, one that mattered to my people—and never asked if he was ready. I failed him.

"You have to toss it off the cliff." I angled my body between him and the watching crowd. "Keep the wings flat. Line it with the horizon."

I took the cord, giving him both hands to guide the launch. The updraft would do the rest.

His jaw clenched. Silence swept over the beach below, heavy and expectant. The sea wind curled around us. Kallias steadied the kite, green wings outstretched, arms firm against the pull.

He released it.

Then it dropped.

My breath lodged in my throat—then the dragon snapped upward, caught by the current. It soared past, the string whistling through my fingers until it drew tight with a sharp tug.

I passed it to Kallias. My heart thudded against my ribs.

I wanted to warn him. Tell him to mind the line, keep it level. But he didn't need me to coddle him.

He was a king.

Sunlight skimmed the kite's hide, catching every scale of painted silk. Far above, Tsunami and Naksula circled, their interest piqued by the stranger among them.

"Get ready to loose it," I said, watching the sky.

"Tell me when." He didn't question why—he trusted me.

That teased a smile from my lips. I stepped behind him and laid my hand between his shoulders. Cold chain met my skin through his mantle.

I shifted, letting the crowd see him fully.

He wasn't a threat. He was our turning point. Through our marriage, Radaan's grain would fill our stores. Our reach would stretch toward the Wild Shores. With his alliance, we'd rival the greatest nations of the world.

The kite dipped, a spark of radiance hovering above the water.

"Now."

He let go.

The display faltered, wobbling in the wind, uncertain in its freedom.

Then it exploded.

Magic burst like dragonfire—violent, radiant. Tendrils of every color erupted, warping the air in a dazzling twist. Kallias' back went rigid, the only hint he gave of surprise.

The kite remained aloft while Father's spell—channeled through Williard—thrashed like the limbs of a squid, writhing around bone and hide. Sunlight winked out behind the growing storm of power. The sky ignited. Magic solidified midair, a flare of blazing multi-color lines.

A beast of light burst forth, mouth yawning in a silent roar. Argos echoed the gesture overhead, wings flaring wide. The gale of his passage ripped at my dress, beating the illusionary beast away from the cliff's edge. The spectral dragon stirred with uncanny life, body churning, neck arcing to follow its real counterpart.

Its eyes locked on us—twin stars, searing and alive. It hovered, beating its wings once as if in approval. Then it turned skyward and streaked into the air, chasing constellations.

The crowd below gasped, a chorus of awe rising as the dragon spiraled higher, its bright tail slicing the dusk. My grin ached across my cheeks, but I leaned into Kallias, his gaze fixed on the sky, head tilted back.

The creature flared—its form blinking white—then shattered. Light burst outward, fragments streaking the heavens in a cascade of color. Cheers erupted from the beach. Kites dropped as people scrambled to reel them in, eyes turned upward to follow the glowing debris. The magical remnants joined the stars above, brighter now, drifting and spinning on unseen currents.

"It's beautiful." The words slipped from me, barely a breath.

"It pales in comparison to you," Kallias said. His voice settled deep, coaxing my gaze back to him. A flicker of a smile traced his lips, his eyes trailing across my face before settling on my mouth. His hand rested at my waist, gentle, a suggestion more than a pull.

The magic of the moment pulled us closer together. My heart pounded against my ribs. Heat gathered beneath my skin. I licked my lips, suddenly dry, and caught his eyes following the motion. His smile vanished.

What replaced it looked hungry—needy.

Butterflies surged low in my belly, urging me closer.

His gaze flicked past my shoulder. A breath snagged in his throat. The spark in his expression died, shuttered beneath a veil of restraint.

"This is the fun part." I pivoted toward Williard, bowing in thanks.

Kallias mirrored the motion and followed me down the cliffside. Laughter broke out across the sand. Lovers dashed into the streets. Older couples lingered in the tide, wrapped in peaceful embraces as they watched the sparks spiral earthward.

Mother and Father stood, waves lapping at their boots. Father's arm curled around her waist, and she leaned in, quiet and content.

I tugged Kallias toward the city.

"And what happens now, Princess?" His voice dropped low, just for me. He moved easily beside me, Greaves shadowing us the moment we hit the shore.

"You'll dismiss Greaves."

The guard arched a brow, his chin lifting, but his eyes never left Kallias. Stars shimmered in their brown depths. I wasn't his queen yet. He wouldn't take orders from me.

"Your demand insinuates you need the opposite," Greaves said, tone flat but watchful.

"This is my people's night. They are too busy to attack him."

Wind surged overhead—another dragon passing low. Kallias squeezed my hand, his elbow tucked in tight, a warning to tread carefully.

"Go. I'll return to my rooms later," he said aloud, voice casual enough to slip beneath the revelry.

Greaves drew in a long breath. His shoulders squared as he pulled himself upright. After a pause, he stepped back. "You were easier to protect before her." The edge in his words softened with a smirk.

Kallias scoffed and spun me toward the winding streets.

We ran.

Through alleys and passageways, past flushed cheeks and tangled limbs. His shoulder brushed mine at every turn, solid and close. A drifting fleck of magic caught on his mantle, clinging like a whisper that he was still a king—racing through the dark as a commoner.

Dragons swept overhead, wings stirring the warm night as we burst into the palace courtyard. We climbed the Spire steps two at a time.

"Where are we going, Nienna?" His breath came quick. He glanced back just as Gyrak and Naneki careened past, yelling as they dove after flickering sparks.

"To the landing!" I called, laughing. My hand dropped to catch his, fingers threading through his without hesitation. His callouses scraped against my skin, his palm rough and warm.

He followed. A king. Older. Wiser. Still suffering my demands, letting me lead.

A crooked smile touched his lips, cautious and fond. But his eyes kept flicking to the corners, the walls, the darkened halls.

He expected betrayal at every turn. Braced for it, even here. Tallon and Eldeiade had carved that fear into his bones.

I hated them for it.

I pulled him into a quiet corridor. Shoved him back against the wall. Kissed him.

He grunted in surprise, mantle slamming into stone. His hands caught my arms, holding me in place. His jaw locked. Whatever emotion darkened his eyes, it wasn't surrender.

My hand rose to cradle the nape of his neck, fingers sliding into his short hair. I tugged him toward me, rising onto my toes. "We're alone."

"For how long?" His words rasped against my lips, wariness flickering and vanishing in a blink.

I smiled into this kiss, teeth grazing his lower lip. His grip tightened around my arms. His hips shifted forward, brushing mine.

"How long do you need?"

A growl escaped, and he spun me around, pressing me against the wall. His mouth claimed me—nothing gentle. No restraint. Hunger devoured every movement—lips parting, tongue slick and demanding.

I melted into him with a moan as my knees gave out. He caught me, hands sliding to grip my thighs as he lifted me from the ground. His hips shoved into me, pinning me against the wall. My head fell back, eyes shut, heat racing through me in a pounding, urgent wave.

His mouth dropped to my neck. The scratch of his jaw teased my skin as he kissed and nipped along the line of my collar.

"You wouldn't need long," he groaned, fingers flexing against my thighs.

A whimper escaped. He held me steady with his legs, tapestry bunching beneath us, one hand rising toward my chest.

"Gods, Nienna, I need you." His voice cracked, dragging back to my lips with unrelenting purpose.

I took all of it. Matched it. Ground against him, chasing the friction I craved. My skin burned. Neck prickling. Nerves flared beneath my scalp.

He tore away with a broken sound. I bucked forward. Desperate. Strung tight and shaking. My pulse thudded in my ears, silencing everything except the rasp of his breathing.

"Please." One syllable. All I had. He was the only soul I'd ever beg.

"I promised your father." His fingers dug into my hips, bracing against my need. He nipped my ear, his breath hot and uneven. "I can't take you. Not yet."

With a snarl, he dropped me. My legs wobbled. Instinct reached for him, but he pressed his palm to my stomach, holding me back. His touch hovered—so close to where I needed him.

He slumped forward, forehead resting on my chest.

"Have mercy, Nienna." He gasped, voice torn. His fingers clenched the fabric of my dress. "You don't know how badly I want to toss caution aside. Take you here. Now. But I gave my word."

He straightened, lifting my chin. Something wild simmered in his gaze—starving and dangerous, barely restrained.

"We will wait."

It sparked a challenge in me. A wicked thrill. He could leash his desire in a blink. Lock it down and choose duty. But when he pressed against me, nothing existed except the heat between us.

My body ached. Still, I met the eyes of a king. Controlled, powerful, expectant.

And I wanted to be the one to break that control.

"Yes, my king." I whispered, biting my lip.

He groaned low, dragging his thumb across my mouth. I darted my tongue out, teasing. His hand dropped, brushing over his belt.

"To the landing."

I looped my arm through his. The walk up the Spire cooled the fire between us, bit by bit.

I could wait. I would. What we had didn't need to be rushed. But sometimes, I longed to erase the caution in his expression. The wariness behind his smile. Years of betrayal by his own son and Eldeiade had left scars that still bled.

He deserved better. I'd give him everything to heal that pain.

"The Spire was found like this?" he asked, pausing to gaze up the hollowed center.

"With the Cireendium? Yes." I leaned over the edge. "Draconia was never home to humans. Some creature must have lived here once. We only made it fit for man."

He hummed, pulling me upward.

At the throne room, I broke into a run out onto the landing, arms flung wide.

Specks of light drifted around us—leftovers from my father's magic. They hovered, soft and flickering, little white fireflies caught in a playful spiral.

I twirled, trying to catch them. They brushed my skin, left gleaming trails down both forearms. Kallias chuckled behind me.

The lights landed in his hair, highlighting the silver at his temples. Others dusted his mantle, scattered bright as fallen stars.

"Feels like warm snow." He cupped my cheek, then brushed a glowing fingertip along my jaw.

"He took it from the ocean. Near the Wild Shores, the sea glows with life. They say it's incredible."

"You've never seen it?"

I shook my head. "No. So Father brought it to me."

"All this—he made it? He's powerful."

I crouched. Caught a few motes in my palm, then dragged my fingers across the stone. "He's a Well. Constantly pulling magic from Argos, storing it in his body. He once held off an entire whirlstorm alone."

"A good reason to honor my promise," he muttered, eyes falling to the markings I'd traced:

Kallias and Nienna.'

"How long does the glow last?"

I heard the judgment in his voice. Laughed. "Do you want to know why the crowd was in such a hurry?"

"With all those boys dragging girls into alleys? I can guess."

"Catch more of these, and I'll show you." I ran across the landing, scooping up the radiant wisps. They melted into my palms, lighting my fingers.

I spun toward him, both palms glowing.

Wiser than I, he held up one hand, the glow faint and cool. Nothing like the sharp, divine light his god gifted him. He raised a brow, gaze flicking between my hands.

"Come." I led him into the palace, careful not to brush the walls. We slipped down a level to his rooms. At the door, he stepped ahead and pressed a bare hand to the panel.

"Do you remember when I said wait?" A twitch caught in his eye, brows pulling tight.

I grinned and nudged the door open with my shoulder. "I haven't forgotten, my king."

"The way you say that." His mutter followed me in.

Greaves hadn't returned. The rooms stood still, thick with silence, lanterns flickering amber along stone walls.

I lifted my chin. "Remove your mantle."

One brow arched, but I remembered the hesitation in his touch the night before. He wasn't ready to let me unfasten it. That time would come; I would wait.

He obeyed, fingers slipping the golden chain free. With deliberate care, he eased the yoke off and set it on the stand.

I reached for the buttons of his vest, but he caught my wrist. "How long does the light last?"

Was he worried a servant would see the glow and know someone had removed his clothes for him? Was he more concerned they would assume some other woman did, or that I was that woman?

"It fades before morning," I said.

He released my hand, and I went to work. Fingers flying, pulse pounding. This was something I'd craved, imagined sharing with the one who held my heart.

Father's magic lingered in everything it touched. I'd seen it many times through the years, glowing at the end of the festival, but this—this piece of my people and culture—always felt out of reach. As I grew, I realized my future husband would reside beyond the sea, far from this moment, far from Draconia.

Now, this belonged to us.

Kallias shrugged free of his vest, muscles flexing. His shoulders shifted, broad and tense. The guarded expression returned, hard and unreadable. Not rejection—something heavier. Something he couldn't silence.

He folded his clothes and laid them on a chair, movements slow and precise. Never careless. Even half-naked, surrounded by temptation, he wasn't rough. He took his time.

Before me, his jaw ticked. Lines cut deep between his brows. He craved this. He wanted me here. But shadows moved behind his eyes—grief, fear, restraint. None of them I could soothe.

"The lovers slip away to claim each other," I murmured, stepping closer.

He scowled, and I raised a hand to smooth the wrinkle from his forehead, fingers trailing a glowing arc along his jaw.

"They catch the magic—unbound by status—and write their names."

I stared at his chest. The silver stubble looked patchy where Kalepsi's fire had burned through. His bandage held clean, no blood seeping through.

Humming, I flattened my palm above his belt and leaned in. My finger brushed over his sternum. His muscles flinched beneath my touch.

"Hold still."

"Nienna." His voice rumbled deep, a low warning.

I drew slow loops, each curve deliberate, letters blooming in bright strokes along his skin. I signed my name across his heart—carefully, reverently. More sacred than any treaty.

'Nienna.'

It wasn't enough.

I claimed him as a woman, but also as a princess. He wasn't just a man I loved, but the one I fought for. He crossed oceans, faced dragonfire. I was so much more than Nienna.

'The Dragon's Heart.'

Perhaps I added more for my sake. But when I stepped back, heat rushed across my skin, chest constricting. My handprint glowed just above his navel, broken where it crossed the ridges of his abdomen. Over his heart, beside the scar he earned for me, shone my name. My title.

"My turn," he growled, voice thick, raw with emotion. "Turn around."

My pulse surged. I twisted, glancing back. A hand tugged my dress loose, rough and impatient. I couldn't breathe. My arms crossed tight as he fumbled.

"Withering laces," he muttered, and I laughed, breath hitching.

Cool air swept across my fevered skin, raising goosebumps. His chest touched my back, warm and bare.

"Gone by morning?" he breathed against my ear, voice barely holding.

"Yes." The word spilled out, more whimpered sigh than sound.

He kissed a line between my shoulders, each press deliberate. The dress parted wider. My upper back bared, skin flushed and trembling under the chill.

I shivered when his fingertip found me.

"Be still." His tone held no space for disobedience.

I swallowed the knot in my throat. His touch moved down, traced the dip of my spine, then slid outward. He exhaled, then gave me room to inspect his work.

I twisted, catching the mirror's reflection.

My skin burned hotter. Across the pale canvas of my back, written in glowing letters—singed into magic and flesh—was a single word.

'Mine.'

Chapter Twenty-Three

KALLIAS

The glow refused to fade. It spread instead—water sloshing against my hands, dragging streaks of iridescence into the basin. My free palm glimmered now, eerie and unnatural. I'd wiped my cheek without thinking; my jaw burned with residual light. Flecks clung to strands of my hair and dotted the hollow of my neck.

The rest belonged to Nienna.

Her name flowed across my chest, pulsing with each heartbeat. A small handprint lingered at my navel, a branded echo of intimacy. Too close. Too knowing. That mark screamed of hunger—mine—for her.

The door creaked open. I stilled. Listened.

Quiet steps. Heavy. Unhurried. No knock.

Greaves.

He passed the dressing room without pause, casting a glance before disappearing into the bedchamber for his sweep.

I dropped my gaze back to her name. Shame curled through me, flushed heat up my neck. He'd call it foolish. Reckless. What was she doing to me—this woman—to an older king who should've known restraint?

"You're lit up like a firefly," he grumbled, returning. His eyes cut over the space, scanning shadows as his hands unbuckled twin blades, setting them on the low dresser.

Then he caught my reflection in the mirror. His brow dipped. His steps slowed.

"Fallione?" I asked, deflecting.

"Out cold in the library." He stopped behind me, eyes narrowing. "Gods, Kal—did you do the same to her?"

His jaw ticked, disapproval etched deep.

He knew my promise to Nereus. I couldn't bed her. But that vow wouldn't hold if someone spotted my name written between her breasts. Thankfully, that darker animal inside me had settled for her back.

Elohios, if it had been her chest…

We would've been covered in the damning light.

"It fades before morning," I said, wiping my face. The rag dragged a smear across my nose and eyes, but at least I was clean.

"She told you that?"

"She's a princess." I kept the rag from soaking the letters above my heart. "She knows the customs."

"If someone–" He bit down on the rest. His gaze met mine in the glass. We both knew what lingered unsaid. Nereus tolerated me, but no treaty meant no shield. If I crossed too far, the man might feed me to Argos and never blink.

"How am I supposed to save you from yourself?" he muttered, turning to tear off his black tunic.

I let the cloth drop, shifting to face him. My hips rested against the dresser's edge. "Sometimes, you can't." He knew that. I'd made choices before, and I would suffer or thrive by them.

"You don't know how hard it was to watch you in that godsforsaken mockery of a trial." He folded his tunic with stiff, angry hands. "I couldn't do anything, and it's my job to keep you safe. And when you wed Nienna? What then?"

"You remain my guard." I pressed my lips together, squinting at him.

He laughed without smiling. "You'll have me here? In your rooms? I've seen how you are with her. Do not lie to me. Don't pretend you'd want anyone near when you…" He grimaced, dropping his tunic on the dresser. "When you consummate your union."

There was more to this than just that. Something deeper stirred beneath the surface, antagonizing him from within.

"You will stand guard outside the room," I said. Measured. Calm. "When it's done, you'd return to my side."

His frown deepened. "What about when she's dressing? When you're asleep? How do I protect you if I'm not there?"

There it was.

His swords hit the dresser with a loud clatter. More knives followed, metal stacking in sharp, discordant notes.

He didn't fear for my safety.

He feared being left behind.

When I married Nienna, it would force distance between us.

He'd lose me. And he knew it.

"Greaves, you are my guard. My chosen." I moved toward him, clapped a firm hand to his shoulder. "You're mine. You've seen her in a nightdress. Gods, I don't want you seeing her in less, but if it happens, it does so in the name of protection. You will watch over our rooms."

"And where would you stick me? The receiving room?" He yanked his belt free with a sharp tug, not meeting my eyes. "What if you take a guest there? How unseemly would that be, your guard's bed in the open? Or should I stand out in the hall through the night?"

"If you don't sleep when I do, when will you?" I scoffed. "You'll stay in the suite."

"And if she refuses?" he asked, his tone clipped. "You know she's not exactly fond of me."

"If I have to rip apart the Golden Palace and build you a wing, then so be it." This had his hackles up. Not even my marriage to Eldeiade had stirred him like this.

His glare slid sideways. "She needs her own protection. I can't guard you both."

"I'll appoint her a Thresher."

He snorted. "She'll be thrilled."

"As thrilled as she is with kahve." I grinned.

That cracked his edge. His shoulders lowered, and he brushed my hand away, stomping toward the bedchamber. His cot sat at the foot of my bed. He slipped a dagger beneath his pillow, then jabbed a finger at me.

"I choose her guard."

"I would trust no one else."

He gave a grunt and dropped to the cot. My brow pulled into a frown. He was older than me, made no complaints, never asked for more. But he shouldn't sleep on stone-stiff bedding after years at my side. His body deserved better.

Groaning as my back slowly relaxed, the tight muscles releasing the strain of the day, I closed my eyes.

He was right. I didn't want him in the room—not with Nienna. The idea of sharing a bed with a woman still felt foreign. If she even wanted that. My jaw clenched, and I pressed my fingers to the bridge of my nose. She wasn't Eldeiade. She craved closeness, not distance.

Which meant things would happen.

The thought raked fire across my skin. I pushed it down. Then shoved harder when more images tried to claw their way forward. No, I wouldn't want Greaves there. But he had to be near. The receiving room was too exposed. He was right. It wasn't an appropriate place for him.

Fallione would have a plan. He always did.

If I was to face a future in Radaan, I'd need both Nienna and Greaves at my side.

Bang!

I rolled before my mind caught up. Cold steel bit into my palm as I hit the floor. Dagger gripped tight, I braced against the mattress just as Greaves burst through the doorway.

A sharp grunt had me vaulting over the bed and toward the attacker.

"Call off your dog," Ronan choked.

Greaves held him in the half-light, blade bare against his throat. His arm locked around the prince's chest, and though he looked reluctant, he let go as soon as the prince spoke.

He was only a guard.

"Knock next time," I snapped, pushing hair from my face. He knew better. Greaves nearly carved him open.

"I came to fetch you—a courtesy. This is how I'm thanked?" He dusted off his riding leathers, smirking. Gods, did he ever wear anything else?

"Who sent for me?" I growled, breath short and sharp. My heart still hammered from the chaos. I sucked in air, forced my lungs to slow, reminding my body I was not, in fact, dying.

"I did."

My gaze shot past Ronan as a shape pulled free from the dark.

Nereus.

White hair stark against bronze skin. His eyes dragged down my bare torso, pausing low. His expression soured, upper lip curling in disgust as he locked onto the faint handprint glowing on my stomach.

Elohios, guide me.

"Ronan. Hall." The king's voice cracked like dry wood, rough and dangerous. His hand rested on the silver pommel at his hip, knuckles bone-white.

Greaves moved in beside me, close and coiled. My pulse drummed in my ears, but I squared my shoulders, lifted my chin.

Ronan's expression froze, disbelief flickering behind his eyes as his gaze dropped to my chest. He gave a low whistle, dragged a hand through his hair, then turned and walked out, leaving me with the father of the girl whose name glowed across my skin.

"Have you broken yet another oath, Kallias Sunspear?" Nereus' glare burned through me, tone cracked at the edge like ice under strain.

"If I bedded your daughter, I would have far more handprints on me."

Anger melded with guilt, swelling inside me. Was there no privacy in this palace? He woke me in the dead of night, and stood fully clothed in dark leather while I wore naught but my underbreeches.

He bared his teeth in response, and I turned toward the dressing room. I wouldn't give him the satisfaction of flinching from this power play. If he had something to say, he could do so while I dressed.

"What's so urgent it couldn't wait for morning?" I asked, tossing the dagger aside and dragging a white tunic over my head. The script on my chest dulled beneath the cloth.

Greaves moved fast, tugging on his own clothes, a blade always within reach.

"I came out of courtesy. Respect that." Nereus loomed in the doorway like a storm held together by bone and rage. "Dress for a walk. But one you may not survive."

I barked a dry laugh, stepping into my trousers. "Threatening me now?"

"I don't threaten. I act."

Gods, this man. Every word is ominous, every look a challenge. I knew his reputation—passionate, rigid, quick to wrath, but fair. I'd heard it all when I agreed to align Radaan with Draconia.

Meeting him? Different story.

That was my fault, though.

Perhaps he would have been more receptive if I'd started off with honesty—not letting his daughter be dragged back home in tatters.

"He will go alone."

Nereus' focus never left me, but he directed the words at Greaves. My guard paused with his sheath halfway to his belt. His eyes cut to mine.

"Another trial?" I asked, sliding a dark green vest over my tunic.

"Perhaps."

Gods, the withering man made riddles sound like death sentences, scorched and vague. My gaze flicked to my mantle as I passed it, heart clenching. This wasn't about me as a ruler, but as a man. If my life were truly in danger, he would've struck already. And he hadn't.

That he restrained himself even after seeing Nienna's marks on my body assured me he wouldn't call for my head.

At least not tonight.

Nereus waited by the doors, and after I shoved my boots on, he left without another word. Greaves stayed behind, and as I followed the king into the quiet halls, Ronan slid into position, falling into step at our backs.

I kept pace with Nienna's father, side by side as we ascended the spiraling path around the Cireendium. Light flickered in its sconces, so dim it cast more shadow than flame. Moonlight did more.

Our footsteps whispered through the silence. No voices. No other sound.

We passed corridor after corridor—throne room, the landing, the heart of the palace. Each one we left behind wound the tension tighter. My bones grew heavy with it.

The path ended in a dead hush. One door stood ahead.

Just as Nereus opened it, Ronan snapped his fingers. A ball of flame zipped past, illuminating a sharp incline.

My jaw locked as my teeth ground together. Worry skated across my nerves. I hated being kept in the dark, unprepared.

The creak of their leather joined our footsteps. No one spoke. The stairs wound forever, and at the top, the space narrowed to a cramped landing with a single door. From the low snarl just on the other side, I knew.

The Nest.

"I don't do this for you," Nereus said, pinching the bridge of his nose. Frustration carved lines deep into his face. "But for her."

"We won't mourn your loss," Ronan quipped.

His father shot him a glare, then opened the door.

Wind slammed into me. A furious roar followed, rattling in my chest. Bones littered the moonlit stone, fragments of shell scattered like shattered armor. Piles of debris filled the space—chewed, broken, old.

A predator's den.

Nereus clapped a hand to my shoulder as I crossed the threshold, then shut the door behind me, sealing me in.

Pale light danced across golden horns as the beast lifted her head, showing her fangs. She sat just a stone's throw away, but I knew her. I recognized the violet scales and the fury in her eyes. The same dragon who'd tried to char me during the trial.

She remembered. And something told me she regretted not devouring me then.

Argos loomed at the edge of the Nest, a mountain of black shadow. His claws sank into the stone. He didn't move. Didn't growl. Just watched, pupils narrowed.

But it was the figure at the dragon's feet that held me.

Nienna.

She sat wrapped in a dark blue shawl, a thin laced nightdress beneath. Her expression froze when she saw me. She scrambled to stand as the beast above her lowered its head, sparks shedding from its jaws.

I flexed my fingers. No sword. No shield. Not even a stick.

Nienna whispered to it, one hand stroking its rigid jaw. The dragon snorted, baring her fangs, then tucked them away. She turned, coiling around a cluster of eggs—massive, rough-shelled, and still.

What monsters would claw out of those?

Nienna grinned and tip-toed through the cracked bones, her pale feet bare. I scoffed at her recklessness, scanning the sharp debris. The floor was jagged, scattered with broken remains—femurs thicker than my arm, splintered in two. Shells as wide as shields littered the black rock.

"Why—how are you here?" she asked, breathless, voice low. She clutched her shawl tight across her chest.

Gods, that dragon studied me as if I were a snack. "Your father dropped me off and wished for the best."

She beamed, all affection and relief. "He brought you to me." Her posture eased as she stepped beside me, leaning into my side. "They're close to hatching. She won't let anyone else in."

"Not even your father?" I asked, flicking a glance toward Argos still crouched at the ledge, keeping his distance.

"Not even the king."

"Yet she allows you to sit at her feet?"

"She sees me as her wingless babe," she said, resting her head on my shoulder. "I'm always welcome."

"And I am... tonight's appetizer?"

She laughed, fingers curling around my arm. "She'll tolerate you because I ask. But this is as far as I'll risk you." Her voice softened. "Dragons are volatile when their young hatch. Vulnerable. And dangerous. Kalepsi doesn't have a rider, so she's bound to kill anything that moves. Man or dragon."

"Hence the distance from her mate?"

"She only tolerates him because of his size," she said, grinning. "Otherwise, she'd chase him off, too."

"Compassionate creatures," I muttered.

For sentient beings, Nienna was right. Without riders, they acted on instinct. Brilliant minds, no temperance. No mercy.

I frowned, pulling her closer. "And the Wild Shores? No riders there."

She nodded, gaze fixed on Kalepsi as the dragon released a croon—low, guttural, and deep enough to vibrate the floor beneath our feet. Loose pebbles rattled.

Perhaps that was why the dragons didn't stay. They would have to fight for territory there. Those dragons—feral, cunning, without empathy—wouldn't reason or listen. Not like the ones here.

We waited, lost in our thoughts, as the sun began to rise.

In Radaan, the sunsets were a thing of beauty. Watching the sun dip below the golden fields after a long day of work—it was beautiful and inspiring. But here, in Draconia, it was the sunrises that brought the world to its knees.

We stayed curled together, my back against cold stone, Nienna tucked in my lap. Her cheek pressed to my chest, my chin on her golden hair. The scent of waterlilies clung to her skin. Lace brushed my thumb as I held her waist.

Our words were soft. Fragments of a conversation between lovers, drifting like smoke. No titles. No weight. Just her. Just me.

Then–

A crack.

Nienna bolted upright with a gasp, her elbow digging into my ribs. Her shawl slipped, falling from her shoulders and baring her back.

Gone was my claim against her skin.

She belonged to the dragons now.

I chuckled, nudging her off. "Go on. See your dragons."

She needed no further encouragement. With a grateful smile, she launched from my lap and darted through the graveyard of a nest. I flinched when she stumbled, heart seizing. One misstep and she'd be skewered on those ivory spikes—but this was her world.

Kalepsi lowered her snout, nostrils flaring as she sniffed the eggs. Her pupils flared, then constricted to slits. When Nienna leaned against a claw thick as her torso, the great dragon let out a soft croon.

A pale egg cracked. A jagged line split the shell, and a muffled squeal tore through the lair. The thing inside thrashed, venting its fury. I drew a knee up, leaning forward, watching.

The top burst open. A smoky blue head pushed through, blinking eyes gleaming like wet river rock. Slitted pupils narrowed as it studied the world, then it ducked back into the shell.

I smiled at its retreat.

The egg exploded. Fragments flew, rattling across the stone. The creature surged out, hissing as it shook off the confines of its prison. It wasn't afraid—it was *enraged*.

Slick wings sagged under their own weight. It staggered, crumpling sideways. Kalepsi answered with a gentle warble, the tone coaxing. The hatchling blinked up at her.

Then it turned and locked eyes with Nienna.

My smile faded.

It bared tiny teeth and snapped. I tensed, palm flat on my thigh, resisting the urge to yank her back. Her voice drifted through the air, soft and steady. She didn't flinch. It cocked its head, predator-like. Her lips curled into a quiet grin as she murmured something I couldn't hear.

Clumsily, it rose. Wings tucked tight, it stood, swaying on legs too new to trust.

It struck.

Its muzzle slammed into her palm—teeth closed harmlessly.

Her laughter rang out, clear and sweet, and relief dropped from my chest like a stone. The little beast, slick with egg and trembling with life, stumbled into her. Kalepsi hissed, batting it aside with a casual flick. It tumbled, huffed, then settled its head on Nienna's lap.

Pride hit me so hard I had to exhale. Dragons adored her. She could have ruled an empire with them and still, she chose to love me. This was her palace, surrounded by beasts and bone, danger and fire. She belonged in the heart of it.

Eggs split, one by one, like oversized chicks clawing into daylight. Only, these chicks could swallow a man whole.

I remained by the wall, spine stiff, as the hatchlings clawed free beneath Kalepsi's vigilant stare. Argos never moved. Whenever I shifted to ease the ache in my back, she hissed as if I'd threatened her clutch.

Even after the last egg cracked, Nienna stayed among them. The firstborn blue clutched her shawl in its teeth, snarling as siblings fought over the torn fabric. They stalked among the bone-pile, sniffing for movement.

Restless.

Argos rose and leapt from the Spire's ledge.

One of the red hatchlings, hide the color of dried blood, nosed at Nienna's dress and nipped the hem.

"No." She batted it away with her finger pointed to its snout, voice firm.

Kalepsi backed the command with a hiss, teeth bared behind Nienna. The redling flinched, twisting to growl at its siblings instead.

Moments later, Argos returned, clutching a thrashing shark in his jaws. The sea-beast dangled like a toy. Compared to the dragon, it barely counted as a meal. Still, it would feed the hatchlings.

Argos landed near the Nest's edge, posture cautious, scarlet dripping from his fangs.

Kalepsi's lip curled in warning, then she returned her attention back to her young.

Apparently, that was permission.

He stepped forward, and a single drop of blood splattered against a dragonling's paw. It stared, transfixed by the crimson spot. Nose twitching, it flicked out its tongue to taste it.

Chaos erupted.

Screeching, the small beast launched upward, wings flapping, and latched onto the shark's tail. Argos released the carcass. The hatchlings shrieked, lunged, and swarmed the prize. Limbs tangled, claws flashed, teeth tore into flesh.

Nienna didn't blink when a chunk of flesh hit her face and smeared crimson across her cheek and down the front of her dress.

My stomach twisted as a gold dragonling bolted for her.

Kalepsi's paw intercepted it, knocking the beast aside before it collided with her.

And Tallon thought he could scare Nienna by feeding some dogs.

In mere moments, only scraps remained. They fought over those too, dragging splintered pieces to the Nest's sunlit edge. There, they sprawled to dry, wings spread like stained silk, bones clutched between their claws.

Nienna approached, her smile sheepish. Dried gore crusted her skin and hair. Her white lace dress bore rust-colored smears. It chafed at my soul to see her covered in blood. I'd seen too much of it on the battlefield—my mind screamed she was hurt.

"And Tallon thought he could scare you." I rose and stretched, working the tightness from my back.

"I assure you, this is normal," she blurted. "It's how they figure out the pecking order."

"Like chickens."

Her jaw dropped, and laughter erupted from her throat. "I'd hardly compare them to domesticated hens." She gasped, eyes bright, breath stolen. "Let me rephrase—they are establishing their hierarchy."

"Spoken as a true princess." I drew her in, and she bit her lip, leaning into my side.

Argos crept toward Kalepsi. She snarled and snapped, sending him to retreat. With a groan, he slunk away, tail dragging.

"He'll feed her," she said, tone filled with contentment. "Then the hatchlings will fly. And the Awakening will end."

"A three-day festival." My thumb traced her bare shoulder. Warm. Whole. Her smooth skin assured me she was well, despite being covered in gore.

"We time them well." She glanced up. "We've done this for centuries."

I nodded. "Then negotiations will begin. Radaan needs a queen."

When her gaze found mine, color bloomed on her cheeks.

Her hand pressed to my stomach, light as breath. "Then she shall have one."

Chapter Twenty-Four

NIENNA

Freya and Edith worked on me for hours. My nerves had frayed well before I stepped into the hall the next day.

The silver tiara nestled into an intricate web of braids, each twist tight and deliberate. They cascaded down my back like the creeping vines through Radaan's halls. My gown shifted from pale blue at the collar to midnight at the hem, a dusky gradient shimmering beneath the lights. Pearls clustered along my shoulders and poured down the center of my chest, flaring wide across my hips.

My black boots made no sound on the stone as I descended to the council chamber. My heartbeat lodged in my throat. I looked the part of a queen, but I felt like a schoolgirl trembling before a boy.

Father wasted no time. When the Draconis returned to work, so did he. I bit the inside of my cheek. I had listened through every negotiation during my engagement with Tallon, but this was different. The man I would marry would meet my eyes from across the table. I would see him—not just his name scrawled on parchment.

My family waited in a narrow corridor outside the council door, and my anxiety surged. This was finally happening. A renegotiation between Draconia and Radaan—a feat I never imagined possible.

Father's expression was drawn, his mouth pressed into a tight frown. He grasped my arms, sliding his hands down to grip mine while searching my face.

"I need to know you want this." His voice strained, ragged with something deeper than worry.

I'd wounded him before with my actions. And now I asked him to give me away *again*.

"My heart belongs to him." My words barely reached the air. I clutched his fingers, my throat constricting. In that room, I wasn't only his daughter—I was a symbol. A bargaining piece.

A queen in waiting.

"Then so be it."

With a sigh, he looped my arm through his. Past Mother and Ronan, we strode forward. The door groaned open, and we stepped into the chamber with our chins held high. Draconis—proud and indomitable.

Kallias rose from his seat, Fallione rising to his right. Greaves hovered near the wall, shadows etching his features. Scribes lined the walls, quills hovering over parchment. Haldor and Zane flanked the entrance, quiet sentinels. There were no formal advisors. Mother, Father always said, was our voice of reason, our wisdom.

Kallias wore his signature green, but the leaf embroidery stitched along his coat was a shade of damp bark. He dipped into a bow, the chains of his mantle brushing the edge of the massive table.

The oak slab commanded the space, broad and scarred, dominating the hard room. The walls bristled with swords and established treaties on display like our kingdom's trophies.

"Welcome, King Kallias Sunspear of Radaan," Father intoned. He led me to my seat—the one time I would sit at his left, with Ronan to my right.

"Thank you for hearing my case, Nereus Draconis, Dragon King of Draconia," he said, laying the title down like an olive branch.

My head swam. No matter what training Mother had drilled into me, Kallias' calm held a note of confidence born of countless verbal battles of wit and word.

"What do you seek in my halls?" Father asked as we all settled. Quills scraped paper, the sound brittle in the vaulted silence.

Though we had an audience, this was private. Here, we preferred quiet meetings—honesty found easier footing in smaller spaces than in the pomp of the throne room.

"I ask for the hand of Nienna, the Dragon's Heart, in marriage."

"To whom?"

A tedious formality, but neither man skipped it.

"*I* ask for her hand," Kallias repeated, expression unchanged. Calm and deliberate, one palm rested flat on the table, emerald ring glinting beside a gold signet, while the other disappeared beneath the edge.

Father leaned back, not in dismissal but with the first breath of casual ease, of informality.

"She was given to your son, pledged as a seal between our lands—a promise. That treaty is broken. Now you ask for her hand yourself. I ask, then, that your grain tithe rise by five percent."

"Done."

I blinked and held still, though my gaze drifted to Kallias. Five percent more in grain alone was a steep demand. And judging by the way Fallione's brow tightened, he hadn't advised it.

But Kallias wasn't bluffing. To him, this was no game.

His eyes—clear, bright, the color of a summer sky—met mine, and he blinked once, masking that familiar twitch. He would pay whatever the price. He would leave with me, no matter the cost.

I stayed silent while the conversation circled. Father demanded. Kallias agreed. Only when Fallione raised a hand did he push back. Grain, wool, timber, stone—it all blurred. Numbers and percentages poured out like water I couldn't hold.

Mother joined the fray when Fallione pressed too hard, and both kings settled in, allowing their advisors to sharpen the edges of each clause.

Would it end today? Could it? Would I walk from this table engaged? Would my parents allow a quick wedding, or stretch it into a drawn-out spectacle draped in lace and wine?

"You must guarantee an heir."

Father's words cleaved through the din. Kallias' eye twitched, and pressed his lips together, buying himself time.

An heir?

I glanced toward Mother. Her frown had deepened, and a thin line pinched between her brows. She wasn't posturing. She meant it.

Kallias inhaled and answered, his tone even and measured. "Can the gods guarantee a seed will take root?" His voice remained steady, but I saw that second blink. He hated the question. "I cannot speak for the gods."

"Draconia seeks a lasting bond," Mother said, tone cool and slicing, her attention shifting from me to Kallias. "One secured by blood. Nienna's marriage to you jeopardizes Radaan's line. If she married your son, her child would inherit the throne. Stability for generations."

A muscle jumped in his cheek. "You want me to remove Tallon from succession?"

Fallione's face flushed red as he raised a hand, but Father silenced him with a glance.

"I'm not telling you how to handle a son who disrespected my daughter. Though I'd hoped you'd taught him better," Father said. "Give her a future, a child with a claim to Radaan."

"As a man, I swear to do my duty by her." His fingers flexed on the table as if he hated saying the words.

"Too old to get it up?" Ronan tossed the comment like a stone.

My mouth dropped. Mother twitched. Father's stare sharpened. Steel locked on Kallias.

I wanted to sink into the floor, vanish into the floor. This wasn't just a conversation, it was legacy. Bloodlines. Empires. And Ronan had turned it into a tavern joke.

But Kallias didn't flinch. His eyes held steady, locked on Father's. The air thickened with tension, and still he didn't waver.

"I cannot swear to things not yet known," he said at last, and Mother's breath hissed sharp. "But Tallon will never wear Radaan's mantle." His gaze found mine again. "He will never be king."

My chest tightened, and my fingers dug into my skirt. That was no idle promise. He was carving a future with me at the center, even if it meant casting his son aside.

Father rubbed the bridge of his nose, elbow braced on the table's edge. "And who, then, inherits your throne?"

"Nienna." Kallias leaned into the chair's curve, the tension slipping from his shoulders. "She will stand beside me. Queen in title and in power. I am older. Likely to die before her. If no heir is born, she shall rule and choose her next mate."

Fallione's face drained of color.

My breath hitched. Not because of the idea of Kallias dying, or remarrying after him. But because he was offering everything. In death, Radaan would pass into Draconis hands.

Unheard of.

Father studied him, squinting. Waiting. Surely a clause would follow. A safeguard. A condition.

None came.

It was reckless. If I married him, and my father ordered a dragon to end his life, we would own his kingdom. Just like that.

Why was he willing to gamble everything—his kingdom, his legacy—for me?

"Let us sleep on this. Prepare for dinner. Nobles will no doubt pester you." Father dismissed him with a wave. "You stay," he added when I shifted to rise.

I pressed my lips together and stayed put. Kallias hesitated, the crease between his brows deepening. He rose, followed by Greaves and Fallione, both silent as they filed out.

Father waved again. "The rest of you, leave."

Scribes shuffled behind riders, doors thudding shut, leaving my family.

"Did he just offer us Radaan?" Father groaned, dragging a hand down his face.

"Only in the event of his death," I replied.

"He's twice your age. He'll die long before you," Ronan muttered with a scoff.

"Silence," Mother snapped. Her slender finger tapped her bottom lip. "He avoided the question about the heir. He doesn't believe he can sire a babe."

My brother leaned back, eyes sharp and teasing. He smirked at me, goading, daring me to deny it. But this wasn't just mockery. He'd called Tallon a bastard before. A slip, maybe. Or something more.

"Old or not, he's well within his prime to–" Father winced, glancing at me. "From what I saw in his memories, that's not in question."

Ronan scrunched his nose in disgust. "You saw them? Like *saw* them?"

Mother sighed, brushing her hair over one shoulder. "The man is a fool."

Her words stung. I valued her opinion more than most, and she thought him foolish, a lovesick boy handing over everything for a girl. But I knew him better than that.

"He's not a simpleton," Father said, watching me closely. "There's a reason he made that offer. Nienna, tell him I'll meet him in my study after dinner."

I dipped my head and rose. They would speak of me once I left—I was certain—but I needed to see him.

My boots clicked through the halls, and I kept my expression carefully neutral as servants glanced my way. Smiles hovered on their lips, eyes curious, searching for signs. They wanted to know if this meant security. Would we feast again with Radaan's backing or go without, cut off from both Radaan and Innaku?

I rapped lightly on the door to Kallias' quarters.

Greaves opened it with his usual discipline, but surprise flickered in his eyes before his mask returned. Inside, I spotted Fallione with his head cradled in his hands. Kallias stood nearby, one hand braced on the table, the other buried in his hair.

When he noticed me, his face twisted in something between relief and resignation. "Everyone out."

His advisor rose, cleared his throat, and bowed before exiting. Greaves followed, footsteps clipped and reluctant.

"What was that?" I asked, narrowing my gaze. He looked like a creature too long in a cage.

Kallias exhaled and winced as he raked his fingers through his hair. He pulled out a chair and gestured. "Sit."

"And if I want to stand?"

"Sit," he repeated, flat as iron.

I took the seat across from him. He leaned forward, elbows braced against the table's surface, fist pressed to his lips, gaze distant.

"You offered Draconia your entire kingdom."

My voice stayed even, though his eyes told me he was still caught in a storm he couldn't navigate.

His nostrils flared as he turned to me. "Because I had no other choice."

"You have Tallon–"

"I burned that bridge," he interrupted. "For you, I gave him up."

I recoiled as if he slapped me.

"No need to feign offense," he said. "It wasn't a difficult decision. The boy makes my blood boil. He's impulsive. Cold. Cruel when he thinks no one's watching. The beast would make a terrible ruler. You are the wiser choice."

He looked away, eyes landing on a mounted fish along the wall. "But more than that—I have my reservations concerning his legitimacy."

His throat bobbed in a thick swallow, but he remained silent, letting that sit with me.

"I heard you call him a bastard," I murmured. "Scythe and I... we listened in. Through the passages."

His frown eased a fraction, and he huffed out a breath. "What else did you hear?"

My expression tugged into a coy grin. "Nothing important."

His hands returned to his temples, circling as if to scrub the thought away. "My concern isn't the throne. Not even the scandal of illegitimacy. I tried for months, *years*, to sire a child." His teeth bared in a tight grimace. "My doubt is that I can produce an heir."

Surprise flooded me. I never once considered that. If Tallon wasn't his, and if he'd tried that long with his late wife ..

Was it her?

Or him?

His jaw clenched as he studied my reaction. "I should have told you. But in Radaan, I assumed you'd marry Tallon. It wouldn't have mattered. And once I left for Draconia, all I thought of was you. Not future babes."

"It does not change anything, Kallias." I reached for his arm, grounding him. "It doesn't matter to me."

"Consider it, Nienna. You're young. I'm twice your age. If I die before you, you'll desire companionship, maybe even children. And think of your people. Draconia will want an heir out of you, not just Ronan. I can't give you that."

He dragged a hand over his face, eyes hollowed out with guilt. "I should've thought it through. I can't promise you a child." His gaze met mine, steady and grave. "Do you still want this?"

I blinked, rage warming my chest, but it wasn't for him. The weight on his shoulders spoke of shame, not indifference. This was not about me at all. This was about *her*—the wife who came before me.

I stood and reached for his chair. When I couldn't move it, he frowned and helped turn it. I straddled his lap and settled close.

His hands gripped my hips. Not possessive, just needing contact. Hunger flickered in his gaze, shadowed by pain.

My fingers threaded into his hair, brushing the strands back. "I want you. I've *only* ever wanted you. If we aren't blessed with a child, then we'll shape another legacy. We are not defined by bloodlines."

"I feel less of a man," he whispered. His eyes closed. "As if I am not worthy of you."

I cupped his face, thumb resting at his temple. He leaned into the touch with a soft, yielding motion.

"You crossed the sea. Braved dragons. Risked everything—for *me*. And you believe you're unworthy?"

"No one deserves you," he murmured, lips brushing my palm. "You are dragonfire and sunlight. A queen waiting to rise."

"And you are my king—tempered steel and searing heat. Exactly what I need. What I want. I will have no other."

I bent to place my lips on his, sealing that promise with a kiss.

Chapter Twenty-Five

NIENNA

Father allowed Kallias to sit beside me at the dining table. Thick bread soaked in soup filled the air with a savory promise—a fraction of what Radaan might offer Draconia through our union. The meal ended too soon. I watched my father and brother disappear with Kallias, the urge to follow tugging at me.

But some matters belonged to men alone. They'd press him about heirs, testing the waters I wasn't sure he was ready to wade.

To the world, Tallon stood as his son—next in line should Kallias fall. But an illegitimate heir held no real claim.

Mine would.

I excused myself and walked toward the kitchens, tremulous thoughts fraying at the edges. Did I even want a child? I was a princess—boiled down to a womb. That was my value. Through my children, alliances would be solidified and Draconia and Radaan would have a peace bound by blood.

Kings sired heirs. That was their duty. My parents were considered unlucky, with only two children and just one male. Other kingdoms birthed many, insurance against plague, war, or misfortune.

If I failed to produce an heir, would Radaan see me as broken? A curse? They believed Tallon was a trueborn son. And after Veridis—after I claimed her at the Celebration of Life?

I could find joy in Kallias. I needed no one else. But would that be enough for them?

The kitchen door groaned as I stepped inside. Steam licked my face. The scent of fish, roasted herbs, and baked grain lingered in the air, warm and earthy. Staff moved in a tide of clinks and soft chatter, nodding as they swept past, hands full of plates.

Gertrude's smile bloomed the moment she saw me. Her hair, pinned into a tight bun, had loosened wisps glowing silver in the light.

"Nienna! Princess, what brings you here?" she gasped, dropping into a low bow. Master of the Spire's meals, and longtime smuggler of pastries.

"I need bean tea."

Her brow puckered. She blinked twice, tilted her head, confused. "Bean tea?"

A nervous laugh escaped. I laced my fingers to stop from hugging my arms. "Yes. A tea made from beans. Do you know it?"

"I have beans, your highness, but I've never steeped them." She pursed her lips in thought and tapped a finger along her chin.

"They're from Radaan." I lowered my voice, insecure by my request. Perhaps it was exclusive to their kingdom, and I was a fool for asking.

Recognition lit her face. She beckoned me to follow. "I've got Radaanian black beans—fresh off the ship yesterday! Never thought of them for tea, but if you're sure..."

We moved between rows of heavy tables and stacks of pots. The area was clean and organized, but packed. With what little space we had, every inch of the Spire had been claimed.

"Yes, though the beans are removed before serving," I said. Truthfully, I had no idea what made it work, only that it eased something in Kallias I couldn't reach with words. I feared the burden of these negotiations was weighing far heavier on him than he'd admit.

"Sit, I'll make it!" She pulled out a chair near a wall where the heat thinned and voices quieted.

I sank into it, breath slowing as Gertrude vanished into the pantry. Around me, the kitchen kept moving. Two girls laughed near a sink. One yelped, then slapped her friend with a wet, limp fish.

A smile pulled at my mouth.

They bickered, teasing over chores and whispered gossip. My chest tightened. Scythe would've joined me here, settled across from me, offered silence or sarcasm. I still had Freya and planned to ask for her and Edith to attend me in Radaan. I wouldn't face it alone. And this time, I'd bring riders. My people. A tether back to who I was.

"Here, drink this while you wait." Gertrude handed me a small teacup filled with familiar green liquid, then bustled away with a rattling mug in her grip.

Mint cooled my throat. Salty water clung to the roof of my mouth. Travelers Tea—brisk and briny—dragged me back to the memory of my brother teasing me. He claimed it was only for riders after a hard flight. Father had scolded him, then passed me his cup. The first time I had it, I nearly gagged. But I smiled through it, determined to show Ronan up. After that, I drank it whenever I could.

Now, it tasted like home. Harsh and grounding. One of the many things I'd miss.

Across the kitchen, Gertrude hummed, bent over a steaming pot. She stirred, cringing at the scent. Her nose wrinkled. She gave the concoction another sniff, then glanced at me with unease.

"This is common there?" she asked, poking the contents again.

"It's a luxury," I said.

She tied her stained apron over a faded gray dress. Frowning, she muttered under her breath as she adjusted the knot.

I sipped my tea and let my thoughts slip toward Kallias. Father was likely prying for answers. Ronan probably couldn't help himself—twisting the topic with some tasteless joke. The conversation about heirs should have ended once Kallias explained I would rule Radaan and my child would follow. Even if it wasn't his.

One generation. That's all it would take to seize his kingdom, break the reign of farmer kings, and root dragons in their soil. My dragons.

Abyss, he was going to die before me.

The thought knocked the air from my lungs. I stared at the empty cup in my hands. He was twice my age. I knew this. But love makes a fool of time. Unless I died in the unlikely event of childbirth, I'd bury him one day.

Life was brutal. It made no room for lovers who found each other too late.

"I fear there's something wrong."

I wiped the grief from my face. Gertrude stood in front of me, holding a cup with both hands. She swirled the contents, her frown etched deep.

"I assure you, it's a simple tea," I said, though I wasn't entirely certain. When Kallias first offered it, there were no spices. No honey or citrus. Just dark, acrid liquid reminiscent of ash and soil.

She placed the cup in front of me with care. I leaned over, studying the black surface. Thick and opaque.

"The color looks right," I told her. I took a sniff and flinched. It wasn't acidic. More musky, with something damp clinging beneath it. Maybe the sea voyage spoiled it. I swallowed down the revulsion, curled my fingers around the warmth, and stood.

"Will you be testing it?" she asked. Worry pinched her face as her eyes locked on the cup as if it were a snake ready to strike.

"It's an acquired taste, and not one I have. Thank you!"

The heat soaked into my palms. I lingered in the hallway, taking a slow path toward Father's study. Ronan's presence in that room still baffled me. He had no filter. No place in delicate talks.

If I caught sight of his blond head, I might toss the tea in his face.

Luck favored him.

As I turned the corner, Kallias stepped out, alone. Shadows deepened to the lines around his mouth. Fatigue dulled his posture. But when he saw me, his eyes lifted, and a strained smile cracked through the weariness.

"How did it go?" I asked, just as Greaves closed the study door behind him, sealing my family inside.

"As well as could be expected." His gaze flicked to the cup in my hand.

I held it out. "You looked like you needed a drink."

His fingers brushed mine as he accepted it. He glanced into the murky depths, nodding once. "Thank you." He raised it to sip.

He froze, holding the hot liquid in his mouth, eyes flying wide.

"What is it?" Panic rushed through me. "The cook prepared them just like tea. Was there a special way to prepare them?"

His gaze darted to the glass at his lips as if he was contemplating spitting the drink back into the cup.

How awful was it that a king would spit it out?!

"Kal?" Greaves stepped up, brows drawn.

Kallias lowered the mug and swallowed hard. His throat worked against the effort, jaw tight, as he turned and glared at the drink.

"What *is* this?" he rasped. "Are you sure this was tea?"

"It's bean tea. What did you call it? Kahve?"

He gave a stunned, breathless laugh. "This isn't kahve. This is... exactly what I'd expect from something called *bean tea*."

"The beans came off your ship!"

"And I deeply regret not bringing kahve beans myself." He chuckled, lifting the cup and swirling it. "You tried this?"

"I never enjoyed it."

"You wouldn't enjoy *this*."

He handed the mug to Greaves, who accepted it with a look of pure dread. He scanned the hallway, desperate for a place to abandon it.

"Your father agreed to the terms today," Kallias said, extending his arm. "Shall I walk you to your rooms?"

"Or yours." I slid my hand into the crook of his arm as he turned us down the corridor. "Will negotiations continue tomorrow?"

"For a few more days, I expect."

I frowned. "You're surrendering to every request."

"You are worth everything I've offered," he said with a hum. "But these things take time. We can have all taxes and details mapped out, but each must be discussed, dissected. And there are matters I haven't yet raised with Nereus."

"Such as?"

"When the dragons arrive in Radaan, they'll be stationed in the Craggs. But—will any of the five be female? Am I risking dragonlings in my mountains?"

I pursed my lips. Father could easily keep the females in Draconia. Kalepsi, Naneki, and Naksula could remain on the island without issue. "Do you *want* dragonlings in Radaan? There's no guarantee they'll lay elsewhere. Though the Andeluith is tall enough, they might be tempted."

"I'm neither opposed nor inclined." He shrugged, and the chains on his mantle clinked together. "But if they're born in my realm, I'd be expected to claim them."

I winced, teeth flashing as we stepped into his rooms. "Best not let anyone else hear you say that."

"It's a fair claim, is it not?"

"It is, but with that logic, Father will keep all the females here. We won't offer any other kingdom dragons unless they can be under the protection and leadership of a Draconis ruler."

"Small details," he sighed, rubbing the side of his neck as he unclasped the chains of his mantle. "All of it must be negotiated."

Greaves passed me, sweeping through each space before he began to disarm himself.

"Mother spoke to me about the wedding." I followed Kallias into his dressing room, where Greaves helped him remove the yoke from his shoulders. "It'll be in true Draconis fashion."

"And are you willing to also endure a Radaanian wedding?" His voice was weary, as if the idea already exhausted him.

"For you? Anything."

His guard grunted, then cleared his throat, placing the mantle on its stand and backed away, like love was a catching thing.

"And you, Greaves?" I asked, folding my arms and eyeing him. "You'll put up with me?"

He leveled a glare at me, jaw tight. "I've survived one wife. I can stomach another."

Kallias flinched, shooting him a warning look.

"I am not Eldeiade," I said, low and sharp. The two might be friends, but he could show some respect.

"Hence why he's bedding you." Greaves untucked his tunic and pointed at his king. "I'll return in an hour."

"Noted."

I looked between them. Kallias made no comment against the jab.

"An hour alone?" I asked after the guard disappeared through the door.

"Which is why he reminded me." Kallias sighed as he pulled off his tunic. "He doesn't eat during the day unless we're without company. This is his moment to escape us both—and fill his belly."

He unbuckled his belt, letting it hang free. I stepped forward, ran my hands along his chest, fingers ghosting over the bandage.

"Seems to be healing." My thumb brushed the linen. No blood. I tugged the knot loose and unraveled the wrap, revealing a long scab stretching across his skin.

"It's been well tended," he murmured. His gaze dropped to my mouth, and his arms slid around my waist as he pulled me into him.

My body met his, the linen dangling from my fingers. His heat soaked through the fabric of my dress, radiating across my skin. Greaves, politics, everything outside this moment—forgotten. Only his eyes remained. Heavy. Hungry.

"An hour is a long time," I whispered, sliding my thumb beneath the edge of his waistband.

"Not nearly long enough." His groan curled in my ears. He dipped low and brushed his mouth over mine. The scruff on his jaw scraped my skin, leaving trails of heat. I lifted onto my toes, pressed harder into him.

He caught my bottom lip, teeth grazing. Then he pulled away, lips brushing my ear. "The things I want to do to you."

Fire roared through my blood. I dropped the bandage and slipped my hand to the nape of his neck, trying to bring him closer. But his mouth wandered to my throat, trailing slow, deliberate kisses across my skin.

My knees faltered. I moaned and gripped his shoulder, clinging to him as the world narrowed to breath, touch, heat.

"I want you," I hissed, hips pressing flush to his.

His smile grazed the crook of my neck. "I know."

Fingers tapped along my spine, teasing the lacings of my dress but never loosening them. The high collar choked me. Warmth bloomed under my skin. I couldn't breathe when he let go like this—when desire silenced his discipline.

With a growl, I slid my leg up his, hooking it high around his thigh. I rocked into him, dragging a groan from his chest. His hand gripped my hip and yanked me tighter. The grind of his body against mine set fire to every nerve.

A messy curse tumbled from his lips. He bent, braced, and lifted me with both hands locked beneath me. I let out a whimper as his mouth claimed mine. He kissed me hard—ruthless—and carried me through his chambers. The pressure against my core teased and tormented, offering no relief.

We tumbled. The bed caught our fall. His hand tangled in my hair as we sank into each other, mouths clashing, teeth catching. Tongues met in a hungry war. He dropped his weight between my legs, settling into the cradle of my hips.

I broke the kiss with a gasp, spine arching. Sensation surged. I tried to flee it—tried to pull him closer. My legs locked behind his back.

"Nienna." His voice cracked, hot breath against my throat. Fingers pinched into my waist. "I need to stop. Elohios, I need to stop."

His words faltered beneath his body's desire. He rolled his hips, forehead pressing to my shoulder with a broken hiss.

"Tell me about the prince."

His demand didn't pierce my haze of pleasure as I threaded my fingers through his hair, coaxing him back to my neck.

"Gods have mercy—what did he do?"

I froze. My breath caught. Was that what haunted him? The idea of Adoni touching me? Soiling me?

With a groan, he pulled away, seizing on my hesitation. He dropped to the mattress beside me, one hand flung toward his lap. Fingers curled in the air, then clenched the edge of his belt instead.

"He attacked me," I panted, heat still burning along my ears and neck. Panic crept in, trailing shame. "He didn't get–"

"I asked for *my* sake." He shut his eyes. One knee bent, boot thudding against the mattress. His palm settled on his thigh. "A few more seconds and I wouldn't have kept my promise."

I edged away, though every part of me ached to keep him there, to chase the heat we left behind. "Then, as a king, you should know." I cleared my throat, grasping for distance in formality. "I've never lain with a man."

His fingers flexed where they rested. "A princess as beautiful as you... surely there were secret kisses."

"A princess such as I?" I laughed. "The Dragon's Heart? Risk offending me, and a dragon might eat you. Many boys *wished* to try their luck. But my parents watched me and my brother too closely. Even now, any girl Ronan pursues, Father intervenes. No, Kallias. I've never kissed another."

"I wish I could say the same." He scoffed. Shame painted his voice. A hand dragged down his face. "Instead, you get someone else's seconds."

The haze left my body, but that comment echoed in my mind. I sat up, heart stuttering.

His eyes snapped open, following the motion. His throat bobbed. Regret broke across his expression, but no words followed.

I cupped his cheek and searched him. I'd never met his wife, but I wished a dragon had devoured her whole. "What did she do to you?"

A flicker of pain crossed his features, but he masked it. "Whatever damage she caused—I brought it on myself." The twitch at the corner of his eye said otherwise, but he kept it buried.

"You didn't *invite* that kind of cruelty. No one does."

"I married her." He barked a bitter laugh and pulled his head from my hand. "Well done. My need has been stifled."

I sank, a frown pulling at my brow. He was hiding something—a wound festering beneath the surface. He kept it locked away, afraid it would change the way I saw him.

"We've a long day ahead. You should rest." He rose, back to me as he adjusted his trousers and fastened his belt.

Negotiations drained us both, but this wasn't about politics. Not really.

I stood, walked to the mirror, and passed him without a word. Fingers smoothed my dress. I fixed the collar he'd loosened. In the glass, I caught his reflection—brows slanted, gaze shadowed as he studied me.

There would be time. A lifetime to unearth every buried thing between us. I didn't need to press now.

I turned with a faint smile—an attempt at conveying his dismissal hadn't hurt me. "Good night, Kallias."

Chapter Twenty-Six

KALLIAS

Fallione droned on about lumber logistics, but my skull throbbed with each syllable. I cradled my head, the ache drilling behind my eyes and draining what little decorum I had left. I would need to save it for the negotiations soon, making my moves as the King of Radaan, but also as a man willing to sacrifice anything for the woman he loved.

The woman I hurt last night.

She masked the pain well. A polite smile had covered the wound I gave her. I never meant to cause it, but there were some things I wasn't willing to share. Some ghosts belonged to the shadows.

Still, she owned me. Mind. Body. Soul.

"Gods." The word rasped past my lips as I rubbed at my temples. We'd marry, vow a lifetime. Passion, loyalty, unity—everything necessary for a future shared between thrones.

But love required truth.

Greaves knew mine. He always had. Since his youth, he stood at my side—whether I confessed aloud or bled it out in the sparring ring, he saw every fracture and flaw.

Nienna asked for that same intimacy, and I shut her out.

I selfishly pressed her for details about the prince, but when she turned the question on me—when she named Eldeiade—I folded. The dead woman kept resurfacing—drawing her back into my mind—into my dreams.

The look on Greaves' face when I rose told me I wasn't silent in the night. Not that it was a restful sleep. I didn't ask what he had heard, and wondered if it was a new development from everyone sticking their nose in my business, or if he was now worried because I was about to marry another woman while speaking of another in my dreams.

Nienna would love that.

Maybe a dragon would put me out of my misery.

"...across the sea, so we should start with a rate of five gold per beam, anticipating Nereus will haggle–"

"How much do we want per beam?" I snapped. The pain in my head pulsed like a war drum. A rough hand closed on the back of my neck—Greaves' thumbs digging into the base of my skull.

I sagged forward, tension unraveling one knot at a time.

"Three would be fair," Fallione replied, tone cautious. "We could survive at two."

He was still walking on glass after I blindsided him yesterday—announcing Tallon's removal and naming Nienna as heir without warning.

"Then we ask for three." I grunted, Greaves pressing into the stiffness coiled through my shoulders. "Nereus doesn't want games. I have a kingdom to return to, and he doesn't want his daughter to be caught in a compromising situation."

Not taking into consideration that I would be the one compromising her.

"Yes, Your Majesty." Fallione gave up the push, his voice tight.

I drew in a breath and rose. Greaves slung the mantle over my shoulders, its weight settling along my spine. My back screamed in protest as I adjusted the lapels and draped the chains.

The negotiations started much like the day before. Tedious. Measured. Formal. All part of the burden I carried.

Even if I was here for selfish reasons.

"We've considered your proposal to allow Nienna to inherit Radaan," Nyxaria said, voice unhurried and smooth, "and we accept." She sat composed, the picture of poise. "However, we have a contingent request."

My headache throbbed again. I forced my focus. "Go on."

"After your wedding, both of you will remain in Draconia for a month."

Fallione stiffened beside me. That silence stretched sharp and tight. Her eyes held mine. A test of resolve between two sovereigns.

A month?

I'd left Radaan leaderless for too long.

"Your Majesty," Nienna broke in, her voice gentler than her mother's, "King Kallias has already sacrificed time away from his realm. Asking more of him is difficult. Why the delay?"

Nyxaria turned her gaze to her daughter. My mind raced. Messenger doves relied on ship-to-ship relay, but Draconia had blocked our waters. Now that the truce held, I could press for their return, establishing the line of communication again, but that would take time—and each day, my unease grew.

"The matter of succession still leaves us..." Nyxaria paused, searching. "Unsatisfied."

"Unsatisfied," I echoed before I could stop myself, cursing inwardly. My tone had sharpened. The king's glare joined hers now.

"I have set the option of the Draconis inheriting my kingdom," I went on, steadying my voice. "And you call that unsatisfactory?"

Nereus leaned forward, bracing his hand on the table. "Never has a Draconis queen been barren. We ask that Nienna remain to ensure nothing interferes with her ability to conceive."

Blood rushed to my ears. My jaw locked.

Would they listen at the door? Monitor the bedding like some kingdoms did? Were they accusing me of risking her health? Or were they worried I would pull back my promise and take Nienna to Radaan—poisoning her womb to keep Tallon in my line?

"Tallon is removed." I matched his posture and tone. "There's no reason to remain here while we consummate our marriage."

His nostrils flared—confirmation I'd struck a nerve.

"Records state you only bedded your previous wife once a month, treating her like a–"

"Ronan." Nereus cut him off before I could.

My head snapped toward him, and the world tilted. Pain lanced behind my eyes. I clenched my jaw. "What records does Draconia keep on the marital affairs of foreign kings?"

He knew. If anyone had seen a sliver of my torment, it was Nereus.

"We've made our request." Nyxaria redirected the topic, but my gaze found Nienna. A flush climbed the tips of her ears as she shot her brother a scathing look.

"I object." My refusal came low, but firm. "I left my kingdom under the care of a war general. My advisor's here beside me. The route home takes weeks. After negotiations, we'll have time enough to prepare the wedding. You ask too much."

Doubt pulsed across the room, thick as storm clouds. I should've eased into resistance—Fallione warned me not to lead with fire—but the demand overstepped. They knew it.

"Perhaps we should revisit this later," Nienna said, lifting her chin. "What's next?"

Nyxaria narrowed her eyes, suspicion sharpening her features. "How many dragons we send to your kingdom."

"I request five." The number Nienna mentioned during her time with the Sols. She'd called it a light demand.

"I will honor that," Nereus said with a brief nod.

"As your daughter, I ask that my brother escort me to Radaan." She straightened her shoulders.

Ronan choked, eyes wide as he turned toward her. "Me?"

There was something in her request, some bold play that I didn't comprehend—but it had her mother leaning back, irises glittering with approval. Nyxaria's thin fingers tapped on the table.

Nereus studied his daughter. "In addition to the riot, I'll allow it," he said at last. "But he returns within a moon."

Suspicion stirred behind his tone. He felt it too—machinations moving where we couldn't yet see.

The women were up to something.

Nienna caught my eye and bit her lip, softening just before she remembered herself. The shift back to polished princess looked almost natural.

I chose trust. "Done," I answered, hating that her insufferable brother would now set foot in my kingdom.

The queen returned to her earlier point. "We still ask that Nienna remain for one month following the wedding."

I turned to my future bride. She was orchestrating something. Her gaze darted from Ronan back to me.

He was key.

His scowl deepened, but he didn't argue. Just slumped in his seat, staring at nothing. She wanted him to escort her, like before. But why?

For safety? She would already have dragons in tow.

Then it clicked.

His dragon.

"On the condition Gyrak is harnessed," I said, the pressure in my skull easing. If that beast pulled our ship, we'd cut the journey from weeks to days. Time reclaimed.

Ronan groaned, burying his face in his hand. Nereus leaned back, watching me with quiet calculation. Nienna ducked her head, barely hiding a satisfied smile.

This was her plan. Every step laid for me. Pride swelled, hot in my chest. Despite the ache in my body, something settled in me.

This—this was what it meant to have a true partner. Not just a queen, but a co-ruler. She wasn't dead weight. She cleared paths.

"It would shorten your travel time considerably," Nereus murmured, fingers dragging through his beard. "You'll remain here until the month concludes. Then return by sea—Gyrak in harness."

"The riot of five will launch four days after our departure," I added. "I won't have dragons descending on my people without my presence."

"Done."

The negotiations rolled on. My headache clung to the edges of thought, and I let Fallione steer the rest, stepping in only when necessary.

When it ended, I gave the formal parting expected of a king—then walked straight to my rooms.

My boots hit the wall with dull thuds, kicked off with more determination than coordination. After removing my mantle, the bed took me without protest, swallowing my aching limbs. The mattress gave a soft creak as I sank, spine throbbing, shoulders locked, my mind still spinning from the meeting.

Greaves muttered something low to Fallione near the door. I didn't catch the words, didn't care to. Every sound grated. Even the rustle of fabric felt like teeth against stone.

My skull throbbed—tight pressure building with nowhere left to go. Muscles coiled across my back, too many nights tense, too little sleep.

I closed my eyes.

Darkness rushed in, thick and immediate.

The seat beneath me offered no escape. Plush and yielding, but I couldn't sink far enough to disappear. Not from her.

She perched beside me at the dining table, poisoning every word that left my mouth with her spite. Across from me, Claydon stood tall, expression raw, pleading for reinforcements at the foothills. His people required protection. I needed to give it.

"I will come to your aid," I said, trying to rise—but my feet refused. Something rooted me to the floor. My own body turned traitor.

"Always to someone's rescue, Kallias. You're a king. Send your soldiers. Truly, you behave like a peasant."

The knife in my hand gleamed beneath the chandelier. I stared at it, wishing I could simply thrash it to the side and be done with her. "I am the king—I will help my people."

"Helping them would've meant avoiding war," she said, her fingers curling around my sleeve. Red nails pierced my green overcoat, crimson on leaves. "You refused to cross the mountains. You wouldn't concede the Craggs. A true king would have known when to yield."

My shoulder twitched. I tried to shake her off. My body stayed still, nerves dead to command.

"Silence."

"That's what you want from me? One of us has to speak the truth."

She shoved my chair back. I lurched, trying to break free, but Claydon blurred, replaced by Gayle. Then Darius. Then Fallione. My entire court assembled before me. Blank-eyed. Silent. Watching.

"You have one duty."

"To protect my–"

Her hand cracked against my face. I snarled and lunged, but the world spun, warped. I slammed onto my back.

She was on me. Naked. On her bed. My voice trapped in my throat as I bucked, powerless. Her laughter rang, shrill and cruel. My clothes—gone. Stripped without my knowledge or consent. Gods, how did I get here?

It was a dream. It had to be.

I threw my arm with all the strength I could muster. The strike landed soft, pitiful. My fingers scrabbled at her hair. Useless.

"Don't touch me!" she hissed, slapping my hand aside. Her claws raked down my chest, not in play—but to wound. Blood welled up, soaking the sheets. Too much. Far too much for scratches that shallow.

She laughed, high and unhinged, dragging a finger through the mess. "Now they'll find you, dearest. They know your secrets."

I roared, fighting against the lead in my limbs. Rage surged, trapped beneath flesh that wouldn't obey. What was happening to me? What had she done?

"Come here, son. Hold him for me."

No.

Tallon stepped from the shadows. Older. Cruel. That cold smile split his face in two. "He's weak. Trails after the girl like a pup."

She leaned close. Her breath hit my lips, heavy with rot and iron. "He'll never sire an heir." Blood-slick fingers gripped my jaw. "I'll make certain of it."

The world blackened, but her weight remained, settled along my hips.

Eldeiade's head lifted. Tallon had vanished. I lay beneath her, half-dressed in a sweat-damp tunic and loose trousers. The fabric barely managed a thin barrier between us.

I growled, driving my hips upward, straining with all that remained. My limbs lagged, slow and unsteady. Poison—had to be poison. Where was Greaves? Had she gotten to him too?

We crashed to the floor, and her scream split the air. Nails dug for purchase. My hands locked around her throat. Her face twisted, shrieking beneath me. Radaan was better off with a murderer for a king than a queen who threw my nation to the wolves.

Her fist collided with my jaw. I hit the floor again, vision bursting with stars. She crawled over me, dragging herself back into place, grinding into my lap. My stomach churned. Her heat seared through the thin layers of fabric. My body betrayed me. My mind screamed treason.

This wasn't duty or legacy. This was something else. Something wrong. Entirely, completely wrong.

Water surged into my nose. I choked—drowning. Coughs raked my chest, and I rolled, the motion too fluid for muscles still dulled by sleep. Pain bloomed as my skull cracked against the dresser's edge. I swore, flailing for Eldeiade. Had she found a new way to kill me?

"Kallias!"

Not her voice. Nienna's.

The fog lifted as I scrambled upright, hacking against the fluid burning down my throat.

Greaves knelt beside me, red bruises wrapped around his neck. A swollen welt pulsed beneath his jaw. Nienna hovered behind him, moonlight casting silver across her hair. She held an empty basin in both hands.

"He's with us," my friend muttered, wiping his mouth with the back of his hand, checking for blood.

Nienna's shoulders dropped as a quiet exhale escaped her. "Get on the bed." No softness in her tone. Not a suggestion—a command. Eldeiade's voice echoed in my skull, and my mind recoiled.

Greaves rose and whispered something to her. I barely noticed. I needed to shake off the nightmare, feel whole again. What kind of king suffered dreams like that? Who lashed out at his friend? I thought the night terrors were behind me, that I'd mastered myself.

He threw a final glance over his shoulder and left, the door sealing me in with Nienna and the pieces I hadn't yet picked up.

"I'm sorry you saw that." My voice scraped dry as I used the dresser to haul myself upright.

She didn't answer. Just stared, her face shuttered and still. After she set the basin aside, she eased onto the bed, moving with a wariness that stung. Like I might bite.

"Please sit," she said, patting the space beside her.

I looked down at myself—soaked through, filth clinging to the fabric. I'd passed out in my clothes after council and missed supper entirely. Had Greaves tried to wake me? Or just let me rest? The ache in my head had vanished, replaced by stiff muscles screaming with each breath.

My knees buckled, and I dropped beside her, back hitting the mattress. "They haven't come in years."

"Do you want to talk about it?" Her voice came soft, cautious.

"No." What man would speak of such things? "But if you ask, I'll answer. You deserve to know everything."

There was so much I hadn't told her. That I feared I couldn't give her a child. That the night terrors still clawed their way free when I let my guard slip.

"Do you want me to leave?"

"No." Elohios, no. I craved her presence. Needed her not to look away. To stay, even now, even like this. To show me she'd have me at my worst.

She lay beside me, unmoving and silent. I closed my eyes, and let the darkness shield me, cover what pride I had left. The bed shifted. A single finger traced the length of my arm, slow, steady. She didn't speak. Just touched me. A tether. Proof she hadn't run.

"Tell me what to do," she whispered. "I hate this."

"What?"

"This helplessness." Her voice barely rose above breath. "I don't know what to say, how to act. You've always been the strong one. I want to help you. How do I fix this?"

I knew that feeling too well. The uncertainty. The fear of saying the wrong thing. Of doing too much, or not enough.

What did I need? What could I give back?

"Let me touch you," I rasped. The words tasted like broken glass. I wanted to spar, to beat this weakness down, bury it beneath bruises and sweat. Instead, I asked. Pleaded.

She shifted. The mattress dipped. Her hand wrapped mine and pulled me to my side. She guided my touch underneath her dress, above the band of her breeches, and pressed my palm to the warmth of her bare stomach.

My breath stilled. My pulse slowed. She didn't see a monster. Not a threat. My thumb brushed soft skin near her navel. I breathed in the scent of her. Waterlilies, linen, warmth.

This was what love looked like in daily life. Quiet, steady, real. The kind people built a world around. The kind I thought belonged to others—never to kings.

Never to me.

"Don't strike me," I said low, the words catching before they escaped. Let the dark hide what shame it could.

I was no small man. I stayed strong. Maintained a warrior's build, a leader's frame—and here I lay, begging a woman not to hurt me.

She swallowed, nodded, and covered my hand with hers.

"Tell me what you want," I said. Not a plea—an exchange. "What must I not do?"

Her brow furrowed. She hesitated. "Do not belittle me. Not in front of others. If you must correct me... do so in private."

I snorted, a wry smile tugging at my mouth. "Likewise."

"Your turn," she murmured, scooting closer. Her fingers rose, hesitant, brushing my chest.

"Don't undermine me," I said. "Disagree in our chambers. Not before the court."

"A unified front," she agreed. "Always kiss me good night."

I raised a brow. "Starting on our wedding night?"

"Or tonight. I wouldn't tell you no."

My eye twitched. A flinch I didn't catch in time. "If I say no—gods help me, if I ever do—respect it."

"I will." No hesitation. No pause. Just her word. She didn't know how much that meant to me.

"Come here," I said, pulling her to my chest. "I don't mean to push you away. But there are things I have to keep for myself."

I wouldn't tell her about Eldeiade. Or what happened in my nightmare. That horror belonged to me alone. She didn't need to carry it—or see me through it. That wasn't part of the life I promised her.

I brushed her hair back and wrapped my hand around her waist, holding her there in the quiet.

"My past is mine," I murmured. "But my future is yours."

Chapter Twenty-Seven

Nienna

The next day, Kallias appeared as if nothing had happened. If I hadn't seen the anguish twisting his expression, the way he fought Greaves off like a man cornered, I would've doubted my own memory.

He walked proud. Shoulders loose, stride fluid, the chains of his mantle swaying with each step. His hair had been combed, face calm, the bruised shadows beneath his eyes faint but there.

He took his place at the table like a man born to it, launching back into negotiations without hesitation. Greaves had mentioned he'd slept poorly the night before. I witnessed the nightmare claw its way free. I heard the broken sound in his voice.

But I didn't understand the cause.

A quiet ache curled through my chest. His last marriage had been miserable—abusive, if I dared name it. And here I was, dragging him into another. He'd chosen solitude, carrying Radaan on his back, content to shoulder its weight alone. Then I crashed into his world.

Our love was neither simple nor planned. But it was real.

Mother and Father carried the discussion forward, and I stayed seated beside them, silent, listening. They didn't brief him in private beforehand—it showed yesterday. He'd need my insight in time, but I couldn't make it obvious I favored him over my family.

"You want my men on the Wild Shores, where your dragons refuse to linger?" Kallias tilted his head, his tone unreadable.

"We can negotiate a fair wage," Father answered with a sigh. "But your people bring knowledge. Mine understand the tides, not the timberlands. I'm asking for shared labor. Our hands, your minds."

Fallione bent closer and murmured into his king's ear. He leaned into him, considering.

"I will trade Vessels," he said at last.

Father's hum was low, pleased.

Kallias understood Draconis worked abroad—our Vessels traveled to the islands of the Kulletti, the Innaki, the Ivetti. If riders could ferry them as needed, his kingdom would gain steady magic, never forced to wait for their return.

A bold counter, but a wise one.

"You ask my people to tread unfamiliar shores," Kallias continued. "I request the same. Send willing participants to help Radaan flourish."

"And who," Father asked, "will give them instruction?"

"Your daughter." He didn't flinch, tone flat as if stating a fact.

My eyes jumped to Mother. Her lips twitched before she dipped in a subtle nod. Joy stirred in my chest. These were moves Tallon never could've dreamed of making.

"The Dragon Riders will obey her as well," Father added.

At that, he bristled. "I object. If she falls ill, or if we're attacked, I must be able to issue orders."

"No. Dragons answer only to Draconis."

A slow breath swelled in his chest. He exhaled through his nose and gave a single, hesitant nod. "Agreed."

"Another thing," Mother said. "We require a traditional wedding."

Fallione frowned, flipping through his pages.

"I'll need specifics." Kallias' eyes narrowed on her. "But there's one issue. I'm not Draconis. I have no dragon to tour the island."

"Argos will fly you," Father replied.

I jabbed my foot beneath the table, catching his ankle. He looked at me, brows raised, smirking in silent defiance.

Kallias deadpanned. "They won't carry a Radaanian."

"He will."

A choked laugh burst from Ronan before he could stop it. He slapped a hand over his mouth, snorting behind his fingers. I glared, warning him with a look.

Kallias blinked. "On his back?"

"In his claws."

"Alive?"

"Or dead." A roar shook the Spire's stones. Argos answering Father's challenge.

I stifled a groan and shut my eyes.

"I will do what's asked of me," Kallias said. "Though I request a Radaanian wedding as well."

My heart surged to my throat. I turned to him, and his gaze met mine, a flicker of mischief behind it.

Mother's brow pinched. "But you will be joined here?"

"The marriage shall be consummated here, and you'll have your month," he agreed. "But my people want to celebrate. Their blessing matters."

"Nienna?" Father's tone opened the floor for me.

I swallowed, fingers clenched tight in my lap. "Are there any ceremonies I should prepare for?"

"My advisors can fill you in." His voice rumbled low. He wasn't just offering tradition—he was asking for trust. I understood what marrying a prince meant. A king, though? That path remained unlit.

"I agree." I trusted him. If Radaan needed a wedding, I would give them one.

"Settled then. Draconia is pleased with this union. Are there any addendums from Radaan?" Father asked.

"None."

"Eamon, ready the treaty. We'll sign tomorrow on the common level where all can witness this joining. A promise of peace—a bright future for us all." He stood, voice carrying the weight of finality.

And just like that, it was done.

After all the heated talks and drawn lines, it felt too simple. But Kallias had risked far more—his life, his pride, even dragonfire—for this moment. For the chance to sign that treaty. For the right to marry me.

Dismissed, I walked past his chambers, though every part of me ached to be there. Instead, I followed the call that drifted through the Cireendium—Kalepsi.

At the Nest's threshold, I laughed aloud.

Chaos ruled.

Dragonlings clambered over Kalepsi's bulk—two perched on her back, another gnawing on a tail spike. She flicked the thick appendage, knocking the offender sideways and snorted, unimpressed.

"They're restless," I said through a laugh, picking my way across scattered white bones. The collection had grown with the clutch. Argos brought fresh kills daily.

The hatchlings caught sight of me and scrambled forward, claws clacking on bone and stone. Kalepsi snarled in warning, hissed, and every one of them froze. Their heads turned in unison. She chuffed, then clicked her teeth—a reminder. I had no wings. No armor.

The smokey blue crept close, head low, neck stretched like a cautious horse. His eyes shone, pupils wide with interest. Pale ivory fangs already pushed through his lips.

I didn't stop. My fingers brushed up the bridge of his nose, then scratched behind the horns. He chirped and followed me, tail swaying, until I reached the heart of the Nest.

Despite the bloodied bones, the space felt clean. Wind poured in from every side, cool and sharp, sweeping the scent away.

Kalepsi waited until I'd settled, then herded her brood toward me. I hummed while a red one flopped down, pressing a warm, heavy head to my lap. With an impatient grunt, the purple dragon clawed her way to the ledge, tail swinging in agitation, sending bones flying. In a breath, she was gone.

Argos coasted past the Spire with a low purr, baiting her to follow.

The red chirped once as if verifying its mother left it with me—alone—in the care of a tiny human. With a puff of air, the beast surrendered, sinking its weight against me. I rubbed the ridged scales, smiling at the absurdity of it all.

I stayed for hours, waiting on Kalepsi. She needed time away from her clutch. They could fly, even hunt, but she wouldn't trust the other dragons near them.

Between lullabies, I broke up two squabbles over whose head got my lap, and three more over favorite bones. When their mother returned, the sun had dipped low, bathing the Nest in copper light.

She needed the break. Her scales shimmered with sweat and blood, a strip of raw flesh snagged between her teeth. Even mothers had to eat.

The moment her claws touched stone, her head swung toward the Spire door. She curled her lip, snarling low.

I followed her glare—and my breath caught.

Kallias leaned against the doorframe, arms crossed. His mouth tugged into a content smile. He barely spared Kalepsi a glance, standing right inside the threshold where he'd be safe. Most wouldn't have risked even that.

"Come get your babies!" I shouted, pushing against the weight of a black-scaled head. The hatchling snorted, wedging in closer and fake-snoring with eyes squeezed shut. I laughed and yanked on its horns.

One growl from Kalepsi and it snapped upright, trilling in surrender. She stalked forward, nosing through my hair. Warm breath lifted the strands. I rubbed the velvet-soft scales framing her bloodied lips.

She lipped at my fingers, purring deep in her chest, then shoved bones aside with a flick of her tail and collapsed beside us. Her stomach hit the stone, and the hatchlings swarmed her. One dug at her fangs, determined to pry loose the remnants of meat wedged there.

I peeled myself up, legs numb, and stumbled toward Kallias. A rib bone caught my foot. He twitched forward like he might catch me, but held his ground. He knew better than to rush into a dragon's nest.

When I reached him, I pressed a kiss to his cheek, sagging into him.

"How long have you been there?"

"Long enough to have six heart attacks from claws or teeth too close to you," he muttered. He shifted, settling back against the stone wall, then drew me into his arms.

"They know better." I sank into him with a grateful sigh. "Did you need me?"

"Always," he said, grinning.

"Should I call you my husband-to-be now?" I murmured.

His eyes crinkled with quiet joy. "The treaty is signed tomorrow. Until then, I'm a king and you are a princess. Two foreign nations."

"You're a little close for a man who represents only that."

His brows rose. "Should I let you go?"

I curled in tighter, resting my cheek on his chest, eyes drifting to the Nest. My dragons dozed, blanketed in bones and death.

"Never."

"Where are you in your cycle?"

Freya choked at my mother's bluntness—but I knew better than to flinch.

"Half-moon," I said, deadpanning as Edith wove strands of my hair into a braid.

Mother hummed and scratched something onto a paper at my desk. "Perhaps we'll get two tries at a babe while you're here," she mused.

"I'm thinking more than that," Freya whispered.

Edith shot her a warning glare, but she only smiled wide, shoving a red curl behind her ear as she buckled my boots beneath my evergreen dress. I hadn't worn green since my return. Back then, it marked my failure. Now it symbolized the path ahead.

"I've been organizing in hopes the treaty succeeded," Mother sighed, pressing a finger to the space between her brows. "But it'll still take days to bring everything together. I worry it won't be as grand as I'd imagined."

"Draconis do their best," I said. "It's not as if we've had months to prepare."

"Thank the sun," Freya muttered under her breath.

Edith cleared her throat, but the young maid didn't yield. She wasn't under Edith's charge, not like Scythe. She only smirked and went back to the laces.

"This isn't just your wedding," Mother said. "It's a message to the islanders. They need to see unity. Strength. This union is proof we can rise from past mistakes and reshape them into triumph."

I pressed my lips together. Brides didn't plan their own weddings. That belonged to their mothers—and mine had claimed the task with both hands.

"Will you need me after the signing?" I asked, straightening the stiff collar circling my neck. The fabric hugged my throat like armor. Her design. I liked how it felt—imposing.

"No. You're free to do as you wish." She turned in her chair. "Did you have plans?"

"I want to take Kallias to the little island."

"For a swim?"

Edith coughed once and fled the room, but Freya's head snapped up, amusement gleaming in her eyes.

"I thought it would be nice to get away for a bit," I said.

"I think you two have *gotten away* quite enough." Her tone clipped. "Betrothed or not, standards still stand."

Relaxed standards. If Tallon and I had been caught wrapped around each other, people would have whispered. No scandal. Only discomfort and gossip.

"I'll honor them," I said. "But he needs a break from the palace, the pressure."

"And your brother can't take him because?"

I raised a brow. "Ronan?"

She let out a defeated sigh, shaking her head. "Fine. But remember—your father may fly over."

Freya tied off the last lace, patted my calf, and stood. "You look beautiful. Green suits you." She winked.

"See her before dinner," Mother added. "She'll need the sand scrubbed from her scalp."

Dismissed, my maid slipped out, and Mother stepped close. Her fingers smoothed the braid over my shoulder, her lips warm against my cheek.

"You'll be spectacular today."

I stood, brushing out my skirts. "Redeeming myself?"

"There was no redemption necessary." She slid her palms down my sleeves, smoothing the creases. "Your father never thought less of you."

But Adoni did.

"Have you heard from the Innaki?" I asked.

Her smile faded into a crease of worry before she shook her head. "Not yet. Their ships should be making harbor soon. I've advised that we wait—let

Galdoni move first. We have enough tasks to occupy us. No use fretting over potential strife before your wedding."

"The Innaki won't truly declare war."

"They might've pressed the advantage, but once you're married to Kallias, they lose leverage. Still, they sailed before the Radaanian vessel made port. They don't know anything's changed. Dragons help them—if they posture now, your father won't tolerate it."

She patted my shoulder, her fingers curling around the crook of my elbow. "Come, my princess. It's time to fulfill your destiny."

The winding route through the Cireendium brimmed with life. Excited voices bounced off the cavern walls, rising into the Spire's height. Crowds parted with murmured greetings, leaving a clear path to the first level—letting their rulers pass.

We made our way toward the auditorium stage. Normally used for island meetings, today it hosted something far more historic. With Tsunami and her obvious fixation on Kallias, Father had refused to hold the ceremony outside.

Ronan appeared from the crowd, offering me his arm. "Last chance to run, Sister," he muttered.

I stepped on his toe.

He snorted, shoulders bouncing with silent laughter. Despite his troublemaking, he was still my brother. His judgment with Tallon had faltered, and he'd swung from detesting Kallias to tormenting him. And yet, I smiled—comforted by the familiar glint of mischief in his eyes as we reached the top.

Kallias wore his signature forest-green overcoat, the gilded embroidery curling like vines. Under it, though, a blue vest hugged his chest. The twin gold designs matched those on the outer layer—a visible gesture, a pledge. A piece of Draconia near his heart.

His gaze swept down my dress, a deep emerald to match him. Beneath the folds, dark trousers peeked from slits in the skirt—stormy-blue patterns trailing into my boots. A statement. I belonged to Radaan now, but my roots still wrapped around the cliffs of my homeland.

At the table, Father extended his arm, and I stepped close, letting him guide me between himself and Kallias.

"People of Draconia!" Father's voice boomed, echoing into the heights above. "Today marks a turning point—etched forever in our memory. A celebration not only of peace, but progress. We have secured a treaty with Radaan."

Cheers burst through the crowd. Fists punched the air, voices roaring with approval.

"I have negotiated the best for our island," he continued, "and through King Kallias and Princess Nienna's union, we gain grain, resources, and an alliance meant to last generations!"

Some faces in the crowd pulled tight with skepticism, and discontent flickered in their narrowed eyes as they glanced toward Kallias. A few shook their heads, but their resistance crumbled beneath the magnitude of the crowd's celebration.

Father lowered his arm and leaned over the sprawling parchment. The parchment spilled over the sides of the table like a waterfall. He dipped the quill, let the excess drip off, and signed his name with broad, black strokes. No blood this time. Just ink.

He signed again beneath mine, scrawling *'The Dragon's Heart'* beside it. Then he handed the quill to Kallias, who accepted it with a slight bow.

His shoulder brushed my side as he leaned into the table, bracing himself as he wrote in the slot once meant for his son. The chains of his mantle swung, catching glints of torchlight above the page. All the struggle, the distance, the fire—it ended in a single name. A simple signature.

He placed the quill aside and straightened. Turning to Father, they saluted—fists to chest—and the room erupted once more.

Kallias turned to me. His smile was rare, unguarded. The corners of his eyes crinkled with quiet joy, though his jaw clenched to cage the emotion.

I dipped low into a curtsy, then slid my hand into the crook of his arm. We descended together, Greaves at our backs.

Sunlight poured through the open doors, striking the stone walls in gold and copper hues. The light caught the rows of faces, their expressions glowing with hope, curiosity, or suspicion.

Before we reached the main floor, the sun vanished behind a sudden shadow. Tsunami trilled, her slit pupils narrowed directly at Kallias.

We didn't pause. We walked beneath her gaze, past the doors, as some of the crowd bent low in reverence.

The dragon snorted, wings rustling like sails in a gale. Then, with a single beat, she launched into the sky.

"She's headed for the landing," I guessed as we climbed the Cireendium's winding slope.

"Is she part of the celebration?" he asked.

"Not on purpose." I kept my smile fixed. "You've been holed up in the Spire for days. The poor beast has been beside herself, trying to get a glimpse of you. Riders have been grumbling about it nonstop."

"You'd think the novelty would've worn off," he muttered.

"You're far too fascinating," I said with a short laugh, slipping free of the crowd. Once we gained higher ground and left the listening ears behind, I lowered my voice. "What were you planning for the rest of your day, my king?"

"I'm to discuss ship placements with Captain Jenson. Wedding details with Fallione. Or yet another discussion about trade with Nereus. Take your pick."

"Would you like to see my childhood hideout?"

"A hiding place?" He glanced down the narrow halls branching off the Cireendium. "I can't imagine there are many."

"It's not here." I slid my hand down to his, fingers threading through his.

His brow furrowed, weighing the cost. "Fallione will be sorely displeased." But when he looked back at me, a grin broke across his face—bright and boyish.

I tossed a glance behind us. "Think we can lose him?"

His guard scowled, as expected.

"He's impossible to shake," Kallias replied.

"If we snuck into my rooms, I bet he'd excuse himself."

Greaves arched a brow. His scowl flattened into a look of long-suffering boredom. Unimpressed by my teasing.

I pivoted down a side corridor, guiding us through a maze of tight turns and narrow stairs. Only one could pass at a time. Our steps fell soft on the stone, swallowed by the quiet. These service passages fed into the Spire from smaller entry points—used by staff to avoid the crowd bottlenecks at the main gates.

At last, sunlight broke through. I led them out to the eastern edge.

Without hesitation, I ducked into a shaded alley. A woman with a basket gasped and dropped into a bow.

"Good day!" I called, not slowing.

The walk through K'bar was brisk. The sun bore down, beading sweat at my temples. My dress clung at the collar, the heat thick against my skin.

By midday, we arrived at the shore. Sand glittered under brutal daylight, white and blinding. A small sailboat floated beside a rocky outcrop. Gulls circled, shrieking above as they scanned the water.

Grinning, I hitched my skirt and climbed into the boat. Kallias eyed the vessel with suspicion, hesitating.

Greaves stopped behind us, arms crossed, his gaze sweeping the horizon. "Who's the captain?"

"I am." I dipped into an exaggerated bow. "Captain Nienna, at your service."

This stretch of beach was a royal secret—hidden, quiet, off-limits to the public. Our own private island offered a breath away from Draconia's tight quarters. A place untouched by court or crowd.

"Have you sailed before?" Kallias asked as he clambered in.

"Often." I grabbed the ropes, lowering the sail. "Greaves, would you be so kind?"

The man stared at his king for a moment, clearly considering whether to toss him overboard or follow orders. With a grunt, he gave the boat a shove. Water surged at his legs before he jumped in, boots thudding beside mine.

Wind caught the canvas, and the vessel shot forward, cutting across the blue.

Ronan had Gyrak and could fly wherever he pleased. This was all I had. My escape. My secret refuge. I came here often as a child. Sometimes Adoni joined me. That memory surfaced, bitter and sour, but I pushed it back. Not today.

The beach wasn't far. A crescent-shaped sliver of land. The eastern shore, shielded by jagged rock, faced away from Draconia. No eyes followed us here.

I pulled the boat into the worn dock and jumped ashore, tying off the line.

Thin trees stretched toward the sun, crowding the strip of sand. Lush vines spilled down stone walls. The ground shimmered, warm and gold, soft beneath my feet. No rocks. No gulls. Just wind and waves and silence.

Kallias stepped onto the dock, eyes taking in the emptiness. "It's peaceful."

"And private." I reached for a boulder, tugging off my boots. "Draconia is all stone and noise. People are always watching. Mother taught me to sail as a girl. This place became my escape—away from Ronan, from the Spire, from everything."

"Your father let a child out to sea?"

"No doubt Argos flew overhead." I shook my head, stacking my boots beside the dock. "But back then, it felt like freedom."

Kallias watched me, his gaze lingering.

"Where do you want me, Kal?" Greaves asked. He stood in the boat, black uniform baking under the day's heat. His eyes flicked to my bare feet, then to his king.

"Wherever's comfortable," Kallias muttered, his attention never leaving mine. "What are you doing, Nienna?"

"Swimming."

"Sun above." He cursed under his breath.

"You've never swum before?"

"Not in the ocean."

"Help me with these laces?" I turned, pulling my hair over one shoulder, offering him my back.

He stepped in close. His fingers worked the knots loose, slow and careful. His mouth brushed my ear, voice low. "Just how far are you stripping?"

"Enough to swim."

"Would that be all of it?"

"Kallias, if you refuse to give me all of you before we wed, you certainly won't see all of me."

A laugh caught in his throat as he dropped his forehead to my shoulder. "Thank Elohios."

The dress slipped. I held it against my chest as the fabric slid down my arms. His lips trailed kisses, the edge of his scruff scratching along my skin—soft and warm and maddening.

With a heavy sigh, he dropped beside me and yanked off his boots. Greaves sat with his back turned, one foot propped along the dock's sun-bleached planks, the other dangling above the glinting water.

I let my dress fall. Cool air brushed my skin as I stepped free of the fabric and shook out the sand. The folds draped easily over the boulder, catching a shimmer of light.

Kallias wrestled with his mantle. I waited, arms folded, watching. He unclasped the last chain, gaze flicking to mine. The conflict there—always layered, always restrained—pinched at me.

"Just catch it," he said.

Some part of me bristled that he still wouldn't let me help remove it, but I caught the heavy gold all the same, setting it atop my dress. Sunlight sparked off the engraved shoulder plates, carving shadows across the fabric.

He peeled off his vest, folded it with rigid care, then stripped his tunic. Still, he refused to meet my eyes. His shoulders flexed, every muscle taut as the shirt cleared his head.

The wound had sealed. Silver strands were growing back across scorched flesh. His chest glistened, a map of hard lines and sharp dips. Pale skin was taut over his abs, and as he twisted, shadows caught along his muscled sides.

No softness remained—just the strength he refused to let fade with age.

He paused at his belt. He glanced over, jaw tight. His gaze drifted across my chest binding, trailed down my torso to the hem of my trousers. Traced the dip and swell of my hips, my bare feet, then climbed back up.

He sniffed. His hands fell from his belt, as if my clothing had sealed his decision.

"Yours are too baggy," I said, crouching to tug at the loose fabric clinging to his calf. "Mine won't drag me down."

"I'm not swimming," he muttered, stepping away.

"Even if I swear to keep my hands to myself?" I straightened and planted my fists on my hips.

A piercing trill cracked the silence. Tsunami swooped low over the treetops, golden wings slicing the sky. She banked, circling wide before crashing down into the shallows with a slap of water and spray. Warm waves surged around my calves.

I jogged forward as she stretched her neck toward me. Her muzzle bumped my chest. I nudged her aside, eyeing the gleam in her stare—she wasn't here for me.

She cut between us, blocking Kallias from view. Her tail whipped past me. I ducked, narrowly avoiding the swipe of muscle thicker than my torso.

Tsunami lowered her head to meet his gaze, one gilded eye narrowing like she was solving a riddle. I shoved at her scaled foot, trying to urge her back into the surf. She huffed, snout twitching as she glanced at me.

"Give us space to swim," I called, shoving again.

She grumbled, a garbled vibration deep in her throat, then sloshed to the side. Kallias lifted a hand to shade his eyes, squinting up at her while she studied him like prey.

"She doesn't do this with my men," he said, lowering onto the sand.

"She dominates the northern skies." I passed him without pausing. The ocean called, warm and inviting. "You wouldn't notice, but the riders know. She's claimed your ship, too. She's curious."

I didn't wait for a response before diving into the waves.

The water pulled and pushed around me as I cut forward. Salt burned my nose. My limbs stretched, slicing through the weightless blue. I broke the surface, tossed the wet hair from my eyes, and searched the shore.

Kallias hadn't moved.

I swam loops in the shallows, each lap a silent invitation. He stayed rooted on land.

Wading back, I gripped my chest wrap and rose from the waves. Wetness sheeted down my skin, curling around my hips. Foam lapped at my thighs.

"Come swim with me?" I called.

His eyes tracked me, dark with hunger. "I don't do well with deep water."

"You can swim, though?" I flicked my hair over my shoulder, droplets spattering across the ground.

"Enough to keep breathing," he said. Final. Closed. That door wasn't mine to open. I sighed and walked up the shore, clutching my wrap tighter.

I flopped beside him. He bent a knee, putting distance between us like armor. Wet sand clung to my skin. I leaned back on my hands, chest lifted, chin tipped toward the sun.

"I almost drowned once." His voice dropped low. His gaze swept over my curves, but his mind drifted elsewhere. "A river runs from Mount Dariel to the foothills. The Velli attacked there, and I learned fast that fighting in water is a thousand times harder than on land."

Sunlight kissed his cheekbones. He looked carved in firelight, jaw locked, throat tight. The memory didn't sit well.

"Thank you," I murmured.

Tsunami curled her massive body around us, resting her head beside Kallias. For a heartbeat, there was no throne. No duty. No kingdom.

Just Kallias and Nienna.

A man and a woman.

Drifting toward a future as bright as the sun.

Chapter Twenty-Eight

KALLIAS

After the signing, only three days remained until our wedding. It was rushed, far from what I wanted to give Nienna, but something nagged at me. A pressure deep behind my ribs. A weight. Radaan called me home, louder with every hour.

Someone knocked before sunrise.

Fallione had explained the expected traditions the day before, but I was still grateful when it was Nereus at my door, not her.

He wasn't always easy to like, a pain in my side more often than not, but that morning, he clapped my shoulder and gave a solemn nod. "It's time."

Greaves stayed behind. The trials—a Draconis wedding tradition—had to be faced alone.

The first: securing a sacrifice for the dragons.

I chose the simplest route—fish. No shame in that, though some might scoff. I lacked both the knowledge and preparation for these challenges. I'd only just learned what they were. Nereus offered quiet guidance, and I took it.

The Draconis revered their dragons, near worshiped. Equal parts divine and deadly. To win their favor, I had to catch a fish, present it, and hope they'd help me survive the next test. Most grooms had already bonded a beast, making them more inclined to assist. I was not so lucky.

As it was, Argos loathed me. And Gyrak would sooner toy with me than lend any aid.

In the dawn's rays, dressed in a tunic and underbreeches, I stepped into the ocean's shallows. Pale morning light caught on the low swells as I carried my golden spear—the same one that pierced mammoth hide. Now, it hunted scaled, twitching bait.

I hunted a small, flat fish. It had a vicious bite—or so I was told—but I was willing to risk it over diving into the waves or trying my hand at a bow or slingshot.

Nereus lounged nearby on the beach, biting into a Radaanian apple. Beside him, Argos dozed, massive and still.

Warm water swirled around my calves. Sand sucked at my heels as the tide retreated, dragging grit between my toes. Every pull of the surf urged me to flee. But this was for Nienna. Just once. I'd never have to do it again.

A flicker. Unnatural brown against the rocky floor. I stilled, watching as another wave passed over the shape. It stirred. A fin shifted slightly, enough to reveal itself.

I braced, lifted the spear, and threw. The blade struck clean through, slicing flesh in one brutal arc. Water frothed. Tentacles shot out—long and whip-fast, each tipped with barbed ends. One touch could take a foot. Nereus had warned me.

I kept my distance, waiting until the creature stopped thrashing. Inch by inch, I edged forward and yanked my weapon free from the ocean floor. A grotesque fish clung to the blade, one side flattened, a single black eye staring up at me. Starfish-like. But wrong. Bulging. Predatory.

As I turned for Argos, a trill split the sky.

Tsunami dropped from the clouds, crashing onto the beach in a burst of earth and sound. Nereus cursed, while his dragon snapped upright, bellowing a roar that rocked through my chest. He surged forward, massive form bearing down, trying to push her off the shore. She clicked and hissed, skimming backward but keeping her head low, gaze locked on me. Sparks flared from Argos' jaws. She spun on him with a shriek, claws tearing shallow ruts in the sand.

I flinched, eyes darting between them, searching for Nereus in the chaos. He'd vanished behind his dragon's thrashing limbs.

Tsunami lunged like a playful pup facing a wolf, jaws snapping at Argos' face. He reared, dodging, then slammed his head down with a warning growl. She curled her neck low, teeth bared. Her body writhed in a herding motion—an instinctual push trying to drive him back, away from me.

Argos snorted, casting a single glance my way before lumbering off and settling where he'd started. A fierce sound rumbled in his throat as he curled his tail around Nereus. The king only shrugged and gestured toward Tsunami.

She tilted her head, unimpressed. With a piercing trill, she dropped to the sand, shoulders hunched, muscles coiled tight. Like a cat ready to pounce, her wide pupils fixed on the fish skewered to my spear.

This was supposed to be my offering. My leverage. A gift to win a dragon's aid in the next challenge. And Nereus wanted me to give it to her? A wild, riderless dragon who had no sense of communication—no tether to a human mind?

She clicked deep in her throat, rank breath wafting over me. It reeked of brine and blood. Impatient, but waiting. Barely.

I clenched my jaw, shaking my head. I would find Nienna, whatever it took. But if this didn't work, I'd be wading back into the sea for another withering fish.

Jamming the spearhead into the ground, I flung the carcass from the blade. With a throaty coo, she lunged forward, and swallowed it whole—no chewing, no gratitude. Then she turned her gaze skyward, sucking in a long breath.

"Elohios, let me dress," I muttered, breaking into a jog across the beach.

My trousers waited near Nereus. He tilted his head, eyes flicking between me and Tsunami with a faint smirk.

"She won't wait," he warned as I tugged my clothes into place.

"Does she even know what she's supposed to be doing?" I fumbled with my belt, grabbed my boots and spear. She had no one to explain the rules. How would she recognize the traditions?

"She knows," he said. "Now run."

I took off toward the city.

No mantle. Only rough-spun trousers and a tunic. This trial wasn't for kingship—I already earned her hand in that. This was to prove my worth as a man.

Tsunami launched skyward, her shrill cry slicing through the quiet. Unlike the others, who spoke in snarls and grunts, she trilled and clicked. Loud. Expressive. Infuriating.

She flew overhead, banking in tight loops as she led me through the winding streets.

I sprinted after her, frustration boiling in my chest. The challenge? Find Nienna somewhere in the city, among homes, shops, alleys. No clues. No hints. Just this dragon nicknamed for her nuisance behavior.

She passed again, shadow sweeping over the road with her giant eye fixed on me. She veered right, and I scanned the narrow lanes until I spotted one leading that way, then bolted down it, boots still dangling from my hand.

No time for footwear. If I paused, she'd fly off, and I'd lose her. I'd never find Nienna.

The ground stayed mercifully clean. No sharp rocks or shards of glass. Just sun-warmed, sandy stone underfoot and perspiration dripping from my brow. My heart pounded a wild rhythm. Every breath tore through my chest.

She circled back again with a fierce huff. I gritted my teeth and turned down another street.

On and on it went. An endless chase. Sweat stung my eyes. My grip slipped on the spear's damp shaft. One boot clipped a corner, yanking me sideways. I caught myself against rough brick, palms scraping across the wall.

Then—finally—a triumphant roar.

I stumbled to a halt, head snapping up. Tsunami dove, wings tucked tight. She hurtled toward the rooftops, claws dragging along the tiles of a rooftop as she pulled up at the last second.

I gasped for air, blinking salt and sweat from my eyes.

Before me stood a simple structure. Same crimson brick as the rest. One door. This had to be it?

Hoping I wasn't about to wake a stranger from peaceful sleep, I entered.

Darkness swallowed the space. No furniture. No light except what bled through a small window.

Grinding my teeth together, I strode into the room, hoping the dragon was correct and she hadn't just played me for a fool.

I crept further, eyes straining for movement. Empty. Nothing but dust and grime caked along the floor.

Stairs curved upward.

Spear held low, I climbed. Slow. Careful. The second level was no different. Shadows, dust, stale air. No footprints. No sign of life.

One level remained.

I ascended. The third story swallowed me whole—black as pitch. No windows. No light. Strange. There should've been one. I crept forward, fingers sweeping the dark.

A breath broke the silence.

Quick. Uneven.

I whipped around, weapon raised.

A body struck me hard. My muscles seized, thoughts spiraling.

And then—her lips crashed against mine, hot and demanding.

My boots and spear hit the ground with a thud. Waterlilies and salt clung to the air, flooding my lungs with the scent of her. My hand caught her neck, fingers tangling in hair I knew better than my own. The other slid along her side, snagging on the heavy belt of metal before sweeping over curves I dreamed of far more than I ever cared to admit.

Her tongue teased the seam of my lips. I shoved her back until brick stopped us, rough and cold. Our mouths battled, all clash and pressure, scraping teeth and swelling heat. The beast in me tore free, ravenous. She whimpered as I pinned her, that plated belt grinding into my hips. I growled, grazing her with the edge of my bite. My hips rocked forward, pressing through steel and cloth, hunting her fire.

The dark fed the animal inside me—made it brutal. Wordless. Nameless. But I knew her.

Her palms flattened against my chest, fingers hovering over the scar carved deep above my heart. That touch told me everything.

"Found you," I breathed, dragging kisses across her cheek, catching her earlobe between my teeth.

"And you have your reward," she murmured, voice husky with heat. The chase had lit something inside her—and Elohios knew how badly I burned. I needed a taste. Just one.

My hand bumped the rigid plates again, armor blocking every path.

"Withering sun, what are you wearing?" I growled, both hands dropping to wrestle with the belt.

"Draconis tradition." Her breath hitched. A soft, wicked laugh followed. "Worn to make men wait."

"So they don't take you into dark rooms?" I scoffed, sliding one hand up her front, over the swell of her breasts, cupping her jaw.

"The hunt tends to stir... instincts." Her words came out in a breath, skin flushed, lips parted.

My thumb brushed along her lower lip. She opened further, right on cue. I pressed between her teeth, and she closed around the digit. Warm, wet, slow—she dragged her tongue over the pad in a greedy stroke.

A groan tore loose from my chest. Fire raced under my skin. Control shattered. I yanked my hand away and claimed her in a bruising kiss. No patience—only demand, hunger, denial. I crushed against that cursed armor, chasing friction, craving the soft give of her body beneath mine.

She whimpered. Nails bit into my skin. "Kallias," she breathed, muffled under my embrace.

I froze, stepped back, hands raised.

"Elohios, help me," I muttered. I wanted her too much. That cursed belt was the only thing keeping me from losing every scrap of sense.

"We need to get to the Spire," she panted, still lost in the dark. A soft scrape of motion. A muffled curse.

"Don't move." I hissed, cursing myself for my own foolishness. Gods, how did men get anything done when they had wives that they were actually attracted to? I adjusted my too tight trousers, grimacing against the blinding need that coursed through my veins.

Using my hands, I doubled over, searching for my spear, hoping I didn't find it blade first. My fingers brushed against the soft leather of my shoes before finding cold steel. Letting out a sigh of relief, I straightened, leaving the tip pointing to the floor in the darkness.

"There, now."

Her hands found my arm, clutching my tunic as I led her back to the stairs.

The city was eerily quiet, and I scanned each street we passed, looking for any sign of life.

"They're all waiting at the palace," she said.

She wore a snow-white dress. The way it hung off her shoulders, it exposed collarbones I could take days exploring. It narrowed at her waist, bound by a skirt of metal scales. It hung in overlapping steel diamonds. Longest in the front and back, where a man would be tempted to lift them.

It jingled as we walked through the barren streets, after we stopped to pull on my boots. When we strode into the clearing, cheers erupted from the gathered crowd as if they were just as surprised as I was that I found Nienna.

I felt exposed, naked, without my mantle. Regardless of how I was supposed to present myself at this time, I was so used to wearing it in front of people that my skin heated, and I cursed the blush of shame that curled up my neck.

Thousands of people were gathered in the clearing, more than were there for the Awakening, all standing on their feet, pressing against each other.

Argos waited at the Spire's base, growling low in his throat. A command. An invitation. A promise of space from the crush of bodies. Other dragons flew around overhead in lazy circles, a myriad of colors.

I led Nienna up the stairs, offering a quick bow to Argos, though it was Tsunami who guided me to the princess.

"Well done, Kallias Sunspear." Nereus' voice boomed, bolstered with magic no doubt. "You've brought my daughter back to us."

There were red blossoms where my facial hair had lightly scuffed her skin across her cheeks and shoulders in passion.

"I claim Nienna Draconis as my bride." I called out for the crowd's sake. Greaves stood at the edge, his face a careful mask—but he knew why I was uncomfortable.

"And you shall have her." Nereus threw his arm wide and we walked into the crowded Spire. As much as I wanted it to be over there, it was only the beginning.

Greaves fastened the last chain of my mantle, his hard brown eyes locked on mine. His fingers lingered at the clasp, full of the things he couldn't say out loud.

I wasn't replacing him. This was no trade. I was taking a wife—a partner who could stand beside me in court, speak her mind, bear the throne's weight with me. He would still be there, always behind me, silent and steady. A shadow in my wake. A blade in the dark.

I placed my hand over his, gripping hard before letting go. He didn't need words. He knew his role—protecting me, guarding Nienna. After a moment, he stepped back and dropped into a deep bow.

My chest tightened. He did it to honor me, but all I wanted was to pull him upright and hold on.

My whole life was about to change, but he'd remain. The constant I could always count on.

Draped in Radaanian green, my mantle polished to a gleam, I strode from my rooms toward the throne room. The space was packed—children perched on shoulders, civilians pressed shoulder to shoulder, eager to fill every last gap. They resembled restless sheep in their excitement. The walls remained bare for now—festivities would come later.

Jaw clenched, I cut through the crowd toward the bright landing. Nienna stood there with her parents, Argos curled at the edge like a coiled beast. His bulk seemed ready to snap the platform in half. When I approached, he lowered his head just slightly, baring a single fang in displeasure.

"Welcome, Kallias Sunspear," Nereus called, his palm resting on Nienna's arm.

"You ask for our daughter's hand in marriage," Nyxaria said, lifting her chin. Her pale fingers wound tightly with her daughter's—a quiet reminder that it wasn't just her father giving her away.

"I do." I stopped before them, ignoring Argos' grumble. My feet braced wide as I met their eyes. "I negotiated for her name. Earned your dragons' favor. Found her in the way a man finds his mate. I've asked. I've come to claim her."

"Do you vow to protect her," Nereus said, "as fiercely as a dragon guards its young?"

"I so swear."

Nienna's nostrils flared. Her breath caught, eyes glimmering with barely contained emotion. She tried to hold her mask together. Part of me longed to shield her, let her rebuild that wall. The rest wanted to see it crack. I needed that fire inside her unchained.

"And will you give her your unbound love," her mother asked, "as deep and endless as the ocean?"

Her peridot eyes dared me to falter. One hesitation, and she'd call it all off.

But I already loved Nienna. Our bond had kindled across the sea, igniting a wildfire neither of us could control.

"I so give it." My chin dipped in respect to her mother's demand.

"And you, Nienna," Nereus said, turning to her with both hands holding hers. "Will you take Kallias Sunspear in marriage? Do you wish for this?"

A tight smile curved her mouth. A single tear slipped down her cheek. She was saying goodbye. I would offer her the world, but she would lose part of hers to accept it.

Doubt spiked through my ribs, waiting.

"I ask for nothing less than to be given to the King of Radaan."

I forced a steady breath, locking my spine as the heat of the sun baked across my shoulders. Sweat beaded along my collar, but I didn't move.

She turned to her mother. Nyxaria pulled her in, kissed her forehead, then cradled her cheeks. A slow grin. A small nod.

"Then you are given."

Nienna faced me, cheeks glowing with color. Her smile spread—brilliant and bold. Chin high, eyes fierce. My princess. Born to fill ballrooms and bend nations to her will. She stepped forward with confidence in her stride and dipped into a deep curtsy.

"I, Kallias Sunspear, Chosen of the Gods, Golden Warrior of Elohios, choose Nienna Draconis—the Dragon's Heart—as Radaan's queen." The words rang strong, sure. No tremble. No doubt. I would have her, if she still wanted me.

Fallione stepped forward, a silk-draped pillow in hand. My pulse pounded behind my eyes. One twitch. Then another. Nienna had promised to wear it—but what if she hated it? What if she refused, here, in front of them all?

What if I was making the same mistake again?

I pulled the velvet cover off in a flourish. Sunlight caught on gold, the scales casting radiance across the dark stone. I lifted the smaller mantle. Chains fine as thread, delicate and glinting.

She didn't flinch. Determination gleamed in her eyes as she met my stare. Her chin tipped upward. Spine straight. She was ready—unlike Eldeiade, she welcomed this.

The metal cooled my fingers as I eased it over her shoulders. The chains shimmered between her shoulder blades, linking the pauldrons in place. Mine were thick, layered with carved gold plates. Hers gleamed with coin-sized scales, shaped like dragonhide—graceful but strong.

I took my time fastening each clasp. With each one I stopped, waiting for her to take it back, to change her mind or tell me she didn't want it.

Yet she never did.

When I hooked the final chain, something shifted in my chest—a deep, resonant note of finality. It was done. No undoing it now. Not after the treaty. Not after the ceremony. After yoking her to Radaan's future—she was mine, and I was hers.

She laid her hand over mine, the gesture firm, mirroring what I'd done with Greaves. She held tight, as if she knew exactly what twisted in my gut.

"Argos awaits," Nereus murmured.

The black dragon let out a low growl and shifted, presenting his shoulder. He climbed with ease, the fluidity in his movement defying his age. Nienna pressed her lips together in a tight smile before moving to him, grasping one thick, scaled leg.

I would ride in his claws. The insult chafed, but I shoved it down. For Nienna, I would–

A scream tore through the air, sharp and ragged. Heads snapped toward the Nest.

Kalepsi leaned over the edge, her mouth open in fury. Deep violet scales rippled under the light, golden horns flaring as she thrashed. The frills lining her neck flared wide, catching the sun.

Argos stirred on the landing, his head lifting toward her. She bellowed again, leaning so far out that stone pebbles skittered loose, tumbling through the air. The crowd below scattered—parents shielding children, bodies rushing the throne room for cover.

Ivory teeth flashed as Kalepsi flung her wings open, sky glowing through the stretched violet membrane.

Nienna moved to my side. Argos huffed, then stepped off the edge, vanishing in a sweep of scales. The female glided down to take his place, landing hard enough to rattle the stone beneath us. Slightly smaller, but no less imposing.

Her tail swept side to side. Pupils expanded, locked on Nienna, then narrowed with precision on me. I wasn't sure which was worse—riding in the claws of a dragon who loathed me, or climbing onto one who answered to no rider at all.

Nienna stepped forward and placed a hand against Kalepsi's shoulder. Her gaze lifted to the beast's face, which chuffed, breath huffing from flared nostrils larger than my skull. After a long, tense moment, she lowered herself to the stone.

Without hesitation, she climbed onto her back with practiced grace. I shifted my stance, eyes tracking the huge claws tipped with golden blades. She settled between the dragon's neck and shoulder, her form tucked neatly in the curve of muscle. The beast turned to me, lips curled in an open snarl. I didn't move. Every second with these creatures felt like a test I hadn't studied for. Dragons bowed to no human expectations.

With an abrupt jerk of her head, Kalepsi growled—an impatient hatchling daring me to hesitate.

"Kallias," Nienna called from above.

My stomach dropped. She expected me to join her.

I trusted her. That would have to be enough. If she believed I belonged up there, then I'd follow her into the sky.

For her, a Radaanian King—born to walk the earth—climbed onto the back of a dragon.

"Dragons and their meddling," I muttered, hauling myself up. It wasn't graceful. Draconis made it look easy. Only years of battle-trained agility saved me from slipping as I found the space beside her. I settled in behind, wrapping my arms around her waist.

"She's letting you ride," Nienna breathed. The wonder in her voice drifted away in the wind.

My thighs bracketed hers. I held her close, my chest pressed against her back. One hand braced against a smooth scale, its surface slick beneath my palm.

"Like a horse?" I muttered.

The dragon jerked, jostling us both. My boots slid, struggling for grip.

"A flying one."

Kalepsi dipped her head, and the motion pulled us with her. My stomach heaved as gravity yanked us into a plunge.

Instinct screamed to lean back. Nienna's hand shot out, dragging me forward. Strands of her hair whipped free from the braided crown, stinging my face. My chest slammed into her spine. Together, we flattened against a wall of muscle and gleaming violet scale.

Wings snapped wide—massive, sun-drenched sails cracking open. The rush of air howled past. In an instant, Kalepsi leveled out, and my insides lagged behind, still plummeting.

Then came the beat—one colossal wingstroke that heaved us higher. Wind roared. The rooftops below shrank, the city falling away in a blur of black and stone.

Nienna's hand closed around my thigh in a firm squeeze. My heart lodged in my throat as I rocked with the dragon's movements, each shift like riding a myth given muscle and bone.

Terror gripped me, an iron fist snaring my windpipe, but even through the dread, I sensed her restraint. The dragon moved steady, wings spread wide over the city. She banked lightly, letting the updrafts carry us instead of forcing the air. Nereus followed on Argos, a dark shadow flying close—our skybound escort.

Kalepsi's gaze never left the Nest. She kept it always within sight.

Nienna's warmth pressed into my chest. Our mantles tangled, chain links catching and clinking with every shift. She flattened herself against the dragon as we passed the last stretch of Draconia. Argos peeled away when Kalepsi veered, banking toward the Nest.

As she approached the ledge, Kalepsi flared her wings. Her hind legs stretched out, aligning her massive body with the side of the Spire. I grunted, sliding down Nienna's back as the dragon adjusted midair. Violet wings snapped taut, catching the lift. Her forelegs dropped hard onto the bone-covered floor, claws thudding like thunder.

Two steps in and her head twisted sharply. Her eyes locked on me—murder gleaming in them.

"Down. Make for the door," Nienna hissed, hand pressed to the dragon's neck.

I grit my teeth and stared down the snarling maw that hovered far too close. Kalepsi had reached her threshold, the calm stripped away, the wild rage returned.

A burst of sparks ricocheted off my mantle as she spat over my head. Her body coiled between me and the pile of dragonlings, still sluggish but stirring—one by one, lifting heads and narrowing eyes at the intruder.

As soon as my boots touched stone, she lunged.

Her screech split the air. She turned on me as if I'd betrayed her, as though even she couldn't believe she'd allowed me on her back. I stumbled a step, boot crunching over old bones. She threw her head skyward, rearing up—then slammed down again, her roar like a cannon blast in my skull.

I hadn't moved fast enough.

I spun on my heel, stalking toward the Spire's entrance. This was her Nest. I was a Radaanian king, uninvited and unwelcome, a stranger too close to her young.

The place between my shoulder blades burned, instinct roaring to turn and face her. A childhood lesson screamed beneath my skin—never show your back to something that can kill you.

From the threshold, I paused and let my shoulders ease. Nienna had dismounted. Calm, always calm, her hand brushed down the beast's snout with reverent care. Kalepsi had folded into a regal perch before her, head lowered to meet her touch.

Majestic—but volatile creatures.

With a final huff, the dragon turned away, lumbering back to her dragonlings. She left Nienna standing alone in her wake.

My chest tightened.

Nienna walked toward me, her mantle catching the light. The gold shimmered over a dress so white it nearly glowed. She belonged in the clouds. Graceful, delicate—but with her chin high and steps sure. Feminine, yes, but untouchable.

The silver tiara still nestled in her gilded hair. Loose strands drifted down to kiss her neck. A sapphire teardrop hung in the hollow of her throat, set on a fine chain that begged for my attention.

Heat spiked through me. My shoulders locked as the familiar ache hit—sharp and hot.

I swallowed, hand bracing at my belt buckle. Nothing separated us but air, yet panic crept in with its cold fingers. She hadn't turned me away—but neither had she claimed me.

Elohios, I'd tear myself in two if that's what it took to make her happy. But tonight still lingered—unknown. She didn't know my body. Not fully.

She had not seen all of me.

"You look pale," she said with a soft smile, slipping her hand through my arm. "Your first dragonflight will do that."

If only she knew where my mind had gone.

Chapter Twenty-Nine

NIENNA

We spent the night on the beach, the celebration mirroring the Awakening. Dancers spun through firelight, while music leapt from the waves and scattered into the stars. The scent of warm bread, grilled fish, and brine clung to the breeze. Draconia rejoiced. My people cheered my union.

I was happy.

Kallias looked more at ease than I'd ever seen him among my citizens. His back still held that rigid pride, his mantle draped with care—but the furrow between his brows had softened. His posture flowed, no longer carved in stone.

Bonfires dotted the shoreline, and drums thundered. The crowd swelled, unraveled, swayed, while formality burned away with the sun. We mingled freely. My parents had vanished hours before, leaving us for the night.

Curled beneath Kallias' arm, I sank into the curve of his side. His laughter rumbled low when a child stomped through the sand, mimicking a dancer's pounding steps. Firelight sparked across their faces, casting wide smiles in gold.

"They're happy," he murmured.

Pride bloomed in my chest. Not the loud, showy kind—but the quiet sort, rooted deep in my soul. Our people felt peace. Hope. And *we* had given that to them. This joy, this safety, was earned.

"Are you?" I brushed my palm over his thigh, tilting my face to meet his eyes through my lashes.

He grunted. A slow smirk tugged at his mouth. "I could be happier."

"Oh?" I shifted. My hand slid inward, settling on the inside of his leg. His muscle jumped beneath my fingers.

"I'm sitting next to a woman who has been nothing but temptation." He twisted, lips brushing my ear. "And I still haven't kissed her."

My nails grazed along the tender space of his inner thigh. A sound escaped him—half growl, half groan.

"Perhaps if you took her somewhere private, you could correct that."

"I'm a king. I leave when it's considered acceptable."

"And if his queen decides it is?"

His teeth skimmed my ear. "Then I suppose I could be persuaded."

I dragged my palm down his leg to his knee, then rose. His jaw flexed, and he stood, legs stiff from sitting too long. Behind us, Greaves straightened. When Kallias turned, I took his arm.

"We're retiring for the night."

His friend inhaled, chasing it with a sigh. He gave a nod, quiet approval shining within the shadows of his small smile. Though wrapped in black, nearly swallowed by the dark, that flicker of joy warmed something in me.

"He's happy for you?" I asked as we slipped away beneath the stars, moving through alleys and broken moonlight.

"He is," Kallias said, his hand folding over mine. "He's always been at my side. This... is new."

"How is it different from when you were with–"

His finger touched my lips. Gently. "Not tonight. Don't sully what we have with her name."

My throat dried, and I kissed his fingertip as he withdrew. It was careless of me. That marriage left wreckage in its wake. He'd been hurt. Betrayed. I shouldn't have brought it up.

"You're the only one I've ever pushed him away for," he said, the words a low rumble. "I have no intention of sharing."

The city was quiet, but my pulse made up for the silence with a frantic beat, pounding louder with every step toward the Spire.

Stillness wrapped around us and I embraced the hush. My skin buzzed. Something sacred hung in the air. Our passion had always lived in the cracks—hidden glances, stolen kisses, moments we couldn't stretch long enough. But now? Now the world knew. My parents had blessed this union. Our people had sung for it.

Tonight, there would be no shame in our consummation. No guilt anchored to our shared love and desires.

We climbed the Cireendium in silence. Kallias stayed close, though he said nothing. Tension settled along my nerves like mist—thick, heavy, impossible to ignore. My mouth was parched from nerves.

The staff had moved our belongings to a new room. A fresh start. A shedding of past lives.

At the door, I paused, and Kallias stepped forward to push it open.

The space felt different from either of ours, expansive, centered by a massive canopy bed—easily large enough for three dragonlings.

"Subtle." He chuckled, walking ahead.

A bath chamber flanked one side, a dressing room on the other. Rich rugs cushioned the stone floor. Velvet chairs and curved sofas stood as sentinels along the walls.

My lips curled as I watched him pace through each space, checking corners. His instincts never rested. So much like his friend—yet where one moved in shadow, Kallias walked like a blazing sun. Power threaded through every step.

His shoulders eased as he returned, nodding at last.

"I wasn't aware there were rooms this large," he muttered, his gaze snagging on the bed.

"You'd be surprised what secrets the Spire holds."

A quiet hum of amusement left him as I guided him toward the stand meant for his mantle. Two wooden mannequins stood side by side—one broader, one shaped for me.

My fingers drifted to the thick chains across his chest, and I watched his face, waiting for permission. His shoulders paused on a breath, while a muscle ticked along his jaw. His chin dipped ever so slightly, cornflower eyes locked on mine.

The first chain slid loose.

With every length that fell, my heart thudded harder. I bore this burden with him now. As his queen, we would rule Radaan together—equal partners, joined in purpose. He no longer had to stand alone.

One clasp remained, the final golden link drawn taut. Butterflies swarmed low in my belly. He hadn't moved, allowing me to undo the weight on my own.

The clasp gave with a soft click. His yoke hung heavy, and I braced as he rolled his shoulders, letting it slide free. His hands closed over mine, helping to lift and place it on the stand.

Then his touch found me—warm and captivating along my chest.

My heart kicked against his palms. My skin lit beneath his fingers, hypersensitive and expectant. I studied his face, and his brow tightened into deep concentration. When his hand brushed my breast, my breath hitched.

The contact sparked through every nerve, and my body screamed for more—to move, tackle him—but I held back. This was an exercise of patience. This wouldn't be frantic. Not stolen. Not rushed.

He closed the space between us, his hips brushing mine. Then—slowly—he began to undo my chains. Each metal link skimmed my bodice with a whisper, a tease, a hint of promise.

My breath came shallow, fast. Every brush of his knuckles tantalized. By the time the final chain dropped, I trembled.

Calloused hands slid along my shoulders as he lifted the mantle away, setting it aside. My fingers found his coat buttons, and one by one, I worked them free. He let the overcoat fall, broad chest rising with a deep breath.

Next came the vest. Then the tunic. I tugged it loose, and he peeled it over his head.

My body purred in approval, knowing he was mine. His strong frame would press against me, moving with hunger and frantic need as–

A gasp shattered the moment.

I spun.

Kallias shoved me behind him, instinctively protective.

Freya stood frozen in the doorway, a steaming bucket in her hands. "Your Majesty—I didn't expect—I brought the bath."

Kallias turned toward me, a look of pure desperation twisting his features. His eyes screamed of betrayal by the fates. "I can bathe you," he muttered, low, husky, on the brink of snapping.

Freya muffled her squeak while I smoothed my palms down his chest. "Patience, good king."

"I've been patient enough," he growled, letting me step around him.

Smirking, I beckoned my maid toward the bath chamber.

She followed, cheeks flushed, shutting us inside. "Sea beneath," she hissed. "I didn't think it would happen that fast! I came as soon as I heard the door!"

"He won't wait long," I warned, fingers plucking the tiara off my head. She snorted and helped me slip out of my dress.

The bath water steamed, infused with fragrant oils. She worked quick, efficient. This wasn't a ceremonial cleansing—it was preparation. Quick and purposeful.

Last night, I had been scrubbed raw. Tonight, only one layer was needed—scented, silken, ready.

After braiding my hair, she draped a silver lace gown over me, sheer and suggestive. The fabric clung to curves, delicate ridges scraping softly across my too-sensitive skin.

"Wait," she murmured, then pulled a single strand of hair loose, letting it curl against my collarbone. "There." She stepped back to admire her work, then gave a low whistle. "He won't be able to resist."

If only she knew how good he was at resisting.

"Thank you. Now shoo." I laughed, nudging her toward the door.

She flung it open.

Kallias sat on the edge of the bed, elbows resting on his knees, hands clasped in a picture of patience. His tunic hung loose again. He stared at the floor.

Then he saw me.

Freya vanished in a blink.

He straightened when I moved to stand in front of him, his gaze trailing down my body, throat bobbing, fingers tightening over his knees. "Any more interruptions?"

"Would you like a bath?" I teased, grinning at his glare. "No? Then the night is ours, my king."

"Thank Elohios." His tunic hit the bed and his hands found my waist. Thumbs pressed into my belly, grounding me.

His gaze roamed—intense, deliberate. My shoulders, my breasts, the lines of my hips beneath lace. He drank me in.

"You've robbed me," he said, voice graveled with restraint and desire. "I should have undressed you."

I cupped the nape of his neck. "Maybe I can make it up to you."

He stood, hands sliding higher until they tangled in my hair. He tugged, gently tilting my head back. A gasp slipped free.

He flinched.

"Is this good?" he whispered.

That soft tremor, the fear buried in his question broke me. I answered without words, pressing closer. My fingers worked at his belt.

"Nienna," he breathed, loosening his grip. "Tell me if I go too far."

His jaw clenched. Something flickered behind his eyes. A shadow. A memory. His breath hitched as he hesitated.

"You can't hurt me."

"I very well can," he rasped. "Don't take it from me. If I cause you pain-"

I silenced his doubts and fears with a kiss. Fierce. Reassuring. Whatever Eldeiade did to him, I had the rest of our lives to undo—one night at a time.

When I pulled back, I met his gaze. "Kallias, I am the Dragon's Heart. You cannot hurt me."

He stared, brow furrowed, digesting my words.

"Now," I whispered, "kiss me."

Something broke free behind his expression, reigniting the heat and need.

He spun me toward the bed and let me fall. I bounced once, and his stare ravaged every inch of me as he prowled forward.

"My queen," he growled, "I have every intention of kissing you." He lifted my gown, kissed my knee, then pressed my foot into the mattress. "And devouring you. Tonight and tomorrow."

My hands clenched the sheets as he shifted the garment higher, nipping my thigh.

His scruff grazed sensitive skin. "And the day after."

My breath stuttered, body trembling, and I reached for him. He crawled up, settling between my legs. I whimpered beneath the weight of him. His mouth met mine in a kiss that depicted desperation. His tongue moved with slow intent, hips grinding to match his tempo.

A growl escaped me, and I hooked my toes in his waistband, shoving his trousers down. They caught on his backside. He chuckled against my lips.

"Easy," he murmured, fingers fumbling with his buckle.

I arched beneath him, hands clutching his sides, eager for relief I wasn't sure how to get. Lust poured through me, hot and demanding.

"We can be easy another night," I gasped. I pushed his trousers off with a breathless laugh.

He caught my thigh, pinning me in place. "Slow down, Nienna," he breathed, lids clenched and teasing gone as the fabric snagged on his boots. "We have time."

My nails bit into his shoulders, drawing a grimace from him. His gaze snapped open with a snarl, hands tightening on my thighs. I hooked my legs around his back, hauling his hips between mine. A gasp rocked through me. Hunger, needy and insistent, burned through every nerve.

There was no slowing, no pushing desire aside. He asked that we take our time, but our bodies didn't listen, driven to give in to the fire building between us. A flickering spark born of duty and respect now roared into a blaze, wild and consuming.

It was not drawn out, or gentle. It was a man and a woman, boundaries razed, giving in to something base and long denied. Rushed, frantic movements, private moans of pleasure—it was my first time with a man.

And I gave it to the right one.

Argos' roar rumbled in the distance, followed by a sharp chirp from Tsunami. Sunlight spilled through the windows, drawing a warm glow across the sheets. I overslept.

Why hadn't Freya woken me?

Then the ache between my thighs brought it all crashing back to me. My skin flushed, and a slow smile tugged my lips.

Kallias lay beside me, an arm draped over his eyes. His naked chest rose and fell with deep, steady breaths, sheets pooling low at his hips. One hand was shoved under the fabric at his lap, and a bare foot caught the morning light.

When did we take his boots off?

My gaze lingered on his arm—tanned skin stretched tight over corded veins. I tilted my head, curiosity tugging. What exactly was that hand doing under there? My smirk returned as I shifted onto my side.

Kallias lurched, diving off the bed. His grasp flew under the pillow as the sheet chased his legs—ripping it off my body.

I yelped, jerking upright as he thudded to the floor.

Then silence.

"Kallias?"

A groan answered. I crawled to the edge, dropping to my belly to peek down at him. He sprawled in a tangle of limbs and sheets, eyes squeezed shut.

"I daresay it'll take some time adjusting to having someone in my bed," he rasped, voice groggy with sleep.

My hair fell over my shoulder as I laughed, the long waves draping down to tease his bare skin. "Not the same as waking up with Greaves?"

He cracked an eye. "We've never shared a bed." He scrubbed a hand down his face, sitting up. "*I've* never shared a bed."

Did he want to?

He held me close last night, breath soft and hot against my neck, long after need had ebbed. If he hadn't wanted to stay, he wouldn't have. I would've seen the hesitation.

A knock froze us both.

We turned in unison, wide-eyed, staring down the door. Me, bare from head to toe. Him, disheveled on the floor. One nudge and whoever stood behind the wood would get an eyeful.

"Kal?"

"We're fine, Greaves!" he snapped.

With a smirk, I crawled off the mattress, tying my hair into a knot as I strode across the room.

"Sun above, woman."

His voice drew my attention, and I peered over my shoulder, catching his head over the edge of the bed. His hair stuck up on one side, but his eyes were locked on my rear. I grinned and added a little sway as I padded into the bathing chamber.

He let me bathe in peace, despite longing for him. There would be plenty of times to make use of the tub, but routine grounded him. This was as new to him as it was to me. I had no years of solitude to break. He did. It would take time to unlearn them.

When I stepped from the bath, he leaned against the doorway.

I wrung my hair, water dripping back into the tub. "Like what you see, dear king?"

His gaze smoldered. Fully dressed, the picture of control. The man was nothing if not efficient.

"I think I do." His voice curled low. "Careful. Kings tend to take what they want."

The memory of a similar warning on the balcony surfaced. Then, he hadn't dared act. Neither had I. Now? That world had burned. We stood in the ash of it, remade.

I pulled my dress over my head, fabric cool against damp flesh. After tugging it into place, I gave him a backward glance. "Could you?"

He pushed off the wall, a slow prowl. Fingers brushed my lower back, light as a breath. He took his time lacing the gown. When he reached my shoulders, he nipped my skin—then kissed away the hurt.

When his lips found my neck, heat pulsed low in my belly. I swayed, aching. But he only tied off the final cord.

"Be calm," he whispered, his hips nudging against my backside. His breath stayed steady, measured, but his body betrayed his calm composure.

Then he retreated, walking into our room without a glance.

I needed a moment to breathe, to pull the storm inside me into a bottle, to pretend I wasn't seconds away from removing my dress for a repeat of last night. Once the air around me cooled, I followed him.

He stood over his mantle, fingers trailing over the golden links. He glanced at me, jaw set. A silent question lingered in his eyes.

Besides Greaves, had anyone helped him don it?

I let my hair fall wet against my back, nudging him aside. I lifted it with care, though its weight felt disjointed. Awkward and heavy. Not an easy thing to place on anyone, but with his help, I managed to settle it across his shoulders.

He said nothing, working his jaw as I fastened the clasps. Knowing his thoughts were churning and not being privy to them was a new form of torture.

"What's on your mind?" I asked.

He blinked, looking down at my hands. "Aside from Greaves and my parents, no one has placed the mantle on me."

A pleasant flush warmed my cheeks, and I bit back my smile. This moment was mine. Something Eldeiade never touched.

I clipped the last chain, and he caught my hand. Lifting it, he pressed a kiss to my knuckles—silent thanks.

Then, he picked up my mantle.

It was lighter than his, shaped to move with me. Still, how the gilded scales draped felt as if they'd slip off any moment. The chains swayed, brushing my breasts, and his fingers skimmed my chest, deliberate and slow, stoking the fire inside me.

Such a simple act. One that would be part of our daily life—and yet it was intimate. Private. This was just as significant as consummating our marriage. A quiet, sacred thing. A vow spoken without words.

This wasn't only routine.

This was ours. A symbol of our future. Together.

"Tasks for today?" I asked after braiding my hair and lacing my boots.

"I need to be briefed by Fallione, visit my captain at the docks, speak to a noble—was his name Elek?—and, most importantly, have a meeting with my queen."

My fingers paused on the boot's final loop. Brows arched. "Oh? What business requires her attention, dear king? Something you need to discuss?"

"Words won't be needed," he said, adjusting the chains across his overcoat. "But I expect her here by midday."

"And if she has prior commitments?"

"Then I suppose a private beach or closet will suffice."

I smothered a grin and leaned back on the bed, ankles crossed. "I'll be in the library until our appointment, then."

"Libraries are dangerous places."

"Agreed. I might need a king to rescue me."

"I could be persuaded to hold the meeting there." His eyes caught mine in the mirror—hot, merciless. Heat pooled beneath my skin, memory of last night flickering like flame.

A knock scattered the moment.

I rose with a sigh and answered. Greaves waited in the hall, his gaze darting past me. A silver-haired man lingered just behind, his expression soft—so unlike the guard's ever-present scowl.

"Until our meeting," I called, stepping into the corridor.

"What meeting?" Fallione asked.

I couldn't stop the grin edging into place as I strode into the hall.

The morning passed in the library, sorting travel plans with my mother. Endless details. We only had one boat capable of carrying a dragon. It needed inspection—and likely repair—before our return to Radaan.

The Dragon Ship straddled innovation. With a bow and stern like any other, it had a flat, wide center for dragons to rest. Only a small few were the right size to both tow the ship, and fit mid-deck.

Radaan's crew would need to transfer aboard alongside Draconis Vessels. Assembling them would take time, and that task fell to Mother and me.

Near midday, Gertrude, the cook, sent a servant to me.

"She says it's about the bean tea, Your Grace."

Mother looked up from her list. Daylight struck her silvering hair, casting a soft glow. "Bean tea?"

"Tell her I'll be there shortly." I stretched my arms above my head, easing the knots in my spine as the servant bowed and took her leave. "It's a Radaanian drink," I explained.

"They steep beans instead of herbs?" Heavy skepticism laced her tone.

"Something like that." I shrugged, laughing it off. "See you at dinner."

"You're leaving so soon?"

"I have a meeting."

"With whom?"

"Kallias."

"Oh?" She tilted her head, eyes narrowing. After a moment, she dropped her gaze to her papers, a knowing smile tugging at her lips. "I hope it goes well for you."

I spiraled down the Cireendium staircase to the kitchen. Warm scents rose—rich broths, fresh bread. The air thickened with steam from bubbling pots. Laughter and clattering metal echoed through the kitchens.

"Nienna—Your Majesty!" Gertrude waved me over, her apron dusted with flour. She bowed, then pulled a small sack from her pocket. "These were tucked behind the pantry. Are they your beans?"

I took the bag, ran my thumb across the faded lettering. *Kahve'* stood out in half-smudged print.

"Yes! These are the beans!"

"This note was with them." She unfolded a scrap of paper. "It says to sweeten and serve with cream. Cuts the acidity."

"Can you brew it?"

"I'll have it in a blink!" She pressed a pastry into my hand. "You must be starving after last night."

I choked on a laugh.

She paled, flushing crimson. "Oh—no disrespect intended! I just meant... you didn't eat much at dinner."

Biting back a grin to capture my mirth, I took the treat with a nod and let her retreat in peace.

Apples filled the crisp—tart and sweet. The sugar on top crunched between my teeth. Its buttery crust reminded me of Radaan and all the different meals there. I wondered what Kallias made of our food. Compared to the continent, Draconia's dishes were humble—simple in taste.

Moments later, Gertrude returned with a mug, steam curling above the rim.

The liquid wasn't dark like it should've been. Instead, it held a soft, milky hue. Familiar scent—earthy and sharp—rose from the cup, tempered by a hint of sweetness.

With a thank-you, I carried it to our rooms, eager to share it with him.

He sat at the desk, papers fanned in disarray.

"You're late," he grumbled as I shut the door. He didn't look up, only separated one sheet from the rest and set it aside.

"For good reason," I said, settling on the desk's edge.

He glanced at the mug, frowning as he shuffled through another stack. "One moment."

I stayed quiet, inching my knee toward his. The front panel of my dress slipped between my legs, revealing pale leggings. His hand found my thigh, hooked it closer, fingers firm as he continued sorting.

Inventories. Schedules. Rough maps and half-scrawled dates.

At last, he sighed and leaned back. "Now. What is it you have for me?"

"Kahve." I grinned, holding the cup out.

He looked into the mug like it held poison. "Perhaps it's better to keep the drink in Radaan."

"No." I laughed. "The cook found a proper bag this time. That other batch was steeped with beans from your ship."

"You made tea from black beans." He grimaced, then shuddered. "That should be considered treason." He sniffed the drink's contents, swirled it. "Kahve's not usually so pale."

"Gertrude found a note. Says it's best with cream and honey."

"Did you try it?"

My brows pulled together. "I've never liked it to begin with."

"For your sake, then." He sighed and took a sip.

He held it in his mouth. Swished once. Swallowed slowly. His lips smacked. "It is... different."

"Do you like it?" I asked, heart sinking when he set it down.

"It's kahve, but not to my taste." His hand squeezed my thigh. "Other things are."

He shoved the chair back, legs braced wide. His hands settled heavy on his thighs as hunger darkened his gaze.

"As queen, your dresses will influence the court." His voice thickened, husky and low. "Hard to believe that slit's practical for a farming nation. Unless you aim to set every man ablaze with raging lust."

"No dragons to ride in Radaan?" I parted my legs, letting the dress spill between them. His eyes roamed the fabric, but it might as well have been sheer. That look could have burned through dragonscale.

"Not a one. I'm told Radaanian's are not permitted to sit astride dragons."

"And husbands?"

His brows pulled together. "Pardon?"

I slid off the desk and straddled him, legs bracketing his hips. "Are women not permitted to ride their husbands?"

His eye twitched. Blinked fast. "I'm not sure that's what the skirts are cut for."

"I best experiment," I whispered, guiding his hands to my rear. "A queen never leads her people where she isn't brave enough to go."

His touch slid beneath my dress.

And I arched into him, ready to lead.

Draconis dresses were in fact fit to ride, be it husbands or dragons.

Chapter Thirty

KALLIAS

Dinner that night tested every shred of my patience. The formal dining hall shimmered with polished coral and carved driftwood, the walls inlaid with shells that caught the lights. Our first shared meal as king and queen beneath the scrutiny of the Draconis court. Nienna kept her hands to herself—but I quickly learned the secret language lovers spoke in silence.

She laughed with the mayor of K'lan, her smile radiant. Deep blue eyes flicked to me, then snapped back to the noble with practiced ease. Fingers drifted along the front of her dress, the smallest one dipping lower. Just enough to catch my attention. A spark of heat flared.

Lust coiled through me like a flame-hungry serpent. She knew exactly what she was doing.

"The tithe has been taken, and we thank you for your grain," Nyxaria said, her voice slicing through the haze. "Dragons have no need for bread. It eases our people's burden."

I gave the faintest nod, letting wine swirl in my glass. "Only a fraction of what's to come."

Nereus lifted his goblet toward me. "To years of plenty."

"To years of peace," I echoed, tapping my cup to his.

Nienna turned, eyes scanning the room before she sipped her drink. She gave the nobleman a polite pat on the shoulder and returned to my side, settling between me and her mother.

"Jakob sends his best," she murmured as I stood to nudge in her chair. The servant behind her flushed and stepped back, robbed of the task. "He hopes to show you K'lan someday."

Her gaze lifted to mine. Light shimmered in her eyes, joy shining raw and honest in her smile. The force of it landed square in my chest.

No performance. No game. Just a shared moment in a room full of people who didn't want me dead. At last, her family let me exist without suspicion. They hadn't ordered their dragons to eat me, which felt like progress. The nobles kept their smiles fixed and no one spat in my direction. That counted for something.

But the miracle wasn't in the tolerance—it was her. She gave me warmth, laughter, fire. Our time in Radaan had been a flicker, a mere taste of what could be. This... this felt real. And it was only the beginning.

She bit her lip, her cheeks blooming pink. Ducking her head, she let her hand fall between our plates.

I sat beside her, brushed her fingers with mine.

"Do you want to visit?"

"I know it well enough," she said, flashing a smile toward someone across the way. "But I'd like for you to see it. You'll never get another chance."

I nodded as a servant placed a bowl of chowder in front of me—steam rising, broth thick with fish and spice. "Then we shall go."

The evening unfolded easy as breathing. Nienna chatted with her family, her fingers sketching patterns on my hand—the same ones I'd drawn across her skin the night before, once hunger of another kind had been sated.

My mouth curved as she traced an infinity loop on my palm, her focus on her mother's words. I wondered if she realized she was doing it—or if echoing the motion came naturally.

After the plates cleared and the lights burned low, I stood as Chief Jehoikim approached.

"Congratulations are in order, King Kallias Sunspear," he bellowed, dragging every pair of eyes at the table toward us. I caught the guarded glances and the polite strain behind tight smiles. No one liked him. But everyone tolerated him.

I squared my shoulders and leaned in, letting my height press into his space. "Thank you, Chieftain."

He spared Nienna no such courtesy. From the way his gaze skimmed over me, bounced to her—I would wager he thought I got the better end of the bargain.

He wouldn't be wrong.

"She's going to be a fiery one," he said with a low, ugly laugh, patting the sash stretched tight across his bulky chest. "Is your kingdom ready for her?"

"She is exactly what Radaan needs," I replied, my voice steady and measured. I eased a step forward, cutting him off from Nienna. "A queen with claws and fangs. I would have no other."

And a passion bright enough to burn away the darkness.

"She could be what your kingdom needs, but I've been hunting for the time to discuss what your people might *want*."

I nodded through his posturing, grunting at the right moments—appeasing the man's desire to debate trades. Radaan had no use for pearls or crystal trinkets, but my ports remained open. I watched Nienna finish her bowl as he rambled on.

She placed her spoon down, and her eyes swept my frame, snagging on the apex of my thighs. A blush bloomed across her cheeks, and she looked away, tucking loose strands of hair behind her ear.

Pride surged through me. I knew exactly where her thoughts had gone.

"More pearls," Ronan slid between us, voice cool, gaze colder, "mean more Vessels from Draconia." He tossed a glance at Nienna, then let his eyes trail down me with open disgust before dragging them back up.

"I grow weary of trade," I said, slapping a hand on Ronan's shoulder with a smile.

His expression soured, jaw clenched, fingers whitening around his glass.

"Perhaps the prince would be more helpful. He knows what Draconia can offer, and what the Kulletti might share with Radaan in return."

I took my leave without waiting for their response, returning to Nienna's side as she stood. My hand found the curve of her back, and I guided her away from the table, my grip tightening around her waist.

The room. I had to make it to our room. I couldn't take her against a wall like some feral boy who hadn't known a woman.

My lungs burned for air. Control frayed with every step. Her head lowered, her knuckles brushing my thigh again and again.

My lips were on hers before I kicked the door shut. Greaves blurred to the edge of my thoughts. I shoved my hunger aside all day, caged it like some wild animal, and now it broke free, savage and immediate.

She moaned when I spun her into the wood, her back arching as she pressed into me, lips parted, neck offered.

"The bed is right there," she gasped.

I nipped down her throat, trailed soft apologies over each mark I left. She wasn't wrong. The plush mattress and blankets waited across the room—but it might as well have been miles. My body screamed for release *now*. Was this a side effect from being celibate for so long—or just *her*? My body's reaction to her taste, her passion?

"Do you *want* the bed?" I asked, bracing a palm against the door. Gods, Greaves still stood outside. I retreated a step for his sake, not mine.

She circled me, fingers curling into my vest, dragging me forward.

Blonde hair flashed to black, and I flinched, grabbing her wrist. She laughed and rushed toward me, but I backed away, mantle slamming against the door.

Her breath hitched, eyes clearing from desire to concern as she searched my face. "What's wrong?"

I frowned, glaring at her hand. Memories surfaced, a storm gathering at the edge of my consciousness, dark and crashing.

My grip dug into the back of her head in a furious attempt to drive the vision away. I pulled her to me and kissed her. Harsh. Rough. Forcing her mouth open, chasing the essence of wine on her tongue. Her lips moved in time with mine. She stumbled as I surged forward. I caught her hips, lifted her. Her legs wrapped around me, fingers tangled in my hair, yanking hard.

Pleasure flared. Then it died.

The wine turned to ash.

I tore my mouth away, choking on the ghosts of my past clawing at my throat. Nienna pulled back, her hold loosening.

"Don't stop," I growled, falling onto the bed with her. Our clothes vanished. The buttons on my trousers gave way under her hands.

Her blue eyes darkened, bleeding into dark brown.

A snarl ripped from my chest, and I snatched her hips, jerking her closer.

I buried myself in her. Not for escape—but to *stay*. Her fire, her brightness anchored me to the present, grounding every nerve screaming with memory.

Those memories were corpses, whispers from the grave. Dust. Eldeiade was dead.

And I would never be treated that way again.

I stifled a gasp as hinges creaked. My eyes snapped wide, mind scrambling to place the figures slipping inside. One edged along the wall; the other eased the door shut behind them

The person moving wore a dress.

I exhaled hard and dropped my head to the pillow with a groan. Sharing a room brought complications I hadn't prepared for.

Freya crossed to Nienna's side of the bed, eyes downcast. She tapped her gently, whispering a quiet greeting. Nienna moaned, rolled into me, and buried her face in my chest.

I tugged the sheet over her shoulders and nodded at the maid. "Draw the curtains."

"You're worse than they are," Nienna mumbled into the crook of my arm.

"The sun waits for no one."

Fabric scraped along the rods, and muted light slipped through. Greaves stood just inside the door, fatigue etched into every line of his face. He was likely sleeping with the staff—and getting less sleep than I did. My rest had been broken by clawing dreams. I placed the blame solely on Nereus and his rifling through my thoughts.

Or Nienna—she stirred things I had buried, dusted off the trauma, bringing it back into the light.

"Will we have another midday meeting?" she mumbled from beneath the covers.

"If my queen requests such, I'm at her disposal."

I tracked Freya as she moved through the room. She swapped out the water basin, raised her hand, and reignited the mage lights. Quiet and efficient, she finished her tasks and slipped out. Greaves followed.

"Mmm. I think we have topics to discuss." Nienna surfaced, pushing hair from her face and resting her cheek on my chest.

"Oh?" I asked, in no mood to get off the bed.

Her fingers wandered to my waist. "Very important ones."

I shifted my hips away, out of reach, and she gave a pitiful whine while I scoffed a quiet laugh.

An invisible weight pressed across my shoulders as I dressed, but I masked the worry chewing at me. Doubt and concern loomed like a stormcloud, but her humming drifted through the room as she combed her hair, a soft and grounding sound—reminding me I wasn't alone.

Not that I would share this burden with her.

A gentle knock was the only warning before the maid returned, tray in hand. Greaves resumed his post inside the door, ever alert—as if the short redhead might maim us with breakfast.

"Thank you, Freya," Nienna said, lifting a steaming cup of tea. A matching one sat beside two slices of bread topped with minced fish.

"There's some for you as well, Your Majesty." Freya dipped her head, then reached for the comb and took over working through Nienna's tangled hair.

I accepted the drink, though the lack of privacy grated. Nienna closed her eyes after a sip, relishing the warmth. A quick sniff told me it was mint—enough to rouse my groggy mind.

The flavor, however, was not.

Hot. Minted. And briny. As if steeped in seawater. I smothered a grimace and lowered the cup, my tongue recoiling.

Freya attempted to busy herself in her task, though her stifled giggle betrayed her.

"Thoughts?" Nienna asked, her smile far too bright and eager.

"It is… salty," I said, clearing my throat. "Unexpected."

"Traveler's Tea. Riders drink it after long flights." She dabbed oil on her wrists, rubbing it along her skin. "It's my favorite—though most don't care for it."

Her eyes sparkled with mischief, nose crinkling as if she'd won some secret wager.

"I'll leave it to you and the riders," I muttered, giving the cup a sideways glance.

Once we were dressed and presentable, we parted ways. She left to find her mother; I returned to my desk to sort through requests from city mayors. K'bar offered a tour of their crafting district—likely an attempt to parade wares and pitch engineering collaborations. Fallione could go in my stead, but with weeks until our departure, a visit might be worth it.

"Kal?" Greaves' voice cut through the rustle of papers.

I hummed in acknowledgment, setting aside the dwindling ship inventory and focusing on the list of island dignitaries. Who else could Radaan lean on while we were here?

When he didn't respond, I glanced up.

His expression said too much.

I schooled my face into the careful mask I wore at court. Blank. Impenetrable. A wall between me and his unwanted concern.

His brows pinched with disapproval, lips drawn in a deep frown. Worry—and something sharper—shadowed his gaze. One hand rested on the hilt of his sword, fingers curled tight.

"Yes?" I prompted, my voice even. I wouldn't volunteer anything. He was my friend, but I had no intention of adding another witness to my nightmares.

He clenched his jaw, frustration cracking through his worry. When he finally spoke, there was steel in the words. "Don't push her out."

"And here I thought you were worried I'd push *you* out." I let out a slow breath, shrugging it off. "Also—next time? Knock before letting the maid in."

He gave a short nod, eyes still locked on mine, but I returned my attention to the stack of documents that promised to keep my mind occupied for a few hours more.

Nienna arrived for the midday meal, carrying a tray stacked with food and a steaming cup of plain, unadorned kahve. I bit back a grin when she set a small plate aside for Greaves, pretending not to see him. The kahve was stale—but still preferable to the fish-flavored bathwater she'd offered earlier.

She perched on my lap while we ate, rambling through topics like ship logistics. She wanted to leave for Radaan just as much as I did. Whether out of concern for what Tallon might wreck in my absence, or because she sensed the importance it carried for me, she wouldn't delay our return.

Something inside me whispered to hurry, that my kingdom was vulnerable without me. But I'd signed the treaty, agreed to remain in Draconia for a month.

And it wasn't as if I could hold the Craggs against Vellos any better than Darius and his Threshers.

Nienna teased me with her scent—that scorching oil she used drove me mad. I responded instinctively, as if her perfume now belonged to me. The blend of waterlilies and sea air embraced my senses, and my body reacted, as if anticipating what came next.

But then she left, claiming the Nest required her.

I let her go, knowing I'd be of no help there. The dragons tolerated me for her sake, and while I trusted they wouldn't scorch me alive, there was still an inkling of doubt.

A knock, followed by "My king," marked Fallione's arrival.

I really needed to ask Nereus for my own study—too many people in my sleeping chambers made my skin crawl.

"News?" I asked, pivoting in my chair.

"The messenger ships are resettling into their posts," he said, flipping through fresh documents. "A few more days and they'll be ready to handle the doves. Also, a sailor caused a scene in K'lan and authorities are demanding gold for compensation."

"What kind of scene?" I frowned. I trusted Captain Jensen's crew, but I should've given them something to do while we lingered. Men grew feral when idle.

"It appears he's destroyed the interior of a tavern during a brawl."

"Destroyed?" I scoffed. "The goods or the structure itself?"

"Both—You remember Ludwig, Your Majesty?" Fallione raised his brows as if the sailor should've made a lasting impression.

"I was barely functioning on the voyage here," I muttered. Locked in the captain's quarters, trapped with a seasick Greaves and my spiraling thoughts.

"Ah, well... K'lan claims damages exceed three hundred twenty gold."

I stilled. That was more than some ships. "Was he possessed? A dragon in human form? Or just feeling ambitious?"

"It took five Draconis to remove him from the building. A rider had to restrain him. He's confined to a cell."

I pinched the bridge of my nose. The struggles of a king bringing his men to a foreign nation without proper preparation or jurisdiction was a discussion needed to be handled with Nereus. No sailor could pay that kind of restitution, but I wasn't about to let him off either. If he destroyed something, he would have to rebuild it.

"Where is he being held?"

"Second prison of K'lan. He's stable and awaiting your command."

Of course he was. The island teemed with dragons. No matter how brawny, if he crossed a rider again, he'd be bones in the sand.

"What started the fight?"

"A woman. What else?"

The fresh reports listed the charges. Apparently Ludwig had assaulted a man over the affections of his wife. Quite a damning accusation. I'd need to speak with him to address it.

Fallione left, but a king's work never ended. Words bled across the page as my skull throbbed. Just as the headache bloomed, Nienna returned.

I glanced at the window, frowning at the faded daylight. Had I really wasted an entire day at this desk? That never happened in Radaan.

"You're right where I left you," she said with a laugh, vanishing into the dressing room, Freya close on her heels.

"I fear kingship isn't all dragonfire and wedding fair queens," I groaned, rising to stretch and follow. My spine cracked with the movement.

"If only," she called. "I've been swimming through lists of Vessels."

I caught my reflection in the dressing room mirror—wrinkled tunic, loose collar, dull eyes. "You'll be choosing who comes to Radaan?"

"Mother has final say," she said, while Freya worked a deep blue gown around her frame.

I wanted to send the maid out. Her presence stole a moment that should've been mine—skin, dress, hands.

"But she's allowing me to take the reins," Nienna continued. "She's managed the trade for years. I've never been involved. But with Radaan now on the table, she's letting me handle it."

"It'll benefit Radaan. I'll put Claydon in charge of assigning tasks. He'll find use for them."

She snorted a laugh. "Like feeding the goats?"

"That or building them new stables in the Andeluith," I added, unfastening my vest.

"The hardest part is choosing." She sighed. "They have the right to refuse, but if I do this well, there won't be any delays."

"They don't have to leave with us," I said, catching Freya's figure from the corner of my eye. "The Radaanian ship can follow."

"Yes, but the more Vessels I arrive with, the sooner Radaan will see my value."

I folded my arms. The worry in her voice struck a chord. She feared they wouldn't accept her. A valid concern, considering our circumstances. But Radaan was mine—I knew its gods, its court, its people. Their faith in me might have been shaken, but I had to believe I've proved myself worthy of their trust.

Fallione had questioned this path—my coming here—not that I was willing to be swayed. We relied on Elohios' favor of honesty. What happened in the Golden Palace was a mistake. But I was being honest with myself and my people by going after Nienna.

And she worried how they would view her.

"You're dismissed, Freya," I said.

She startled, bowed, and slipped out. Greaves followed without being asked, sensing he'd outstayed his welcome.

"Kallias." Nienna looked over her shoulder. "Now who's going to help me with my boots?"

I prowled across the room, snatching both boots in one hand. She turned, fists propped on her hips as I closed the space between us. My body herded her backward until her knees knocked against a plush chair, and she fell into it, laughing.

"I think I can manage," I said, sinking to my knees.

Her dainty feet were soft, wrapped in sheer stockings. I curled a hand around her calf, smoothing the fabric of her trousers as I drew it down. "Do you doubt your value to my people?"

She scowled and let her head fall back, eyes to the ceiling. "Not my value—I fear they'll see me as..." she wiggled her toes as she struggled to find the right word, "tainted."

I hummed and slid the boot up her foot, tugging the laces tight. "Tainted by whom?"

"Myself," she laughed. "I seduced you, remember?"

"And yet, in Radaan—and Draconia, from what I've seen—people tend to lay the blame on me." I tied the lace, tucking it clean. "Which is where it belongs. They'll be slow to accept you, yes. But my reputation took the hit."

She leaned forward, placed her bare foot in my lap.

In my mind's eye, a different boot—high-heeled, sharp—slammed into my chest.

I blinked the vision away, gripping her ankle harder than necessary to steady myself.

"You think they'll forgive me for trading my betrothed for his father? That they will accept a queen who was found splayed on their king's desk?"

I hooked a hand behind her knee, dragging her closer. "It's bound to happen again," I said, the words a promise.

She laughed and surrendered to my pull, letting herself fall into me. I kissed her with care, corralling the hungry beast inside me. She needed reassurance, not to be devoured.

That would come later.

Chapter Thirty-One

KALLIAS

After dinner, Nienna led me to the private dining room—the same cramped space where Nereus had invaded my mind, my memories. A phantom touch tingled across my scalp. Even with Nienna here, her presence did little to quiet it. I would never carry magic, never allow another soul into my thoughts again.

He'd unearthed ghosts in mere breaths. A shiver crept through my veins, but I stifled the shudder.

"Great, *two* old men." Ronan leaned back in his chair, feet tossed onto the table. He crossed them at the ankles with a dramatic flair.

"Be civil," Nyxaria warned, eyeing his boots with disdain.

Nienna turned to Greaves. "We'll be fine."

He gave her the briefest glance before fixing on me again. His stance held tension—solid, watchful—not out of disrespect, but habit.

I nodded my assurance. "Go. I'll check in before I turn in."

He dipped his head without a word and took his leave. Part of me longed for the relaxed version of him I had in Radaan—the friend who laughed with ease and walked at my side, not in my shadow. Here, there were too many ears listening, too many eyes. I missed his company.

"He's a good man," Nereus said, swirling amber liquid in his cup, staring after Greaves.

I drew out a chair for Nienna beside her mother. "Saved my life more than once," I muttered.

That left the spot next to Ronan for me.

"A decent guard is hard to come by. A loyal one? Rarer still." Nereus reclined in his seat, cup in hand, nodding as if to himself.

As I sat, the prince inched his boots into my space, and I smacked them off the table. They thumped to the floor, and he rolled his eyes, tipping his chair on its back legs.

"How goes the search for Vessels?" Nienna's father asked, sipping his drink.

"Harder than expected." She sighed, resting her head on her mother's shoulder. "We need candidates without families or ties to the islands. That list is short. And sifting through the rest? Tedious."

"Then tighten the net." He grunted. "Kallias and I will settle which riders will fly to Radaan. Then search for their Vessels."

Nienna squinted, gazing at the wall. "That would narrow it down significantly."

"They only work with certain riders?" I asked.

Nereus nodded. "Too much pressure otherwise—lightens the load. And you don't want just anyone poking inside your brain."

His eyes cut through me—sharp, deliberate. I'd built walls around my memories. Surely he couldn't have seen more than I allowed.

"It's a symbiotic relationship," Nyxaria added. "The two have to get along to anchor the flow of magic. Both sides have to agree."

"Some refuse pairings outright," Ronan said. "Either side reserves the right to decline the connection."

I deadpanned. "I can't imagine anyone willingly lets you in their head."

He scoffed. "I'm royalty. I don't answer to the common man. Just as no one expects Father to power the mage lights."

"We are royalty," I corrected. "And we answer to every man."

Nereus lifted his brows, chin dipping in agreement as Ronan's pride took the hit.

A dragon roared outside, and I glanced up at the ceiling.

"You plan for dragons to hold the Craggs?" Nereus pulled my attention back to the table.

"I want them scattered through my watchtowers," I said, resting a hand against my thigh. "A visible threat to deter the Velli."

"You think they'll invade again?" Ronan's tone held genuine curiosity.

"The Velli are..." I paused, thoughts pacing through old wounds. "Persistent and restless. It took too long to push them into a treaty. They never made it far into Radaan, but I never crossed the Craggs either. Perhaps I should've. Still, after years of war, I want something that keeps my people safe. A show of force."

"Then I'll send five bulls," Nereus said. "The largest I've got. That'll ease our tithe as well as provide you protection—but are you prepared to feed them? I won't have complaints about them snatching livestock."

"There's plenty of game in the mountains." Nienna shot me a look, smirking.

I cleared my throat, swallowing a laugh. "They'll be fed," I said. "Their protection's worth the cost."

"And the riders answer only to my daughter. If there's fault or crime, she handles it—or they go home."

"Understood." The words tasted like iron. I'd need a full list of which dragons returned with us—and everything Nienna knew about their riders. Strangers who believed themselves above the law had no place in my kingdom.

"Speaking of crime," Nyxaria mused, turning my way. "Have you heard of your man, Ludwig?"

I drew a breath, steadying it, and Nienna perked up, intrigued.

"I have been informed about an incident in K'lan, though I've yet to speak with him."

"An *incident!*" Ronan laughed. "He tore a tavern apart with his bare hands."

"I should've known you were there," I groaned.

"He's a beast of a man." Nereus shook his head. "Haldor claims he took down five of my men before they knocked him out. All over some married woman."

"Captain Jensen's respected," I said, lips tight. "Fallione picked him for speed, trust, and precision. I wouldn't have boarded just any ship to cross the sea. The captain earned my confidence—and that extends to his crew. I'll speak to Ludwig myself before passing judgment."

"You'll remain here for a while yet," Nyxaria said. "Perhaps we can find work for your men. Let them earn something to take back to their families."

"Send them to the Wild Shores," Ronan offered with a shrug.

His mother tilted her head in thought.

Nienna's frown deepened. "To do what?" she asked.

"Log, build, forage. Keep them away from the cities if tensions rise." Nyxaria lifted a shoulder. "It's a sound prospect."

"You'd send my men to the island your dragons refuse to stay on overnight?" I gave her a tight smile. "I won't ask of them what I'm not willing to do myself."

An idea spawned in my mind.

"If you insist on sending them, I'll go as well," I added. "For a few days."

Nienna sat upright, eyes narrowed to slits. Her face screamed she was guessing at my plans and I almost chuckled at the way she wore her feelings on her sleeve in private. In the dining hall, she would have remained composed, and no one would have been able to decipher what she was thinking.

"It'll take time to get there and back," Nereus murmured, more to himself than to us. "I'd have to leave Argos or use the Dragon Ship."

"It's still under maintenance," Nyxaria reminded him. "Preparing for the voyage to Radaan."

"I admit, I'm intrigued by these shores," I said. "Another continent? This chance won't come again."

Fallione wouldn't be pleased—not when alliances and trade deals waited to be forged with the Draconis populace. But he could manage those.

Nyxaria's gaze slid to her husband. "I'll stay with Ronan. No one knows the Wild Shores like you, Nereus. You could show Nienna before she returns to Radaan."

Nienna's head whipped toward her father, braid swinging. She'd never been there, but judging by how the Awakening and its lights affected her, she wanted to. Her mother must've sensed my plan, and supported it.

"Round trip takes a week by ship," Nereus said, sniffing. "We drop off your men, keep them out of trouble, and send for them when you're ready to return."

That would give them close to three weeks of work.

"Make sure they have two days to spend what they earn before we depart," I added. "And we leave at month's end. No delays."

Nereus nodded, and Nienna's gaze drifted to me—down my chest, then up again. She pressed her lips together.

My body burned with the urge to sling her over my shoulder and carry her to our room.

Instead, I stayed seated.

The meeting—if it could be called that—felt easy. No pretense or forced formality. The family tossed jabs, shared opinions without bracing for impact. It reminded me of dinners with the Sols. Untroubled. Honest. Almost joyful.

Eventually, we retired to our rooms.

"No guard," Nienna muttered, cutting a glance my way. "We don't have to be quiet."

"You never are." I backed her into the room, kicking the door shut.

The kiss landed messy. Greedy. Two bodies aching after a day spent pretending we weren't starving. My fingers tangled in the laces of her dress. I tugged once, then gave up. I broke the kiss long enough to shove a hand behind me to bolt the lock.

"No interruptions," I growled.

Her eyes widened, but her lips curled with a devious grin as she retreated a step.

"You want to be caught?"

"By you." She bit her lip, voice low and coaxing. This was her hesitant place, unsure how to ask, but knowing exactly what she wanted.

I let her drift back, unhurried, unfastening my vest one button at a time. I didn't stop watching her as I removed my tunic—the shift of fabric, her every breath. My hand slid to my belt. I loosened it, steps closing the space between us.

She hadn't removed a single scrap of clothing. Still and composed, she waited for me, wordless. Anticipation clung to her like perfume. She liked when I undressed her, made her feel wanted, piece by piece. A gift meant only for my hands.

Heat surged beneath my skin. That hunger in her eyes, that silent plea—it was for me. Not for a throne. Not for a king. Me. Pride swelled in my chest, pleasure racing behind it, snapping at its heels.

But I was in no mood to take things easy. Slowing down wasn't an option—not tonight. Not after the endless restraint, the hours spent pretending my hands didn't ache to be on her since dawn.

The buckle slipped free, and I crossed the room in a breath, wrapped my arm around her waist, and tossed her onto the bed. Her gasp cracked through the air, chest slamming into the mattress. Her cry was soft—surprised, not afraid.

I didn't give myself time to think.

Her skirts bunched in my fist. I yanked her trousers down her thighs—then stopped cold.

Dark bruises stained her legs.

My breath vanished. Veins iced. I stared at the four brown ovals on her thigh, one more across from them.

A handprint.

"Kallias?"

Her voice echoed as if down a corridor. My heart rammed into my ribs.

Red welts on arms. Bruises hidden under crimson silk. Black hair covering what little remained. Whispers and rumors that I abused women—that I was a monster. That my charm masked something vile.

I flinched.

The memories surged—shadows I thought I'd drowned. I tried to shove them down again, but it was like submerging my fist in a jar of water. The more I pushed, the more they surfaced.

Eldeiade had been cruel. Vicious. And when she started the rumors, it didn't matter what I said. The court believed her. A king who beat women behind closed doors. That's who she made me.

It took years to undo the wreckage—years marked by silence, strategy, and deliberate distance. I refused her hands, dodged her reach, turned every gesture into a line she couldn't cross. Each rejection became a quiet tally, a shield forged from restraint. And now... now Nienna wore the evidence Eldeiade once claimed I left behind.

I hurt Nienna.

There were days I *wanted* to strike Eldeiade. I pictured it more times than I'd admit—yet I never lifted a hand. Her cruelty simmered in my blood. Fermented.

I endured her abuse, waiting for the day she'd go too far and I could call for her head without guilt.

But Nienna?

She was the one sacred, pure thing I claimed in my life. And now her skin mirrored the very accusation I spent years disproving. The lie had found shape again. This time, in someone I cared for.

Tangled on the bed, her trousers slipped low, the dress caught between her thighs like a shroud. The soft rustle of fabric sounded far away.

"Kallias?" she whispered.

I looked up.

Not just eyes. Her whole face watched me, open and unguarded. Irises like seawater. Confusion blooming beneath furrowed brows.

Passion drained in an instant, dying in a puff of smoke. What filled me wasn't cold—it was hollow. An emptiness that gnawed at my ribs.

"I'll be back," I said, the words gravel in my throat. My voice cracked, breaking the air between us like something fragile.

She was not Eldeiade.

"Wait—talk to me."

I backed toward the door, my legs moving while my mind stayed trapped. Thought splintered under the torrent of emotion rising in waves.

Disgust churned first, then shame, then a deeper rot. Not fear of her—but of myself. A pathetic man hunted by echoes that never faded. Her bruises dragged my past into the light and held it there. A living nightmare.

I snatched my tunic, the linen rough in my grip, and shoved it over my head. My fingers found the lock and turned it before my mind caught up. The door swung wide, and I pushed through, desperate for air free of her scent.

Greaves stood there, blocking my path.

His brow snapped into a frown as his gaze dropped to my chest. He stepped aside, but flinched when I stormed past.

He followed.

Failure. That's what this was. A reminder that no amount of progress could erase the scars. Life would always find a way to throw this back in my face. There was no escaping it.

"Where in gods' name do they spar here?" I snapped, fingers buried in my hair.

Greaves didn't answer. He just picked up speed, and I followed. The hallways stretched quiet and still, but I rushed through them, skin on fire.

He led us through the Cireendium, then down to the first level, past the grand floor where we'd signed the treaty. Turn after turn, Greaves moved as if this route had become familiar, like he'd walked it more than once since we arrived.

We stepped into a vast, windowless chamber. Lanterns burned low along the walls, their flames flickering gold over stained wood painted in concentric circles.

A training room, similar to the one I recognized from our boyhood drills.

Weapon racks lined the edges—swords, staves, spears. I walked straight to the shortswords. A spear would've kept him at a distance, but I craved the heat of close combat. I wanted to feel the sting of every strike. Let Greaves knock the guilt from my bones, draw penance for my sins.

Black stone walls loomed around us, matte and lightless. The air pressed heavy, gloom wrapping me like a second skin.

Greaves rolled his shoulders, loosening his stance. I tested the weapon in my grip, adjusting to the unfamiliar weight before I stepped into the smallest ring. He moved to meet me, gaze dipping to the blade in my hand before drawing his own.

As soon as steel cleared leather, I struck. No warning. No hesitation. I threw myself into the clash, a flurry of slashes and parries. Each blow shoved memories deeper. The ringing metal drowned my thoughts.

Greaves slipped inside my defense and seized my wrist. "What happened?" he hissed, breath sharp through clenched teeth.

I wrenched free. He let me go, stepping back, eyes locked on my feet. My chest heaved. A twitch shivered under my eye.

He had asked me the same question once—after the first night with Eldeiade.

With a growl, I lunged. We fell into motion, blades snapping and twisting in tight arcs. Each movement deliberate. Every counter mattered. One mistake could brand us both.

He ducked beneath my guard and clamped an arm around my neck, lips at my ear. "She's not Eldeiade."

"Then why does she remind me of her?!" I roared, swinging wild and hard.

He grunted, rolled free of my reach.

"Why do I see black hair instead of blonde? Why does my mind betray me?" My blade came down again. "Why can't I forget?!"

My muscles screamed. Each strike slammed against his sword, arms shaking from the impact. Pain told me I was strong, that I was still standing. Not the beaten king who hid from his wife.

Or was I?

Was this fighting? Or flailing in her shadow?

Her ghost laughed in my mind. Delighted. Triumphant. I'd pushed Nienna away—and Eldeiade was winning.

I turned and hurled the sword. My scream cracked through the chamber.

Kallias Sunspear, King of Radaan, a pawn in his dead wife's game.

Steel scraped across the floor, echoing sharp. My rage throbbed beneath my skin. I needed to break something. Prove I wasn't weak. Prove I could still feel.

"Kal–"

"You wouldn't understand," I spat, even though he did. He heard the whispers and rumors, saw the stares I endured. Witnessed her cruelty, the jabs I never dodged. She had broken me—the one person I was supposed to trust.

"Pick up your sword, Kallias."

I turned, teeth bared. Nereus stood in the doorway, expression unreadable.

Greaves shifted aside, the loyal guard once more.

"I said, pick it up," Nereus snapped, his voice rising.

"This isn't your business," I bit back, holding tight to the chaos boiling in my chest.

He drew his sword, stepping into the ring. "You married my daughter. That makes it my business."

He swung—not fast, not reckless. Just enough to force movement. I ducked, dove for my blade, and caught it in time to block.

Greaves fought fair. Nereus did not. He struck with a power I couldn't match, strength too sharp, too sure. He had to be using magic—each blow faster than the last, each step more relentless. I barely had a chance to breathe before his sword came again and again, forcing me out of our circle.

His teeth flashed. "Where's your light now, King of Radaan?" He dipped under my guard and slammed the hilt against my ribs. Air left my lungs in a wheeze.

Gods. He *was* using magic.

I stumbled sideways, lungs clawing for breath.

Elohios, hear me. Lend me your strength.

My sword arm flew up to block another strike, but my skin—pale, bare—offered no protection. No glow shimmered beneath the surface. No flicker of light answered my plea. Only silence.

"You've let your past chain you," Nereus said, stepping back as his blade dipped in a slow arc, tip brushing the ground.

My chest rose in heavy, rattling breaths. Pain throbbed deep in my ribs, a steady beat beneath the louder cry of pride.

I was being schooled by a man years my senior. Why did that bother me when I was content to let Greaves batter me?

Because he was my wife's *father*. He knew I hurt her, though I couldn't imagine how.

"My past was buried. Forgotten," I rasped, each word gravel on my tongue. "*You* dug it up."

"Buried, yes. Forgotten?" He gave a small shake of his head. "You might not be new to a union. But marriage isn't about rule—it's about surrender. It's a single soul, split and shared."

My grip tightened on the sword's hilt, knuckles whitening with the effort. "She doesn't need to know."

"You're right," he said, softer this time. "But *you* need her to."

My gaze fell to the floor. No one deserved to carry it, to relive those horrors. To voice it aloud would only stir the rot, drag the past into the open where it could fester in daylight. Yet if I left it buried, would it be any better?

Was he right? Would her knowing help anything? Or would she believe me weak for my flinches, my craving for control?

Would she regret her marriage to a weak king?

"Ready yourself!"

Nereus rushed me again. Steel collided, the blow jarring straight through my arms and into my ribs, which flared with pain.

"Show me your light!" he roared, eyes blazing with fury.

Elohios. Honesty. Truth.

Who was I lying to?

Not her.

Myself.

Brightness flickered in my veins—weak, unsure, barely rising.

This wound was mine, no one else's. But if I left her in the dark, if I allowed her to believe her love had somehow broken me, if she bore guilt for something she never caused...

Forgive me.

Radiance burst from within, lacing my skin with gold. Cracks split across my arms like veins carved in fire. Nereus cursed, lifting a hand to shield his eyes as the brilliance blinded him.

I stood in the glow. My chest heaved. My sword hung loose at my side.

I could carry the burden of my past. I had before.

But Nienna did not deserve to suffer for my actions.

She was my partner, not a crutch. Two halves of a single soul—we rose or fell together. And I had no right to guard a wound she had already reached for with gentle hands and open truth.

"I'm done," I said, the words raw.

I turned from the fight, dragging my aching body to the rack and placing my sword back into its cradle. Behind me, Nereus didn't follow. He watched in silence, unreadable, as if measuring the shape of something that had finally cracked open.

Each step stung. Bruised ribs. Tight breath. But those wounds would heal.

The one beneath? That aching, blistered gash in my soul?

Only she could mend that.

Chapter Thirty-Two

NIENNA

He just left.

I sat on the bed, turned Freya away when she came to help me into my nightclothes, then collapsed onto the mattress, trying to figure out where I went wrong.

My trousers were folded beside my boots. The mage lights cast a faint glow on my thighs, bruises blooming soft and dusky across my skin. I stared at them, as if they held the answers.

A small voice whispered his late wife's name—blamed her. Were the marks of passion too stark a reminder for him? Had I scared him away by wanting too much, too openly? Did I need to quell my desire, become more distant?

I dragged a hand down my face and cursed the silence, the unknown. How was I supposed to fix anything when he wouldn't talk to me?

The door flew open, and I jumped to my feet as Kallias strode in, his shoulders rigid, every step a thunderclap. A storm brewed in his gaze, wild and churning, and I braced myself to face his anger—then, he kissed me.

His lips crushed mine, not harsh but desperate. Pleading. He cupped the back of my head as if he might never let go. I wound my arms around his neck, grounding him, anchoring him. A promise—I wasn't going anywhere.

He smelled of sweat, steel, and something warm beneath—cinnamon and heat, like the edge of a forge. Like home.

"Forgive me," he whispered against my mouth. A lock of silvered hair slipped down between us as he rested his forehead to mine, eyes still closed.

There was nothing to forgive. But this wasn't about me—it was about whatever haunted him, whatever he still carried. If he needed assurance, I'd give it to him.

"I love you," I breathed.

While lavishing him with tender kisses, I stripped him of guilt, of fear, of clothing. I made sure he knew he was wanted and adored without condition. No matter what happened, I would be his. Nothing could change that.

Later, after we lay tangled together, the moonlight painted his chest in soft silver. I traced the scar that had once condemned me from a sketch, and he traced soothing infinity loops along my back.

"You did nothing wrong," he murmured, barely audible. His eyes stayed shut, as if speaking into the darkness offered protection.

I shifted, chin resting on his chest, gaze pinned to his face. "Then why did you leave me?"

His breath caught, his hand faltering against my spine.

"You know about my previous marriage through hearsay and rumors. Through gossip. But not the truth." He paused, jaw tightening. "Eldeiade had a gift for manipulation. She could charm a room and twist a crowd to bend to her whims. I was younger than you when we married. My parents died, and the throne demanded a queen. She was chosen."

He scoffed, bitter.

"She was beautiful. And I thought that would be enough."

I shot him a glare, but his grimace said he knew better now.

"I had no idea how wrong I was. Her mask cracked the night of our wedding when she–" He hesitated, gritting his teeth before he continued. "Gods, saying it aloud makes it seem so trivial. Pitiful. A man should be better than this."

I braced my elbow on his chest and rested a hand over his heart. The heart that was *mine*—not some dead queen's. "Tell me."

His eyes opened, sadness pulling one corner of his mouth into a crooked smile. "You're nothing like her—everything she wasn't. Every day with Eldeiade was a battle. She chipped at me with insults and commands, made mockery a ritual. She wore me down like a plow through a field. Nothing I did ever pleased her—and that was just in public."

He turned his face upward, staring at the canopy above. His jaw clenched as moonlight caught the pain in his eyes.

"She wanted an heir more than anything, but she was volatile. She'd strike me, belittle me. Refused to share her bed." He paused, as if tempering the memory. "Not that I tried after that first night. I was a tool to her, a means to an end. When I stopped trying, she accused me of striking her, blamed me for her injuries. Spread stories, rumors that I abused her. Called me a beast in a gilded mask."

He fell silent.

"But she got what she wanted: a child. And I was finally free."

"Was it the bruises?" I asked, soft as a hush, careful not to shatter the moment, to break the spell over us.

He nodded, sitting up. A broad hand peeled away the sheet, revealing the faint smudges on my thighs. Small banners of our passion.

"They brought everything back. What she said about me. What people believed." His voice shook. "But seeing them on you... I wanted to kill her. To drag her from her grave.

"Last night, I wanted to ground myself in you—and left her marks on you instead."

My breath hitched, and I tilted my head. "You think being rough was too much for me? Stand up."

He hesitated.

"Go on. Shoo. To the mirror."

Grumbling, he rose and crossed to the polished glass. I let my gaze trace the lean power of his form, then turned him by the arm.

His back bore red welts. Dozens.

"Seems I can hold my own," I purred, fingers sliding up his jaw to bring his face close. "But if you ever need me to slow down, I will. If something reminds you of her—tell me. I won't treat you like a child, or think less of you. Don't bear it alone."

His forehead dropped to mine, the weight in his chest easing with the breath he exhaled.

"In so many ways," he murmured, voice thick, "you're my first."

Warmth surged in my blood, pride thrumming through every limb.

"And you will forever be my last."

Chapter Thirty-Three

KALLIAS

It didn't take long to ready a small ship. The day was spent coordinating between Captain Jensen and the Draconis captain, Wylyn. Nienna was kept occupied preparing for departure, and by the time evening approached, I managed to slip away to K'lan and seek out Ludwig.

The jail was cramped, humid with the stench of sweat and old iron. A single glance at the sailor explained how he'd held his own against a gang of men. He stood taller than me and broader by half. The cell barely allowed him to sit, let alone pace.

He rose when I entered, bowing low. His head nearly scraped the bars—though I doubted they'd contain him if he chose otherwise.

"Your Majesty!" A worried frown cut across his weathered face, fingers twitching at his sides. His beard, thick and tangled, barely veiled the grimace underneath.

"Sailor," I said, sweeping my gaze over his stained tunic and threadbare trousers. This man, a Radaanian in Draconis chains, represented more than himself. He reflected on all of us.

"I beg your pardon, my king. I didn't mean to cause any trouble."

"Trouble?" I arched a brow and took the nearby chair, the chain of my mantle clinking with the motion.

"You must be a busy man," he said, fumbling. "Many things need your attention—more important than me, I'm sure."

He apologized for the inconvenience, not his actions. Interesting.

Greaves blocked the door behind me, keeping the Draconis guards at bay. This was a Radaanian matter. I'd deal with the fallout and payment with Nereus later.

"My people deserve my complete focus," I said, motioning for him to sit. "Start talking. Why dismantle a tavern?"

He dropped his gaze and sank to the cot, the wood groaning under his weight. "I didn't want the woman—they be sayin' that."

"I'm not here for Draconis accusations, sailor. Tell me the truth."

His fingers scratched the back of his neck as he sighed. "Well, we were just drinkin', tryin' to pass the time. Petty little to do 'round here. And we best not linger out in the open or them beasts might think we're a snack. You know how it is. And a man was—he was mistreating his missus, you see. Wouldn't sit right if I didn't say somethin'."

I resisted the urge to pinch the bridge of my nose, knowing where this headed. "Tearing apart a place of business is hardly saying something."

"Told him he ought to rethink his behavior," Ludwig continued. "Then she smiled at me, and he done struck her." He shook his head, breath catching. "Couldn't stand for it."

"So you retaliated."

"With a might bit more fervor, Your Majesty."

"And the others? I can assume the men you fought were just innocent bystanders?"

"Little lady was hidin' behind me, my king." He looked up, earnest. "What's a man to do when a woman wants his protection?"

Now I saw it. In his mind, he hadn't started a fight. He'd answered a call. I couldn't fault him for his actions. But this wasn't about morality—it was about diplomacy. This strained relations between Draconia and Radaan. We needed our people to get along, and tavern brawls were hardly the solution.

I exhaled, pressing my hands to my thighs. "May Elohios bless your honesty, but you're indebted. You may have acted with honor, but your timing was poor. We're guests here. You can't strike a Draconis again. Not for any reason. Understand?"

His chest deflated, gaze dropping like a scolded child's. "Aye, Your Majesty."

"You'll be released," I said, "and escorted to a Draconis vessel. We sail for the Wild Shores at first light."

His face drained of color.

"You are to work the island with Jensen's crew—earn your keep. And your pay will be docked to compensate for the damages."

"I've heard stories 'bout them shores... You're leavin' us there?" he whispered.

"After I walk it with you." I met his stare without flinching. "If islanders can swing an ax, so can a plainsman."

"They say dragons won't even land there..." His words trailed off, the tremble of fear unmistakable.

Sailors were notoriously superstitious—rumors clung to them like barnacles to a hull. But I expected better from my men.

"Where I go, you go," I said, the weight in my voice leaving no space for dissent. My bond with Elohios might feel frayed this far from Radaan, strained as though stretched too tight across the sea, but faith wasn't rooted in proximity. He would protect us. The Draconis had worked those shores for years. If they managed to survive, I had no doubt my men would walk away unscathed.

I rose, turned, and left the room without a backward glance.

At the desk sat an older rider—Haldor, the same one who'd restrained Ludwig. Thick arms crossed over his chest. Behind him, another Draconis lingered, posture stiff with quiet disdain.

"Release him to Captain Jensen. Escort him to Wylyn's ship," I ordered. "He's confined to the deck until the vessel departs."

Haldor's eyes narrowed, slow and deliberate, as if weighing whether he needed to obey a foreign king. I didn't wait to see his choice. With his silence in my wake, I moved through the tight, sunless corridor, then out into the open air.

I'd never get used to how narrow these streets were, or how tightly the buildings hugged one another like huddled sheep before a storm. The island felt overcrowded, breathless—a place wrapped in endless ocean, yet starved for space. A single outbreak away from being wiped out by a plague.

Greaves followed without a word as we wove through the stone alleys, unhindered by guards. The lack of their presence felt oddly freeing, like walking Reem's streets in childhood—before the mantle, before its weight. Here, the threat of blades in the dark didn't linger. The greatest predators flew above, scaled and clawed, and yet they doubled as protectors.

Tsunami soared overhead with a curious chirp. Her tail undulated behind her like a streamer caught in wind. I watched her vanish between rooftops, unsettled by her capricious nature. She lacked the discipline of a trained mount. She needed a rider.

Then again, who was I to guess at Draconis' affairs?

At the Spire, the evening passed in ease.

At dinner, I found myself watching Nienna more than I listened to the chatter. She moved with fluid grace between nobles, her voice a steady current in ever-changing waters. One moment she spoke of pearls with the Kulletti; the next, she detailed a coconut blight with the Ivetti. She smiled through a striped bass debate with a local mayor as if it were nothing more than idle sport.

At her age, I had fumbled through court like a colt on ice. It had taken me years to command a room the way she did now, with softness instead of sharpness. Where I once barked to be heard, she whispered—and the whole table leaned in to listen.

Perhaps it was the dragons. To be raised in the Nest would forge anyone in fire.

Later, we joined her parents in their private dining chamber. Nereus passed me a goblet of spiced mead, the closest Draconia came to cider. I took a long sip. It filled my chest with warmth, the heat spreading to my skin in a slow, pleasant hum.

Talk of the upcoming journey continued. Nienna chattered about the ocean lights, her voice full of breathless wonder. Nereus looked on with that peculiar mix of pride and longing only fathers carried.

Guilt nipped at my resolve. These were her final weeks here. Final nights in the only home she'd ever known. I was stealing her from them—taking her away from everything familiar.

And yet, I would give her more.

A kingdom. A legacy of her own. Nienna had dragons, but she deserved more than sea air and tides. She needed land beneath her feet that stretched to the horizon—a sky unbroken by cliffs and towers. Here she would be stifled, smothered like a vine trying to take root between cracks of a building.

She would either wither, or her roots would shatter the foundation.

When we returned to our chambers, she was careful with me, her movements gentle, her gaze unwavering. Her kisses held no ghosts. Her hands carved away every memory until only Nienna remained.

She wasn't a shadow tainted by my past. She was light. Real. Present. Mine.

The ocean wind flung Nienna's hair behind her shoulders, exposing pale skin to the sunlight. She tipped her head back, face tilted to the sky, a wide smile lifting her lips. Her deep green dress snapped and twisted around her legs, the fabric caught in the tug of salt-laced gusts.

I leaned against the ship's railing, feigning admiration for the endless blue. My chest clenched against the emptiness stretching in every direction. No trees. No cover. Just open sky and the gnawing thought that some great-winged monster might pluck me up and carry me away.

Argos' shadow rolled across us, and the massive black beast emitted a low, mournful groan. His golden eye fixed on Nereus, who stood with his captain, bent over a map.

I counted myself fortunate to remain above deck—far from Greaves, who battled for his life. He'd fared poorly from the first swell, unable to keep down so much as water. The man could stand against Velli spears, but a ship's gentle sway undid him—a blow to the poor man's confidence.

"Look!"

Nienna pointed toward a fin slicing through the water. A whale surfaced, exhaling a misty plume. Its dark bulk carved through the surf, magnificent in its grace.

Then Argos dropped from the sky.

The whale's tail arced above the waves just as the dragon's claws struck. Blood sprayed into the air. Water churned beneath them, a whirlpool of violence as Argos wrestled to lift the creature. It thrashed free with a heave, slipping from his grasp. With a grumbled growl, the dragon wheeled and soared back toward Draconia.

The voyage to the continent passed with little else to note. My men shifted and paced, nerves running thin. The Draconis crew did what they could to ease their anxiety. Nereus offered reassurances, claiming no monsters lurked the forests. Any deaths came only from natural causes.

By the next morning, land rose on the horizon. Hills thick with trees stretched toward the sky, but along the shoreline, the forest had been pared back. Stumps dotted the sand, and felled trunks lay in neat rows. Several ships waited at makeshift docks carved into the shore.

As we disembarked, a man approached—leathery skin browned by sun, face wrinkled like dried fruit. A wide-brimmed hat flopped over his brow, matched by his baggy clothes that hung loose on a wiry frame.

"King Nereus!" he shouted, voice booming across the waves. "Good to have you!" He pulled the man into a back-slapping hug. His clouded gaze caught on Nienna and me, and he paused.

Nereus gestured between us with a flick of his hand. "Barchalk—my daughter, Nienna. And her husband, King Kallias Sunspear of Radaan."

He recoiled, eyes wide, jaw slack. "She married the king? I heard about the–" He clamped his mouth shut as I lifted my chin, stiffening. "There were whispers of news... but not that she married. Beg your pardon, Your Majesty." He bowed deep, snatching his hat from his head.

"Well met, Master Barchalk," Nienna said, gaze drifting to the busy shore.

"We've come to offer aid," I added, drawing the man's confused stare back to me.

Nereus slung an arm over his shoulder, guiding him toward the sand. "They'll be with us a few weeks yet. Might as well put the foresters to work."

They weren't forest men. Plainsmen. Sailors. Used to wind-bent trees and open fields—not the dense thickets of western Radaan. Still, I let the Dragon King's words pass without correction.

Nienna slipped her hand through my arm as we stepped from the gangplank. Greaves followed close, face pallid, desperate for solid earth under his boots. The thud of our steps vanished beneath the clamor of saws and shouted orders.

Men hauled timber, stripped bark, sawed lengths into beams. Lumber flowed in a steady rhythm from the forest to the ships. I frowned at the camp. No buildings, only canvas tents. No roots in the land. As though they could vanish by dawn.

Nienna's fingers squeezed my arm. Her expression stayed calm, but I felt the tension beneath her skin. The sand crunched underfoot, bleached so white it forced me to squint toward the distant treeline. They logged with precision, neat and orderly, but no signs of regrowth marked the cleared ground.

If they meant to settle, they'd need space. But if they only wanted wood, they should treat the land as a farm—harvest, then replant.

Simple thoughts. A farmer-king's thoughts. Likely not ones that ever crossed a Dragon King's mind.

We followed him and Barchalk to a canopy shading a table.

"Any developments?" he asked.

"Nothing new, though the blasted snakes remain a nuisance. Bite at the workers, but that spirit trick still works. Splash it on their faces, and the slithering things pull back quick."

My brow knit as I glanced at Nienna, who only smiled. Snakes, then. Harmless enough, apparently.

"I notice your dragon stayed behind," Barchalk added.

A flicker passed over Nereus' face. He brushed a leaf from the map on the table. "Argos is... reluctant to linger."

I made a quiet sound. "They sense danger—but are content to leave their riders here?"

The king's gaze turned sharp, and his tone lost its warmth. "If I believed there was true risk, I wouldn't have brought my daughter."

Nienna's grip tightened—a silent plea to let it go. Perhaps Draconis trusted their dragons the way we trusted our gods. But I questioned it. Where they saw guardians, I found creatures with instincts sharper than words.

I held my tongue and leaned closer to study the map.

The northernmost shore, where we docked, sprawled out in precise detail—but to the south, the ink faded into emptiness. Eastern and western coasts had lines and names, but the interior remained untouched. The blank space hinted at a single truth—they never strayed far from this point.

"One day, we'll send cartographers deeper," Nereus said, noting my study.

"We're still mapping northern Radaan," I replied, understanding all too well.

Barchalk let out a wheezy chuckle. "We've lived on this planet for countless years and have yet to see it all. Strange, isn't it?"

I sank into a sun-bleached chair beside Nienna. "Why haven't the other islands pushed to settle here?"

"Dragons," she answered. "The wildlings fly south. The islanders know what they become without a rider."

"End up like Prince Adoni." Barchalk spat at the ground, then winced and darted a look at Nienna. "Begging your pardon, Your Majesty."

"It's the truth," Nereus said. "We hold the Wild Shores because we have the airpower to force our way here. No other island nation can claim that. If it came to war, they'd sit on the water like kindling."

"But we wouldn't strike without cause," Nienna added.

Her father and Barchalk exchanged a glance. The land was rich, tempting—a valuable resource worth fighting for, if Draconia hadn't already laid claim. I rested a hand on her thigh, subtle but firm. She didn't want to go down that road.

The rest of the afternoon passed in talk of trees—measured clearing, careful strategy, rotations and cuts. Nienna answered questions when they came, always polite, but her gaze kept drifting past the tents, toward the untouched forest, thick and shadowed.

We dined on the beach. The workers erupted in cheers when they discovered we'd brought Radaanian grain. My men chuckled. Simple bread, nothing to us—yet it raised spirits like fire on a cold night.

As the sun dipped below the water, I left Greaves with our mantles and slipped away with Nienna. The breeze nudged her skirts, tugged at my sleeves. We rounded a bend in the dark shoreline, out of sight, where she dropped onto a smooth stone and yanked at her boots.

"They won't eat you?" I asked, lowering myself beside her and peeling mine off. "No tiny monsters waiting in the water to poison your feet?"

She laughed, already standing, wriggling out of her trousers. "Oh, you'll be plagued for sure."

"There are worse ways to go." My voice deepened, body heating, as she bent over to step free of them, knowing there was nothing beneath that dress. But this moment wasn't about me. She had waited her whole life for this—freedom, wild waves, and sky.

"You'll meet your end as an old, old man," she said. "In your sleep, next to me."

"You want me to die in your arms?" I rolled my trousers to my knees, smirking. "Sometimes I swear my heart will burst with you."

She glanced back, smile curving. Mischief lit her face. "Your heart is that full?"

I moved close, brushed my mouth against her neck, catching the faint salt on her skin. "I'll show you tonight."

She shivered, then bent to knot her skirts at the knees. The hem hiked above her calves as she walked into the surf.

We stayed out until blackness swallowed the horizon. Then the water came to life.

Nienna stepped forward. Her bare feet dipped into the waves, a slight glow along the crests. Each step caused a flare in the luminescence. She laughed, breathless and soft, and ran through the shallows. Pale strands of hair flew behind her, catching moonlight as she moved. Blue light burst from her movements, reminding me of her father's magic.

I reached down, dragging my fingers through the tide. A radiant glow clung to my skin, gleaming like stardust.

The world shrank. No kingdom. No throne. Just her, and the crash of luminous waves.

We wandered for hours—knee-deep in glowing surf, toes sinking into warm sand. Shells crunched beneath us as I laid her down on the beach, stars wheeling in slow arcs overhead.

My tunic became a pillow. Her head nestled close beside me. Everything stilled.

And she was right.

My heart brimmed.

Whatever waited back home—war, duty, pressure—I could face it. For once, I wasn't drowning or crumbling under the pressure.

She curled into my side, leg draped across mine. "Kallias?"

I answered with a low hum, my fingers threading through her tangled hair. Above us, the stars blinked in silence, the only witnesses to our stolen moment.

"What are you going to do with Tallon?" Her voice carried hesitation, as if the question pained her to ask.

"I'll banish him to the Valley Beneath." No other answer existed. Elohios would guide me when we returned to Radaan, and Fallione would stand at my side. The valley where I cast the lost and irredeemable—Tallon belonged there now.

"I doubt your people will accept that."

"Then I'll name him a bastard."

Her breath warmed my chest. "After a lifetime of calling him your son?"

The thought soured my stomach. She was right—Radaan had built its future on the assumption he would inherit the mantle. That certainty would be torn away, and without an heir to take his place, the kingdom would be left staring into a void, an uncertain future.

"Do you see him as your son?" She lifted onto her elbows, eyes searching my face, storm-dark and sharp with feeling.

"Maybe—at one point." My throat closed around the words. "There were moments, as he grew beside Eldeiade, where I saw it—brief flashes of what might've been. He kept his distance, but I caught it in his eyes. That hunger. He wanted a father."

I clenched my jaw, unable to meet her gaze. The stars above held no judgment, only cold light. My mistakes meant nothing to them.

"I don't know when it changed. The want twisted into something darker. He's my greatest failure—not for what he became, but because I let it happen. I stood back while a monster raised him, and for some reason, I expected him to be different, that he'd rise above it."

She held still. Quiet.

"He attacked me."

My chest locked up. I turned to her, sharp and fast. "When?"

"One night he—he followed us to the balcony. I didn't see him." Regret strained her tone. "It was when we knew—when we realized it couldn't ever work. After I left you, he confronted me. Accused me of sleeping with you."

She was here. Safe. An ocean away from him. I brushed hair from her cheek, letting the moonlight spill across her skin. Rage smoldered in my chest, but she was unhurt. Whole.

"He always suspected it," I said. "He thought you were trying to replace him. That wasn't my plan. I was prepared to give Radaan to him. Every decision I made pointed toward shaping her for his rule. Until you."

"And now I've changed everything." Her smile softened as she leaned into my palm.

"I won't pretend to know what's ahead. The future's uncertain. But I'm her king—Radaan will follow me." I ran my thumb across her lips.

She caught it between her teeth, then drew it into her mouth. Her tongue traced the pad, teasing, warm. Heat surged through me like a lit fuse. My pulse drummed in my throat.

"And as her king," I said, "I have a duty to produce another heir."

I shifted, rolling her beneath me in one smooth motion. Laughter burst from her lips as strands of hair fell across her face. I brushed them aside, pressing my weight into the cradle of her hips.

Exactly where I belonged.

"Do your best, my king."

Greaves found us knotted together, limbs entwined, calling out that Nereus demanded we return to the ship. Sand clung to our damp skin, buried in every crease, and we made our way back like two young lovers caught in the throes of passion.

Nienna lent me youth. I wasn't blind to my years—my joints refused to let me forget—but her presence woke a piece of me long buried. She moved with radiance, and her brightness inspired me. It hinted the world didn't have to be so bitter, so bleak.

The moment our boots hit the dock, a sound cut through the night.

A scream. High, shrill, strangled. It split the air with jagged force and ended in a sharp snap.

We both turned to the sky. I'd heard dragons before—but this call didn't match any creature from Draconia.

"In the ship, Nienna." Nereus stood at the rail, arms folded behind him, eyes locked on the stars. "You too, King of Radaan. These shores do not welcome wanderers after sundown."

No protest rose. Exhaustion pulled at me, and I followed it to our cramped berth. Sand gritted in the sheets, clinging to sweat-damp limbs, but I couldn't bring myself to care. I lay on my side, and Nienna pressed in close, tucking herself against me, guiding my arm around her waist. I nestled my chin into her hair, breathing in her scent, her warmth.

She endured more talk the next morning, sat through another round of tree assessments without protest. Ludwig, once a logger, made himself useful among the Draconis—but Nienna's eyes wandered toward the forest. When her gaze turned pleading, I claimed fatigue and excused us from the talks.

Someone passed around Traveler's Tea, something about salt and sweat, but I politely refused the cup of minty fish water and followed Nienna, who offered to pick more herbs for the tea. Basket in one hand, my arm in the other, she tugged me toward an overgrown stretch of beach. Greaves stayed behind. His slow blink and reluctant step back said it all—he knew why I dismissed him and wasn't happy about it.

Thick foliage spilled across pale shore, wild and tangled. My chest ached, longing for Radaan. The sun's quiet warmth on my face. The soft roll of hills draped in forest. A hollow ache stretched inside my soul—one only my kingdom could fill.

Our boots struck dark soil where grit gave way beneath a canopy of palms, shifting into thicker trunks. Shade pressed down, and my mantle cooled against my shoulders.

Nienna stared up at the treetops, her eyes wide.

I smirked. "Mint grows on the ground."

She laughed and bent to cup a red bloom, fingers careful around the thorns lining its stem. Her cheeks flushed with heat and the trek's exertion.

Sweat trickled down my spine; the forest air pressed against my skin—humid, heavy. The scent of crushed blossoms, rich soil, and the faint sweetness of waterlilies clung to her clothes.

"If you weren't a king, what would you be?" she asked.

"Dead," I snorted. I'd never had another option. The throne had always been my destiny.

She rolled her eyes and wandered deeper, one hand gliding along the bark of a gnarled tree. "I think I would've liked to explore. There's so much no one's ever seen."

Sunlight broke through the canopy, striking her scaled mantle and scattering it in prisms. She knelt by a patch of mint, brushing the leaves with a delicate touch. When she looked back, her eyes stole my breath. She belonged in wide-open spaces. Draconia would never be enough.

"Someone might've seen it," I said, resting a shoulder against the tree. The gold chain of my mantle dug into my joint. "Whatever made that noise last night might have eaten them."

She pointed at me. "You're not wrong."

"As thrilling as it is, most explorers die before they return. And those that do come back bring more scars than stories."

With a sigh, she plucked a sprig of mint, twirling it between her fingers. The gray sleeve of her dress slipped off one shoulder, skin gleaming like marble in the shade. A beautiful temptation.

"But still—imagine the adventure."

I cocked my head. "Is your life not thrilling enough, my queen?"

She purred, letting her gaze trail over my body. "Oh, things have been plenty exciting lately."

Heat flared beneath my skin. I squatted beside her, plucking the sprig from her hand. "That's not spearmint."

She blinked. "Looks like it."

"A hazard of marrying into an agricultural kingdom." I shook my head. "You'll need to learn the difference. Spearmint's sweeter. Smoother. Lighter on the tongue. Leaves a man wanting more." My gaze slid down her frame, settling on her mouth.

"This," I said, lifting a darker leaf, "is peppermint. Stronger. Sharper. Bolder." I held it up between us. "See the veins? Deeper. The taste stays—but it cuts first."

"They grow so close," she breathed, her tongue skimming her lower lip. Eyes locked on mine. "How can you tell them apart?"

"Practice, my queen." I leaned in, advancing on her.

She lost her balance and tumbled back with a startled laugh. I smiled, crushing the leaf between my fingers, hovering above her. My mantle spilled down her chest in a soft, gilded cascade.

"We're supposed to be gathering mint." Her breath hitched, body already strung tight with expectation.

"I never agreed to those terms." I settled between her thighs, and her gaze followed my hands as I undid the fastenings at my collar. Lips parted. Knees pulled in beside me. "I came to watch."

"Me pick herbs?" she asked, laughing under her breath.

The last link slipped free, and I shrugged off the mantle. It landed in a gleam of sunlight. "To watch you come undone."

The sun poured over bare limbs. I folded my clothes with care; hers landed wherever they fell. A picture of my life. My calm and her chaos. I'd never sought to anchor her—only to move with her whirlstorm.

Later, green smears streaked across us. The scent of mint clung to sweat and warmth. Sunlight traced the lines of our bodies, and the world faded to birdsong and distant waves.

"Kallias?" Her breath brushed my cheek. Eyes shut. Voice soft with exhausted satisfaction.

"Hmm?" I kissed her forehead, tucking my arm beneath her head. Numbness crept down my fingers, but she was so perfect. I refused to move.

"I love you."

My chest ached with those words. I still wasn't used to them. They came after mad desire, after heated pleasure. Simple, unadorned—but I devoured them like a starving man.

"You'll grow tired of me." My hand tightened on her hip, as if my body rejected the idea.

She giggled, fingers stroking the stubble creeping back across my chest. The gray mocked me. A reminder of years between us.

A booming roar exploded in the distance.

I flinched, and Nienna bolted upright, every muscle wound tight. Leaves and twigs tangled in her hair, and she stilled, breath caught in her throat, eyes trained north.

When she spoke, horror filled her words.

"A dragon is coming."

Chapter Thirty-Four

NIENNA

I knew that roar. Deep. Earth-throttling. Argos.

I scrambled for my clothes. A seam tore as I yanked my dress over my head. My skin crawled, heart raging to a chaotic pulse under my ribs. "They never come—not without a rider."

Kallias dressed with precision, each motion quick, exact. Determination drew harsh lines across his brow, shadowing his features with concentration.

I bit my cheek, trying to steady my unease. "They fly in at first light, rest through the heat, and leave before dusk. A dragon doesn't arrive this late in the day unless–"

"Let's go." He cut me off, fastening the last clasp of his mantle. He grabbed the basket, dirt still dusting his silvering hair, but I didn't stop to brush it away. I bolted for the shore.

My instincts screamed to run, but brambles snagged at my steps. I tripped twice, steadied myself, forced my pace to slow. Panic surged like a tide. My fist clenched around my skirt as though the fabric might anchor me. Leaves whispered, branches shifted—nothing escaped my ears.

We broke through the treeline just as Argos dropped from the sky.

My hand flew to my mouth. He spiraled downward, wings faltering under his weight. The left buckled. He crashed into the beach with a guttural cry, the impact rattling the ground.

Father stood apart from the tents and men. Alone. Hands folded behind him. Chin high. Shoulders stiff as he watched the wounded creature right himself with a weary groan.

Whatever brought Argos here, Father had chosen to face it.

Kallias' hand settled at the small of my back with a gentle push. I didn't need more. I descended the hill in long strides, breath catching at the sight before us.

The dragon's wing hung limp, its tip dragging a trench behind him. Labored breaths hissed from his flared nostrils. His head lifted and snapped at the air, gold eyes narrowed to fierce slits. Massive claws shredded the shoreline, spraying white sand.

I reached Father's side. Wind tugged at his beard. He never blinked—his gaze held fast to the dragon, locked in a wordless exchange.

He drew in a breath, and fury hardened his features.

Argos mirrored him. A snarl curled his lip, and he dropped his head, rumbling deep enough to shake my bones.

"I ride for Draconia," Father said, stepping forward.

"What happened?" I stayed close, matching his hurried steps. His dragon wore no saddle—it would be a long ride. And if he collapsed mid-flight, both of them would die at sea.

"The Innaki are coming."

Laughter burst from me, disbelief masking my fear. "You're joking. A messenger, maybe. Surely not an attack. Galdoni wouldn't dare."

"They'll breach our waters in two days."

Sea beneath. He dared?

I watched, frozen, as Father climbed onto Argos' bare back. Horror curled tight in my belly. The Innaki had never launched a real threat. Sharp tongues, yes—insults wrapped in politics—but never open war. *No one* had.

They knew we had *dragons*.

Kallias stayed behind me, quiet. Steady. There'd be no talking Father down. He would not remain idle while raiders approached. Not when his queen, the riders, and his people were in danger.

Ronan and Gyrak could defend the island. Mother could rule if needed. But this—this need to be at their side burned in his marrow as fiercely as it did in mine.

Argos lifted his head, muscles flexing, pain twisting his form.

"He can't fly!" I screamed, surging forward.

Kallias caught me around the waist, pulling me back while Argos threw himself into the air with a strangled shriek. The left wing wobbled. He veered and dipped with a shriek. Father jostled like a doll strapped to a charging horse.

My chest clenched. I grasped at the feeling, as if I might hold them to the ground with sheer will.

With strangled grunts, the black dragon struggled into the sky.

No backward glances. No hesitation. Only a king riding to war.

I couldn't stop him.

I spun, ripped from Kallias' grasp, feet pounding the sand—then stopped. Looked back.

He stood, head tilted, watching. He didn't speak. Didn't push. He let me choose. With a flick of his chin, he gestured toward the ship. I didn't need to wait for him, for his permission. He'd follow my lead here. He gave me the helm.

And I took it.

We set sail before nightfall.

Out on open water, dark clouds pressed low, swallowing the stars. A dense weight settled in the air, wind thick with storm-salt. At the prow, I kept my eyes on the horizon. Dread sat heavy on my shoulders, silence anchoring me in place.

I scanned the sky until it blurred. Listened for wingbeats. For a distant cry. For anything.

When the first drops of rain kissed my cheeks, they mingled with tears I couldn't hold back. If Mother had been there, she might have stopped him, tempered his fire.

But she wasn't.

Instead, I searched the dark for a black dragon.

Kallias stayed near, his presence a barrier against the sea's howl. Rain plastered my hair to my face as the waves bucked beneath us. When water breached the deck, he took my hand, pulled me below.

His arms wrapped around me. Heat seeped through chilled skin. One heartbeat steadying another, chasing away my dread.

Small red-painted ships blocked our path to Draconia. Cannons lined their decks, harpoons glinting along the rails, sharp and waiting. Sails waved in the breeze, a golden banner slashed by a crimson scythe snapping at their peaks.

"They think they can cut us off?" I scoffed. How could they? Just men in boats—until I scanned the sky and my stomach soured.

No dragons.

"Where are your riders?" Kallias' calculating gaze locked on the enemy formation. "They wouldn't hold this line without something up their sleeve."

"There's no defense against dragonfire." I shook my head. "Unless you're the King of Radaan," I added.

He alone had survived it. Wood and iron were no match for dragonflame.

A roar cleaved the air, pulling our eyes east. A red dragon shot low over the raiders, its cry sharp as tearing silk. My nails dug into the railing as harpoons arced upward, metal tips catching the light like stars.

With a squeal, it veered, spiraling through the sky.

Lightning struck.

A white-hot bolt cracked across the clouds, engulfing the creature midair. My heart stopped, a scream lodged in my throat. Kallias swore under his breath. The red tumbled, wings limp. Its rider—barely a dot—clung tight as they plummeted together.

Then a shadow dropped from above us.

Gyrak.

The black dragon descended with devastating silence, fire erupting from his maw. The nearest raider ship ignited in a bloom of heat and light, wood splintering as flames tore through hull and sail. Screams rose beneath the roar of flames.

I gasped, rooted to the deck as the charcoal beast ripped through their line.

"Now!" Kallias twisted toward Captain Wylyn and shoved me down behind the rail. "Take us in! Straight for the island!"

Gyrak vanished again, folding into the clouds. The sea boiled where he'd flown, only wreckage left in his wake.

The remaining ships scrambled. Red sails dropped as wind caught their canvas. Crews shouted, trying to close the gap.

But we were already moving.

A Draconis sailor stepped forward, rolling his shoulders as he looked up at the mast. Confidence swept through me. The gale shifted. I bared my teeth at the distant ships.

They were too slow. Too late.

We were Draconis.

Our ship surged like a living thing, the deck pitching underfoot as if shoved by some invisible hand.

At the heart of the vessel, a man stood still. Fingers spread. Palms angled toward the boards. His jaw clenched, sweat gleaming across his brow. Power swirled around him, rippling through the planks and rigging. Wind howled past us as magic grabbed hold and dragged the ship forward.

No sails needed.

We hit the wreckage with a shudder. Burning timbers shattered against the bow, bodies twisting in the surf.

A flash of blonde hair surfaced—brief, unmistakable.

"Kallias!" I gasped, leaning over the edge, scanning the burning mess. Smoke curled off scorched beams and shattered hulls. Blood spread in ribbons across the water. "A Draconis!"

A pale body bobbed amid the carnage, blonde hair stark against torn limbs and tangled strands of black. My stomach churned as we sped past, leaving the corpse adrift in reddened waves.

"Can your people summon lightning?" Kallias didn't flinch. His tone was all steel—calculated, detached. A king assessing damage.

"That's why the dragons aren't attacking," I whispered. Rage pressed tight against my ribs. "We won't burn our own, even if they're the ones calling the storm."

"What's stopping the Draconis on board from turning on the raiders?" He didn't waste words. Just followed the logic.

"There's too much variation." I tightened my voice, layering it in fury. "Some Vessels barely hold enough magic to light a lantern—others don't know how to sail or swim to shore without getting harpooned."

A lump of pale flesh bobbed in the wake. Bone jutted through both ends.

My people.

Galdoni would pay. With his life.

On our ship, the Vessel faltered. His color had drained to ash. I caught him as he collapsed, arms limp, head slumping against my shoulder. His fingers twitched, pouring everything into the spell that carried us home.

"Thank you," I murmured, brushing sweat-soaked hair from his brow.

Kallias shifted beside me as the ship slowed, his mantle chains clinking with the motion. He stood angled between enemy sails and the dock ahead, unreadable.

The Vessel sagged fully against me.

"Your Majesty, he's spent," another sailor said, easing the young man from my grasp.

I pressed a hand to the Vessel's chest. "When he wakes, bring him to me—or to Queen Nyxaria."

The man nodded, grunting under the weight as he carried him below deck.

Behind us, the red sails held their distance. They flanked the harbor mouth, watching, waiting—but not attacking.

"Negotiating?" Kallias muttered.

"Father would never." I spat the words, hiding the tremor beneath them. I couldn't see Argos. No sign of Father. Only dark clouds, broken sky. Doubt he made it home at all, gnawed at me.

"Your mother would."

As we approached the dock, four guards waited in full silver plate. The sight jarred me. Draconis summoning the guard? At port? Absurd.

The ship docked in silence. No voices. No commands. Even the water felt still.

Greaves stumbled behind us, boots slapping wet boards. He looked ready to vomit. Hopefully, he'd keep his feet for what came next.

A figure sprinted from the shadowed city—black leathers flapping, goggles shoved onto his brow. Ronan's face was carved from stone.

"The dragons are grounded. The island's surrounded," he barked. "Mother's handling talks. That bastard Galdoni has our people—using them as shields."

"Innaku doesn't have enough Vessels for every ship," I snapped, keeping pace as we hurried through the city. "We never gave them that many."

"No, but he's hiding them. We don't know which ships they're trapped on. It's chaos without Father."

Panic gripped me. Cold. Crushing.

"Where is he?" I asked, voice low but sharp. I wanted to stop, shove him against the wall, shake him until the truth fell out.

"Argos crashed off the eastern shore. We managed to get them to land, but the flight took a toll on them both. Argos can't move his left wing. He's landlocked."

"And Father?"

"He flew through a storm on a dragon that shouldn't have made the trip," Ronan bit out. "He's unconscious. But alive. No injuries."

Air returned to my lungs. I straightened, spine iron.

He needed me more than ever now.

Kallias placed his hand at the small of my back, anchoring me with that simple touch.

I wasn't alone. I had my mother's mind, my brother's fire, and Kallias' unshakable presence.

Let the Innaku come.

They'd regret this show of force.

"What does he want?" I burst into the war room, breath catching when I saw my mother at the head of the table. Not Father.

Haldor looked up. Flight leathers hugged his frame, a line of pearl studs marching across his right shoulder to mark his rank. His goggles dangled from one hand, the other braced against the map.

"You," Mother answered, glare fixed on the red fleet clustered around Draconia. Light skimmed the gems in her crown, but no shadows dimmed her fire.

"Bold choice," Kallias growled, stepping closer. His gaze swept the map's coastline, calculating.

"He knew nothing of you, King of Radaan," she said, repositioning a black dragon on the eastern shore. "Until he saw your ship docked in our harbor."

"And now his demands have changed?"

Mother met his stare without flinching. "No."

His jaw flexed. Fingers drifted to the hilt at his hip. His attention shifted to the cluster of ships to the east, pausing on the largest one guarded on all sides.

"The Draconis Vessels will be there. And here." He traced south, then west. "If he knows I've made her queen, they'll also be stationed to the north. Cut off your reinforcements."

Mother shook her head, the corners of her mouth tight. "We can't be certain."

"Queen Nyxaria." Kallias' tone brooked no argument, and she stiffened with a glare that could pierce armor. "I've fought wars my entire life. Draconia has never seen a battlefield. Trust my word."

Her nostrils flared, but no protest escaped her lips. He wasn't just some farm lord; he was the Golden Warrior. Chosen of the gods. Untested in sea warfare, perhaps—but war was his mother tongue.

"What do you advise?" she asked, brittle but listening.

"Greaves, fetch Fallione," Kallias said. The guard vanished with purposeful strides.

"Does Galdoni have spies here?" he continued. "Any chance he knows Nienna has been named queen?"

"Every Innaki was sent back the day before your arrival," Mother replied. "He shouldn't know."

"Then we move as though he thinks Kallias is still rotting in the dungeon," I said, catching onto the rhythm of his plan.

"What's his leverage? Wheat?" Kallias asked, face sharpening, voice tuned to war. The relaxed man who once smiled in mint fields was gone. What remained was a general, a strategist.

"And our people," Ronan cut in, posture taut as he stared through the window. Hands folded behind his back, so much like Father.

"He plans to starve you out, then," Kallias said. "He's severed your fishing routes, blocked your trade, grounded your dragons. You're overpopulated and short on food. He's not pressuring you—he's letting time work for him. Galdoni believes he has the upper hand."

"We'd fly before that," Ronan snapped.

"We *meet* him before that," Kallias corrected. "Is he aware of Nereus' condition? He didn't know he'd be sailing into that storm. He expected you to come to him. What's the state of the red?"

"Elmo's alive. The diversion was successful," Ronan replied. "Two riders burned out their magic, shielding him from the blast."

"He's counting on you to fly. It's a gamble. If he downs your dragons, what's left? Where are your forces? Your battleships?" Kallias' words cut through the room like drawn steel.

Haldor slammed a fist on the table. "We've never needed them! Our beasts have never failed us."

"And now you suffer for that blind trust. *If* you lose your dragons, you lose your island."

Cold pooled in my gut as my gaze cropped to the map. Adoni's death had been an accident, but perhaps it also cracked the door, igniting his father's fury. The storm aided his cause. He saw his chance—and took it.

This wasn't the end, either. Once he claimed Draconia, he'd set his sights on Ivetti and Kulletti. Or worse—join forces with the brutes and crush us between them.

"Meet him," Kallias said, tapping the ship Galdoni had fortified. "If he's reasonable, draw him to shore. If not, take your strongest Vessels and face him on the sea. Call his bluff."

"The Innaki no longer feed our people," I added. "He only holds leverage through the lives on those ships."

"Can you feel them?" Kallias asked, scanning our faces. "The Vessels? The riders who lent them power—can they sense where they're being kept?"

Haldor clenched his teeth. "Once the magic's given, it's gone. No tether remains."

Kallias sighed. "Then we don't know where your people are."

Mother's voice broke the silence. "He will not set foot on our shores. We'll go to him and hope the man has an inkling of sense."

If he was anything like Adoni, he didn't.

Chapter Thirty-Five

NIENNA

Radaan's mantle rested across my shoulders, its dragon-scale finish whispering with each step as I moved through the Spire's halls. Beside me, Kallias wore his golden yoke—not just a symbol of weight and duty, but a declaration of wealth and abundance. Its gleam alone stripped the Innaki of the one thing they still lorded over us.

Radaan stood as the only alliance Draconia required.

We stepped from the Spire into open air. My gaze lifted, and a smirk tugged at my composure. Storm clouds ringed the Nest, thick mist veiling the sky above. The dragons hidden there remained unseen by any looking skyward.

Not all of them were grounded to the sand. Several took their rest in the heights.

Chin raised, shoulders square, I followed Mother and Ronan with Kallias at my side. Father was still asleep, unable to be roused. Greaves, ever stubborn, had argued to come despite his sour stomach. Kallias relented eventually, though not without a hushed standoff in our rooms that made me hide my grin.

Four riders flanked us: Haldor, Zane, Mikal, and Erwin. Aside from Father and Ronan, they were the strongest we had. Following close came four of our most powerful Vessels, saturated to the brink. Riders had poured into them until their bodies thrummed with magic.

We boarded a smaller craft under a white flag. The sea lay flat, unnervingly still. A mirror waiting to shatter. I'd never seen the ocean so calm—as if it held its breath before unleashing a storm doomed to swallow us whole.

As we neared the outer ring of Innaki raiders, fire licked at Ronan's fingertips. Guilt seethed beneath his placid exterior, thick as smoke. He'd taken his first lives today—two of them being our own people. That grief had hardened into rage, and it now burned for the Innaki.

Their ships parted.

Relief brushed against my unease. One test cleared, so many more to go. Kallias' arm flexed underneath my hand, steadying me. His presence lent me a confidence I never had before. I was not alone in this. He'd faced the Velli countless times in a similar manner—face to face, blade at his back, head high. He would guide me through this. Not by command—but at my side.

Another line of ships gave way. The hush deepened, broken only by the whisper of oars slicing water.

Clouds sank lower while fog licked the masts.

We said nothing. Moved only as much as necessary. Our vessel slipped into place beside Galdoni's warship—a monster of a thing, its hull slashed with crimson warpaint like it had gored a whale or two and kept the stains as a show of dominance.

A carved merman sneered from the ship's bow, trident pointed toward the distant Spire.

Ropes flew, and lines were fastened. Innaki stared down at us—dark hair, sun-browned faces, blow darts leveled in grim silence. When the boarding plank slammed into place, Mother held firm.

We ascended.

King Galdoni had always repulsed me. Something about him strained every ounce of my patience and self-control. Once, I pitied Adoni for the pressure his father put on him. Now, I recognized it for what it was—poison passed down like inheritance.

The man stood tall with black hair slicked back from a proud brow. He wore his people's traditional skirts. Gold chains danced against his thighs, ending at his knees, while red pearls and jewels wound through his belt. A stark white sash hung across his bare chest.

Muscles rippled under his tawny skin, and a sick smile stretched his lips as his gaze skipped over Mother and Ronan before locking on my mantle. Then they found Kallias.

"Ah, truly you waste no time, Kallias Sunspear," he drawled, voice slick as rancid oil. He turned his disdain on Mother, feigning a sorrowful shake of his head, as if he somehow blamed her for my marriage. "Queen Nyxaria, I fear you've lost your most useful bargaining chip."

Fire nipped at my bones as my spine stiffened, but I forced my jaw to stay loose. Let him think I simmered. He'd never see how much I hated him.

"King Galdoni, we've come to seek peace." Mother's voice was silk over steel, smooth but unmoved. "Between our nations."

"It might've been better sought before your daughter murdered my son." His words oozed pity. A performance. Prudish, as if he were speaking to a child. "Yet here we are. Someone had to challenge the myth of Draconia's greatness. You've outgrown your little patch of sand."

My fingers twitched, desperate to curl into fists at my sides. He *dared* insult her—us—on our waters.

He waved a hand. "Alas, I welcome you to my table."

A line of Innaki warriors stepped forward with guarded, severe expressions. Crimson-painted skin, dart tubes strapped to their sides. They brought a table from behind the king's quarters, setting it in the center with unspoken precision.

"However, the King of Radaan is not welcome."

Kallias didn't blink. He met the island king's gaze without flinching, though his stare promised retribution. With the barest nod—controlled, sharp—he dipped into the smallest of bows. "I've claimed the Dragon's Heart as my own," he said. "You summoned her, and by extension, you've summoned me."

Galdoni's brows twitched at the reference to my title. The only thing he or his son ever cared about.

"He sits, or we leave." Mother smoothed the folds of her gown with regal disinterest. "And before you answer, ask yourself—can you account for all of our dragons?"

His gaze slid to the mist-choked Spire.

"Is that a threat?" he asked, head tilting, curiosity slithering into his tone.

"Draconis do not threaten," she replied, taking her seat. "We act."

Ronan and I took seats on either side of her. Kallias settled beside me. With hands clasped on the table, Mother waited.

Galdoni let loose a booming laugh and dragged a chair out before dropping into it. "You've always amused me, Nyxaria. But tell me—did your husband fall in the storm? We saw his dragon in pieces on the beach."

"Perhaps I'll answer," she said, tone light as idle weather talk, "once you count your dead from the two raiders we destroyed."

A flicker of shadow passed over his face, and his snide grin wavered. "Forty-eight. And two of your own. Truly, you should be more careful."

Ronan's fingers twitched. The wooden surface beneath his palms darkened with the flameless heat radiating from his skin. He sacrificed two of our own to ensure my passage through enemy ranks. That guilt clawed at him, fed his rage.

"Galdoni," Mother said, her tone steady, "our nations have known peace since their founding. You *and* your son knew the risk of coming to our isle. Yet, you sent him anyway. And you know Tsunami has no rider. While we regret Prince Adoni's death, you are just as responsible."

He leaned back, his smile slipping like a mask gone slack. "You've unsettled my kingdom. Destroyed our trust. And now you dare place the blame for my son's death on me?"

His eyes landed on me. I held his gaze, spine rigid, ready to fight.

"He came for *her*." He sneered. "I told him she wasn't worth it—a sullied princess, discarded like–"

"You want a dragon," Kallias said, slicing through the venom. Galdoni's mouth snapped shut, like a hawk's beak.

"My son died by her hand." He forced calm into his tone. "That alone merits the demand. It's a fair ask."

"Done," Ronan cut in, lips curling into a vicious grin. "A fleet's already on its way to Innaku."

Galdoni froze, his gaze returning to the cloud-wrapped Spire.

It had been Kallias' idea—drag the mist low, mask the dragons, and pull them out of range from the lightning. Hidden. Waiting. We knew what the island king wanted, and we would give it to him to get our people back—just not how he expected.

"You wouldn't dare scorch Innaku," he growled. "You need–"

"Grain. Cloth. Crops?" Kallias tilted his head.

I brushed the mantle chains with my fingertips. "We need nothing from you now, Galdoni."

His skin flushed crimson. "I have your Vessels."

"And we will have your island." Mother shrugged. "You may be king of the Innaki—but when your islands burn, what shall you rule?"

"You owe me for my ships and men."

Kallias' knee brushed mine. He felt it too—Galdoni was unraveling. We had him. No allies waited to save him. The Ivetti would never shelter him, and the Kulletti were just as likely to slit his throat as they were to offer him safe harbor.

"And you owe us for the grave insult to our name," Mother snapped, "for attacking our shores, wounding our dragons, and spilling Draconis blood. And you believe you get to make *demands*?"

"The goods you once supplied," Kallias said, "Radaan now delivers."

"Surrender our people and leave our waters," Mother added, "and we'll call back our riders."

"This means war," Galdoni hissed. Rage turned his face to stone. "There's no undoing this."

"We're already at war," Ronan bit out, voice low, heat laced beneath it. "The only question is—will you die this battle or the next?"

The island king glared, each plan he cultivated crumbling behind his eyes. He reached too far, stretched thin by greed.

"You want to fight?" he muttered, then let out a soft chuckle. "Have your Vessels. Own the skies if you like. But we own the sea." His gaze landed on Kallias. "You think your goods can sail across oceans I command? We will see."

"We're finished here." Mother rose, her chair scraping the wooden planks. "Our people—all of them—shall be delivered within two hours. Only when the last pair of boots is safe on our shores, will I call our dragons home."

"Get off my ship!" he snarled.

We turned from him, backs straight. Mother and I crossed to our boat first while Kallias and Ronan remained behind a moment longer, watching him seethe.

Once we were all safely aboard, the ropes were cut and the Innaki retreated, letting the plank crash into the waves. My heart pounded as I studied their cannons for any sign of movement, ready for betrayal.

But Kallias' tactic held, and our ship sliced toward shore, powered by the Vessels' magic.

"You were beautiful," Kallias whispered close to my ear, wind ripping the words away before another caught them.

Pride warmed my chest. Our generations-long peace with the Innaku was shattered—but our people would return. And our dragons were safe, either curled in the Nest or along the beach.

On the shore, we waited.

The sky dimmed as small boats ferried the Draconis home. Mother sat with a scribe, marking each name. There would be no more losses. Two was our final cost.

Hope flickered higher with every face that stepped onto the sand. Artorius circled above, wings skimming the treetops, reporting fewer raider ships with each pass.

Families flooded the beach. Cries rang out—relief, grief, joy. Tears soaked tunics and hands gripped arms tight. But Mother never moved until the last elder stepped from the final boat.

She embraced the woman, whispered assurances, then passed her to a guard. Her gaze found mine.

The beach pulsed with anguish and glory, fear braided through relief, while voices full of questions carried low on the breeze.

Would they return? Could Radaanian ships outmaneuver the blockade? Would they twist our strength against us again?

Mother's fingers drifted down my arm, her whisper barely louder than the wind. "It's time."

She stepped away without hesitation, and Ronan moved with her, his face unreadable. Kallias lingered, eyes flicking between us—this wasn't part of the plan.

But there was nothing left to debate.

Our people wept with their families. They trembled in uncertainty. And Galdoni had already made his move.

He had reached for the Dragon's Heart. He would reach again.

I lifted my chin and strode toward the Spire. "Light the pyres."

The command rose from a place older than thought, deeper than flesh—an instinct, a promise written into my bones.

The sky split open.

Dragons burst through the mist, wings unfurling in violent elegance. Their roars shattered the silence as they dipped low, then climbed, circling once before banking toward the enemy ships. Bronze, onyx, copper, scarlet—every scale caught the dusk like a spark.

The hush that fell was immediate and total.

Kallias turned, gaze fixed on the horizon.

Then came the fire.

The roar of it cracked through the sky.

Cheers erupted on the shore. Cries of joy, revenge, justice. Their dragons had been used, their families held hostage. Those actions would never go unpunished. No one would hurt or threaten my own and get away with it.

This was my vow to them.

We were Draconis.

Our enemies were naught but ash.

Chapter Thirty-Six

KALLIAS

The dragons torched everything. Fire poured over the raiders' fleet, their hulls erupting in bursts of flame, splinters, and limbs scattered like kindling across the sea.

Nienna didn't flinch. She turned her back on the blaze, spine straight, head high—leaving ruin in her wake.

When I arranged her marriage to Tallon, I expected the usual mold of royalty: sweet, sheltered, easily steered. But she wasn't raised to bend. She carried the heat of dragonfire and the brilliance of sunlight. Fierce, brilliant, and on my side.

Radaan needed that fire. That edge. Not another polished diplomat, but a weapon sharpened to defend its borders. Someone who would burn down a threat without flinching.

I always thought I'd shoulder the burden alone. Make the brutal choices, carry the guilt. But today—she showed me she could carry it too. She would kill for those she loved. Radaan needed that steel, that ruthlessness.

Pride surged in my chest as we moved through the Spire. The halls swelled with voices, windows crowded with onlookers. Laughter tangled with disbelief, wonder thick in the air.

Without ships, what could Innaku do now? Rebuilding a fleet would take years—and Draconia would be ready for them.

Based on the fervor with which the dragons flew, it would be a wonder if Galdoni even survived.

Nienna passed our floor, her steps leading upward through the winding Cireendium. "I want to see my father," she murmured.

I caught the note of weariness in her tone, the quiet fray at the edge of her resolve. She leaned into my arm, fingers curling against my elbow for support. She was exhausted, drained by the demand the last few days had put on her.

"He never should've risked the storm." A heart-heavy sigh chased her words. "What good did it do?"

"I can't imagine he would have listened to anyone but Nyxaria," I said, rounding a corner into a bright corridor.

"Don't sound so smug."

A chuckle slipped out. "I would've done the same. Charged through wind and sea to reach you? I wouldn't hesitate." If the Velli laid a hand on Nienna, I'd make the last war seem merciful, child's play compared to the havoc I would wreak among them.

"If I ask you to stop," a hint of desperation lingered in her tone, "just *stop* and *listen.*"

The way her father dismissed her warning and flew off without a backward glance bothered her. She wasn't only clever—she was intuitive. Sharp. To ignore that was to discard a blade mid-battle. I wouldn't make the same mistake. I'd be a fool to toss her opinions aside.

Outside the door, I framed her face with my hands, pressing a kiss to her forehead. "You are the other half of my soul. To disregard you would be to rip out my heart."

A soft breath escaped her lips. She kissed me once, quick and chaste, before stepping inside.

The hairs on the nape of my neck bristled. I wasn't supposed to be here. This was Nereus' domain. His air. His walls—but I remained at Nienna's side.

The space pulsed in deep blue. Couches dusted in navy velvet circled the spacious receiving room, cushions plush and welcoming. We passed through two quiet chambers and into the bedchamber.

There, the king lay still beneath a canopy. Gauzy curtains swayed in the breeze, hazy gray daylight bleeding through the open window.

He didn't look broken—only asleep. His face full, skin warm. Beard trimmed. Hands resting together over his chest. His silver signet ring caught the light, a flicker of authority untouched.

"He looks like he's sleeping," Nienna whispered. She eased down beside him and brushed his hand. A twitch answered her touch, but his eyes stayed shut.

"It wasn't magic that drained him?" I asked.

"He didn't use any," Ronan answered, appearing in the doorway.

Sun above, I couldn't imagine the children just walking in unannounced when their father was well.

"He hit his head," the prince continued. He tossed me a frown before moving to sit near Nienna. "We think it happened when Argos hit the sea. He didn't even send a flare. We heard the dragon's scream and sent Artorious and Naksula to pull him out, while I carried Father back."

Nienna shook her head. "I told him not to go."

"When have we ever listened to women?" Ronan smirked.

"A wise man listens to anyone with a knowledgeable word," I said.

"Father would've listened to Mother," she muttered with a sniff. "Argos never should've flown to the Wild Shores—let alone made the return without rest. What is it with you men and your black dragons?"

"We protect what's ours." Ronan raised his brows at me like I was meant to back him up. "He'll wake in a few days."

"And Argos?" Nienna's voice dipped low.

Her brother paused. A muscle jumped in his jaw. "Might take longer."

She read his face, as if searching for answers. "Will he fly again?"

"You couldn't stop him from trying." He shrugged. "But I doubt he'll sire another clutch."

"What happens to the hatchlings?" I asked.

She stroked her father's hand once more, then stood. "They'll find riders—or fly south."

"With five going to Radaan, perhaps more will choose to stay," Ronan muttered, barely masking his irritation. As if the very idea of dragons leaving was a personal insult.

I studied him—sun-bleached hair pushed back by worn flight goggles, blue irises bright with fierce loyalty. Smile lines had already begun to form at the corners of his eyes. He would make a fine king one day—once he matured.

"Only time will tell," Nienna said with a shrug. "Ronan, let Mother know we won't be at dinner."

Back in our rooms, she stumbled toward the bed. I bit down a smile and shut the door behind us. Greaves had finally been sent to rest—he needed it. The past few days had taken their toll, and though my body screamed to lie down, Nienna required care.

She collapsed face-first onto the blankets, limbs spread wide in a very undignified heap of exhaustion.

"I'm afraid you'll need to bathe before sleep, my queen," I called, unlatching the chains at my shoulders. The laces of my tunic came loose as I headed for the bath chambers. Praise Elohios—Freya had drawn a hot bath. Our delay at Nereus' side gave her just enough time to prepare.

"I'm a queen," Nienna groaned. "I do what I want."

The golden yoke slid from my shoulders, its links clinking as I set it on the stand. I unbuttoned my vest, peeled off the rest, and bolted the lock to our door.

"You are a queen." I crossed to the bed, then rolled her onto her back. "But even queens don't always get their way."

Her eyes roamed over my naked body and she bit her lip. "Too tired."

"I have no intentions beyond seeing you clean." I frowned at how her mantle twisted around her neck. "Start with that."

She groaned but rose, her fingers fumbling with the chains while I loosened the side laces of her dress. In moments, the mantle hung beside mine, and I pulled her dress over her head.

She kicked off her boots and wriggled out of her trousers, flinging them across the floor. I gathered her up. My back ached in protest, but her body sank against my chest, warm and limp, her breath feathering against my throat.

Once we were scrubbed and rinsed, I plucked a limp sprig of mint from her hair and carried her to bed.

I kept my word—held her close but nothing more. Rest claimed us fast. Not only had the past days drained our bodies, facing down an enemy nation demanded a level of energy that would take time to recoup. Sometimes mental fatigue was worse than physical.

So I held her—and let the queen of Radaan sleep.

"You're with the living!" Nienna burst into the private dining room, flinging her arms around her father. He wore his leathers, calm as if it were any other morning.

She kissed his cheek and dropped into the seat beside him.

"I didn't know I was ever with the dead," he muttered, nodding my way as I pulled out a chair.

"You might as well have been, for all the good you did." Nyxaria sighed, pinching the bridge of her nose, while Ronan threw his boots onto the table like a delinquent court jester.

"I heard you torched Galdoni's fleet," Nereus said, sipping from a cup of flavored fish water. The minty, briny scent wafted through the room.

"If they want war, they'll get one." Nienna shrugged. "They've got years of shipbuilding ahead of them."

"Forty percent of their workforce was on those ships," Nyxaria added.

"Should've flown to Innaku to remind them not to mess with us," Ronan grumbled. "Elmo's scorched from nose to tail. We were too far to shield them properly."

Nereus turned to me. "You had a hand in the strategy. Thank you."

"I'm no sailor," I said. "But war is war, and that much I understand. Hiding the dragons in the Spire was a trick we used in the Battle of Gad at the base of the foothills. We lured the Velli in, then dropped the charge from the mountain."

"When was that?" Nereus asked, tipping his cup.

Ronan snorted a laugh. "Was Nienna even alive then?"

The king choked, and the corner of my eye twitched with the urge to put the boy through the nearest wall.

The rest of the evening passed easy. Nienna's family folded me into their little group without pretense or suspicion. I'd told myself for years all I needed was

Greaves, that anything else was a liability. People always wanted something. But Nienna didn't take—she and her family gave. Their only condition was that I protect her.

When Ronan summoned us the next day, I was suspicious. He never brought good news—but Nienna laughed it off.

His rooms were suspiciously tidy—a mockery of Tallon's mess. He waved, beckoning me to his desk.

"This is the Dragon Ship's layout," he said, sliding aside a stack of letters and placing weights on the blueprint corners. "Gyrak's nearly too big. We keep livestock penned here normally."

He tapped the ship's main deck, where space had been constructed for a dragon's bulk.

"He can make the flight, but he'll be starving when you land. You'll need to plan for provisions."

He stretched, locking his hands behind his head like his part was done.

Nienna lounged on the couch, flipping through a book. Greaves stood watch at the door, as always.

"There's not much before Reem," I noted. "Some pastureland between the port and the palace. He might have to veer west. There are some sheep farms out that way. How many will he require?"

"No cattle?"

"Are you making menu requests?"

Ronan scoffed and rolled his eyes. "After that flight? Four sheep. And he'll need to be grounded for a day."

"Done. Anything else?" My gaze drifted over the table. Shells and stones anchored the paper—childhood habits clashing with royal council duties. But the documents beneath told a different story. Orders. Reports. Rider logs. Proof of the boy's responsibility and level of maturity.

A word caught my eye.

'Radaan.'

I knew that handwriting.

After shoving aside the blueprint, I scanned the letter.

"Oi!" Ronan snapped, reaching, but I angled away, pulse spiking.

'Nienna is homesick. I worry about her.'

My throat dried. This was the missive Tallon sent to summon Ronan. That rat never worried about anyone other than himself—unless it served him.

'Fyrn says she doesn't sleep at night.'

Cold prickled my scalp. My eyes darted to the date. Days before the assassination attempt. He and Fyrn had been fooling around already?

"Look, I meant to toss it," Ronan muttered, trying to reach for it again, but I stepped clear. My ears roared.

"Kallias?" Nienna's voice sounded far away.

My gaze narrowed on another line.

'Without magic.'

"Did you tell him?" My words came rough, torn. "You told Tallon she was a poor Vessel?"

Ronan blinked, confusion playing over his expression. "We never talked about it."

The answer from Elohios was blood, but it hadn't been mine—I knew in my bones I hadn't sired Tallon. If he was half Velli, he could use blood to control others. I had checked Egath, locked him away while my bastard son ran free.

How did he know Nienna had no magic? Could the Velli sense that?

The pieces slotted into place, the letter's words swirling along the page. My hands trembled. Gods, it was bold—even for Tallon. Banishment was no longer a just punishment. This was treason, attempted murder. He would hang for this.

Someone banged on the door, startling us all, then it burst open.

Fallione barreled in, white-faced and grim. He ignored the room, heading straight for me. In his outstretched hand, a tightly rolled scroll from a messenger dove, its seal broken.

My stomach dropped.

One look, and I knew.

Every instinct screamed. I felt it like a blade at my throat.

The letter fell to the desk as I took the scroll. My heart slammed against my ribs while the mantle's damning weight pulled on my shoulders.

A hush fell over the room.

I fingered the broken wax seal and read the words that would shatter us all.

'Tallon has taken Radaan.'

Secret Clubs

AND OTHER NONSENSE...

If you want to be part of the cool kids club and get sneak peeks—sign up for the newsletter so you don't miss a beat!

Newsletter Sign-Up!

I take a bow

THANK YOU

When I started writing Between Flames and Deceit, I thought it was going to be a short 90k romantasy. Something short and fun. Well, here we are ending Between Love and Ruin on yet another cliffhanger. Yes, this is now the Dragon's Heart Trilogy.

I would like to thank each and every one of my fans for putting up with my pantser ways and just hanging along for the ride—no matter the ups, downs and squiggles between.

For those of you who might not know, I ran a kickstarter to fund a special edition of Between Flames and Deceit. During that process, I allowed people to buy tiers to name characters (and Dragons!) so I must give credit where credit is due:

Freya – Fillie (Thank you for not choosing anything crazy!)

Artorious – Jessie

Naneki – Bethany

Guglielmo/Elmo – Melanie (So of course he's red!)

Naksula – Kacie

A huge thank-you to my Alphas: Shannon and Millie! My Betas: Kate, Brittany, Ashley and Leann! And my Editor: Erynn Snell. You guys are the best team a girl could ever ask for!

Lastly, I would be remiss if I did not thank my loving husband who got me into this mess of publishing and my bestie Jessie who has supported me through thick and thin. You guys are the best!

M.A. Frick

M.A. Frick is a mere peasant.

Once upon a time, she read to escape the world. Now she writes to create them.

Not only the mother of worlds, but the mother of three children—she is joined by her husband who supports every adventure, no matter how absurd it may be.

9 781965 611043